THE SHADOW FABRIC

MARK CASSELL

www. **THE SHADOW FABRIC** .co.uk

H

HERBS
HOUSE

First published in Great Britain in 2014 by Herbs House
An independent publishers

1

Copyright © Mark Cassell 2014

For more about this author
please visit www.markcassell.co.uk

ISBN 978 0 9930601 0 6

Printed and bound for Herbs House

First Edition

For all the black cats out there

THE SHADOW FABRIC

'Old sins cast long shadows.'
– early 20th-century proverb

CONTENTS

VENEERS

Unable to blink, I shot a quick glance around the dining room. My heartbeat stormed my head. I had to get out of there, I had to leave the other men to it. These brothers had a lot of hate to throw around.

The black fabric draped across the table and chair, tracing every contour. It flowed over the wood like liquid. Hugging tight whatever it touched, it turned everything into a shadow, a silhouette, a featureless dark blot of its former self. The way it moved defied physics.

My throat clamped around a cry that came out a whimper.

I had no idea what Stanley intended. The strange fabric didn't travel far from his hand, and where the material ended, it rippled and pulsed, pulling further away, yet unable to claim more of its surroundings. The more it unfolded, the dimmer the room became. My skin itched as it sapped the light.

Victor and Stanley stood facing each other: Victor, with his eyebrows pushed together, the ornate blade clenched in a fist, and Stanley, with his jaw tight and a twitch at the edge of his mouth. In Stanley's grasp the fabric quivered, its material reminding me of the way midday sunlight reflects from the surface of a swimming pool, the ripples a criss-crossing of movement. It was peaceful to behold, hypnotic almost. But this thing was dark and stifling to observe.

There was nothing remotely tranquil about this.

I wanted to leave them to whatever absurd game this was…yet my feet refused to move. The familiar ache in my knee rushed through my body, drumming in my skull, telling me I was useless. Since the car accident the knee often was useless. I couldn't leave Victor, I knew that. The man looked as terrified as I felt.

"I hate you, Victor." Stanley's nose was no more than a thumb's width from his brother's.

"No," Victor gasped. His hand shook, his knuckles whitening around the knife. "Don't!"

I didn't know who or what Victor spoke to. Was it Stanley? The shadows? The knife?

In a blur of darkness, shadows coiling his arm, the blade slammed into Stanley's chest. Blood spread and he staggered back.

Victor's eyes widened. Clutching the weapon, he stumbled from the fireplace, away from his brother. The knife slid out, sucking at the wound. A jet of scarlet misted the air, and then oozed.

I could only see darkness...so much darkness, and my lungs went tight.

The fabric—the Shadow Fabric—closed around Stanley's buckling legs.

The remaining material swept from the table, away from the violin case. Black tentacles whipped and grabbed Stanley. The darkness enfolded him as his eyes glazed over. It dragged his body along the carpet a short distance and tightened its grip.

My jaw muscles twitched as I clenched my teeth.

The Fabric began to shrink. Still in its embrace, the last I saw of Stanley was his dead stare.

"Vic..." I whispered, and gripped the back of the sofa.

My boss dragged his eyes away from the retreating shadows and stared at the knife. Behind him, the mantel clock hammered out several seconds before the weapon slipped from his hand onto the carpet, where it bounced with a red splash.

He fell to his knees. "Oh God."

The Fabric vanished.

I dashed across the room as much as my leg would allow and staggered to a halt beside him. Sobs wracked his frame as I grasped his bony shoulder.

On the table next to where Stanley had been standing was the violin case, still open like a crooked yawn.

A million thoughts tumbled through my head, but I couldn't find the words. I'd been Victor's chauffeur for no more than a day, and already I'd witnessed him stab his own brother. What the hell?

I don't know how long I remained like that, holding him, with light creeping reluctantly back into the room. Victor shouldn't have been surprised that the shadows had taken his brother. After all, those shadows—the darkness—are associated with all that is dead...or should be dead.

Silence clogged the air like we were buried in a tomb.

For some of us, there is a moment in our lives where all we've believed real is whipped out from under us and we're left to survive in a world that's a lie. All the things in life we've taken for granted are sheathed in a weak veneer, behind which stands the shadows.

For me, this was one of those moments.

CHAPTER 1

After a year travelling the world, I stood before Periwick House, a retreat used for long-weekends by those wanting to ease off the accelerator of modern life. In rural Kent, such quiet-time could be found. I had no choice other than to be there; it's where I lived. I was one of two men who did, the other being the owner of the place, Richard Goodwin. The remaining rooms were for visitors.

Three storeys, with a hint of Georgian influence, the House stretched up and outward. Its terraces and sweeping wings clawed into the woodlands and surrounding grounds. In keeping with the original architecture, various annexes and extensions provided the services expected of any retreat: a restaurant and bar, a pool, a gym, spa and beauty treatment rooms.

I squinted. Perhaps some of the first floor rooms had new curtains. It was difficult to tell with sunlight glinting off the windows. On the roof, the weathervane looked like it had been polished, or even replaced.

It's the only home I could remember. Not for much longer, though. Having lived there for two years, one of which spent travelling, I needed—finally—to go it alone. It felt good to be back, that I couldn't deny. And strange, certainly, after such a long time away. I'd left England to discover myself, but still the frustrations remained.

Spring sunshine pressed on my neck as I headed for a weathered table where a jug of orange juice and two glasses waited. I shrugged off my rucksack and swung it to the ground.

Further out in the gardens was Neil, half-swallowed by daffodils, and as gangly as the saplings behind him. It was Monday, and his passion for the job was evident as always. He pushed the barrow with his back straight and chin high. We acknowledged each other with a nod.

"Leo!" a voice bellowed from behind me.

I turned and shook hands with Richard Goodwin, the only family I had and we weren't even related. He hadn't changed since I last saw him. Yes, this was my home. Kind of.

Cigar smoke hung around his shiny dome, stifling the scent of mown grass. Topped with a contagious grin, his roundness creaked into a chair. He squashed his cigar into the ashtray and looked at me. "It's good to have you back."

"Good to be back." I sat opposite him and watched cigar smoke spiral and disappear. The chair, although hard, was more comfortable than the one I had been squashed into on the aeroplane a few hours before.

Goodwin poured the juice and handed me a glass. I mimed a 'cheers'.

My parents had died sometime in a past I didn't quite remember. Having made a promise to a family I had no knowledge of, this man gave me a room at the House. It wasn't just my family I couldn't remember, I didn't even remember me. I knew only what Goodwin had told me after I bombarded him with questions. In the early days, I was surprised my persistence hadn't annoyed him. If it did, he never once showed it. Everything he shared was as though he spoke of someone else. It was weird. There were blanks up until the car accident, gaping chasms throughout my life. That's why I called this my 'new' life. I had recollections of various childhood memories, yet little in the adult bracket. I was able only to recall snippets and fragments. Goodwin once took me to the house where I grew up, yet nothing remotely stirred my memories. According to him, as soon as I was old enough, I'd moved out and didn't have much to do with my family. And so, he couldn't help me with my latter years.

My past, like a jigsaw bought from a charity shop, was untrustworthy.

I often found that curious. Why wouldn't I have much to do with my family? Did I disown them? Did they disown me? There was only so much Goodwin could tell me. Whenever I tried to piece anything together, my head wanted to cave in.

Goodwin nodded. All I'd known was this man's generosity.

"Thanks for having me picked up," I said. "Appreciate it."

"No problem." He leaned forward.

"What is it? You excited to see me?"

He laughed. "I have a job for you."

"Oh?" I almost choked. This was unexpected. "Already?"

"I will ask how your travels were in a minute, Leo."

"Straight to the point." I wanted to relax after the flight, uninterested in talk of work.

He knocked back his juice, immediately topped it up, and held the glass in both hands.

"Tell me more then." I looked beyond him; the House loomed over us. I needed to start a new life.

"His name is Victor Jacobs and he needs a driver. A chauffeur."

I tapped a finger against my glass. Sunlight lanced from the rim. "Been a long time since I worked."

"You remember anything?" Goodwin placed his drink down. "From before the accident?"

"Something with cars, maybe. Still not sure. If I really, really think hard, I can see a car park."

He didn't blink.

"But that could mean anything." I shrugged and clenched my teeth. After all this time the frustrations remained. "Goodwin, my past is still a mystery.... Tell me about this Victor guy."

"The man runs plenty of errands in his line of work, dealing with antiques."

"Thanks." I didn't know what else to say. After a year, I didn't expect this as a first conversation. But, at least it was a step towards a new life.

"And tell me, how were your travels?"

I leaned back and the chair groaned. With birdsong a chorus from the trees, enhanced by the aroma of grass and the juice set before us, I felt refreshed. I'd almost forgotten how this place felt.

"Apart from food poisoning in Vietnam," I said, "it was inspiring."

"Good."

A pair of wood pigeons flew across the eaves. My forehead prickled with sweat.

"Was educational," I added. "Eating different foods, meeting different faces."

"A different world?"

I nodded. "Thanks to you." It was a simple coupling of words, often overused. This man had paid for my trip, a round-the-world ticket to go wherever I wanted. All at his expense. The card statements must've contained row upon row of acronyms followed by numbers, beginning a year before at Heathrow with GBP.

Thanks to Goodwin, I had twelve months' worth of crazy tales and amusing anecdotes. There were times of sadness and hilarity, tears and inspiration. I wanted to tell him of my moments of confusion, doubt, and denial, of how it soon became a journey of self-discovery, to learn of a new me...even though I couldn't remember the old one.

Goodwin scratched his cheek. "A year is a long time to recount over a glass of juice."

"I wrote a journal...kind of. Lots of scribbles."

His head tilted. "That's good."

"Might let you read it," I said. Mostly it contained a load of shit, I knew that. Full of hazy memories. Some I even doubted were real. In truth, they felt like dreams.

"Only if you wish." From his pocket, he pulled a cigar case and a disposable lighter. Moments later, he grunted amid a plume of white smoke.

"Got something for you." I dragged my rucksack towards me. After a rummage in the front pocket, I handed him a small packet. "Nothing much. Just something to say thanks for everything."

He beamed and unwrapped it. Perhaps he took his time, but for me time seemed to slow down. It was starting already. Being there, at the House, everything always slowed down.

Sunlight glinted off the contents finally dropping into his palm: a Zippo lighter. He read the engraving: *Godwin. A Good Friend.*

I stared at it. Already it felt like ages ago when I'd bought it, trying to get the man behind the counter to understand me.

Goodwin laughed. "Thank you, Leo. Thank you. *Godwin?*"

I shrugged and took a gulp of my drink. "Got it in Hong Kong."

"It's great, thank you."

We finished our drinks in silence. Again it was as if time dragged its heels through the gardens.

Eventually, Goodwin slid his chair back. "Come on."

We trod the gravel path separating Periwick House from the gardens, which would eventually take us round to the main entrance. Towering conifers hid the rest of the complex from view—I'd always called this place a *complex*, whereas others called it a *retreat*, which was more accurate. It was, after all, a retreat for those seeking escape from the world beyond these trees. I simply wanted to escape from the House itself. Not long treading the countryside soil, and already I wanted out. I had no past, no home to go to. Something was missing. Although I had Goodwin to thank, there was something not quite right for me here. It was like my brain couldn't breathe.

A short distance from the approach to the House, running parallel with the drive, I heard the rhythmic beat of a tennis ball. The year before, Goodwin hired me a coach, but it wasn't my thing. It didn't help that after the accident my knee wasn't up to anything strenuous.

Through the chain-link fence, behind the courts, a horse and rider cantered towards the stables on the edge of the woods. Riding, that I could do—easy on the injury, provided I didn't stand on the stirrups for too long. Next to the courts stood a shed that hadn't been there before, and on its door a poster proclaimed a concert was being held at the House that coming Saturday: *New Tide Chamber Orchestra*. On the far side of the gardens a line of oaks gave way to white canvas. It was an impressive marquee which definitely hadn't been there a year ago. I guessed that was where the concert would be held.

Several more strides took us beneath the portico to the House's entrance, flanked by bay windows which felt absurdly like open arms. On the other side of the doors, I met Dean, the manager, and we shook hands. He greeted me as Goodwin pushed his cigar into a trough of sand. With manicured fingers, he handed me a keycard and I thanked him. Dean was the sort of guy who wore too-tight trousers and never needed a shave. He'd grown his hair longer.

Goodwin said goodbye and I watched him walk to his office. I glanced at Dean whose grin annoyed me. Pursing my lips, I slowly breathed out.

So, there I stood, inside the lobby of my home. A marble floor stretched before me, ending in a mahogany reception desk. To the right, Goodwin's office door closed behind him. Beside the door was the restaurant and bar area, and further to the rear, a swimming pool. Off to the left were beauty treatment rooms and the spa, the gym and the fitness studio. It all linked round to the pool. I looked forward to getting back into the gym, and the pool. On my travels, I'd kept up with my fitness as much as possible—though I found it hard when a foreign city begged exploration. Even after all the exploring, nothing had cleared my mind to help me piece together memories.

Dean returned to the desk. It was tidier than it used to be.

Beside him, a marble staircase swept up to the bedrooms. The way it twisted into the ceiling always made me think of a spiny tail of some great beast. Up in its belly was my room: the Vivaldi Suite, number thirteen. Goodwin had number one—the Holst Suite—which left the others for visitors to enjoy solitude, spiritual awareness, and personal enlightenment.

Enlightenment, that's what I needed. That, and my memories.

I was home, though I felt like a visitor.

CHAPTER 2

I didn't get to relax much on my first day back in the UK. In the afternoon, I was in London meeting Victor at his flat. I immediately got the impression Goodwin had convinced his friend that I was right for the job. Having known Goodwin for two years—even though he'd known my family my entire life—I found it curious he'd never before mentioned Victor.

Was I going to accept a job as a chauffeur? Not an ideal job, but what really is?

After shaking Victor's hand, I nursed crushed knuckles; the man had a mighty grip for a small guy. He gestured at a sofa, and paced before the room-length window, staring at his feet. He wore neither a tie nor any shoes...and he didn't wear any socks, either. As he moved, his suit's bagginess accentuated his spindly limbs, and behind him, the grey expanse of London wallowed beneath a clear sky.

The sofa folded around me and as I made myself comfortable—not too comfortable, this was a job interview after all—a lady with patterned fingernails handed me a mug of tea. The way she avoided eye contact with him suggested she wasn't Victor's daughter.

I reached out and made certain not to be scratched by her talons. Her perfume lingered. It clawed my nostrils.

His place didn't have a TV, which I found remarkable—books were his thing. They were everywhere, whether flipped over like a tent or stuffed with markers. In places, precarious stacks of them rose from the wooden floor. Shelves lined two walls, where sections of reference volumes ranging from music to sea creatures remained untouched. The empty spaces, however, shared a common thread: the supernatural.

From somewhere behind me, I heard a door close.

"I won't be seeing her again," Victor said. "She makes a crap breakfast as well."

I wanted to ask *as well as what?* but thought better of it.

"My friend," he added, "how was the journey over?"

Calling me his friend made me smile, having never before met. "Long way from the village to the city."

"I have never been a fan of public transport. Smells. I grew up in Sevenoaks. Not far from Mabley Holt and Periwick House." He placed a hand flat on the glass and squinted at the only cloud in view. "Things are different here. Up here."

Up was accurate, geographically from Kent as well as in altitude: Victor's flat stood on the outskirts of London, on the eighth floor.

"Nice place." In all honesty it was too contemporary for me. One day, I'd have my own place, and it wouldn't look like this. But that felt so far away. First, I needed a job.

In a flat like Victor's, with the cooker—which even had a pile of books on it—in one corner and a bed in the other, it was difficult to relax. There were two doors: one through which I'd entered, and the other I guessed to be the bathroom. This place was certainly large enough for him and his books. I sat on one of two sofas, the only one almost free of books, and between them crouched a coffee table. Plastic and very 70s.

On the table, upturned and impressive, lay an aged book. A peculiar symbol squinted from its worn spine: two triangles with facing apexes, one hollow, the other solid, and separated by a crude X. There was no title.

"I don't like it," Victor said.

I dragged my eyes from the curious tome. He spoke of his flat and not the book.

"It serves a purpose," he continued. "A base if you will. I long for the simplicities of village life, where a population of no more than a hundred can chirp a friendly hello to one another on a morning dog walk. Somewhere I could go for an evening jog without needing to check my back pocket. Here, shadows follow us wherever we go, Leo. Even Mabley Holt isn't without its fair share."

I wasn't sure what to say. The guy spoke about shadows. What the hell was he on about?

He blinked and said, "How's Goodwin? How's the House?" He raced across the room to stand before a bookcase. I began to suspect he was mad.

"He's well," I said after a moment. "House is thriving, and he's hosting a classical concert this weekend." I wanted to know more about the job in question, I didn't want to talk about the House or Mabley Holt. Or Goodwin.

Victor gave me a strange glance.

"Tell me more about this job," I said. This was about me, after all.

"When can you start?"

"What does it involve?"

"I need a driver. A chauffeur if you like. I can't drive. Are you interested?"

I laughed. I needed a new start. A job. A new life. This wasn't turning out how I'd expected.

Victor chuckled. "Would you like to start today?"

I raised an eyebrow.

"It will be cash in hand, my friend," he said, "and I'm a generous man."

Goodwin had been more than generous, and now with Victor standing in front of me, I felt a little overwhelmed. *New life*. And today was all about my future. I needed this, even though being a chauffeur wasn't my dream job, and perhaps it would remind me of my past. Somehow.

"Okay," I said.

"Good." He threw me a car key and I snatched it before it hit me in the face. It was one key and one fob, the BMW badge shiny and unscratched. I couldn't remember what car I used to drive, but I was certain it wasn't anything too expensive.

As I stood up, I had a flash of memory—it happened sometimes, seeing I'd lost most of it—where I drove a car. It was red, yet most recollections often featured something red, a significant colour. Red is also the colour of danger, something we've all come to learn. Even Mother Nature gives dangerous or poisonous creatures a hint of red: the black widow spider with its red hourglass stamp on its abdomen, for instance.

An hourglass... Often the image of an hourglass would tease me, the twin bulbs reflecting sunlight. Maybe the sun, or possibly something else. As quick as it came to mind, it would vanish. And as always, I'd be left with nothing more than frustration.

That's what I felt then, and I ground my teeth.

Victor pointed at my mug.

"Finish your tea," he said, and pulled on a pair of leather gloves. He flexed his fingers. "Then you'll drive me to a bookshop."

New life.

With a wall of books behind him, I doubted he needed any more books, but I needed the money. I needed this.

I squeezed the car key. This was a start.

* * *

Victor already had his seat belt off, and as I pulled up the handbrake, he leapt from the car, eager as a kid. He wore shoes now—still no socks—and the leather gloves made his hands appear feminine. We were parked in an alleyway opposite a shop simply called *Books*. Its filthy windows and peeled frontage made me wonder what it was like inside.

"You can come in." He slammed the door.

I followed, and moments later stepped over an unstable threshold. The bell above my head clanged and I hoped the thing wouldn't fall from its housing. An aroma of coffee and books filled my nostrils.

Victor already stood at the counter, behind which stood a burly man with the heaviest of scowls.

"Victor Jacobs." A shiny scar wriggled down his face.

"Lucas."

I scanned the stacks of ready-to-tumble books. Near an archway stood a pile of split boxes, and bookshelves lined the walls, floor to ceiling. In comparison to Victor's flat, this place was even more untidy. A thin layer of dust covered everything. The room wasn't large, made smaller by the crammed boxes, and led to a larger area beneath an archway framed by shelves held up by dubious brackets.

The two men didn't shake hands, and I was ignored.

"Good to see you." Victor peered up at the proprietor. It was as if he wanted to say something else, yet somehow couldn't.

"Still searching?" Lucas asked. There was little friendliness about him. "Still playing the game?"

"It's not a game, Lucas."

"It was once, remember?" He held Victor's gaze.

It annoyed me, being ignored like that. I walked closer to Victor.

"We were a lot younger," he said.

"What brings you here?" There was something in the way Lucas said it. "What do you want?"

"I know I should have come to see you sooner. It's been too long, my friend."

"We were friends once," Lucas said through yellow teeth.

"We still are. Still can be."

"Are you kidding? After what happened?"

I bounced my eyes between the two of them. What was all this?

"It wasn't my fault." Victor's voice was small.

"You left me out in that jungle."

"That was long ago."

In his youth, Lucas probably hadn't been bad looking, but the scar, the way it cleaved his face from forehead to chin, was ugly. I was thankful I had no scars like that. Having survived my accident was lucky enough, walking away without any visible scars even luckier. On the inside? Perhaps my brain looked like that.

I tried not to stare, and wondered how the big man got it.

"Yes," Lucas said. "It was a long, long time ago."

"I had no idea—"

"Look what they did to me." Lucas pointed to his face.

I wanted to look away. What the hell were these guys talking about?

"Why are you bringing this up again?" Victor's shoulders slumped. "Time passes. Fast. Sorry I've not visited sooner. I should have, I know."

"It matters little to me."

Victor's eyes lingered on the man's face, and then scanned the shelves around the room. "So much has happened between then and now."

"And scars are permanent," Lucas said, and followed Victor's gaze. He still didn't acknowledge me. The scar twitched and his eyes narrowed.

I thought perhaps he would punch Victor, and I wasn't sure how I'd cope with that. After all, I was his driver, not his bodyguard.

Victor propped his elbows on the counter. "Lucas, I still think about that time."

"And you think I don't?"

"Please, you have to understand how it was for me. I nearly drowned. I'm sorry."

"How about me? How about when they tortured me?"

My heart lurched. What had happened to him? Were they in a war? Which jungle was this?

"Lucas, seriously, my friend, this was years ago."

"And I haven't seen you in years."

"I know and I'm sorry."

"You've said that far too often. Back then. And now."

I felt a little awkward here, although I didn't want to leave. Should I wander around the shop, have a nose through the books? I needed something to read. The last book I'd read was shit and I'd left it on a seat at the airport. I couldn't even remember the title.

"It still pains me," Victor said. "I was helpless. You know I was found floating—"

"I was there for days. In their hands. The evil little bastards."

"Lucas—"

"And I still sleep with the light on."

This I found hard to believe. Such a large man as Lucas, and he found comfort with a light on at night?

"What do you want, Victor?" He leaned forward, his knuckles ready to burst from fists which pushed into the counter. I was impressed Victor didn't flinch. I would have.

I reckoned Victor could handle himself here, so I headed for the archway. It was intriguing, no doubting that, but it was no place for me. Their voices faded, absorbed by paper, as Victor mentioned a book about leaves. Victor didn't seem the sort of man into gardening, nor anything green, I had to admit. Perhaps the 'save the planet' kind, but not as in grass and plants. I found it odd that we'd come to see a man he hadn't contacted in years, all for a book he could buy in a garden centre. Or find on the Internet, for that matter, though I couldn't recall seeing a computer at Victor's flat.

Jungles and Victor almost drowning? Lucas tortured? I thought of Vietnam, but that was just a United States thing, wasn't it? Sure, both men were probably old enough to have served in that war, but they're British. I guessed they could've been journalists or photographers. I had no idea.

I shuffled along the corridors, sometimes sideways—and I'm not a big guy. Tall and short stacks of books heaped the floor in places, and it was a challenge not to knock any over. This place was more treacherous than Victor's flat. I reached a corner and the shelves shot into the distance. Running parallel with them, the occasional strip light flickered. Some were dead.

I thumbed a few books as I scanned the rows, and soon made it back to the front of the shop.

The bell clanged and I heard Lucas greet a new customer with a bellowing hello. No names, this time. And friendlier.

I stepped aside for a young lady whose blonde curls filled my view. Her lipstick flashed a thank you. Victor stood near the entrance, holding the door open. A fire engine thundered up the road. Its siren filled the shop.

The girl hovered in the crime fiction section. She wore tight black jeans and a red jacket. I caught her eye—or rather, she caught me looking—and I turned away. I didn't want to come across as some kind of pervert.

Victor's eyebrows squeezed together, looking like his normal self. He turned to the proprietor. "Thanks, Lucas."

The man didn't reply. Again, it was as if I didn't exist. The rude bastard.

We stepped into the street and I noticed Victor's empty hands. I wanted to ask about Lucas and what had happened between them. The jungle? Torture? Victor nearly drowning?

Having only known him for a couple of hours, I settled for, "On the drive over, I saw a huge Notcutts."

"Eh?" He stopped as I dug in my pocket for the car key.

It was a lame comment and I knew it. There had been a reason why we'd come to that particular bookshop. "Yeah, the garden centre we passed coming off the motorway. They'll have books on gardening. You're looking for a book about leaves, right?"

For a moment his face remained blank, and then it cracked into the widest of grins.

"I just thought you could look there." I thumbed the key fob and the BMW unlocked with a clunk. Sunlight burst from the bodywork, near blinding.

Victor laughed. A couple of passers-by eyed him with amusement.

Once in the car, I clicked my seat belt into place with deliberate attention.

"*The Book of Leaves*," he said, as I released the handbrake, "isn't a book on gardening. Not at all. There are many kinds of leaves, my friend. Many kinds."

"What do you mean?"

"The word 'leaf' can also mean *sin*."

"What are you talking about?" I didn't know what to make of the guy.

"You'll find out in good time," he said.

CHAPTER 3

With Victor talking about sin, I'd not pressed him further. He was my boss after all. I drove him back to his flat in silence. Besides, he seemed to have a lot to think about. I enjoyed the quiet, and I enjoyed driving the BMW. It was a silver 7-series with less than a hundred miles on the clock and most of those were mine.

I hadn't been back in the UK for long, and I already needed some time on my own. I left Victor at his flat and drove to the House. Raised voices in the lobby rushed towards me as I sprinted from the car. Rain pummelled the ground, the borders and driveway erupting. Lightning cracked the sky.

Beneath the portico, I shook myself. Relief, and I wasn't sure whether it was the release of atmospheric pressure or that my first day at work was over. Or perhaps it was because I was finally in from the rain. The distance I'd covered wasn't any further than twenty metres, yet my shirt stuck to my back.

Two people, anoraks dripping, blocked my way into the House. Voices spat from beneath the hoods.

"Pam, listen to me, I—"

"Shut up, Mick, not interested."

"I—"

"No."

"I—"

"Excuse me, please," I said. This was ridiculous.

"Pam, the—"

"Mick." A hand shot from a sleeve. It yanked the other's collar. "Shut up. We're late. It's late."

"Excuse me," I said again, trying not to allow anger to leak into my voice. It was difficult. "Please, may I pass?"

"What?" The woman, Pam, spun round, her lips tight as if they'd been glued shut. I guessed Mick wished they were.

"Can I get through?"

Her feral glare held me for a second, and with a tut she pushed Mick backwards and he bumped the doorframe.

I felt sorry for the guy.

"Inside, you." It felt as though the words were for me.

My boots squeaked as I hurried across the marble floor towards the staircase. No one manned reception. Goodwin's office door was open, so I nosed in. He was shrouded in smoke while opposite him a woman, her face as sharp as her suit, spoke rapidly. Each word leapt around the room. "Even a hurricane wouldn't stop this event from going ahead."

"That's what I like to hear." Goodwin waved me in. "Leo, meet Jocelyn."

The woman beamed and slid her briefcase onto the desk. She stood up and in one stride met me at the door.

Goodwin added, "This is the son I never had: Leo."

After two years, I still didn't know how to feel about that.

"Pleasure." She extended her hand.

"Hi." I wasn't sure which dwarfed me more, her heels or bosom.

"Jocelyn is our event organiser," Goodwin explained. "The concert this weekend is in her more than capable hands."

"That it is," she said.

Goodwin puffed on the cigar.

"Well," she added and grabbed her briefcase. Her engagement ring bulged between small fingers. "That about wraps it up anyway."

"Don't rush out because I'm here." I backed out of the office. "Need to chill out for a bit. Not used to working."

That was an understatement. I still couldn't dislodge images of Lucas being tortured.

It wasn't long after I'd made it to my room, showered, and gotten dressed, when a knock on the door stole me from my thoughts. Goodwin entered and stood beside me at the window. We peered through the rain-smeared glass.

"Once I get on my feet, I'll be out of here," I said. "Thanks for all this."

"You're sticking with the job then?"

"Yeah." I thought of how Victor didn't wear any socks.

"Good." He gripped my shoulder. "Victor knew you would and said that you're a worthy ally."

"When did you guys speak?" Maybe there was an edge to my voice.

"A moment ago."

I nodded. "Talking behind my back?"

Goodwin laughed.

"You two known each other long?" I wondered if he knew Lucas. They were all the same age—or thereabouts—and perhaps Goodwin could tell me more of their history.

"Too long," Goodwin said. "Victor was there when the House first became what it is now. We shared ideas for its renovation and expansion. He and his brother had a hand in the first few years. Indeed, to get it established. They soon began to follow their own…er, lives."

"What's his brother like?" I imagined he was just as cranky.

"Stanley? I haven't seen him in years, nor have I spoken to him since…" Goodwin moved closer to the window. Twilight deepened his frown. "Do you fancy going out somewhere tonight?"

CHAPTER 4

Tuesday

In contrast to the evening before, I squinted as sunlight glared from the parked cars. My boss jogged towards me, weaving between vehicles and bollards—no socks. His shoes splashed the remaining puddles. Water soaked his trousers and he didn't seem to care.

"Good morning, my friend," he said. He intrigued me; I couldn't deny it.

"Hello, sir." I didn't know how to address the man.

"Call me Victor. No one calls me sir. Sounds awkward. False. I'm no larger than anyone else."

He had a point. "Fair enough, Victor. Where're we off to?"

"A little further than yesterday," he said. "Out of the city. Heading down to Tunbridge Wells."

I knew the journey, and as was often, I wondered if I'd ever lived there. No matter where I visited, memories still wouldn't return. On that hour's drive—unlike my first day as his driver—there was hardly any silence. After the standard exchange about weather, we soon spoke of my travels. Which was when I didn't shut up.

Eventually, Victor asked me a simple question. "So, do you remember much of your past?"

I didn't know how to reply. Half of me wanted to tell him to mind his own business, the other wanted to admit it scared the crap out of me. Slowing the car on approach to a red light, I stared too long at the road sign.

"This lane is fine, keep going," he said without taking his eyes off me. "I know a lot about you. As much as Goodwin's shared with me."

The traffic light turned green and it failed to register, my focus pushing through the colour. The car behind me honked. In the rear-view mirror the impatient bastard, a mobile phone to his ear, frowned at me. I wanted to flick him a finger, but didn't think it wise in front of my boss. Further back crouched a red convertible, whose driver was a pair of sunglasses in a blonde flurry. As I brought up the clutch, pain stabbed my knee and I stalled the engine, the traffic light changed back to red. Another look in the mirror and fury burned in the driver's face. I didn't give a shit, yet I still raised a hand to apologise, and quickly started the engine again…only to make three or four car lengths in progress before coasting to another red.

I wasn't sure how to feel about Goodwin having shared information about my past. Not just that, but sometimes I'd forget that I've forgotten everything before the accident. It was strange to admit. "Then you know as much as me."

This ended our conversation and I'd not meant it to.

Victor gave me precise directions, and when we reached the outskirts of Royal Tunbridge Wells, he explained we were not heading into the town itself. Again, I wondered if I'd ever lived in this area.

"An acquaintance of mine," he told me, "Montelius. Next right. Just here."

I swung the BMW off the road and took us down a driveway loosely paved between rows of gnarled trees. In front of us, smothered in ivy, stood a cottage beside a riverbank. In the rear-view mirror the convertible from earlier shot past.

On foot, gravel crunching, we strolled towards the front door. Before we reached it, a female voice carried across the generous colours of the garden: "I'm over here, Cubs."

For a moment that name confused me, then I realised it was an abbreviation of Victor's surname, Jacobs. From a row of box hedging a lady emerged, her smile shaded beneath a wicker hat. I couldn't see her eyes, but what I saw of her face looked old. Cruelly, I thought she looked ancient.

Victor cut across the grass and I hurried after him.

Stepping around the hedge, the lady tugged off a dirty glove and dropped it. Her dress mirrored the flowers around her. With wrinkly hands and delicate precision, she stroked Victor's face.

"Nice to see you." Polly's eyes focussed on something beyond us, into a space reserved for her. "And you've brought a friend."

Her touch was as soft as those wrinkles suggested, and equally the warmth in her face proved welcoming. There was a faint smell of earth on her hands.

"Leo, Polly." Victor winked at me. "Polly, Leo."

"Good to meet you." I stood rigid. It was surreal to allow someone you've never met before to stroke your face.

She lowered her hands. "You're handsome."

"Cut it out, Montelius," Victor said. "He's not here for you. He's my driver. A friend of Goodwin's."

I didn't know what to say.

"Georgie." Polly reached down and stroked a golden retriever. I hadn't noticed it join us. The dog brushed against her legs as it led us into the cottage.

Inside Polly's home, we came to a table underneath a painting of a Mediterranean landscape. It somehow filled the room with more warmth. I avoided taking the chair facing a magazine and a pair of spectacles. Victor sat beside Polly, the two of them at an angle from me. Georgie, back straight, sat by her feet. She tucked her chair in. I could smell furniture polish and cakes. Such an odd combination. A floorboard creaked from the hallway.

"Annabel," Victor said, "how are you?"

A young woman walked around us to stand beside Polly. Her hair was pulled into a tight, short ponytail. Her brow creased as she took us in, spending a second too long on me. In contrast to Polly's blank gaze, this woman's eyes penetrated the core.

Her features were as thin as her voice. "Fine. Who is this?"

I felt more than uncomfortable, which irritated me.

"Leo's my driver." Victor wore an expression difficult to interpret.

I stood, and without wanting to, I offered my hand. Her shake was cold and limp.

"Annabel," Victor added, "is Polly's hired hand."

She picked up the spectacles and the magazine. Her ponytail whipped as she left the room.

Polly's smile wrinkled her face further. "Pleased you could make it." She slipped on a pair of sunglasses and hid her floating eyes.

"I'd never turn down the offer of tea from you." Victor beamed.

"But," she added, "I've not had a good morning."

"Oh?" Victor leaned forward. "What's wrong?"

"I've been waiting on a delivery and now it's not coming. I have to wait until the end of the week."

Victor grunted. "What happened?"

"Lame excuse." Her laugh was humourless. "Not enough hands apparently. The annoying thing is, they're local."

"Do you want me to help? What is it?"

"It's okay, I can wait. It's just some furniture. Not much at all, really."

"No, honestly." Victor glanced at me. "It wouldn't be a problem for us to collect it."

I nodded. "Of course. The Bee-Em is pretty spacious, you think it'll fit?"

"I would ask Annabel," Polly said, "but they're heavy. Only a set of chests. They would fit in your car, yes."

I drank my tea in silence while Victor and Polly talked. I didn't mind too much, I was content listening. Occasionally they'd include me, but the conversation would soon resume between the two of them. Polly was thankful that we'd help her with the chests. It seemed that I wasn't just a chauffeur, I was also some kind of haulage guy. It was still a job.

CHAPTER 5

Victor and I entered the antique shop, and from a threadbare sofa, an old man glared at us over a paperback: *Treasure Island*. I wanted to laugh; all around him suggested quite the opposite. Behind him a female mannequin pointed at the ceiling. The other arm was missing. She wore only a leather waistcoat, and someone had crudely drawn a smiley face on her. Dusty, inappropriate junk smothered the place. And it stank of old umbrellas.

"Can I help you?" He folded the book and dropped it on a cluttered table. His clothes were as old as his wares, and his face looked older than Polly's by another century.

Victor strolled up to him. "I'm here on behalf of Polly Montelius, she—"

"Ah, yes." The man grasped his knees and eased himself up. "About time I moved, I've been there all morning."

"Apparently you have some chests for her?" Victor added.

"Yes, yes." The old man waved a hand. "Terribly sorry I couldn't get them out to her."

On a sideboard was the mannequin's arm, and wrapped around it was a row of watches. I liked one, so had a closer look. It was old, the face scratched, and the metal casing tarnished. Something about it made me pull it from the wrist and fasten it to my own. I lifted it to my ear, its ticking sounded different from modern-day watches.

As Victor explained our intentions, from the corner of my eye, I saw movement, and my stunned face stared back. The mirror, framed in split wood, was cracked in the corner. The filthy glass gave my reflection a strange darkness. It made me look tired. Perhaps even haunted.

The old man had left the room and Victor thumbed a yellowed comic. It looked close to disintegrating.

The door behind us crashed inwards and a stack of magazines tumbled to the floor. A violin shifted sideways and fell against a glass case. It played a sustained note as if to announce the arrival of the grubby man running into the shop. An overcoat billowed in his wake, and his bloodshot gaze speared us through tousled hair. He barged past me and rushed to the counter. A cloud of stink followed him.

"Where…" he began, and then coughed. "Where is he?"

Victor, having taken a step back, had a hand inside his jacket. His eyebrows twitched. "Who?"

"The man who owns this place. Who else?" He clutched to his chest a long and thin box, about the length of an average school ruler. There was dirt beneath his fingernails. His eyes darted around the place. The guy was a tramp, surely? Most likely drug addicted too.

"He's out the back getting something for us," Victor told him, still with a hand inside his pocket. It made me think he had a gun in there. Perhaps he did. How was I to know?

"William!" The tramp's voice filled the shop. "I have something for you."

My pulse quickened. I expected him to go crazy, to smash up the place. I didn't like the way he shifted from foot to foot as though he trod on hot coals. And his eyes were on fire. Red raw. Maybe he'd been crying. I decided it could be nothing other than drugs.

From out back, William shouted, "Hang on! I need to send someone around with them. The damn stupid boy isn't answering his phone."

"What are you talking about?" The tramp's filthy face twisted into a grimace as if in agony. "William, it's me. I have something to sell you. I need to get rid of it."

I exchanged glances with Victor and he shrugged, slipping an empty hand from his jacket. No gun. He wouldn't have a gun—it wouldn't suit him.

"I'll be there in a minute!" William's voice sounded muffled.

Again, I admired the watch on my wrist. I listened as it counted out more than a minute. When the old man came back, maybe I'd enquire about it. I now had a job, so I could afford a little welcome home present to myself.

When William returned and saw the tramp at the counter, his eyes shot from me to Victor. "Please, I have customers."

The man clenched his jaw. "I don't care."

"Josh, you look terrible." William's voice softened. "What happened?"

They knew each other? Perhaps this guy wasn't a tramp, and if not, why was he filthy? I took a step back, trying not to wrinkle my nose.

"I have to get rid of this." Josh slid the box across the counter. "I don't want the responsibility."

"I can't take it." The old man knocked it away. "I want nothing to do with this."

"You have to!" Josh slammed a hand down and the counter rattled. "They've killed the others!"

For a second, I couldn't breathe. What the hell was this?

"I told you," William said, "I want nothing to do with you."

Josh's hands curled into fists, the knuckles white. "You have no idea what I've gone through. I'm the last one. They're all dead. The witch came."

Victor grabbed the man's shoulder.

"Get off me," Josh screamed.

Victor didn't flinch and that impressed me. He did oblige, however, and stepped back.

William looked worried. This wasn't good for business.

"What do you mean by that?" Victor's forehead wrinkled, eyebrows knotting. "You said 'a witch came'?"

"It did," Josh yelled, "because that's what happened."

Victor glanced at me as though he knew what was going on. He faced the man. "Who are you?"

"He's no one," William said. His breath sounded panicked, his face red. "Don't listen to him."

"Listen to me," Josh whispered through brown teeth. "Take the thing."

"I can't take it."

"They've all been killed!" He lunged across the counter, arms outstretched.

Victor yanked Josh backwards and whirled him around. "Leave him alone."

The man leaned back and swung a fist. I was about to shout a warning when Victor blocked it. Another swing followed and Victor crouched, sweeping his leg in a blur. The man crashed to the floor.

Victor stepped aside, gloved fists raised in defence. "Leave."

The man's eyes burned into Victor's.

"Now," Victor added.

The watch still on my wrist, announced several passing seconds. Its tick filled my head. Still the man lay there wide eyed, his coat bunched around his neck, legs tangled. His chest rose and fell. Eventually, he moved and slowly nodded. He pushed himself up, and with a hung head, staggered towards the door. It was still open. I expected him to shout something, but he didn't. He vanished into the street.

The black box remained on the counter and William, with his hands clamped against the back of his head, eyed it. "I don't want this."

Victor approached him. "Are you okay, my friend?"

"More to the point," William replied, lowering his hands, "are you?"

Victor flicked his eyes at the box. "May I?"

William didn't take his eyes from it. "If you wish."

Victor reached out and paused. It was difficult to read his face, but he came across as both scared and excited. He stroked the top of the box and tapped a finger on its lid. He then traced its edges with a thumb, inward to the clasp, and flicked it with what I could only describe as respect.

The old man's lips had tightened.

Victor lifted the lid and I glimpsed red fabric before he snapped it closed. He mumbled something.

"Keep it," William said, his face blotchy. He pointed at me. "And you keep the watch."

I'd forgotten I still wore it. I looked down at my wrist. "But—"

"Your chests will be in the car park. My son will be there shortly. Please leave."

Victor nodded his thanks. "Let's go, Leo."

I followed him to the door, seeing the box disappear into an inner pocket of his jacket. William already sat in his chair, reaching for *Treasure Island*. Outside, beneath a warm sun, I kept pace with Victor. So, I was his driver, that was fine. The occasional lugging around of furniture wouldn't be a problem either. I thought about that sweeping kick, his ninja move, and the possibility he had a gun. Thinking of that, I began to wonder if I'd made a good career choice. It wasn't a career, it was only a job…temporary.

At least I didn't need to be his bodyguard.

On the way back to Polly's cottage, with the chests secured on the back seats, I drove in silence. Minutes after leaving the shop, Victor's eyes had closed and he now gently snored. I wanted to wake him, and was thankful the journey wasn't far—I doubted I'd last much longer. I itched to know what hid in the box, yet I managed to remain as professional as I could. I had no right to pry into his affairs. My curiosity returned to Josh, the guy in the shop who'd said people had been killed. What the hell was he talking about?

Although a short drive, it felt like a long one.

Once at our destination, I nudged Victor awake and we heaved the chests into the lounge. He remained thoughtful, with few words spoken. Soon, his anxiety turned to almost excitement. In the dining room, with tea at the table and Annabel now elsewhere, he leaned towards our host.

"Polly," he said. "I have the athame."

I frowned, misunderstanding him. I believed he'd quickly said, *If I may?*

He opened the box and I craned my neck to see. I had to know what was in there. As before, all I saw was red, only now I recognised it to be silk. I leaned further. Held between the delicate folds of cloth lay an ornate knife, its hilt a twisted knot of silver. The curved blade ended in a nasty point and reflected the red of its surroundings. The mirroring of the fabric made it appear as though blood coated it.

I thought of Josh saying something about witches. The guy must've been hallucinating. Totally loopy. Yet, there was something about that knife. And certainly, there was something in the way Victor held the box. Light glinted from the blade.

"What does it look like?" Polly's lips were tight.

Victor placed the box on the table. He still wore his gloves. "Beautiful."

"How did you come by it?" Polly asked, her voice no more than a whisper.

"By chance. Pure and simple. At the antique shop."

"I don't believe in coincidence." Polly's voice was so soft, I leaned closer. "These things happen for a reason."

"Perhaps," Victor replied.

"How do you know it's the one we've been searching for?"

"Because of its markings."

Polly stroked her face. "It was last seen in Bohemia, in a small village where superstition clouds judgement."

"Witches." Victor glanced at me.

Again, I thought of what Josh had said. Did a witch kill the others he'd spoken of? Was that what he believed? I didn't know where any of this was leading. I looked at the car key in my hand. I'd been gripping the damn thing so tight there were marks in my palm. I put it in my pocket and sat up straighter.

Polly rolled the tea cup between her hands. "It goes by another name."

Victor nodded. "Often referred to as The Witchblade."

"Yes," Polly said, her voice much stronger. "Of course."

I had to remind myself I was getting paid for this bullshit.

As Polly's lips parted to say something else, an electronic warble pierced the atmosphere: four beeps vibrating in Victor's pocket. He blinked and his hands clamped the case. Then he retrieved his mobile phone. It was one of the old ones with actual buttons. He stabbed it with a rigid finger.

"Stanley," he said and grunted, glancing at Polly.

Silence.

"Leo," Victor added, "you'll meet my brother later."

CHAPTER 6

Leaning against Victor's car and squinting at the rain, I looked up to where I guessed his flat was. The rain cooled my skin. I felt as though I needed to be cleansed after the strange morning I'd had. I glanced at my watch—the watch I didn't pay for—and it agreed with my stomach: lunchtime. After returning Victor home, he told me to wait for a few minutes.

As I considered getting back into the car, I saw him emerge from the building. He held an envelope.

I moved towards him.

"Pay day, my friend." Victor slapped the envelope into my hand. He'd taken off his shoes and now stood in a puddle. The water covered his toes.

"Vic—" I began, not knowing what to say. He was paying me already?

"You can go home now," he added. "Come back later, at six. You'll get to meet Stanley."

I scratched my chin. "It's Tuesday. This is my second day, and they haven't even been full days."

"Bah!" he replied. He reminded me of Scrooge, yet the weight of the envelope suggested otherwise. "There's a bonus, given today's lucky find. Go home or go out. Either way have yourself a jolly afternoon. Oh, and here's a mobile for you. Take it, I've put my number in there. Goodwin's as well, plus a few others. If it rings, answer it. Make calls to whoever, whenever, wherever. It's all yours."

"Er, thanks." The words were lame, as they often are when someone shows you ridiculous generosity. Goodwin—now Victor. If there's anyone out there with a cynical view of the world, then trust me, there are good people around us. When we're surrounded by the good guys, it energises the soul. They might sometimes prove hard to find, and I know occasionally the good can turn out bad…there are many bad eggs.

"Keep it charged and don't lose it." His feet splashed the puddle. "Be here bang on six."

"Will do, Victor."

"You have a good afternoon." He jogged back towards the building.

Wage packet in one hand, I managed a quick, "You too!" as he disappeared. The door closed behind him and cut off his slapping footfalls.

It was strange to hold a pay packet—money I've earned. My money. A new life was starting.

In the car, I thumbed the lock and relaxed—some would call it paranoia, but I'd call it being sensible; it's London after all and not Mabley Holt, population 97. After eyeing the car park, I gave the envelope my full attention. I tore it open and took more care when shaking out the wad of notes. I counted £500 in twenties and £500 in fifties. I was glad, perhaps even *relieved* that I favoured combats and the compartments they sported, as I wouldn't trust such an amount of cash to sit unguarded in a jeans pocket waiting to be lifted.

Or perhaps someone may rush at me from anywhere and attack me. Again, I scanned the parked cars: no carjackers, nor potential muggers.

Not paranoia, just being sensible.

I had my first pay packet and was high on life. My new life. Everything was going to be okay, even if today there'd been talk of witches and a drug addict saying people had been killed. All nonsense, of course. That guy in the shop had been hallucinating. He was paranoid.

I hoped.

CHAPTER 7

"Who the fuck is this?" Stanley pointed at me. "How much does he know?"

Victor placed one hand on the back of the scuffed sofa and the other on my arm. "This is Leo. And he knows enough."

I wanted to say I didn't know anything, but kept quiet. My cheeks warmed and it took a lot for me not to move. I glared at Victor's brother.

In three strides, Stanley stood before Victor, still holding the TV remote. The buttons looked sticky.

"Why do you need a friend with you?" His jaw muscles flexed with his biceps. "Scared to be in the same room with your own brother?"

I couldn't believe this guy. Already I hated him, and I wondered if I'd ever met anyone quite as obnoxious. I wanted to leave.

"Stan," Victor said, "you know I can't drive. Leo is my driver."

"I'm a friend of Goodwin," I said as my jaw relaxed.

Stanley, clutching the remote in a massive fist, ignored me.

"Okay, okay." He backed away from Victor's face. "I've got something to show you."

"So you said in your text." Victor walked the length of the room and slumped into an armchair beneath a poster of a Harley and a bikini-clad girl.

"Help yourself to a seat, bro."

Arms folded, I strolled towards Victor as he lifted a leg and hooked the ankle on a knee. Stanley—the guy was a bad egg—pointed at him.

"You didn't get dressed properly." He laughed. "Still forgetting to put your socks on."

Victor remained silent.

I lowered my eyes and tried hard not to shake my head in disbelief. I also tried not to wrinkle my nose—the stink of recently fried chips pleased me in knowing I'd not long ago eaten salad with my pasta.

In the corner of the lounge, at the end of a well-trodden rug and propped against a curtain, was a violin case. Stanley headed for it, threw the remote onto the sofa and lifted the case.

"You know the story, Vic." He stood in the centre of the room. "Back in the Great Fire of London it burned with the rest of the city."

"You have it?" Victor dropped his leg with a thump and leaned forward. "We've been searching too long."

I stared at both of them in turn.

One side of Stanley's mouth curled upwards.

"Since we all got together, Vic." He patted the case. "Long ago. Back when you wore ridiculous outfits."

"I liked the 70s." Victor clenched and unclenched his hands. He seemed to always wear those gloves. The leather creaked.

"Sure you did."

"I know Goodwin's given up believing in it." Victor sank into the cushions. "That and *The Book of Leaves*. Clocks it all as just legend. Polly's certain of the existence of everything. Always has been."

"Well, the blind bitch has always seen the world differently."

Victor grimaced. "Don't speak like that."

I gaped at Stanley. This guy was unbelievable.

He eyed the case. "Out of all of us, I was the one who found it."

What had this irritating bastard found? A violin? How special could a violin be? I thought of the Witchblade—or the *athame*. Coincidence there, with Victor finding it at the antique shop. Yet now, Stanley revealing something on the same day—another coincidence. Polly didn't believe things happened by chance, and I was beginning to feel the same.

"How did you find it?" Victor asked.

"Ah, contacts." Stanley slid the case onto the table, knocking aside several takeaway boxes. Rice scattered and a pair of flies took to the air. He slapped a magazine to the floor.

Victor stood up, lips parting.

A fly buzzed near my head and I waved it away.

"Well," Stanley said, "here it is. The Shadow Fabric."

The case, I'd assumed, would hold a musical instrument. A violin. But no...as Stanley popped the lock and pulled it open, the Shadow Fabric proved to be what its name suggests: a roll of black fabric, loosely bunched in places, the material somewhere between silk and velvet. It played with the room's lighting which gave the illusion it wasn't entirely there. The way it toyed with the senses, the way something wasn't quite right about it, I felt I had to immediately avert my eyes or I'd get caught out. Sussed. It was as though I allowed something to see me...or to see *into* me; into my being, burrowing into my core.

I shivered.

Stanley stepped away from the table, mouth set. "Victor?"

"Huh?" He dragged his gaze from the Fabric.

Stanley pointed at Victor's jacket. "What's that?"

Victor brushed his fingers along the box protruding from an inner pocket. The Witchblade.

"Something I wanted to show you," he said. "You're not the only one who's found something."

Yeah, I thought, coincidence.

Stanley reached for the violin case. "Not *The Book of Leaves*. I can see that."

Victor shook his head.

"That book has been a pain in the arse for the last three hundred years." Stanley slammed the case closed.

The pressure in the room shifted. With my vision sharpening, I inhaled the suddenly untainted air—such a relief to no longer see and feel the Fabric.

"That's the athame." Stanley's eyes widened. "Right?"

Victor nodded, saying nothing. It was difficult to read his face.

"You trying to hide it from me?"

"Of course not." He shook his head. "I brought it over to show you. You're as much a part of this team as anyone. You deserve to see it."

"I thought everyone had abandoned me."

"You're lucky we didn't. But you're my brother, Stan."

Stanley's mouth twitched. He pulled the violin case open again. "Well, this is why I wanted you here."

My eyes took in the Fabric once more; the thing shimmered. The air turned stale and my head hurt, my lungs were tight. I wanted to run from the room. No, I wanted to leap out the window—the nearest exit.

Victor slid a hand into his jacket and pulled out the slim box. He placed it onto the table, locking eyes with his brother.

It was Stanley's turn to say nothing.

"And this…" Victor said, then flipped open the box, "is why I came."

Stanley sucked air between clenched teeth. He held Victor's gaze and tugged at the Fabric, caressing the material between thumb and forefinger. He lowered his eyes to the Witchblade.

"You're not wearing gloves!" Victor held out a hand, fingers splayed. A warning.

"*You* are, as always, you little weirdo."

"Yes." A crease down the centre of Victor's forehead separated his eyebrows. He pulled off his gloves with fumbling speed. "You can't touch the Fabric."

"What are you talking about?"

"The Fabric, Stan." Victor offered him the gloves.

"That's just it…" Stanley swiped them away with his free hand, the other was a fistful of black folds. His neck stretched and he pushed his face into Victor's. "You've always thought yourself better than anyone else."

"Stan—"

"Mister fucking clever."

"Please—"

"All our lives you've been the one to follow others…"

Victor gripped the Witchblade with his bare hand. I'm not sure when he had taken it from the box. Where was this heading?

Stanley's face had turned scarlet. "And now you're barking orders at me."

"Stanley, listen—"

"The problem with you…" Stanley yanked the Fabric from the case. "You've never known whether you want to be the pigeon or the statue. Most of the time you just allow people to shit on you, without moving a muscle. Me? I don't stand around, I'm the one who carved the statue."

"Stanley—"

"No!" His brother slapped a hand onto the table. "I'm the architect who designed the square that statue stands in!"

This was turning nasty and I didn't know what to do. Then I remembered Victor's sweeping kick, bringing down the guy in the antique shop—he could look after himself.

Still in Stanley's hand, the Fabric flowed over the table like liquid, turning everything into a dark shadow of its former self. The edges of the material rippled, seeming to tug as though desperate to grab more of its surroundings. As it unfolded, the light in the room dimmed.

The two brothers stood nose to nose. Victor with the Witchblade tight in his fist, and Stanley with the Fabric quivering in his.

I couldn't blink. The presence of the Fabric clamped my head. I threw swift glances around the room. Someone wanted to stab me in the back, to kick me in the nuts. To shoot me in the head. I had to get out of there, I had to leave Victor and his brother to it.

"I hate you, Victor." Stanley's mouth twitched.

"No," Victor gasped. The Witchblade shook, his knuckles white. "Don't!"

I didn't know if he said it to his brother or the Witchblade. Then I saw it was neither. It was to the Shadow Fabric. It pulled his hand...and the blade slammed into Stanley's chest.

CHAPTER 8

The tendrils of Shadow Fabric released Victor's wrist and recoiled from the Witchblade. Stanley staggered backwards. The blade sucked out from the wound and blood spread down his shirt like an obscene inkblot. His eyes wide, mouth agape, he still clutched the Fabric. The tentacles whipped the air once, twice, and returned to the main seething mass.

My lungs tightened as I watched Victor stumble, the Witchblade now gripped in a red fist.

Stanley gulped as blood drenched his shirt. The Fabric slipped from his hand and closed around him. It dragged him along the carpet. His eyes glazed as the shadows curled inwards. Only a pale face and a bloody torso remained.

The darkness hovered, shrinking moment by moment, and I saw only Stanley's dead stare.

I clenched my teeth so hard my jaw hurt.

Victor's mouth opened and closed, no more than a step from the twisting shadows, watching as his brother eventually vanished.

Silence.

His eyebrows twitching, Victor looked at the Witchblade.

"Vic…" I whispered, my throat dry.

Beside him, over a gas fireplace, stood a mantel clock. It hammered the seconds into the room. The Witchblade slipped from his hand and thumped on the carpet, leaving a red stain.

He fell to his knees and lowered his head. "Oh, God."

The Fabric faded to grey and folded into itself. And disappeared.

The combination of streetlights through the curtains and the artificial light in the room was almost physical. Without the Fabric's cloying presence, I could breathe again. Such a welcome relief.

Victor's shoulders trembled.

I lunged forward, charged into motion. With the Fabric no longer tainting the air, there was nothing to worry about. Energised and feeling happy and guilty—ashamed of my light-heartedness—for I knew I didn't deserve this happiness when there crouched Victor, his brother's blood at his feet. I stopped beside him and grasped his shoulder.

"Vic—" I swallowed. "Victor…"

The Witchblade glistened red.

My jaw slackened. Blood. Murder. And there I was, an accessory. I'd seen those arms of shadow extend from the darkness which Stanley held, thin tentacles clamping Victor's wrist and pulling the knife into his brother's chest.

I'd been this man's chauffeur for little more than a day, and already I'd witnessed him kill his brother. What the hell was this?

It was supernatural. Paranormal. Whatever this was, it proved the unfolding of a reality I'd assumed was as solid as a paperback in hand. Everything beneath and around us was not as black and white as we believed. All things in life which surround us and are taken for granted since we first came to be, are false. There's a lot more to what we see, feel, smell, hear, taste….

"Shit," I said. "What's going on?"

Victor said nothing. His sobs quaked beneath my hand.

"Get up, man." I squeezed his shoulder. "Victor. Get up."

He shook his head; whether in denial, or in answer to me, I didn't know. One thing was certain, what I felt in the grip of his bony shoulder told me this man's previous vitality had been drained. It now leaked from him in whimpers, seeping just as Stanley's blood now soaked the carpet.

"Victor, please." I was thirsty.

He said nothing, although this time there wasn't any movement, not even a sob. I let go of him and stepped back. The mantel clock clanked 8 p.m.—the chiming mechanism evidently missing or broken.

This was murder, yet there wasn't a body.

Victor lifted his head and his eyes focussed on the Witchblade. He closed a hand around it and in jerking movements got to his feet.

I took another couple of steps back, unsure if it was just to allow him more room, or because the man had a knife and he'd used it only moments ago. Being a little further away made sense.

He went to the table, avoiding the yawning violin case and grabbed the Witchblade box. He opened it.

Such a small box and looked more innocent than the instrument case, though both housed something equally curious and dangerous. Of course a knife wouldn't be as innocent as a musical instrument, if that was what had been inside it. No matter the ornate qualities and monetary value of the knife—the *athame*—its blade was deadly, and having seen the Fabric's power, no wonder Victor had tried to persuade his brother to borrow his gloves, for whatever good they might've done. Victor apparently had some idea of what was going on. The Witchblade, the Shadow Fabric; I again wondered about coincidence of finding them. There was none of that here.

Victor hid the bloodied weapon from view and snatched his gloves from under the table. Finally, he saw my expression.

"Don't worry." He pulled the gloves on. "We can fix this."

I tilted my head.

"I think," he added, and stood up.

"Victor? Stanley…"

"I know, I—"

We both spun to the crash of the front door, the sound reverberating in the room. The light fittings shook. My immediate thought was that the Shadow Fabric had returned, and my breath stuck in my throat. Victor's eyes bulged.

A hooded figure charged into the room. Perhaps the Fabric had manifested into human form, wearing black with something red across the head. No, this slight figure, feminine, was entirely real: black jeans and a black hoodie, red scarf and sunglasses.

She stopped and waved a gun in our faces. Knowing a bullet lurked a mere trigger-pull away, a coldness ran through me. So many things in my past remained hidden from me, and I was certain up until then, I'd never before been confronted by someone holding a gun, its muzzle a deathly O waiting for me to do the wrong thing.

The red scarf was taut over her mouth, sunglasses hiding her eyes. The only feature which stood out was a blonde wisp of hair that arced beneath the hood.

"The knife," she said, her voice muffled. The gun moved from Victor to me, and then to Victor again.

My heartbeat pounded my ears. It tuned out everything. All I saw was the gun. In my head, I screamed for Victor to hand the damn thing to her.

His already slumped shoulders dropped further and he held out the box. She grabbed it, and with a flick of the thumb, it popped open and snapped shut. One swift movement, all without the barrel of her gun wavering. Leaning towards the table, her head tilted for a view into the violin case. Apparently satisfied with its gaping emptiness, she circled us and paced backwards, reaching the door.

As she left, she said, "Don't follow me."

Silence poured into the room.

I stood with Victor, a patch of blood at our feet. From outside, a car engine roared, followed by a screech of tyres. I snapped my head up and leaned towards the window as a familiar red convertible disappeared down the road. The bitch had been following us since yesterday, and most likely had been following Victor for a lot longer.

I squeezed the cash in my pocket and followed Victor's gaze.

Blood.

CHAPTER 9

Wednesday

When we stare at something and don't quite see it, lost in our own head and someone talks to us, we're reluctant to lose that eye-locking trance. We're conscious of our staring eyes, we look without seeing. At that moment, I must've appeared as though I scrutinised the poster on the wall. I'd been there for a while, waiting outside Goodwin's office. Apparently, he was busy and would be right with me.

"Thinking of going?" a voice drifted over my shoulder.

I focused on the poster: *New Tide Chamber Orchestra, this Saturday.*

The resident beauty therapist stood beside me. An attractive girl with dark hair over slender shoulders. Her figure would make any man do a double-take. She continued when realising I wasn't going to answer.

"I reckon it'll be cool to go, and ticket sales have gone well according to Gina Godfrey. She's one of my clients." She laughed and added, "And a bit nosy."

Her perfume filled me up. I tried to smile and doubted it reached eyes reflecting a night of duvet-kicking. After leaving Stanley's house, I'd driven Victor home. The journey dragged with few words exchanged. I imagined a driving instructor would feel the same on the way back from a test centre having to drive a pupil home after a failed test. Wanting to say something—anything—to reassure him all can be fixed. No matter the tears, the frustration, the disappointment, all can be rectified with practice. As far as my drive went, there were no words of consolation. Things couldn't be fixed with a few hours of practice. Someone had died. That someone—the man's *brother*—was dead. And to top it all off, a cloud of shadow had essentially eaten his corpse.

Pretty fucked up.

As gorgeous as this young lady beside me was—Natalie had worked at the House for as long as I'd been there—her presence did little to reassure me of the nicer things in life.

"Not sure." This was the first thing I'd said all morning. I had ignored Dean at reception. He'd seen me approaching the office and buzzed Goodwin for me, but I didn't acknowledge the man. Even when he'd called across the foyer to inform me Goodwin would be with me, I didn't thank him.

"It's Wednesday. Mid-week. Was it a heavy night?" Natalie's expression softened me.

"Could say that." I nodded. "I'd like to go, yeah, but…"

"Need a date?"

I didn't know what to say. Hunger stabbed my stomach.

She pulled her handbag tighter over her shoulder. "See you later."

I watched her walk away and all I thought of was the Shadow Fabric taking Stanley's body.

Dean was talking on the phone, something about the marquee and the concert. It was a big event for a village such as Mabley Holt.

Goodwin's door opened and there he stood. Smoke plumed about his head like a deformed halo.

"How are you?" He waved his cigar into the room.

All morning, I'd rehearsed a kind of speech, to get the story out, to tell Goodwin of Victor's family visit. Of course, faced with the only family I had, my tongue wouldn't move. My lips twitched pathetically.

Goodwin's eyes widened, the cigar halfway to his lips. "What's up?"

I collapsed into a leather armchair.

"You don't look yourself." He circled the desk and sank into his chair. It creaked.

The words in my head were as swollen as my tongue. Finally, I managed, "Victor."

He jerked his head back. "Everything okay with him?"

"Last night," I sputtered, "we went to see his brother…Stanley's dead."

"What happened?" It was the first time I'd heard the man raise his voice. He pressed the stub of cigar into the ashtray and lit another.

"Victor's fine." I dragged a hand from my forehead to chin, squeezing my jaw. I'd forgotten to shave. "As fine as anyone can be after watching their own brother die. He killed him."

"How?"

"Victor had a knife and Stanley had some black fabric. It came alive, Goodwin. I've never seen anything like it…it moved, took hold of Victor's hand and made him kill Stanley."

Goodwin nodded. I was conscious of biting my top lip.

"The Shadow Fabric took Stanley," I added. "It folded around him and took the body."

Goodwin's thoughts wrinkled his forehead.

My fingernails continued to rake the stubble. "Never seen anything like it. Stanley's body vanished into the shadows!"

"Leo, everything's going to be okay."

"The man should hand himself in. Shit. I should go to the police. I witnessed a murder, Goodwin. A man died. He was stabbed. Killed. He's dead!"

"Yes, he's dead, and you also saw him disappear into the shadows. That in itself should make you realise this isn't an ordinary situation."

"Murder is not an ordinary situation. It doesn't happen every day."

"Unfortunately, it does." Goodwin glanced at a photo on his desk. It showed a gentleman with familiar round features standing beside a Rolls Royce. "Mankind's own evil killed the greatest human being I ever knew."

A clock bounced the seconds around the office. It wasn't often he spoke of his family. All I knew was that a young Goodwin witnessed the unmotivated murder of his father. I didn't care about any of that right now. All I cared for was having seen Victor murder his brother.

"Goodwin, you know what I mean."

He ground out his cigar. "Let's go for a walk." He stood up.

An invisible belt had been pulled across my chest, its buckle cranked to the tightest notch. Reaching out with shaky hands, I gripped the desk and hefted my body up. My legs were weak, my knee throbbed, and my heartbeat slammed in my skull. I paused, clenched my teeth, and stood straight.

"Come on." Goodwin's voice floated from the doorway behind me.

I plodded into the foyer, following Goodwin. We headed past the spa, the massage room, the gym and its adjacent studio, and made our way through the windowed portal along the pool area that took us onto the rear terrace and into the overcast morning.

The echoes of someone sweeping came to us and Goodwin slowed as we rounded a corner.

"Hang on, Leo," he said, and then in a louder voice, "Suzy, please don't leave boxes of products around."

This annoyed me. I had more important things to discuss than a box of cleaning products.

The young face of one of the House's newest employees appeared. She ambled over and threw me a toothy smile. "Hi, Leo."

I nodded. There was a deadness in the corners of my mouth. She faced Goodwin. "They've just been delivered and I didn't see the point in taking them to the storeroom before I used one, and it's not for long. These tables out here need a good scrub."

Goodwin's shoulders relaxed.

"It's all good," he said. "I don't like seeing boxes hanging around, that's all. It makes the place look untidy. Besides, the housekeepers have a habit of leaving cans of polish around."

"That's never me."

"I know it's not. You're doing okay."

We left the terrace and stepped onto a gravel path, while behind us the sweeping resumed.

"Fresh air," Goodwin mumbled, and he led us between a row of laurel hedging. To our right a water fountain bubbled onto lily-pads, and on the left a stretch of grass featuring a sundial pointed to aged willows. The gravel path would eventually take us to the edge of the estate, beyond which lay open farmland.

We walked in silence for a while, my chest no longer tight.

"It was unnatural," I finally said. "These things just don't happen."

"I know."

"Do you?"

Our pace slowed.

"Yes, I do. Victor and Stanley, Polly and myself, we're wrapped up in something which is *super*natural."

I thought of Stanley enveloped by the Fabric, its presence overwhelming as I'd stood helpless. And I wondered about the supposed witch and who else had been killed. Nothing was coincidental.

"We're against it, please know this. We don't relish being a part of it. It came upon us a long time ago, and ever since then, we're involved. To the end."

This was all new to me, making me wonder what else Goodwin had kept from me.

"Tell me what happened, Leo."

I told him, sparing nothing, recounting even the smallest detail. It was important. From Stanley's obnoxious who-is-this moment to the point where I had a gun in my face.

"Stanley is gone," he said once I'd finished. "No one can survive the Fabric. It's sad to know he's dead, but of the four of us, it's better him. He was too…he was too volatile. Especially after what he did."

"What?" I doubted I'd be surprised by anything that man had done.

"Only Polly knows exactly what happened, but know this: Stanley was not a nice person."

"Got that from the moment I met him."

"Indeed. All I will say is that the three of us need you. You're strong, Leo. You have a good head on your shoulders, no matter how strange everything yesterday appeared to be. I shall not lie to you, it is going to get worse."

I stared at him.

"Stay with us," he added. "Stay strong."

I wanted out. I didn't want to stay here. Perhaps I'd go travelling again. I watched my feet kick at the dirt. "What is the Shadow Fabric? Where did it come from? What's the deal with the Witchblade?"

"Victor is the best person to speak with, he's the brains when it comes to details. He has the literature."

"He has."

The pathway came to an end, and so did our walk. Spread before us, the countryside failed to provide any security. Having now experienced a total shift in perception, I couldn't find peace where once I would. The two of us stood silent, yet my head was filled with noise. Too much, and I knew it.

"I think…" Goodwin chewed the words around an unlit cigar. "Victor is going to need you now more than ever. Don't see him as just your boss. You're more than just his driver."

A tractor crept across a field, and I squinted to keep it in sight. My lips were pressed together, my jaw aching. It was almost as if Goodwin didn't give a shit about Stanley's death. What precisely had that bad guy done to Polly?

From the corner of my eye, Goodwin's lighter flared. Smoking tobacco leaves snatched the fresh air away.

* * *

I needed answers to this madness, and maybe I drove too fast into London to Victor's flat. By the time I stood outside his door, beating my fist against the wood, I fancied I could still smell Goodwin's cigar.

It seemed like minutes had passed, yet likely only seconds, when Victor's glazed eyes peered past me. At least he'd managed to open the door. The stink of alcohol pushed itself into the hallway as he staggered sideways. He mumbled and waved me into his flat. I guessed I'd have to wait for sensible answers.

Thin lines of sunlight leaked around the curtains. He slammed the door and after walking into me, dropped to where he'd evidently been sitting. The sofa shifted a small distance and knocked a stack of books. The top few tumbled. Several empty wine bottles rolled away from his bare feet and short-lived laughter erupted from his throat. His lips were stained purple, teeth black. Even his loose shirt—yesterday's clothes by the look of it—showed a few splashes of the stuff. His head wobbling, he stared through me. The failed light in the room darkened his sockets and his chin glinted with silver stubble.

"It's all shit, my friend," he said. "We've lost. I've lost. The whole bloody human race has lost."

Swearing didn't suit this guy. I ignored him, went over to the window and yanked open the curtains. It sounded like wings taking flight, beating once in the air. The drapes flew against the bookcases.

Victor hissed and spat as though the sunlight burned him.

It was late afternoon and the sun was fierce, yet comforting. Ever since leaving the House, I'd been unable to stop replaying everything in my head. The moment which most haunted me was Stanley's dead face being swallowed by darkness, the Shadow Fabric.

Victor pressed both palms into his eyes and mumbled curses.

"Too many shadows in here, Victor." I didn't mean it as a joke.

His laughter bounced around us, a humourless uproar that faded into a chuckle, occasionally repeating the word *shadows*.

I went into the kitchen, and by the time I finished making coffee, he was snoring. Placing the two mugs on the table, I switched off the lamp. Could his dreams be at all peaceful? I sank into the sofa opposite him and grabbed the large book I'd noticed when first meeting him. It creaked as I pulled it open. Sunlight illuminated the title page: *Necromeleons*. I'd never heard of it, and sure as hell didn't know what necromeleons were. Perhaps once I did, and I'd forgotten. The word itself intrigued me, let alone this stained tome with its tatty binding. The title reminded me of the word *chameleon*. With an anonymous author, no publisher listed, nor a year of actual publication, this book cried for further questions.

Across from me, Victor snored into a cushion.

Turning a couple of pages, the not-unpleasant smell of old paper wafted up and I scanned the text. From what I could tell—given my limited knowledge of languages—it was a mixture of Latin, German, French...perhaps others. As I flipped another page, a single sheet of paper, torn perforations and dog-eared, slipped out. I snatched at it. Scribbled in pencil were two columns: one side was Latin, the other in English:

Necro – corpse
Mortuus – dead
Occultus – hidden
Pedibus – walk
Umbra – shadow
Textum – fabric
Folium – leaf

Necro, meaning corpse? I flicked back to the title page again: *Necromeleons*. Necro-chameleon? A corpse that changes? My stomach churned. None of these words offered any reassurance. Maybe it was Victor's handwriting, I wasn't sure.

I put the piece of paper to one side.

Thumbing more pages of the book, it proved solid with text for the most part, and occasionally an illustration leapt out at me. Some were portraits of the average 16th- and 17th-century ladies and gentlemen, while others depicted orgies of creatures, bloodied and frantic in the rituals of feasting; burning witches at the stake; cats, frogs, dogs, and goats; each surrounded by diagrams. There were even a few images of the sun and moon and planets in alignment.

Voodoo, the occult, what was all this? I thought of the man in the antique shop. Witches and witchcraft? I wanted to laugh.

One image stood out, a full page sketch. It illustrated a man climbing from what I first saw as a tunnel or a mineshaft, perhaps. On closer inspection, I knew it to be a vortex of shadows. The way the artist had shaded around the figure, it appeared as smoke, but having seen the Shadow Fabric at work, I had no doubt what it was. This scene took place in front of a brick wall, its masonry sharp and precise. Not much detail, simple straight lines of any bricks and mortar structure. The artist had spent more time drawing the man himself. Smartly dressed, difficult to pinpoint the era which his clothes suggested; ambiguous, even down to the featureless shoes. It was his face— such incredible detail; his head abnormally stretched, pulled sideways and downwards, warping his appearance. The skin of his face drooped like it melted. It wasn't so much the dripping skin that I scrutinized, it was the man's expression. Was he actually smiling?

About to flip to the next page, I realised my error. The man wasn't climbing out of the shadows, but *into* them. Again his expression grabbed me.

I browsed each of the 623 pages, trying to understand passages and failing every time. I closed the book and ran my fingertips along the spine and across the strange symbol. Those two triangles facing one another, one hollow, the other solid, with their apexes separated by a curved X, represented something. Throughout the book, it was referenced several times. What the hell did it mean?

I reached for another book, this one about metaphysics by a man named Robert Fludd. Published in 1617, its title was incredibly longwinded, *The Metaphysical, Physical, and the Technical History of the Two Worlds, namely the Greater and the Lesser*. Another scrap of perforated notebook paper marked a page depicting a simple black square, and nothing else apart from the words 'et sic in infinitum' written on all four sides. In pencil on the bookmark, and what I assumed was the translation, were the barely legible words: *and like this to infinity*.

The book's title was in English, yet German and Latin dominated its pages. Those five scribbled words troubled me as much as the image in the aged tome at my feet, the one with the man climbing into the shadows, his melted face not a mask of pain, but of enlightenment?

And like this to infinity…

CHAPTER 10

Thursday

The smell of coffee shot up my nostrils and a gloved hand fell away from my shoulder. Victor placed a mug on the table as I pushed myself up. The sofa groaned with me. I didn't know where I was. Books everywhere...then I remembered: Victor's flat. Necromeleons. Corpses. The Shadow Fabric. And Stanley was killed.

"Morning." Victor pointed at Fludd's book in my lap. "Bedtime reading?"

"Not quite." My tongue stuck to my teeth. I rubbed my eyes.

"No nightmares?" Victor asked and leaned back against the sofa, linking fingers around his mug. He looked much better than he did yesterday.

"Did you have any?"

"In light of what's happened?"

"Yeah." I caught the book before it fell. My elbow popped as I placed it on the table.

"You need answers," he said.

"Yeah." The coffee was too hot to drink.

"I know Stanley was not a good person. Everyone knows that. His death is another in a long line of casualties."

"You say that like it's a war."

"It is."

I thought about that for a second. "I spoke with Goodwin," I told him.

"I knew you would. We, the four of us, that is..." His mug almost touched his lips. "Three now. But I hope you're going to join us."

I managed to laugh, but it kind of fell from my lips.

He raised an eyebrow. "That sounded sinister, didn't it?"

I nodded. "There's still four, if you include me." I said it without thinking. Was this really what I wanted? I thought again of Victor holding the Witchblade, its edge dripping his brother's blood.

Victor's eyes widened just a fraction. "Thank you."

"Tell me everything, Victor. From the beginning."

"The beginning is a tricky place." He leaned forward, elbows on knees. "Along with Goodwin and Polly, we are up against the darkness hidden beneath what surrounds us. Everyday life is not as solid as you'd think. The Shadow Fabric is a powerful concentration of evil. Monstrous energies exist in its every thread."

"How did it take Stanley away?" I thought of how the man's dead eyes disappeared into the folds of the Fabric.

Victor shook his head. "Up until now, I've only read about it. I have never witnessed it."

"How old is it?"

"The Fabric predates the 17th century, for that's when its existence became truly evident. Evil has, after all, been with us since time immemorial, and through the ages it has manifested itself in countless ways."

"I felt the evil when Stanley opened the violin case."

"It was the practice of witchcraft that threw its potency to dangerous levels when witches across the globe stitched the Fabric. They channelled through one another the shared burden using gateways of darkness."

"You're kidding?"

"My friend, I'm afraid not."

I didn't know what to say.

"The Fabric's power," he continued, "escalated with each stitching of a new piece."

"Stitching?"

Victor held up his hand and flicked his eyes at the window. "That's where the Witchblade comes into it."

My eyes followed his. Another blue sky.

"To give some kind of timeframe here," he continued, "a reign of unceremonious witch hunts took place about twenty years before this city was ravaged by the Great Fire in 1666. Have you ever heard of Matthew Hopkins?"

I shook my head.

"Hopkins," he said, "was the self-appointed Witchfinder General, responsible for the ruthless persecution of countless witches, and it is to him that the athame is said to have once belonged. According to records, he sent to the gallows more witches than any other witch hunter. He was only twenty-four at the time and his career spanned little more than a year. There were many easy targets. The accused were often elderly women living as outcasts from the local community. Never a problem for anyone to accuse an unfriendly neighbour with a deep frown or too many wrinkles. Or eyebrows joining in the middle. Anyone with an unfortunate and unattractive appearance was a candidate for trial."

"That's ridiculous."

"Another cause for suspicion was the Devil's Mark, as was called, which came in obvious forms such as warts and moles. Birthmarks, of course. A blemish, no matter how faint, would suggest the Devil has marked them as one of his own. Any such mark would confirm suspicion. The theory was, every witch who kept a familiar—a demon disguised as an animal—fed it with drops of their own blood. These imps would feed at special teats. A wart or raised mole would prove suitable."

My lip had curled upwards. This was disgusting.

"Of course," he said, "many *were* witches. The problem was, people began doubting the Witchfinder General's integrity. Judges queried him about the trials and his means of determining whether the accused was a witch or not. They suggested it was nothing short of torture and persecution. His fees, too, were equally questionable. Don't get me wrong, Leo, I don't condone such behaviour if the man was a fake. If he was making money from a town's superstitions and unfounded finger pointing, well, he knew a witch when he saw one. He simply became misguided in his quest."

I pinched the bridge of my nose, frowning.

"Anyway, Leo, you may wonder where I'm going with all this. Well, it was the tools he used."

"Right." I couldn't care less for a history lesson. A man had died.

"He had a number of assistants known as witch-prickers. So we're back to the Witchblade. It was with a knife the witch-pricker would make a decision."

"How?"

"They'd prick the accused with the blade, concentrating particularly around the Devil's Mark. If they didn't bleed, then there was no doubt about it, they were a witch. This brings us full circle, right back to the authenticity of the witchfinders."

"Huh?"

"They used retractable blades to make more money."

"Oh."

"Precisely. These blades were nothing like the Witchblade, they were in fact pins, or simple metal spikes. The Witchblade, throughout known records, is referred to as an athame and has nothing to do with witch-pricking."

"Doesn't matter to us anyway, Victor. That bitch stole it from you." I reminded myself how it felt to look down the gun barrel.

"Yes." His eyebrows weaved across his forehead. "We need to get it back."

"Thought you might say that. So what is an athame? What's it got to do with the Fabric?"

"An athame is a knife traditionally carried by a witch for ceremonial purposes."

"What? Are you saying this guy Hopkins was a witch? You said he owned the Witchblade."

"Plenty of evidence suggests he owned it, yes. Whether he was a witch himself…"

"What does that mean? He used it on witches?"

Victor nodded. "His assistants would use the retractable pins to make money on the falsely accused, while Hopkins used the athame on a true witch. So, the blade's powers never drew blood. It absorbed it, and so proving the accused was in fact a witch."

"If the knife was used for ceremonial purposes, I guess Hopkins stole it from a witch."

"Quite possibly. Or someone gave it to him with the knowledge of what he could do with it. Ultimately, it means the

Witchblade's origins are wrapped in as much mystery as the Shadow Fabric."

"You don't really know where it came from." My jaw tightened.

"There are references to it being forged in a place called Beneath, and we know it has power over the Shadow Fabric. A dangerous weapon ordinarily, fusing with whomever holds it. It feeds on your deepest emotions." He rubbed his face. "That's why the Fabric made me kill my brother."

"Victor—"

"The combination made it happen. The blade heightened my hatred for him...my fear of him...and with close proximity to each other, the shadows powered up, took charge and literally forced my hand."

"Tell me about this." I pointed to the book on Necromeleons. It sat in the centre of the coffee table beneath the smaller one I'd fallen asleep with.

"*Necromeleons*. Not to be confused with the *Necronomicon*, which is the Book of the Dead. However, it isn't too far from its origins. The dead."

"Nice." I shook my head and lowered my eyes. My feet fidgeted.

"*Necromeleons* is proving a bugger to decipher. Some passages remain impossible. Typically the ones I know to be important. I've been translating that hefty volume for a very, very long time. It's not as easy as translating its smaller friend there, Fludd's book."

"They're in mixed languages."

"It wasn't uncommon practise to write mysterious works in a mixture of tongues."

"Of course."

"The 16th-century astrologer Nostradamus completed his most famous works in a combination that included French and Latin. It was said to throw off the Spanish Inquisition. Interestingly, one of his verses prophesised the Great Fire of London. Most likely a coincidence."

"That's just confusing." I folded my arms tight across my chest.

"Fludd's book wasn't written in a mix of languages. It's only that particular copy. I have no idea how Lucas came by it."

"The guy…" I almost said *'who was tortured in the jungle'*. "The guy with the bookshop?"

"That's him."

"What about *The Book of Leaves*?"

"I'll get to that later. Back to Necromeleons."

"Yeah." I chewed my lip.

"A necromeleon is what we call a living dead being."

"A zombie?" I kicked my feet and leaned forward, a stack of books tumbling over. "This is ridiculous."

"Please, Leo."

"This is a load of shit."

"No, believe me, it's not."

"You're talking about zombies."

"They're not zombies."

My face grew hotter.

"Not entirely," he continued. "Unlike zombies in fiction, the necromeleon doesn't last long. There's only a brief spark of life. A piece of the Shadow Fabric essentially charges the awakened corpse. At the same time, it feeds off the dwindling energies. Eventually, once there is no longer any life force to drain, it dies again."

"Hang on, slow down." I scratched my stubble. "You're telling me the dead can walk?"

"Yes. Reanimated by the properties of the Shadow Fabric. Whether in its entirety and close proximity, or as a single patch detached from the main bulk of the Fabric."

"Shit. You say it so matter-of-factly."

"These are facts, Leo."

"Necromeleon. Chameleon?"

"Quite possibly, yes. The changing from death to life. Taking on the substance of what surrounds it, or penetrates it. Namely the shadows."

"Who wrote it?"

"Anonymous, and it goes back centuries."

"I can see that."

"The majority of it is a collection of works and records spanning the last four thousand years. Although it does contain the odd reference or two dating back to the beginning of time."

I laughed. "Of course it would."

"This battle has been going on since darkness gave way to light. A battle we're caught up in without the world even knowing of it."

"Good versus evil."

"That's what it always boils down to, certainly."

"How'd you guys get caught up in all this?"

"The passing of generations and circumstance."

"Circumstance. Like me."

"Yes."

"Who are you Victor?" I leaned back, shaking my head. The cushions smothered me. I tugged at one and shoved it aside.

"Throughout the years there has always been an 'us'. We have no name. We've been incorrectly referred to as the Shadmen, or even Keepers of the Light. It means nothing. We are who we are, following past generations on a quest now diluted by science and technology. A quest once as strong as any superstition and spiritual belief with roots to the time when man first discovered that fire can hold back darkness."

I wanted to believe—I almost *did* believe, given I'd witnessed the Shadow Fabric do its thing—yet something told me it was a windup. All jokes on me, guys, come out from behind the curtain.

Victor's voice strained as he added, "We are here to protect and serve the world without humankind actually knowing it."

"The Fabric." I tapped a fist against my chin. "It's a concentration of evil, I get that. And it has the power to bring back the dead. Why did Stanley have it? Why did you want him to wear gloves?"

Victor, his eyebrows twitching, didn't answer immediately. Eventually, he said, "I don't know how he came by it. We've searched for a long time, ever since we became involved. No one has seen it for three and a half centuries. Since 1666 to be precise. Fire is a means of its destruction. And according to records, there have been many attempts. Yet always there remains a thread or two, just enough to manifest itself again. The Fabric's near destruction started The Great Fire of London. Followed, or possibly traced, to Pudding Lane. Maybe it was chased there, being carried by someone with either good or bad intent, who knows? Maybe it had expanded into such a mass it travelled of its own accord. Back in 17th-century London there were many shadows..."

"Travelled. How is that possible?"

"Once the Shadow Fabric is powerful enough, having absorbed enough life force to become an entity in itself, it can move with ease."

"An entity?"

"A being born of darkness. The Shadow Fabric is already sentient life, and once strong enough, it would be able to haunt."

"Like ghosts?" This was getting too much. Ridiculous.

"Haunt or haunting, and I'm not talking about poltergeists and spirits. They are a very different kind of haunting. In this context, it's a term used for travelling between planes of existence. We are on one side, and darkness is on the other. That place is known as Beneath. Once charged with enough life force, the Shadow Fabric can be a gateway. And so other entities could come through."

I rubbed my face. This was all incredible stuff, and I felt like I was in a dream. "So the Fabric exists on stolen life force."

"Yes." Victor nodded. "In the 17th century, whichever group of people were after it, their intentions were just. Much the same as ours. And so, in a bakery, they held it back with the Witchblade. Pinning it to the ovens, as far as I'm to understand. An ideal place to burn it, wouldn't you say? Clever. Fire was on hand. And they used it. The fire spread and many people died...yet saved the entire human race."

"Here we are, present day, and Stanley found it."

"As for the leather gloves..." He sat up—the more he'd talked the more the sofa swallowed him. "Leather is dead flesh, if you think about it. Without life force to energise the Fabric, wearing such gloves enables it to be safely handled. In theory."

"I see." That explained why Victor always wore gloves; it made sense now. At least the part about the gloves. The rest? Simply incredible. I didn't know what to believe.

Victor shot to his feet, startling me, and I blinked.

"Let's get breakfast," he said.

I was relieved. My appetite for knowledge was temporarily satisfied, but my stomach had been rumbling for a while. And I had a headache.

CHAPTER 11

After a late breakfast at a café a short distance from Victor's flat, traffic was good to us and we soon stepped into the foyer of Periwick House. A woman approached us from the reception area. Dressed in joggers and a t-shirt, she looked older and fitter than me. She had a gym mat rolled under one arm, her red hair bouncing against the towel around her neck. She crossed the marble floor as though she flew, her movements mirrored by an inverted image. I vaguely recognised her, but wasn't certain from where. Perhaps I'd seen her around before I went travelling. As always, I didn't trust my memory.

Behind her, a man and a young girl tried to keep up. The woman beamed at Victor. "I hope you'll be in my class tomorrow morning. Yoga, remember?"

"Katrina," Victor said, "I think I need it."

They hugged. Brief, almost awkward.

Behind Katrina, the girl tugged out an earphone. "What else is there to do round here, daddy?"

"Whatever you want." The man had round shoulders and a red face. There was a likeness between the two; father and daughter at a guess.

Shrugging, the girl popped herself back into the music. The man sighed and his eyes seemed to retreat into their sockets.

"Last few weeks have been quiet, Vic," Katrina said. "Missed you last week."

I looked at Victor. It didn't surprise me he was into yoga. After all, he'd displayed remarkable agility with his ninja move at the antique shop. And I found it interesting he hugged his yoga instructor.

"I've a lot going on," he said. We both had a lot going on: Goodwin was expecting us. He'd arranged a meeting with Polly. I'd been invited too.

Katrina looked at the pair who stood next to her. They didn't look interested. "Everyone has an excuse."

The man tried to smile in reply, but failed. He eyed his daughter.

Victor started to walk off and apologised to Katrina.

She and her two followers remained in the centre of the foyer while we headed for Goodwin's office. From behind us, Katrina said, "You always have a lot going on. See you tomorrow."

As if knowing we were there, Goodwin's door opened and he greeted us, an unlit cigar clamped between his teeth. He nodded, then his gaze shot over my shoulder. I didn't realise Polly had entered the foyer. She wore the wicker hat and sunglasses. About five paces back was Annabel, her face set. Georgie was in the lead, being the guide dog he was. It seemed we were all on time.

When Goodwin shook Victor's hand, there was an unspoken exchange…and something else from Goodwin. I sensed Victor's previously re-energised self dwindling, being there with both Goodwin and Polly must have reminded him again of the loss of his brother. Even though Stanley had betrayed the others in some way, the group was now broken beyond repair. The link these guys once had would never be the same.

I'd never be the same.

After pleasantries, we entered Goodwin's office. As the last to enter the room, Annabel pulled the door closed and stayed there. I lingered near the window as the others sat around Goodwin's desk. He'd tidied it. The windows were open, fresh air failing to eliminate the smell of cigar smoke. Birdsong drifted in, but was drowned by the sound of scraping chair legs.

Of everyone, Victor was the smallest. And it wasn't only his slight frame giving that impression—everything smothered him.

"Victor." Polly turned her head in his direction. "I'm sorry to hear about Stanley, I truly am. If there's anything I can do…"

"Thank you." Victor's frown somehow dragged at his mouth.

Goodwin inhaled and rubbed his head. It was difficult to read his face.

"However," Polly added, "I'm uneasy with your driver being here."

What the hell? I was about to defend myself when Goodwin said, "You have a problem with young blood?"

"Not at all." She shook her head. "I'm uneasy that—"

"Leo deserves to be here." Victor straightened his back. "He stays. Besides, not too long ago we had a similar discussion about Annabel."

Across the room, the woman in question showed no response.

Victor's forehead creased. "On top of that, he witnessed the Fabric's power first hand. It made me kill my own brother."

No one said anything.

He flexed his fingers and pulled each glove tighter in a slow, exaggerated movement.

"It did," I mumbled.

"Plus," Victor continued, "I've told him much already. He's in this with us, and has agreed to help. With everything."

Goodwin raised his chin.

"Very well." Polly's lips tightened. "Apparently the Fabric has turned up, finally."

"It has." Victor nodded.

"And Stanley's death…" she added, and paused, "shortly followed its appearance? Is that right?"

Victor gave a breakdown of Tuesday evening's events. His voice was soft, and when he spoke his brother's name, his hands curled into fists.

"And after the girl took the athame," he concluded, "she looked into the case, satisfied the Fabric was no longer in there. Then she left."

Silence clung to every surface in the office, and eventually, Goodwin coughed.

"Um…" He ground out his cigar. "Stanley visited me this morning."

Victor's head snapped up, his gloves now tight balls of leather. "What?"

"He isn't dead, Victor."

Polly kept silent. Again, her lips whitened.

"Impossible." Victor's eyebrows quivered. "Goodwin—"

"I saw him. He came to my office and sat where you are now."

"I—"

"And his handshake was as real as you and I."

"But—"

"That man was dead, Goodwin." I shook my head. "I told you. I watched him disappear into the shadows. Dead. The knife wound was deep."

Victor nodded once.

"In the chest," I added. "Didn't miss his heart. No way."

"He was here." Goodwin frowned. "He's alive."

"What was said?" Victor pulled at his gloves and wriggled his fingers.

"He told me he was sorry he'd not contacted me. Any of us. He understood why no one had contacted him. He said he was sorry for everything but I didn't believe him, of course."

Polly fidgeted.

Victor pushed back his chair, dug in his trouser pocket and pulled out his mobile phone. After rapid thumb movements, he jammed it to his ear. His eyes darted from person to person and lastly fell on me. None of us moved, and after several seconds, he lowered the phone. "Straight to voicemail."

I thought of the folds of shadows, and the man's dead eyes vanishing.

"If he's back," Polly said, "then he's a necromeleon."

"No." Victor still gripped his phone. "Necromeleons are cold, walking dead things. With dead eyes. Black like bottomless pits."

"His eyes were Stanley's eyes." Goodwin tilted his head. "Nor did he act like I'd imagine a necromeleon would."

"You'd know if you saw one. They walk how a dead man should. Stiff-limbed and cumbersome. Not slow as such. Kind of lethargic. Sleepy."

Goodwin shifted in his chair. "Is it possible the Shadow Fabric can bring the dead back to life? Actual life, and not undead life?"

Victor chewed his lip. "There are passages in that book I'm failing to decipher. Confusing texts of haunt, the vessel that the Fabric could be. Haunting. Also tongues. Something about tongues. The Fabric is powerful, certainly. That is evident. It was a small roll of Fabric which came out of the case, yet its power is immeasurable."

"And it disappeared with him," Polly said.

"We're back to square one." Victor nodded.

Goodwin leaned forward.

"I can't believe this is happening," he said, shaking his head. "It's Thursday and this weekend is a big deal for the House."

Polly's eyes shot towards Goodwin. "Victor thought his brother was dead, and all you can think about is—"

"It's okay, Polly," Victor interrupted. "Really."

"Polly," Goodwin added, "you of all people—"

"Goodwin!" Victor's voice filled the room.

For a moment, no one said anything.

"So," Goodwin murmured, "where did Stanley find the Fabric?"

"He never told me," Victor said.

"He's alive." Goodwin lit another cigar. "That's why I've brought you all here. He told me he has the Fabric, but didn't wish to reveal his supplier."

"What else was said?" Polly asked.

"It was a short visit." Goodwin frowned. "Though he also told me he no longer trusts you, Victor. And for me to do the same. You're not to be trusted either, Leo. You're a liar, apparently. Everything you told me yesterday was fabricated bullshit."

"Goodwin, he—" I began, not really knowing what to say. Stanley was such a bastard, what was his problem? And I thought he was dead.

"Of course," Goodwin added, "I don't believe a word of what he said, saying the pair of you attacked him, threatening him with the Witchblade when he revealed the Fabric."

"What?" Victor shouted. "That's—"

"I know, I know." Goodwin raised a hand. "Don't worry, I told you, I don't believe a word. Anyway, he said he wrestled you both and escaped. That was about it."

I shook my head.

"Do you…" Victor swallowed. "Do you think he wants to stitch?"

"That's what I've been thinking." Goodwin pulled at his shirt collar. "And if so, we must stop him."

* * *

I shoved the car into first gear. As I pulled away, the tyres lost traction and the BMW wheel-spun on the gravel. We headed away from the House a little too fast.

"Okay," I said, "let's get back to the Fabric. Why's it so important to find? And what did you mean by *stitching*?"

"You need to know more about the Fabric." Victor slipped his mobile back into his pocket. He'd tried Stanley again, without any answer. That's where we were heading, to his house.

"Well, tell me."

"Before there was light, there was the primordial darkness, and that was all and everything. The universe was simply one big nothing. And then there was light. The creation of the Earth. Fish. Ape. Man. Whatever you want to believe, whichever religion you follow and whatever your god, it doesn't matter. Before us, there was a darkness and then there wasn't."

Driving with one hand, I rummaged in the glove box for my sunglasses.

"No one knows when it first became substance, morphing into the Fabric itself," Victor continued. "As I said earlier, it was the concentration of evils from the witches of the 17th century that put the thing into overdrive. There's a power—a force—within the Fabric, which is all evil. The larger it is, the more powerful it becomes."

I glanced at him.

"Its power influences everything and everyone around it," he said.

"That's what I felt when Stanley opened the violin case. It was sickening."

"Yes."

"You've never seen the Fabric before?"

"That's right. We've been searching for it since the 70s. Since we first came together. Our group was a little larger then."

"How many others were there?"

"A few. But that's another story."

"Oh." I didn't want to know about anything else. Not yet, anyway. There was a lot going on and I was still trying to accept everything. This madness.

"Not only does it have mental and physical influence over man and animal, it can also charge actual shadows in its close proximity."

"What does that mean?"

"It can make our everyday shadows move of their own accord. Shadowplay."

"This gets even more incredible, Victor."

"Remember, I've been deciphering this for nearly forty years, and haven't been in the presence of the Fabric until the other day. That was the first time I felt its influence. Makes you think some odd thoughts."

"Yeah." I grimaced, remembering how I'd felt as though death was moments away.

"No one knows the range the Fabric has to control normal shadows without even touching them. It influences the shadows around it, manipulating them, no matter how weak they are."

"The Fabric is potentially dangerous wherever it is."

"Certainly. Such control over individual shadows only lasts a little while...the charge, or life, gradually ebbs into nothing."

"Control? Why didn't the Fabric move any of the shadows when Stanley pulled it from the case?" I opened my window a fraction and fiddled with the climate control.

"It wasn't strong enough maybe." Victor pulled his gloves tighter. "I'm not sure. Its intentions were clear."

"Yeah." I thought of the blade slamming into Stanley's chest, remembering his dead eyes.

"Immobilising the shadows is a problem. Holding them at bay is achieved with the Witchblade or a blazing fire."

"I remember, and you also said the blade heightens your fear."

"And hatred. But it can still be used to restrain the shadows. To pin them down and immobilise them. The athame would absorb the remaining energies from an individual shadow and render it impotent. Lifeless. Back to normal."

"Using fire or the knife can hold back the Shadow Fabric," I said. Was I accepting all this? Perhaps...

"Yes."

"This is all theory, right?"

"Yes."

"The knife can stop an individual shadow, but can it stop the Fabric?"

"It can temporarily restrain it, certainly…"

"Actually stop it?"

"I've come across no evidence of that."

"As you say, the larger it is, the more powerful it gets. Can the Fabric get any bigger?"

A white van took up the rear-view mirror. The driver wore a red cap pulled low over the eyes.

"Oh, yes. Most certainly," Victor was saying. "It has the ability to drain life, making it much larger. So it can sustain itself, if you like. In the meantime, the only way it can grow is to be stitched."

"Ah, right." Again, I flicked my eyes at the mirror.

"This is where *The Book of Leaves* comes into it," Victor said. "Finding the book and destroying it is imperative. It contains the most concentrated evils in shadowleaf form."

"Shadowleaf?"

Victor began to say something when the roaring of the van distracted him…and it smashed into us.

I fought with the steering, the rear end swinging out. I managed to bring it round, but the front wheels caught a collection of potholes and the car bounced. It jerked us in our seats as though a giant shook the car. A wheel thumped downwards and then up, and my arse lifted from the seat. The steering went light.

A tree surged from the woods: wide trunk, brown and green everywhere.

After the explosion of airbags inflating, silence rushed into the car.

CHAPTER 12

Being in a car accident is an awful experience. Regardless of blame, the lump in the pit of the stomach and the few seconds which follow, both mess with the head. Although I remembered nothing from my accident two years before, this one felt a thousand times worse. I couldn't think why, which was odd. It was as though this was my first. I had an impressive No Claims Discount somewhere. Amnesia is a bastard.

Victor said, "You okay?"

The airbags had deflated and the smell of fireworks and foliage stuffed my lungs.

I rubbed my head. "Um. Yeah. You?"

"I'm fine, I'm fine."

My head was fuzzy, a little confused as to what precisely happened. All I remembered was how dangerously close the van had been. Did he ram us?

Both of us alive, the engine dead and the windscreen a mass of white splinters, the car sat crooked against an embankment. Victor's window was gone and glass sprinkled his lap and the foot well. He was lucky not to have any cuts. Brambles bulged into the car and a thick stem of thorns rested against his chest.

Subconsciously, I yanked up the handbrake and twisted the key to switch off the already silent engine. I popped my seat belt and shrugged out of it, tugged the door lever and shoved the door wide. Given the angle of the car, gravity swung it back and I managed to stop it with my palm before it slammed shut again.

"Shit." I hooked out a leg and clambered from the car, still with one hand against the door. Once steady on my feet, I prevented it from swinging closed with the backs of my legs.

Victor brushed aside my offered hand as he climbed out. He grunted. His face sported a scratch on his left cheek. I'd missed it before because it was along the jawline, where I sometimes miss when shaving.

"Bloody hell," he said.

"Victor, I—"

"Oh, it's not your fault, Leo." He waved a hand at me. "You couldn't have done anything."

"But—"

"This is getting out of hand, and it's going to get worse."

I watched him as he pulled his phone from a pocket.

There was no sign of the white van.

CHAPTER 13

Victor made some calls. The first couple were to personal contacts. One for a replacement car, and the other to a guy to drag our wreck from the bushes. While we waited, Victor spent the whole time on the phone, quietly talking. I didn't overhear much. I sat on a tree stump and stared at the ground. I knew I was getting deeper into this. Whatever this was. And as the week went on, I found myself accepting it. Accepting everything, including what I'd always believed was impossible.

The response time was excellent. No more than half an hour passed and we had an identical replacement car. Another half hour after that, Victor and I stood in the shadow of his brother's house, hip deep in nettles. There was a cat flap. I couldn't imagine Stanley owning such a pet. A snake, maybe. Or a tarantula.

"Stanley would go mental if he knew I had this." Victor twisted a key in the lock. The man's resolve was admirable—someone had tried to kill us. The only injury he appeared to have was the scratch along his jawline, whereas my neck ached and my knee throbbed.

With a gloved hand, Victor shoved open the door. "Are you okay?"

"We've just had an accident. You haven't said much about it."

"Neither have you."

"True," I said.

"You drove us over here with a large scowl on your face, my friend."

"Who was it, Victor?"

"The van driver? We can only assume it was our mystery girl."

"That's what I thought, but—"

"I know as much as you right now."

"Really?"

Victor frowned. "You don't have to doubt me."

I rubbed the back of my neck. It clicked when I stretched.

"Are you okay?" he said again.

I nodded, and a moment later, he stepped into the kitchen, avoiding an overturned bin. I followed. The stink of food—bad eggs—shot up my nostrils, and the echo of a dripping tap bounced off chipped tiles.

"Sadly," Victor announced, "this kind of mess isn't unusual."

Microwave meal boxes and empty milk cartons, plus all manner of other rubbish, had spilled from an open refuse sack, and required a big stride to avoid. Bits of sticky fluff clung to the skirting boards, and in places, dubious liquids pooled on the linoleum. The worktop, littered with crusty plates and chipped mugs, acted as a playground for the flies. I counted six just on one congealed lump of ketchup.

Before we left the kitchen, Victor reached out and tightened the tap.

We paused in the hallway. To our right an uncarpeted staircase led upstairs, and in front was a closed door shielding us from the room where Stanley had vanished into the shadows. Victor went to open it, and a peculiar expression darkened his face. I thought of what we'd witnessed in that room. Almost stumbling, he shot up the stairs.

"Search quickly, Leo," he called from the landing. "Look for anything to tell us how Stanley came by the Fabric."

Squinting after him, I marvelled at his agility. One moment, he stood beside me, and the next, he flicked a switch. A bare bulb spotlighted his face and he disappeared round the corner. I headed up the stairs, my knee aching with each footfall.

The area mirrored the lack of house pride downstairs: wallpaper, skirting and carpet revealed years of neglect. The landing reeked of damp, and reluctantly, I pushed open the bathroom door. The stink crawled into my brain. Nothing shone or sparkled—not that I'd expected it to. With a shower curtain half hanging from the rail, and a cracked toilet cistern lid, there wasn't any recent evidence of use. No damp towels or pools of water in the sink or bath, nothing to suggest Stanley had been here of late.

I left the room, breathing again, took a few paces and entered another room. Neglected as elsewhere; empty, apart from several cardboard boxes huddled in a corner. I knelt beside them and thumbed open the nearest. Dust leapt into my face.

Wrinkling my nose, I whispered, "Dirty, filthy bastard."

Inside wasn't what I'd expected, although I wasn't sure exactly what it was I had been expecting. Porn mags. A whole load of them. I opened the next box: a few broken pieces of crockery and a spoon. Coat hangers, the wire kind, occupied the last box.

"Leo!" Victor's voice sounded stifled. "Anything?"

I joined him in the main bedroom. "Nope."

Victor stood tiptoe on one leg, the other hooked off the ground. The rest of his body was in the wardrobe. A tongue of clothes licked him while hangers chattered like teeth. A double bed with duvet and pillows askew took up most of the room. On it sat a laptop, booting up. Apart from the wardrobe, the only other furniture was a scuffed chest of drawers with clothes heaped on it. Next to a blinking digital clock was something pink.

I picked it up: a business card for an escort agency.

"Nice," I said, and dropped it, wiping my fingers on my trousers.

"What's under the bed?" Victor still had his head and hands in Stanley's clothes.

"Do I have to?"

"Yes."

"He's not been here for a while." I crouched beside the bed. "Unless he never washes."

"Stanley's hygiene has always been questionable."

"You're not kidding." The closer I got to the carpet, the more I wanted to puke. Under the bed lay a haze of dust, a few socks and some underwear. Nothing else. My neck ached and blood pounded between my temples. Slowly, I got to my feet. "All due respect to him being your brother, but this guy's got issues."

Victor closed the wardrobe doors. "I know."

The laptop's screen asked for a password.

"Do you know anything about computers?" he asked, and sat on the edge of the bed.

"Not much." As always, such a question reminded me of the immense hole in my past. I didn't even know if I'd worked in IT. I had a basic understanding of computers, nothing more. After a moment, I walked around the room and stood beside him. "You have any idea what the password could be?"

His shoulders slumped. "No. This thing may contain a clue where he got the Fabric from. May even tell us where he is now."

"Guess," I said. "You never know your luck."

"Knowing my brother, it'll be something lacking imagination."

"Besides porn and prostitutes, what else does he like?"

"Please, Leo."

I didn't reply.

"Something obvious," he mumbled.

The view from the window wasn't much: houses, telegraph poles, an odd tree here and there, and a lot of back gardens. Most were as unkempt as Stanley's, and next door's featured a collection of busted and buckled toys. Every one a bold colour like chunks of broken rainbow tangled with grass. A garage clung to the side of the house.

"What car does he drive?" I asked.

"An Audi. When the TT came out, he wanted one immediately." Victor straightened his back and pulled the laptop closer. "I never knew where he got the money from. He became obsessed with it. Given his otherwise slovenly nature, that car didn't suit him."

"Try that."

Victor spoke out loud as he typed: "Audi TT…no."

"Without a space?"

He tried. "No."

"Worth a shot."

His lips twitched as his fingers darted over the keys, and with each slam of the Enter button, his frustrations grew. "This is impossible."

"You find anything in his pockets?"

"Receipts."

"Could be a clue on one of those," I suggested.

"What, for his password?"

"No, where he's been recently. I don't know."

"They're on the floor." He flicked an eyebrow towards the wardrobe. "They all point nowhere."

I scanned the receipts while Victor punched the keys. Each time he hit the Enter button, the sound snapped. There were about a dozen receipts, mostly cash paid at the local supermarket—the guy liked his lager and pizza. One was for the purchase of a laptop. Others were for DVDs, each on separate occasions: The Matrix, The Expendables, and a few other similar movies all starting with the word *The*. The date of two particular receipts interested me.

"Victor, strange question. Do you remember The A-Team?"

"Eh?" He stopped banging the keys and glared at me. "Of course I remember. Stanley loved the series. Even if he was about thirty when it first came on TV. He's always been immature. Why are you asking?"

"He bought a DVD of the remake on the same day he got himself this." I tapped the laptop.

"I see where you're going with this."

I shrugged. "Worth a try. I've done that before when it's come to passwords. Anything I see on a desk." It was all I could remember about my use of computers.

He prodded the keys.

"No luck," he said. "Funny, when he got the TT, he used to call himself Mr TT. After Mr T. Get it?"

"Yes." I grimaced. Stanley had always been a fool, it seemed.

Victor froze and we locked eyes.

"Mr TT is too short for a password," I told him. "How about M-I-S-T-E-R?"

He punched it in and hit the T button twice, paused, and hit the Enter key.

It worked.

He threw gloved fists into the air. "Well done, Leo."

I moved closer as he popped up empty folders while the email program loaded. No more passwords, and soon Stanley's personal correspondence crowded the screen. Victor used the cursor to scroll down a stream of junk mail, pausing occasionally. Going back a few days before the Shadow Fabric incident, a collection of emails with the subject header, *re package*, proved interesting. We read the most recent first.

> *From: tulipmoon73*
> *To: stantheman*
> *Subject: re package*
> *I will see you then. Make sure no one follows you.*
> *TM.*

Victor clicked the column header and about a dozen emails between tulipmoon73 and stantheman listed on the screen. The first one referred to a telephone conversation they'd had. Others contained references to the package itself.

> *From: stantheman*
> *To: tulipmoon73*
> *Subject: re package*
> *Thanks for all this tulip. victor and the others will finally listen to what i have to say. they'll have me back in their pathetic group. thanks for giving it to me. Maybe you and me can meet up properly sometime. when I get the fabric i'll have the power. we can share it.*
> *S*

Victor said, "Stanley never shares anything."

> *From: tulipmoon73*
> *To: stantheman*
> *Subject: re package*
> *I'm pleased you'll put it to good use, Stanley. But no, we can never meet properly. I'm sorry. Know that you deserve the Fabric.*
> *And that the Fabric deserves you.*
> *TM.*

Stanley's reply was short and to the point:

From: stantheman
To: tulipmoon73
Subject: re package
Don't know what your missing.

There were a few more exchanges before Tulip Moon suggested a time and date. It was on a Sunday night, two days before Stanley had shown his brother the package. The meeting place was a pub car park. I remembered the uninviting building as I'd driven into the area.

"Tulip Moon," Victor murmured, and accessed the other folders, finding nothing else of interest. Internet history provided us with no further clues.

My neck ached and all I wanted to do was sit for a while.

"That's it," Victor said and set the laptop aside.

"At least our mystery girl has a name. Guess it's the bitch who we've run into a few times," I said.

"Yes," he whispered between tight lips, and folded the laptop. "Or who ran into us…"

"I don't get it. Why does she want us dead?" I thought of the cap-wearing driver, and the girl with the hoodie. One and the same, it was almost certain. Red cap, red scarf. I remembered staring down the gun barrel. "And why didn't she shoot us when she had the chance?"

"I've been wondering about that." Victor stood up. "Why go to the trouble to run us off the road?"

"Maybe it was a warning. After all, she didn't come back."

We went downstairs. Victor was still hesitant about going into the only room we'd not yet searched.

He flexed his fingers and pulled his gloves tighter. "We've got what we came for."

"No, Victor." I put my palm against the door. "We should check everything."

He grunted, his eyebrows frozen above wide eyes.

"We need as much information as we can," I added. "If there's anything else, it'll be here."

I nudged open the door. An odd smell punched me in the nose.

The open-plan room remained almost as we'd left it. The violin case on the table yawned wide, and on the carpet the bloodstains had dried black, yet those two reminders of what had occurred only days before was not what took our immediate focus.

A shrivelled corpse sat against the wall. The skin wrinkled, tight to the bone, and grey as storm clouds. Naked. It was male.

CHAPTER 14

The stink of the corpse reached down my throat and threatened to pull out my stomach.

"Shit," I said. I couldn't believe what I was seeing.

"Quite." Victor's eyes were wild, and the scratch along his jaw wriggled as he ground his teeth. "If Goodwin hadn't said Stanley visited him, then I'd assume this was his body."

"Whose is it then?"

Victor's frown deepened.

My voice was small as I said, "You guys say Stanley isn't a necromeleon?"

It took him a few moments to answer, and when he did, he tore his eyes from the corpse. "The Fabric needs a body to inhabit. To possess. A necromeleon by definition is a changed corpse."

"Of course." Again, I was annoyed. Over the last few days, that had been happening too often, which in itself annoyed me further.

"This is someone else. Are you okay?"

"Honestly?" I shook my head. Somehow, I managed not to puke.

Victor grabbed my shoulder, the glove creaking as he squeezed. My head thumped with a heartbeat and my neck throbbed.

To my knowledge, I'd never before seen a dead body. The sunken eyes were a pair of tiny beads inside a skull. Not a head, a skull. The skin shrivelled in uneven ridges of miniature peaks and valleys. Gaping nostrils in a nose cavity of shrunken flesh, and below it, the mouth; a rictus suggesting nothing short of terror. Sparse grey hair hung from the dome of the skull, clumped across the forehead. It reminded me of a Halloween mask.

I allowed my eyes to drift over the torso, the ribcage in defined hollows and curves, the navel just a bowl of wrinkles. The genitalia, in amongst a patch of dark hair, only a fold of lumpy skin. The arms and legs were spindly, knobbly sticks ending in curled digits of a claw-like freeze.

My palms were clammy, and there was a tightness in my throat.

I helped Victor search the room for further clues. We came up with nothing. I often found myself glancing at the corpse, its wilted eyes staring at the ceiling as if in hope of an angel's rescue.

* * *

Within an hour we were back at Periwick House, almost running towards Goodwin's office. The image of the corpse would not dislodge from my head.

As Victor knocked four beats into the wood, from inside the office, I fancied I heard a door thumping closed. Maybe. As we waited—me with a streak of impatience—I strained to hear something more, if indeed I'd heard anything in the first instance. Nothing. No voices. Goodwin wasn't on the phone. At least I didn't think so.

"Dean said he was in here." Victor knocked again, waited one second, grabbed the handle and pushed.

On the opposite side of the office, the French doors allowed the evening sunshine to flood the desk. From the ashtray a stub of cigar curled off its final wisps of smoke. We strolled into the room calling Goodwin's name. Behind us the door swung shut.

Victor darted into an adjacent room.

As I peered around the bathroom door, a peculiar whirring noise drifted towards me. A mechanical hum, loud at first, gradually reducing in volume. No sooner had I heard it, it stopped, or possibly faded. My ears were hot, and I guessed it was my imagination.

"Where is he?" I said as Victor came back into the office and headed for the desk. Cigar smoke clogged my throat and I coughed.

Victor grabbed some papers, his eyebrows twitching. In slow motion, he placed the sheets down. Both hands, their splayed fingers straight, supported his weight. His head lowered, and a strange noise drifted from his throat.

"What is it?" I asked.

He nodded at the papers. "Invoices."

Standing straighter, he took one gloved hand from the desk, while the other walked a short distance forward and stopped. The forefinger tapped repeatedly over a particular sheet. The drumming of the leather-tipped finger filled the office. I leaned over and read the page. The descriptions were nonsense to me. The only word I understood was *hypodermic*, and the quantity of the order was a hundred. There were three invoices from separate pharmaceutical suppliers.

"Syringes?" I said. I didn't understand. Why would Goodwin need those?

"Tranquillisers, mainly," Victor whispered. "Plus general supplies."

"What kind of supplies?"

"For hospitals."

"What?" This made no sense.

"I don't know what it means."

"This is crazy, Victor." My hands became fists.

"Welcome to my world."

I glared at him.

"Goodwin hasn't been sharing," he said.

"What do you mean?"

"Secrets."

I shook my head. "Okay. One day, I see moving shadows, and the next day, some crazy bitch tries to kill us. Then this afternoon, we find a dead body. Fucking great."

"Yes."

"And now this."

"Please, Leo…"

"Shit!" So much noise in my head.

Victor nodded. "These supplies aren't for any ordinary hospital."

"And what does that mean?"

"A mental hospital."

My heart wanted to explode. "What's his signature doing on this stuff?"

"Precisely."

"What's going on, Victor?" No more madness today, thanks—I'd had my fair share so far. I'd had my fill for the week...and Thursday wasn't over yet.

"I really don't know." He stepped back from the desk and shook his head. "It's not just these invoices troubling me..."

"How about the corpse at your brother's house?" My jaw muscles flexed, making my teeth hurt. "Does that trouble you?"

"It does."

"What else then, Victor?" I managed to relax my fists. "Don't keep me in the dark."

The corners of his eyes crinkled, his mouth humourless. "Dark secrets."

"What are you talking about now?"

"I don't think we can trust Goodwin anymore." From beside the telephone, he grabbed a jotter pad. Holding it by the ring-bound edge, he handed it to me: a doodle.

Goodwin had drawn an hourglass.

CHAPTER 15

With thoughts of an hourglass, we headed for my room. I didn't understand it, and I felt sick. Victor said nothing else after we found the doodle. I doubted the hourglass meant anything to him, whereas to me it meant much more. Occasionally, over the last two years, the image of an hourglass haunted me; whether in a dream or memory, I couldn't place it. Or was it all in my head? Why would Goodwin draw an hourglass? Was it just that, a doodle, nothing more? Was it coincidence? Polly didn't believe in coincidence, perhaps Victor shouldn't either. Not only was I facing corpses, I now puzzled over Goodwin's place in all this. What the hell was going on?

We were halfway up the stairs when Katrina blocked our ascent. She took hold of Victor's arm and the pair came to a standstill. She wore jeans and a shirt, no longer looking like the resident yoga instructor, and her hair flowed over her shoulders in a wave of auburn.

I leaned back against the banister, looking up at them.

"Victor." Her smile faltered. "What's wrong?"

"It's been a long day, Katrina."

Below us, I heard Dean talking about the orchestra's arrival on Saturday.

Katrina frowned. "All the more reason for you to come to my class tomorrow."

"I'll do my best."

"Victor, come on. Dwindling numbers over the last few months has got me thinking that Goodwin will get rid of me."

His mouth curved up slightly. "That won't happen."

"And I've always relied on you being there."

"I know."

"Be there at eight?"

"I'll try." He rubbed his cheek. "I can't promise anything, though."

"What did you do to your face?"

"I'm okay. Long story. Long day."

The two of us must've looked weary—I wanted to lay down and close my eyes, even for five minutes. And I wished this woman would piss off.

To me, she said, "You look after him."

I stepped aside, allowing her passage.

"See you tomorrow," she called over her shoulder. "And bring your friend."

On the way to my room, Victor phoned Polly. With no answer, he tried Stanley. "Nothing."

I wasn't surprised about Stanley not answering. But Polly? Could we trust her? And Victor? Was I able to trust him? Goodwin proved to be hiding secrets, yet what was Victor's deal? Was he one of the good guys? Was I still a good guy?

We reached the Vivaldi Suite, my sanctuary. As I slipped the keycard from my wallet, I paused at the door. Busy with his own thoughts, I doubted Victor noticed my hesitation.

Was I on the 'good' side? I had no memory for most of my adulthood, remembering only the past two years. Before then, nothing, other than scraps and flashes. Nothing whole. That was worrying, to lose trust in yourself. Not good. Trust? If I couldn't trust Goodwin, and definitely not Stanley, whom could I trust? Fair enough to doubt Polly, as I'd not learned much about her, but Victor?

Dark shadows clung beneath his eyes.

I thumbed the keycard into the slot and the light changed from red to green as the mechanism clicked.

"What would you say to Stanley if he answers?" I opened the door and he followed me in.

Victor remained silent and headed for an armchair by the window. He'd already taken his shoes off and, with one foot tucked beneath him, sank onto the cushions. He passed his phone from hand to hand.

"When you're ready," he said, "please take me home."

"Give me a few minutes."

I went to the bathroom and left him sitting there looking how I felt: beaten and drained. And he was supposed to be used to this kind of thing.

Pulling the light cord, I reached behind me to lock the door and went to the basin. I gripped the edge, puffed out my cheeks and let out a long hiss. My reflection came across as troubled-looking as Victor. I didn't know what to make of the information we'd found in Goodwin's office. A man I'd trusted for the last two years, who'd taken me into his home, and proved a true friend, hid a big secret. Syringes and tranquillisers, and a list of medical supplies an average business owner—for a place like Periwick House—would not have any use for. But a mental hospital?

I'd had enough for today. I wanted to talk about it, and knew I wouldn't. Couldn't. My ears were ringing. Taking Victor home sounded like a good idea. When I joined him, he hadn't budged, rooted in a trance.

We stayed in my room for a while longer, each with a glass of water. Victor sipped his like it was vodka. Maybe he needed something stronger. I knew I did.

CHAPTER 16

Friday

Goodwin laughed at me. All teeth, eyes closed. Black smoke billowed around his head, and with the moon full and flanked by storm clouds, his bloated silhouette engulfed the view. Lightning stabbed the darkness and a crack of thunder drowned his bellows. His fingernails shrieked down the window, slow and deliberate, sharp to the ears. Louder than his laughter, more intense than the lightning. Chipped glass sparked as though energised by the electric atmosphere, the sound as relentless as an angle grinder.

And yanked me from sleep.

Ten seconds—maybe ten minutes—passed as the hammering in my chest subsided. My ears still hummed from the echoes of the dream.

I kicked off the clinging bed sheets. Hooking my legs out, I blinked at the alarm clock: 3.33 a.m. I'd only had around four hours of sleep. My back ached and my head buzzed. Many thoughts kept me awake the night before. Evidently my tired brain eventually shut down and took the anxiety into my dreams.

I got up, pulled my combats on and opened the doors to the Juliet balcony. As I leaned out, the air rushed into my senses. The patchwork of woodlands and fields stretched away in a grey weave, and above it a bright night's sky. No light pollution here. Stars were sharp points in an almost cloudless expanse, with a low moon covering the countryside in a soft ambience.

A shiver ran through me, but I welcomed it. It cleared my senses.

I didn't know what to think anymore, I didn't know whom to trust. Digging hands into my pockets, I scanned the heavens and recognised a few constellations. Goodwin had educated me once, shortly before I'd set out on my travels. Sitting on his balcony we shared a few beers and he identified the sky's more interesting ones, giving me a brief insight to the mythology behind each: Perseus, Andromeda, Cassiopeia. Goodwin proved educated in many respects, and precisely how educated was yet to be learned. Syringes? Tranquillisers?

The countryside of Mabley Holt was quiet no matter what time of day, and often the only movements were of animals and farmers—the village, given the surrounding maze of lanes, was lucky not to be a place to simply pass through.

A faint rumble of approaching vehicles floated on the night. Two pairs of headlights—several miles to the east—approached from the direction of Sevenoaks, and came to a crossroad that led to the next village, or down towards Mabley Holt. The other headed directly to Periwick House, which is where they turned. Halfway along the lane, with woodland on either side, they stopped.

I leaned over the railing and squinted. The iron chilled my hands, and my breath plumed. What were those vehicles up to?

A car and a mini-bus pulled up, the moon reflecting from their windows. The car's headlights shut off and two people got out. Moments later, the mini-bus manoeuvred away from the car. Its headlights jerked as it entered a field and approached the woodland on the perimeter of the House grounds. It came to a standstill, its lights spearing the trees. Drenched in moonlight, a number of people climbed—or stumbled—from the rear, while a pair of statue-proud men stood on either side. The car headed back to the crossroad.

This wasn't right. I toyed briefly with the idea of waking Goodwin, then thought of the man's doodle, crazy as that was. But what was going on down there in the woods? I made a swift decision. I'd make it to the copse in little more than three minutes.

I wedged my feet into a pair of trainers, struggled into a t-shirt, and grabbed a jacket. I snatched my wallet and phone, and wrenched open the door. Ten seconds passed and the soles of my trainers slapped the stairs in a two-at-a-time descent. Remarkably I felt no pain—not even a twinge—from my knee. Somehow, I managed to get my jacket on.

Reception was quiet, and soft lighting paved my sprint into the gardens. Thirty seconds more took me between rows of

Neil's immaculate lawns and flowerbeds. Their fragrance filled my nostrils. I charged over loose gravel and the occasional stretch of paving. My arms pumped forward and back, and another minute found me hurtling towards the far reaches of the grounds. I leapt over a low wall and out amongst the orchard, careful not to lose footing on the lumpy ground—at least it was spring and there wouldn't be any fallen apples hiding in the shadows.

My head thumped, the cold air rushed into my lungs in short bursts. I charged with the end in sight. At the edge of the orchard, ducking a low branch, I made it to the fence and without hesitation, hurdled the wire. Rusty barbs and rotten posts shot beneath me as I crashed to the ground in a squat. My thighs absorbed the impact before I straightened.

My knee still didn't hurt.

Breath controlled, head hammering, my veins fired with adrenaline, I scanned the terrain ahead. Drenched in blue shadows and moonlight, the trees and the mini-bus were no further than another thirty-second sprint.

Gritting my teeth, I ran low. Hunched, keen to remain out of sight, I made it to a reasonable distance, keeping to the shadows on the fringe of woodland. As quiet as my shaking legs allowed, I shimmied from tree to tree, keeping one eye on the activity, and the other on where I placed my feet, careful not to snap twigs.

Beside the copse rose a steady hillside, and in places, vertical spears of rock jutted between tufts of grass and brambles. The line of trees ended at the hill, and on the other edge the mini-bus sat. The passengers, all men—at a quick count a dozen—were handcuffed and being led into the woods. They wore identical overalls. Four more men flanked the group. Each held a torch in one hand, and an automatic weapon in the other.

My mouth was dry. Guns?

The mini-bus still rumbled and drowned what was being said, yet I could tell there was a lack of hostility. Even though held at gunpoint the cuffed dozen didn't seem reluctant in any way; they trundled along, restrained, passing through the torch beams. With each footstep the torchlight broke off for a moment, and then continued to lance into the woods, only to repeat the process. All the while, the four men held their weapons horizontal and directed their captives towards the hillside.

I had no idea where they were being taken. As far as I knew it was only grass and trees out there. Though clammy from the sprint, a coldness crawled up my spine. None of this made sense, all so close to Periwick House. I thought of traditional war movies, the ones where prisoners are taken out into the fields for execution. I shuddered—I didn't want to see that.

A yellow light spewed from the hillside and burst into the woodland. I squinted into it. What was going on now? A mechanical hum emanated from the hill. The headlights and torches paled in comparison as the light grew. The prisoners shielded their eyes with cuffed hands.

A gruff command urged them onwards.

The hum stopped and I saw a widening doorway—an entrance into the hill, something I'd never known existed. I still squinted into the light, my heartbeat in my ears, and I realised I held my breath. I slowly released it. From within the light, shadows moved. Something was emerging. I thought of the Shadow Fabric, and wondered if this was where it hid. My pulse quickened. The shadow blotted the entrance to the cave. Here amongst the trees near Periwick House a group of prisoners were being taken to a secret cave. Was the Fabric going to take the men into its folds? No. No Fabric; it was a man. Nothing supernatural here. Someone had stepped onto the threshold between the cave and the copse. A bulky someone, an unmistakable frame silhouetted in the entrance to that cave. Round, proud and familiar.

A plume of smoke billowed around it, creating phantoms in the near-blinding light—Goodwin. That man kept a lot of secrets.

I crouched lower, dug in my pocket, and yanked out my phone. I thumbed Victor's number.

CHAPTER 17

The automatic doors slid aside and I looked at my watch: just after 7 a.m. and already the supermarket hummed; mostly men in overalls grabbing a newspaper, crisps and a can of Coke. Victor had suggested meeting there first thing. It was a short distance from his flat.

He rounded the corner and saw me. He pushed a trolley containing several bunches of bananas and a copy of *Fortean Times*.

I walked over to him, resisting the urge to run. "Half of me wants nothing more of this," I said.

His eyes narrowed. "And the other half?"

"Since I've been back, more and more shit has happened to make it difficult to walk away. And now, what the hell's going on with Goodwin? You have any idea?"

"Leo, trust me, I don't know. Really. You said those men followed him into that cave?"

"Yeah."

He continued further along the aisle. "We're getting deeper, you know we are."

"And that's why I can't leave," I whispered, not wanting a lady beside me to overhear. Bread rolls packed her basket. "I've seen too much."

"My back's killing me," Victor mumbled as he grabbed some radishes. "Tulip Moon ramming us off the road."

"And yeah, that. Why hasn't there been another attempt on our lives?" I asked.

"Just mine, Leo. Don't worry."

"I'm in this too." I was. To the end.

"You are." His trolley veered to the left and crashed into the display racks. "Bloody wheel."

It wasn't just the trolley he swore at, his frustrations reflected my own.

"Really didn't want to drop you off last night," I told him. "Knowing Tulip Moon is still out there."

"It's okay, I stayed at a friend's."

"Oh?"

"Yes." He glanced at his shopping list. "Remember the woman with me when you first came to my place?"

"Yeah." I remembered her patterned fingernails and the way she'd avoided eye contact.

"I slept at hers," he said.

"You amaze me, Victor."

"Pass me four of those." He pointed to a row of semi-skimmed milk. "The large ones."

"Tell me more about Goodwin's doodle. After last night, I need to know more."

"I don't know everything."

"You know more than me."

Victor shrugged. "The doodle was of the Hourglass. A contraption suspected to have its alchemical roots in the early 17th century. Constructed by Robert Fludd for his experiments."

"The guy who wrote the book with the longwinded title." I guessed this was heading for another history lesson.

"Yes. Fludd, the philosopher and scholar. His illustration of the primordial darkness, *And like this to infinity*, is said to be linked to the Hourglass. A black square no less, yet often compared with a shadowleaf."

I thought about the car accident. "You were talking about shadowleaves when we got rammed off the road."

"What would you like for breakfast?" He managed to pull the trolley away before it hit the bacon chiller.

I'd lost my appetite these last few days. "I'm good with whatever. Keep talking."

He threw a packet of smoked bacon into the trolley. "Fludd was a remarkable man behind many historically influential works: science, medicine and philosophy. He journeyed throughout Europe seeking the knowledge of mystics, scientists, musicians, physicians. And alchemists. With the wisdom he gained on his adventures, it is said that he constructed a piece of apparatus to harbour a person's evils. He succeeded with the Hourglass."

"Harbour?"

"To contain it in solid form. A kind of physical projection."

"And Goodwin's doodled it on a notepad." Doubt dripped from my tongue.

"I believe he's found it."

"Thought you guys were a team." I remembered the cave mouth as it opened, giving way to Goodwin's silhouette. Victor moved off and I stared at the back of his head. I dragged my heels like a kid.

"From what I've learned of the Hourglass," he continued, ignoring my comment, "I understand that strapping it to a witch would create a shadowleaf. The most powerful kind of shadowleaf. Solid black. Absolute evil."

In my first history lesson back in Victor's flat, I learned about the Witchfinder General and his cruel ways at collecting the shadowleaves. "This has something to do with the Witchfinder."

"Precisely. Each shadowleaf, an essence of their evil—a token of badness—was collected by him and his assistants."

"*The Book of Leaves.* I guess it contains all the shadowleaves from the witches?" I couldn't believe I was going down this route again, yet I'd seen the Shadow Fabric's power…and so much more.

"Yes." Victor grinned, but it was short-lived. The trolley's wheel shuddered and shot sideways, and he managed to avoid the legs of a guy with muddy boots. He was almost twice Victor's size. "Sorry, my friend."

"It's cool," the man said in a voice tiny in comparison to his chest. It surprised me.

Once out of earshot, Victor said, "The shadowleaf of a witch was attached to each page to document every successful trial. There were hundreds collected during the Witchfinder's career span."

"Why would someone want to keep them? And how did the Witchfinder come by the Hourglass?" I also wanted to know why Goodwin had drawn the damn thing and how he'd found it, if indeed he had. And, what the Hourglass meant to me, if anything.

"No one knows how the Witchfinder came by it. Nor why he'd want to keep such things. That, along with the Witchfinder's death, remains a mystery."

"How does this Hourglass work?"

"According to sources, of which there are very few, the Hourglass is strapped to the hand. Turning it over as you would any ordinary hourglass, the sand runs from one bulb to the other. Only difference being, the white sand runs darker. From a special compartment inside, you will find a shadowleaf."

This was getting into the mad stuff again. "How big are these things?"

"A leaf? As large as your thumbnail. Maybe bigger."

"And how does it contain a witch's evil?"

"Alchemical properties in the sand itself. A person's *shadow*, in the ethereal sense, is their darker side. A place of unbalanced morals, ethics and ideals. To collect such refined evils, they are made into shadowleaves."

Five days ago, I would've laughed this off. It sounded like the biggest load of shit, yet I saw the truth behind it. I didn't know how to reply, so I simply nodded.

Three dozen free-range eggs went into the trolley. Victor saw the look on my face. "A couple of those with a couple of bananas, added to milk, make a fantastic smoothie. Very good for you."

I began to doubt having breakfast with him was a good idea.

"As a rule," Victor explained, "the leaves can only be contained in a layer of dead flesh. Leather."

"Same as the Fabric," I said, and thought of Victor's attempt to get his brother to wear gloves when handling it.

"Yes. So there is no life force to interfere with its dormancy. The pages in *The Book of Leaves* are leather."

"Are there white leaves?"

"Black ones from witches and criminals. Anyone who's sinned. There are no white ones on record. The only white ones would be from a nun, and no one has ever tried that as far as I know. Most people's would be a light grey. No one is guilt free.

No one is entirely innocent. The lighter the leaf, the less likely it could be stitched."

"Ah, yeah, stitching." I remembered Victor suspected Stanley of wanting to stitch the Fabric.

"I'll get to that in a moment."

I realised I gripped the trolley. With surprising reluctance, I let go. As I did, Victor pushed off round a corner and down another aisle. He still fought with the trolley and managed to steer it where he intended, then stopped.

"Every sentient being on this planet is charged with a life force," he said. "The extinguishing of such contributes to the darkening of your shadow. All life is sacred, no matter how small. Even the accidental stamping of ants over a lifetime would contribute to grey flecks in the sand."

I frowned. "Everyone's leaf would be grey."

"Not just committing a sin, but also nasty thoughts, unsavoury actions or intent, are also factors. So even if you've not killed somebody or something, your shadow would be nearer black. Depending on the level of immorality."

With two hands, he took from a shelf the biggest jar of Marmite. "Now this stuff is great with radish and bacon."

His shopping list annoyed me now. I just wanted to know about the Hourglass, and I certainly didn't want to know what he had in mind for breakfast. Once we reached the cereal aisle, I intended to grab some Coco Pops or something.

"Okay," I said, "you're saying a shadowleaf can be a darker grey if you've committed small crimes like fraud and robbery. The stuff you just shouldn't do, but no one's harmed, yeah?"

"Yes." Victor nudged the trolley sideways so not to scrape the racks. "For different crimes, those leaves would come out in light or dark greys. If someone is truly evil, it turns black. No one's perfect. We would all reveal various shades of grey. Anyone with a sickness in their head tilts their shadow—and their shadowleaf—towards black. The sicker their thoughts, the more black grains of sand…so the blacker their leaf."

"And you reckon Goodwin's got it." My mouth was dry. What was Goodwin playing at?

Victor stopped again, eyeing the tinned fruit. I waited for him to announce that pears or pineapple made a great accompaniment to Marmite and bacon. He didn't. "It was assumed to have been destroyed in the Great Fire of London. Which I've always doubted. No one agreed with my arguments. Goodwin certainly didn't believe it existed. Ever. In fact, he made a great effort trying to convince me."

"If he had it all along, I guess he would do that." I dropped my gaze, and when I looked up, I saw in Victor's face a sense of betrayal. I felt sorry for him. He'd known Goodwin much longer than I. "Let's get back to stitching, Victor."

After a moment, he straightened and moved off. "Stitching is essentially what it suggests, only without a needle and thread. A person's life force is the needle and thread. A stitcher, as he or she is commonly referred to, holds a shadowleaf in each hand. The potency of evil within those leaves drains the energies of that person, extracting the spark of life from their very being, absorbing every ounce of energy, eventually killing them. Sucking them dry. All that is left—"

"Is a dried corpse."

"Yes."

He didn't have to say it. I knew the implications of our discovery at Stanley's house. The corpse must've been the remains of someone who'd stitched shadowleaves. "Stitching the leaves together, they make the Shadow Fabric, right?"

"Yes."

"How much can a stitcher stitch?" It sounded stupid, like a tongue-twister.

"One life force has the potential to stitch two leaves."

"Stanley is finding people to stitch," I said, and wondered who that corpse once was.

"Quite possibly. I don't know where Stanley managed to get the shadowleaves from, though."

"Does he have *The Book of Leaves*?"

"He got the Fabric from this Tulip Moon person, so he may well have found the book, too. Although we didn't find any evidence to suggest that."

I didn't want to say what I said next. "You think Stanley and Goodwin are working together?"

Victor slowly shook his head.

"Think about it," I said. "Goodwin has the Hourglass and can make shadowleaves, and he's got something going on in that cave in the woods."

"If Stanley has the Fabric and is stitching, then yes, it is possible."

"He admitted Stanley came to visit him."

"He did."

"Why would he say that to us?" My jaw ached as I clamped it tight. "None of this makes sense."

"It will soon, my friend."

I wasn't looking forward to that moment.

We made it to the cereal aisle and I stared at the shelves without actually seeing anything. "If Stanley has the Fabric, what's stopping him from making necromeleons to stitch the leaves together."

"The dead cannot stitch."

"No life force."

"That's right."

"So," I said, and grabbed the trolley. The metal was cold beneath my grip. "Let's get this straight. We have the Witchblade, now missing, that once belonged to a 17th-century Witchfinder. It's the only weapon powerful enough to stop the Shadow Fabric. This is a type of entity. And it's missing, though maybe Stanley has it. The Fabric can turn people into zombies...sorry, *necromeleons*, and not only that, is a gateway for other entities to cross over into this world. This is called 'haunting', and is possible once the Fabric absorbs enough life force. A man's life force can be drained if he stitches a pair of shadowleaves. These shadowleaves are bad thoughts or wrongdoings turned into something solid, something of substance, and they're extracted by using an Hourglass that's been missing for centuries. Possibly Goodwin has this. Something else that's missing is *The Book of Leaves*, a collection of shadowleaves from 17th-century witches. Finally, seeming to be the bad guy here, is your brother Stanley, who's playing some twisted game, and no one knows the rules."

Victor said nothing as I peeled my fingers from the trolley. He just stared at me.

Finally he said, "Yes."

"I get it. I guess." And I did, mostly. Except one thing. Goodwin's role in all this.

Victor's slow nod was a reflection of precisely how I felt.

"White shadowleaves," I said, "aren't evil enough to drain a stitcher's life force."

"That's right."

"And they're not actually leaves." I didn't know why I said that, because I knew they weren't. I just had to say something else.

"They don't come from trees." He frowned. "They come from men, and we are all just like trees. We grow from seeds, we live, we die…some of us live a long time, watching others fall."

"And," I added, "some are chopped down."

Victor's phone rang, and I was thankful for the caller's timing. My last comment had been morbid and pointless. He answered and listened, and…

"What?" he yelled and shoved the trolley. It crashed into the shelves.

He ran for the exit.

I wasn't hungry anyway.

* * *

The two of us stood in the hallway outside Victor's flat. He glared after the landlord as the lift doors closed, and we stepped into chaos. Afternoon sunlight drowned the room, highlighting the bedlam.

"What the hell is that woman searching for?" Victor demanded. The bookcases—those remaining upright—were empty, some of the shelves either broken or askew.

"You think it's Tulip Moon?" This wasn't a random burglary.

"Of course it is, Leo. She's already tried to kill us."

"She's even torn your books up. Why would she do that?"

As well as books, cushions littered the place, and pieces of busted furniture poked between them.

Victor grunted. "This is hell."

"I guess she's under the impression you've got the Fabric."

Victor's eyes glistened. "She looked inside the violin case. She knew it was gone."

"Stanley has the Fabric now."

"There's no proof he has it," he said. "If he's actually alive."

"Goodwin said—"

"Can we trust Goodwin?"

That was a question often on my mind. I knew the answer, and as always, I pushed it aside. I nudged a cushion with my foot. "We can only guess that Stanley's got the Fabric."

"Assuming he has, how does Tulip Bitch know either way?"

"That's why she's searching for it. She doesn't know."

He picked up a hardback at his feet.

"Maybe no one believes our story," I added. "Maybe they think you're hiding something."

"Why would I lie, if that's the case?" His face reddened. "Would I lie about killing my own brother?"

"You didn't kill him." I hated being reminded that he stabbed Stanley. I hated the image that always followed: the Shadow Fabric taking the body. But then, I hated the mistrust I now had in Goodwin. Not to mention seeing a dried corpse and being in a car crash. I hated everything about this.

"I did kill him," Victor murmured. "You saw him. He was dead."

"Goodwin said he was alive. He said Stanley visited him."

"And I said we can't trust Goodwin. We found those invoices. You saw the handcuffed men in the woods, and you saw Goodwin there."

I pulled up my sleeves. It was getting hot in there.

"Tulip Moon must be working with Goodwin." He glanced at the book in his hands, then hurled it at a wall. "This is outrageous."

I froze, not knowing what to say. My heart sank seeing him like that. Disregarding the missing cushions, he collapsed onto the sofa. He winced as his backside thumped.

"Polly." He pulled out his phone. "I must call her."

"Are you sure we can trust her?"

He looked up at me. "We have to, Leo. We have to." He stabbed the buttons and put the phone to his ear. His eyebrows wriggled.

From somewhere down in the street a car honked.

"Still no answer." He lowered his hand.

"Okay, Victor, let's think about this," I said. "According to your landlord there was no sign of forced entry."

"Yes," he mumbled.

I bent down and dragged free a couple of cushions. Books slid off them with a soft thud. I offered one to Victor, which he dismissed with a wave of a gloved hand. I shrugged, dropped it at his feet, and placed the other beneath me as I sat opposite him.

"Could it have been Stanley?" I said. "He disappeared in the shadows. Maybe he came here the same way."

A smile tugged Victor's lips. "Anything is possible when it comes to the Fabric. You're learning."

"Whoever did this is looking for something. Do you think they found it?"

"Apart from many first editions and the book of *Necromeleons*, nothing is worth taking. From what I can see, they're still all here."

"Then what were they looking for?"

He shrugged. "Whoever's responsible, whether it was Tulip Moon or Stanley, is desperate. Things are coming to a head."

I nodded. "Do they think you've got *The Book of Leaves*? They want the shadowleaves, maybe?"

Victor's lips moved without uttering a sound.

Leaning into the sofa, I considered finding more cushions, but couldn't be bothered.

"This is a total mess, Victor." I didn't mean his ransacked home.

Victor's rounded shoulders quivered for a moment. Then he laughed, long and loud.

CHAPTER 18

Victor and I jogged down the pathway leading to Polly's cottage. I still felt stuffed from the late, and very rushed, breakfast we'd eaten at a café on the way over. The morning had almost disappeared while we cleaned up the mess of the break-in. By the time we sat down, I was ravenous.

Victor pounded the front door. He'd only just rung the bell. Rain trickled down my neck and I pulled up my collar, which did little to stop it.

"Polly?" He peered through the window, his foot sinking into soft earth. It sucked at his shoe as he came back onto the path. "Polly!"

A quick thumbing on his phone, he tried her mobile and home numbers. Inside her house, we heard the shrill tone of an electronic warble, and then the deeper ring of a landline phone. His eyes darted around, settling on nothing.

"She's still in there." Victor tried the handle. It didn't budge. "Either that, or something's wrong. She never leaves home without her mobile."

"Should Annabel be with her?" I asked. I couldn't help feeling sorry for the guy. Everything around him was falling apart, and he was beginning to doubt everyone. Just like I was.

"Always on weekdays," he mumbled.

Attached to the cottage was a garage, its door not fully shut. I dashed to it, grasped the handle and pulled. The mechanism groaned and clanked, failing to open all the way. I ducked beneath it, Victor beside me, and a heavy smell of damp, oil, and paint washed over me. It was bare inside, save for a few rusty paint cans. The rest of the shelves held a layer of dust. One wall housed a door and Victor ran for it. Luck, it seemed, allowed him to open it and he disappeared.

I followed as he darted into each room, continuing to call Polly. I scanned for signs of recent activity, any evidence of her using the sink, sofa, coats, shoes. Anything at all. Georgie's bowl was almost clean, with several crisp pieces of meat remaining. Hard to tell how long ago it had been used—I knew for certain I hadn't been a detective in my old life.

Victor thundered up the stairs. He still shouted for Polly between the occasional creak of a floorboard.

I remained in the kitchen with a sense of déjà vu. First Stanley's house, now Polly's. Unlike the day before where the house was in a mess, this one was tidy. All things at hand—as it should be for any blind person. Walking around someone else's home was strange, everything unfamiliar—stranger still to be in a blind person's home. All appliances and gadgets had bumpy stickers attached to them. In the corner of the kitchen next to the microwave sat a small printer with a stack of paper protruding from it. It looked like an all-in-one scanner and printer. I nosed through some of the papers in ignorance—I can't read Braille. This place had such a warmth to it; a real home, and it felt wrong to snoop.

"Leo." Victor's voice rolled down the stairs. It sounded faint, yet eager. There was something in it which unnerved me. I thought again of the corpse in Stanley's house. An image of those shrivelled eyes, gaping nostrils and wispy hair came to mind. I couldn't handle seeing another dead body.

I took the stairs fast and followed the sound of rustling. Victor sat at a dated computer station, and hadn't switched it on. The room looked like a study.

"It's okay," Victor said. "We don't need to guess any passwords. I think we've found what we're looking for."

"Polly?" I said. "Where is she?"

Victor shook his head. "I don't know. I'm really worried."

"But—"

"All this paperwork belongs to Annabel."

I scanned the room, and agreed. "She's Polly's assistant. This must be her office."

"Yes, but it's this which concerns me." His eyebrows quivered as he held out a sheet of paper.

I took it from him.

"And that," he added before I managed to read what he'd given me. He pointed to something behind me.

Underneath the small window which gave a view of trees and little else, stood a chair. Simple, wooden. Nothing special. Propped against it, however, was a violin—without its case.

That case was back at Stanley's house.

My heart crammed my throat. "Victor?"

"Precisely, my friend." He eyed the paperwork he'd given me. I'd forgotten I held it. It was a hire agreement for a Transit van rented from a Tunbridge Wells company, dating back to Tuesday, only three days before. At the bottom, the named signature was Annabel's.

"What the—" I tossed it away. "You're telling me Annabel tried to kill us?"

"This doesn't prove it."

"Victor, the bitch rammed us off the road." Next to where the paper had landed was more proof. Red, like a beacon, it stood out in contrast to the black and white of the room, glowing amongst the collection of files and computer equipment. My feet were rooted and my knees locked. I wanted to pick it up.

"Leo?"

My eyes must've been bursting from my face, and I felt my cheeks redden. Finally, with a mental shove, I grabbed it. Victor mumbled something.

"This…" My tongue stuck to the roof of my mouth as I straightened. "This proves everything."

It was a red baseball cap.

"What?" One of his bushy eyebrows arched. "Why?"

"The driver of the van wore this…when we were rammed, this was the last thing I saw. And then we hit that tree."

"Oh."

"Yeah. Exactly."

"But Annabel was with Polly that day. All of us were in Goodwin's office. Annabel was there. She came with Polly. Drove her as always."

"Polly stayed with Goodwin for the rest of the afternoon. That would allow enough time."

"You're right." Victor's shoulders slumped. "How did she get the van there? She drove Polly to the House by car."

"It was all perfectly planned."

Victor's eyes fixed on me.

I rubbed my neck. "Knowing that we'd meet at the House, she'd parked it nearby, ready to follow us. She waited for us to leave."

"Why only ram us off the road? If she is Tulip Moon, she's got a gun. We know that. So why not get out of the van and shoot us?"

A familiar thought crashed into my head, the gun pointing at me. "I don't know. Maybe it was more of a warning."

"Of what?"

"To stop searching for Stanley. Or the Fabric. Stop searching for *The Book of Leaves*, maybe. I don't know." I hated not knowing, yet I was getting used to it. I didn't know my past, and now my present made no sense either.

"Lots of questions." Victor grabbed the hire agreement and scrutinised it as though hoping further information would leap from the paper. "If this is the case, then she's close to accomplishing whatever her goal is."

I thought about Victor's book, the one titled *Necromeleons* and its illustration of the man who climbed into the shadows. My head throbbed. "And what could that be, do you think?"

"If Annabel and Tulip Moon are the same person, then she gave Stanley the Fabric."

"They have to be the same person."

"That, my friend, is all we can assume."

"If she gave Stanley the Fabric, maybe she wants it back. You reckon she ransacked your flat looking for it?"

Victor's lips thinned. "Certainly possible."

"Why give it to Stanley in the first place?"

"She knew his arrogance wouldn't keep him quiet. He'd end up showing me. And I had the Witchblade."

The man in the antique shop—the guy called Josh—had claimed a witch killed the others. I asked a question which wouldn't have come easily a week ago: "Is Annabel a witch?"

Victor didn't answer me directly. "Annabel's cunning, and if she managed to set all of that into motion, she's definitely a key player. She knew Stanley and I would meet to show each other our finds. Sibling rivalry…as it always has been."

"She played you guys off each other."

Victor tugged at his collar. "She's clearly sharper than any of us, and she knew the athame would feed off our fragile relationship."

"Knowing how the Fabric would react."

"She knew I would kill Stanley."

"And she wanted him to die," I said, thinking of his dead eyes as they disappeared into the shadows.

"She knew the Fabric needed a dead body to energise it. To recharge it and bring it back to power."

"But Stanley's not dead." This was getting confusing. "Goodwin said so."

"Then her plan has failed."

"More questions." I shook my head.

"We can assume it was Annabel who stole the Witchblade from us."

"Not sure about that, Victor. She didn't look like Annabel."

"Who else could it be? She disguised herself."

Again, I thought about the gun pointing at me. "I don't know."

"And we still can't trust Goodwin."

"What's his role in all this?" I bunched the baseball cap in my hand and threw it down.

"No idea," Victor said. "Polly's in danger. We have to find her. Annabel's been up to all this right under her nose."

"Taking advantage of Polly's blindness. Sick."

"She's playing with all of us. Me and Stanley in particular. Polly's vulnerability, too. Using all of us. Now we even doubt Goodwin."

"We have every right." When I thought of Goodwin, it was as if my brain boiled.

"Annabel wants the Fabric for her own means. To whatever end that might be. Throughout history there has always been someone opposed to the Shadmen, and to us. Someone in opposition to those who've kept darkness at bay throughout the ages."

I shook my head again. Crazy. All of it.

"And now it's beginning again," he added, and stood up, "after three and a half centuries."

CHAPTER 19

Skipping lunch we headed out again, this time to meet Lucas. But not at his bookshop. Victor didn't reveal what the man wanted, and he remained silent during the entire journey. I was getting used to that, though I suspected it had something to do with *The Book of Leaves*. We were in the countryside, even more rural than Mabley Holt, approaching a farm. As I drove us past several outhouses, avoiding a horse that had evidently got loose, I missed the name of the place. I pulled up, and Victor got out first. When I slammed my door the horse charged off.

Lucas stood near a row of corrugated barns, his overcoat flapping around his boots. He slapped a crowbar in his palm.

"Lucas," Victor said. Mud squelched as we strode towards him.

Across the yard from a barn, another horse stuck its face out into the cold afternoon. Its breath plumed as though fed up to be held in what I initially thought was a derelict barn. The smell of animals and hay clogged the air.

The man ignored Victor and stepped towards me. Unlike the first time I'd met this guy, he addressed me by reaching out a hand. "We haven't properly met."

His grip was as firm as I'd expected from such a large man, and cold, rough. Where his cheek sported a deep cleft from forehead to chin, his hands were a mess of spidery scar tissue as if a hundred razorblades had once danced over them. I recalled their conversation in the bookshop, about torture, the jungle, and being held for days, imprisoned while he believed Victor had abandoned him.

I kept quiet, eyeing the crowbar. I didn't like the way he swung it. When we parted, I noticed Victor stared at it. He said, "What's going on, my friend?"

Lucas's jaw muscles rippled. They tugged at the scar. "I told you. I'm not your friend. Not anymore."

I expected him to swing the crowbar at Victor's head. Perhaps it had all been a ruse, we weren't there for Victor's *Book of Leaves*. Once Lucas finished with Victor, he'd do the same to me, the only witness. The guy was massive. We had little chance against him. I doubted he'd even stop there. He'd finish us off, being certain we were dead, leaving us at this quiet farm. I could almost see the revenge in his eyes, feel it in the chill breeze.

"I have contacts," said Lucas, and as he spoke, it was as though he shrank. The crowbar became only a tool. "These days, I rely on them. One reminds me of myself when I was younger, and he has a gift for it. I've been getting him to do a lot for me of late."

I was conscious of my tight forehead, and after an effort, I relaxed. Where was this heading?

Lucas stroked the crowbar as he added, "He was here, the last I heard from him. At this farm."

"Why are we here?" Victor's voice was unusually tiny. "Have you found it?"

"*The Book of Leaves*. Possibly Thomas has found it."

I couldn't recall anyone mentioning a Thomas before, but I kept quiet.

"Why didn't you tell me on the phone?" Victor said, "Why all this secrecy?"

"I didn't hear from him when I should have," the big man replied, "which is unlike him. And because I'm true to my word, Victor, I've brought you here. This is your game."

"What happened to him?"

"There's a saying of wanting a job done right, you do it yourself. Well, here we are, just like old times." Lucas didn't smile.

"You could have told me this on the phone."

"I owe you nothing."

"You've traced the book for me. You must believe you owe me something."

"Victor, shut up." Somehow, Lucas grew upwards and outwards, looming over his old friend. "I said I'd do this for you. We're going to find Thomas. And your book."

Victor's eyes flicked to me, and I raised my eyebrows. Lucas grunted and headed for the farmhouse. It wasn't too far. I hoped we weren't going to find any corpses.

Flanked by great oaks, the farmhouse seemed in better condition than the surrounding buildings. The windows looked recently installed, and pot plants lined the path to the front door. A pair of gnomes guarded the edge of the garden. Lucas stomped up the path. With crowbar and swaying coat, he made the gnomes look ridiculous. He threw a glance over his shoulder and raised the weapon. I reminded myself it was only a tool.

When we reached his side, I expected a swing to take off Victor's head. This paranoia was now irritating. He lowered it and crammed the metal edge between frame and door. He pushed his weight into it and the wood splintered. Maybe Victor flinched, I wasn't sure. Perhaps it was I who'd flinched. I did exhale, certainly. Then I remembered how Victor overcame the guy in the antique shop. Victor wasn't worried.

The wind swept among the trees, and dry bracken drifted over my boots. I kicked it, though my eyes remained on the crowbar.

A laugh rumbled in Lucas's throat. "You guys really think I'd lure you here to kill you?"

The wind chilled my eyes and I blinked.

"Don't flatter yourselves," he added. "Especially you, Victor."

My boss didn't say anything.

Inside, a strange smell like overcooked dinner reminded me I was getting hungry. Poor light greeted us in the hallway. I knocked the door back into its frame, the splinters holding it ajar. It didn't quite block out the sound of the wind.

Four pairs of muddy Wellington boots sat upside down on a rack. Mum, Dad and two girls, going by the colour and size of them. Above them, a family portrait confirmed it. One of the girls wore a tiara, and the other sported a wide smile. An impressive grandfather clock peered from the other end of a worn rug where a staircase vanished into darkness. A smashed mirror crowded one wall, its shards scattered over the floor, reflecting the gloom. Something about a shattered mirror was reason enough to doubt the sanctuary of this place. Plus the knowledge that we were breaking and entering. I was no longer hungry.

I ran my hand over the radiators. Hot. "What the hell are we doing? This isn't right." I looked again at the portrait. Where was the family?

"How much do you know, Lucas?" Victor nudged some glass with his shoe. It tinkled as the shards slid over each other.

"I was in two minds to contact you." Lucas's voice filled the room. "But I'm good to my word."

Victor repeated his question.

"I know enough to be worried." Lucas didn't come across as a man to be worried about anything, and I again wondered about this pair's history. What was it with these guys?

Victor glared at him. "Worried about what?"

Lucas ducked into a side room to our left, the crowbar gripped in a white fist. I followed him.

The first thing I saw was another broken mirror, void of nearly all glass. Beneath it stood a side-unit, and there the glass peppered its surface. Fragments covered the sofa and, as though someone lay on the floor, a pair of legs poked out from behind. A lamp flooded the scene and spotlighted the muddy trainers. One lace was untied, the trousers almost flat over the shins. My pace slowed as I entered the room, mouth dry. Lucas dropped to his knees.

"Thomas." The crowbar thudded beside him. "Who did this?"

The lamp bathed the body in yellow light, adding to the harshness of the flesh. Shrivelled to the bone like the corpse we found at Stanley's house, its clothes hung loose. Spindly limbs protruded from the sleeves. Mud and straw covered it, and dozens of mirror shards pierced the skin. They glinted. The head was little more than a skull with tiny beads for eyes, the hair only wisps. Stuffed in the mouth, a large shard forced the jaw wide. Wrinkled cheeks split and curled up into a hideous grin. A few teeth lay on the carpet.

My stomach lurched and I gasped, then coughed. I nearly spewed.

"Good God." Victor's voice hissed from behind me. He grabbed my shoulder.

"Thomas," Lucas said again, shaking his head. His eyes were closed. "I am so sorry I brought you here."

"This is your contact," I said.

"Yes."

"How—" I shouted, then in a softer voice, I added, "How can you tell? This could be anyone."

Lucas stood up and groaned as his knee popped. He held a crumpled piece of paper. "Because of this."

Victor snatched it and his eyes barely scanned the text. I glimpsed the words before he screwed it up: *Farm, Book, Graves.*

Beside the corpse's hands lay a mobile phone. Lucas grabbed it and thumbed the buttons. A red light flashed, its battery almost out. "The last number he phoned was mine. He told me he'd found it."

I couldn't take my eyes off the shard buried in the corpse's face. "Found what?"

"Victor's book."

"The police," I said. "Why didn't you call the police?"

"The first thing I did was call Victor. This is his territory. Despite everything, he needs to be here. He wants the book."

"Where is it?" Victor looked around the room. "Is it here?"

"As far as I know, yes," Lucas said. The phone bleeped and the screen went dark. He dropped it on the sofa. If he intended to leave it there, I wondered about fingerprints. This had to be reported…and here I was, an accomplice. I looked at the mirror fragment in the corpse's mouth. What the hell happened here?

Victor's frown looked painful.

"Thomas followed a trail to this farm," Lucas added. "The answer is on that paper, Victor."

"Graves?"

"Yes," Lucas mumbled. "That's what it says."

Again, I wondered if he was going to strike Victor. This time it would be a fist in the face; the crowbar too far to reach for any instinctual reaction. The man's eyes were tiny. His scar twitched.

"We must leave," Victor announced. The ball of paper disappeared into his pocket. He straightened his back as he added, "But not before we have the book."

Lucas turned slowly. "I wanted out of this shit years ago, Victor, yet you still bring me back."

"Luc—" Victor began.

"Bad enough when I shave that I remember you left me to die, and here you are again." His voice rumbled. "Back in my life, stepping through my front door and asking for help."

"You were willing."

"Because I am more than you." Lucas loomed over Victor. His arm straightened and I waited for the punch. "I am so much more than you, Victor."

"Guys, calm down," I shouted, and their heads spun in unison.

Lucas's lips whitened as he said, "Keep out of this, boy."

"What happened to this man?" I asked, desperate to keep my voice even.

No one spoke for a moment, and I felt my cheeks warm. My heart hammered.

"His life force has been drained," Victor eventually said. "That's obvious."

"It's not obvious to me. Seriously, what about the glass?" I thought about the corpse we'd found at Stanley's house. There were no broken mirrors there.

"The Shadow Fabric has returned," he said.

"We already know that." Then I thought about Stanley vanishing into its embrace and I looked at the near-empty mirror frame. "What did it do, come through the mirror?"

"Quite possibly."

"Possibly?" Spit flew from my mouth.

"I don't know everything."

If Lucas wasn't going to hit him, perhaps I would. "That corpse is like the one we found in Stanley's house, remember?"

"I can't forget that, Leo."

"Too right." I turned on Lucas. "And you? You ever seen this before?"

Lucas eyed Victor, the corpse, and then me. His head bobbed and his scar twitched.

"What are we going to do now?" Victor squinted into the shadows beneath the stairs. I understood why. It was dark there.

"The Shadow Fabric could be here, right?" I said.

"Yes. And the Witchblade would be bloody handy right now."

I wondered how that ornate blade could help us, and I remembered him explaining that it had power over the Fabric. It could hold it back apparently. I hoped I'd never get into a situation where I needed to witness that.

"What's with all these broken mirrors?" I asked, no longer wanting to hit him. In truth, I knew I couldn't. The thought of actually hitting him, hitting anyone, unnerved me and I wondered about my past. I shivered, hating, as I often did, the absence of memories.

"I have no idea," Victor said. "Lucas?"

"Nope, can't help you there. I've never seen that before."

"You've seen a shrivelled body like this before, then?" I said and bent over the body. The stench climbed into my mouth, down my throat, and made me gag. I clamped tight my jaw and wrinkled my nose. I don't know why I needed a closer look, perhaps it was to bring my thoughts to the present, away from my past. I scratched my chin and heard my watch. Its tick reminded me of my mortality, counting the seconds towards my death.

"Drained, yeah, but not pierced with glass." Lucas crouched beside me. "Help me check his pockets."

"No. You do it." I straightened and tried to breathe normally. "He's your friend."

"Suit yourself." Lucas searched, careful to avoid the glass. The body shifted and the head tilted. With a rustle of splitting skin it detached from the neck and fell sideways. The shard stopped it from rolling further. My stomach lurched.

Victor's voice floated over to us. "This is not looking good."

Lucas leapt to his feet and faced him. I was relieved the sofa and coffee table separated them. "Did you think that when you knew I was taken by the tribe?"

"Lucas." Victor shook his head, his eyes pleading. "We have more important things to deal with now."

Lucas held another piece of paper. Circles and lines covered it.

"A map?" I laughed. "You're kidding me."

"X marks the spot?" Lucas grinned. There he was, rummaging through the pockets of his dead friend, and making jokes. Looking at his scar, I wondered if he'd deserved it. The way it twisted his face made him look cruel. I imagined he could be very cruel, given the chance.

Victor ran a gloved hand over the bookshelves, his eyes glazed. I doubted he even read the titles. "What does it show us?" he asked.

Careful not to kick the corpse, Lucas collapsed into a sofa and held his find beneath the lamplight. "He found the graves. He knew where *The Book of Leaves* is."

Victor's eyes widened. "Where?"

I couldn't believe their coolness. What was going on? Here they both were, talking casually about graves and a book which apparently contains *sins* or something, all with a dead body—drained of life force and spiked with glass—laying at their feet.

"This is mad." I closed my eyes and breathed out. The air whistled as it escaped me. I no longer wanted to be sick.

"The graves are on this farm," Lucas mumbled. "On the grounds."

"What?" I said. "What sort of family bury their dead in their own back garden?"

Victor said, "When you have as many acres as a farm, you can do just about anything."

"Isn't there a law for burying the dead?" The skull, choking on glass, looked back at me. *I'm dead*, it queried, *What about what's happened to me? Isn't there a law about this?*

"Let's get out of here." Lucas headed for a door.

"Hey," I called after him. "Where is the family who lives here?"

Victor's glance told me he'd been thinking the same thing.

Lucas paused on the threshold, the crowbar gripped in both hands. He remained silent.

"Let's find the graves first," Victor said. "We can't wait too long."

"Why the hurry?" I said, and believed I already knew the answer. I stole a peek at the corpse. The lamplight reflected from the mirror shards.

Victor tugged at his gloves. "Because the shadows may return."

I looked at my watch, and for a moment, I thought the shadows coiled around my arm, but it was only the poor light.

When I looked away, the first thing I saw was the shattered glass of another mirror. This one was small, its silver frame broken, nested in reflecting splinters.

"All these broken mirrors…" I said.

Victor's eyebrows twitched, and so did his lips.

"In your books," I added, "you ever read anything involving mirrors?"

"Reflections," he mumbled. "Reflections of haunt."

I wanted to laugh, yet couldn't. There was something in the way he'd said it.

"What?" Lucas's voice disrupted the momentary silence. "What do you mean, haunt?"

"Haunt," Victor said, "is a term used when referring to an entity's means to break onto this plane of existence."

I recalled a conversation the day before about haunting.

"I didn't know that," Lucas said, then disappeared into the other room. His voice came back to us. "There are more broken mirrors here."

With the back of a hand, I wiped sweat from my forehead. The sound of my ticking watch reminded me of more time spent with the corpse. I had to get out of there.

"Come on you two, we're going." Lucas returned to the room. He was pale. "Let's leave Thomas."

I looked down at the body and hoped he'd died before the shard entered his mouth.

"Vic—" I began, wanting to say more, yet I didn't know what. This was all complete bullshit, and I wondered just what the hell I was doing with these guys. Why did I still play Victor's game? I should've run the moment he killed his brother. Then I remembered. It wasn't Victor who killed Stanley, it was the shadows. And was Stanley dead? Apparently, he was walking around like nothing had happened. Crazy.

As we walked into the adjacent room, glass crunched underfoot. In the corner, an upright piano sat with its sheet music open on Boccherini's *Minuet*. Lucas stood at the back door, beyond which a pathway wound through an immaculate garden. He unlocked it and stepped outside. The wind rushed in.

"I think this map makes sense," he said as we joined him. "I reckon all we have to do is head out past the barns and find a pond. Or a lake, depending on the scale of this thing, and get to a tree line. Not sure how accurate this is."

Victor tugged at his gloves. "Then we'll follow you."

We left the house, and I couldn't help thinking of the corpse laying there, its head detached, the mirror shard cleaving the face in two.

CHAPTER 20

We followed Lucas, passing tractors and other machinery, and came to a row of barns. The last was set away from the others and looked derelict. Its doors swung in the wind. One rattled against the corrugated panels like it laughed at us. It was all I could hear.

I left Victor's side and peeked in. A strong animal smell hit me, and the semi-darkness revealed a circle of hay bales. The centre contained what could have been a pile of rubbish, possibly even clothes. I thought of the family in the house.

"Victor, I'm uneasy about this," I said as I caught up with him. He was a few paces behind Lucas. The crowbar swayed in the man's grip.

Victor's mouth turned down. "Me too, my friend. A lot is riding on us finding *The Book of Leaves*."

"Yeah," I said. "About that…"

"What?"

"Sins?"

"Just don't think about it."

That was difficult, given everything I'd so far witnessed. Things had gotten messy way too fast. And what the hell was Goodwin's role in all this? I'd lost all trust in that man, and I had no idea where any of this was going.

We came to the edge of stretching fields, the barns and machinery now behind us. Lucas was already through the gate and into a field with sheep. They stared at him, bleating their disapproval, and then began to amble away. Lambs bounded between their legs. I was certain I'd never seen so many lambs in one field before, yet as always, I doubted my memory. The noise was incredible.

"Lambing season," Victor explained. "And by the sounds of it, they're hungry."

Still no farmer in sight, and again I thought of the family…and the dead body we'd left in the lounge; Thomas.

Lucas headed for the woodland in the distance without looking over his shoulder. The wind bit my neck and I yanked my collar high. I glanced to the sky, suspecting rain.

When we reached the graves, I wasn't sure they were that at all; simply five mounds, covered with years of woodland growth, each peaked with a rock and moss that almost glowed.

"You serious?" I said. "You think these are the graves."

Lucas turned, his eyes piercing. "That's what the map says."

I held up my hands. "Okay."

Set back from the graves, closer to the tree line, and beside a possible path, was a weathered fence. In places, barbed-wire cut into the trunks, and rotted posts dangled like hanged criminals. Or witches.

"Graves," I said. The more I thought about it, the more they could be graves. I'd been expecting something more obvious, like those found in a church graveyard. Wooden crosses and statues, or something similar.

"I know they could be anything," Lucas continued, "but given our location it has to be here."

A few splashes of rain fell, and in moments it smashed through the branches. "Great," I said.

Lucas yanked up his hood, his face now in darkness. "Of course it would rain just as we find the creepy graves." He rammed the crowbar into the ground and scrutinised the map.

"The trail ends here?" Victor stood beside him and peered over Lucas's shoulder. Standing on a muddy bank, it was the first time Victor could be taller than the other man. "This is where your Thomas believed the book to be?"

Without a word, Lucas screwed up the paper and shoved it in his pocket. He grunted, which was all I'd expected from him. I wished these two would settle their differences.

"So there are five graves, and we're going to dig them up?" I couldn't believe this. We weren't just breaking into houses, we were now robbing graves. "We haven't even got shovels."

Lucas pulled from his pocket a collapsible shovel, the type metal-detecting enthusiasts use. It was ridiculous to think he intended to dig up a grave with that little thing. "The book is buried to the north of the smallest grave."

"Nice," I said, eyeing the small mound and thought of a child buried beneath it. The sadness to lose a child must be unbearable.

In his other hand, Lucas held a compass. He flicked it open. The needle pointed at a rock a few paces away, and he strolled to it and kicked it.

"Have some respect!" I shouted. "That could be another grave."

"Here. Maybe," he said.

The rock was large and flat as a suitcase, and covered in grime and leaves and moss. I wondered how much we couldn't see.

"It's a good enough marker as any." Victor held the crowbar in both hands. I hadn't seen him pull it from the ground. Mud caked its pointy end. He dragged it over the rock and removed some filth. Something red showed through, faded paint perhaps. Dropping the crowbar, he wiped the surface clear—as clear as he could given the years the rock must've been there.

Victor picked up the crowbar and stood back. "Recognise it?"

Both Lucas and I said, "Yes."

It was a symbol. I'd recognised it immediately; from the book in Victor's flat, the one titled *Necromeleons*. Two triangles with facing apexes, one solid and the other hollow, separated by a curved X…making it resemble an hourglass, in fact. It was almost insect-like, too.

Rain flattened my hair and trickled down my face. I mopped it with my sleeve, which was already wet, and failed to dry my skin.

Victor wedged the crowbar between the rock and ground, and leaned on it. It moved a fraction, and settled when he let go. "Heavy."

"Looks like it," Lucas said. "Leo, over here."

I circled Victor and stood beside Lucas. I wasn't happy about this, though knew it had to be done. There was something important about *The Book of Leaves*.

"When Victor moves it," Lucas said, "we pull. Got it?"

The moss was cold and soft, tricky to hold onto given the pelting rain. My fingers clamped a jutting edge. I bent my legs and braced my back, shoulder to shoulder with Lucas, and could smell his breath: coffee. Victor gripped the crowbar with both hands and leaned into it. The rock lifted and we pulled. It moved up and sideways, sliding. My foot slipped in the mud, Lucas's too. We regained our footing and heaved with renewed strength. The rock shifted and Victor almost sprawled over the crowbar as it went all the way under.

"Yes!" Lucas's bellow was lost in the sound of crashing rain. Straightening, Victor pushed the rock with both hands as Lucas and I continued to pull. It slid away further from its earthy housing, and as one, we leapt back from the rock as it settled again. My back screamed and I wondered how the older men felt. I didn't voice my ache, seeing that neither one even grunted when handling it.

Lucas passed the small shovel to Victor, who began scraping the mud with it. He dug into the ground and hacked gouges in the earth. Deeper he went. Mud chipped away and revealed nothing. The rain pooled in the hole and Victor got filthier.

"It might not even be here," I said. "Could be further up there."

Lucas followed my gaze, saying nothing, while Victor continued to dig. He now hunched over the hole. In one hand, he held the crowbar like a walking stick, supporting himself as he dug with the other.

"It's here." Victor threw the shovel aside and held up the crowbar. "The symbol proved that."

Lucas sat on the rock, eyeing the hole as I peered over Victor's shoulder. There was something metallic there, rusted and muddy. The rain made it difficult to see. Victor dragged the crowbar along its edge and teased away some earth. Eventually, after more scraping and poking, he stabbed the crowbar into the ground beside it.

High above, the branches creaked. It felt like the trees warned us of our desecration, telling us we should leave it buried.

With a slurping sound, a metal box, big as a briefcase, erupted in a burst of clumpy earth. Victor pulled it out and stood up. His gloves were slick with mud. Nudging Lucas from the rock, he placed the box down and stood back.

The three of us stared at it. The sound of the rain attacked the woods with renewed force. It was like we were three modern-day pirates who'd dug up buried treasure. I thought of the antique shop where Victor and I collected Polly's chests. The owner of that place had been reading *Treasure Island*. This rusted box, however, sitting atop that moss-covered rock, was nothing like those chests. This was smaller, flatter and a huge lock hung on one side.

Victor grabbed the crowbar and swung it down on the lock. The rusty clasp broke and shot across the ground. It came to rest beside the middle grave.

"That was easy," he said.

Lucas reached for the box, and stopped. His hand almost touched it. "Victor, you should open it."

"Thanks," he replied. This was the first time I'd witnessed anything other than hostility from Lucas. There was a lot said during that moment.

Victor pulled up the lid. It creaked and didn't move any more than a thumb's width. He wedged his fingers beneath the edge. I imagined something biting his fingertips off, and thought it absurd. There was just a book in there, nothing more—maybe. A book of sin, apparently. Worms perhaps, but nothing with teeth. When he yanked harder, the metal disintegrated in rusted strips, tearing his glove across the palm. It didn't cut through.

Inside was a book wrapped in cloth.

Victor inhaled sharply. His face said everything.

"Amazing," Lucas said.

"Well done, men." Victor held it to his chest.

"Don't you want to check it's in there?" Lucas took the crowbar from him.

"I'm not opening it here."

"Why?" I asked, eyeing the bundle.

"Because the Fabric could be somewhere around us right now." Victor glanced at Lucas. "Look what it did to Thomas."

"Yeah, Vic, good point." Lucas calling him Vic didn't go unnoticed, and Victor raised an eyebrow at me.

I stepped towards the nearest grave, the littlest one, making certain not to tread anywhere near the other mounds. I wondered what stories lay beneath my feet. "Who were these people? And why would your book be buried with them?"

Victor came up beside me. "I've no idea."

Lucas stabbed the crowbar into the ground. "We should get out of here before the Fabric comes."

Victor's voice was barely above a whisper. "It's already here, there's no doubt about it."

"Of course it's here," Lucas spat. The hate surfaced again and I pictured him swinging the crowbar at Victor's head. "What else could drain the life force of the poor bastard who'd found that damn book for you?"

"Let's go," Victor said, and walked away.

"What about the family?" I said, thinking about the rack of Wellington boots, particularly the little pairs. "We should find out what happened to them."

"We're returning to the house anyway," Victor said. "We may as well search while we're there."

* * *

Back at the farmhouse, habit made me wipe my feet and scrape off the mud as best I could. Victor and Lucas waited patiently behind me. When I finished, neither one bothered to clean their shoes. They left muddy prints behind them. Did these men have any faith in finding the family alive?

Water dripped from all of us.

We found the family in the kitchen-dining room, and the stink slapped me across the face. I gagged. The four still sat at the table, meals untouched. Flies buzzed around them and the food. Lucas coughed and Victor grimaced.

"Disgusting," I mumbled into my hand.

All four were seated as though nothing was wrong, only they were dried husks wearing ill-fitting clothes, drained of life force. Unlike Thomas, there was no sign of mirror fragments. Each had their head bowed, hands clasped together as if in prayer, about to enjoy their meal together. I thought of the Wellington boots, wondering which of the little ones had worn the tiara. I thought of the graves out in the field, then looked at the book under Victor's arm.

"This is mad." My stomach twisted, and my mouth went dry. Somehow, I managed to say, "I'll be in the car."

I only made it as far as the next room. The shadows moved. All of them. It was as though the grey light of the wet afternoon had forced the gloom indoors. Shadows folded on my periphery. They snaked around furniture and drooped from the ceiling. Darkness closed in.

"Guys!" I shouted, backing up.

Thundering feet rushed behind me and the pair stood on either side of me. One of them inhaled sharply.

"Run!" Victor cried out.

They charged towards the kitchen and I followed, squeezing past the dead family. Lucas knocked a chair and one of the corpses fell sideways. It sprawled across the floor in a plume of dust. I leapt over it just as something crashed behind me. I glanced back and the gloom pushed through the doorframe. Wood split and the wall crumbled.

Darkness rushed through the house after us.

My knee ached and I wondered how the hell we would outrun this thing. I didn't believe it was the Fabric, the shadows were too clean. I knew that was a strange thing to recognise. Fresh, clean shadows, not cloying at all. Unlike I'd sensed when the Fabric had absorbed the light at Stanley's house.

As we reached another room—this house was bigger than I'd first thought—I heard wood explode and the crackle of something else, soft thumps of what I guessed to be the bodies hurled out of the way.

I passed another mirror, its shattered glass crunching beneath my feet.

From another room, the piano played a haunting tune. The sound of splintered wood and a hurricane of wind echoed through the house. It blasted apart furniture and ornaments. Everything else clanged and shattered as the shadows leapt from where they'd lain dormant only moments before.

We rounded a corner entering the hall, and as Lucas ran past the grandfather clock, its tick overpowered my pounding heart. And its panels exploded in a rush of darkness. A loop of shadow coiled around Lucas's legs and tripped him. He smashed into the wall. A hammering rain of wood and clock mechanisms swallowed his yell.

The shadows reared up and reached for his head. His hands slapped about, flailing blindly. His eyes were glazed.

I stopped running and started for him, when Victor shoved me aside. Before I managed to say anything, he lunged for his old friend. He kicked the shadows and stamped on them. His jaw clamped tight and determination squinted his eyes. With one hand, he tugged at Lucas, and with the other, he clutched *The Book of Leaves*.

The shadows broke in places, dispersing like oil and water. Too weak, perhaps, for such an attack. For a moment, Victor and Lucas held one another. Lucas gave a sharp nod as he regained his footing, and Victor pulled him towards the front door.

"Go!" he shouted.

I stepped back, my arse hitting the wall. The presence of the shadows—although not as menacing as the Shadow Fabric—flexed its muscles. Its energy charged through the house. Shadows beneath the Wellington boots erupted in grey bursts, like phantoms awakening on the other side of reality. My breath was rapid as I eyed the door.

Lucas had already yanked it open and staggered towards his truck. It was parked further up the driveway. Rain still pummelled the ground. Victor made it to the car and started tugging at the handle. Mud streaked his face and caked his hair, his eyes wide and his clothes filthy.

With the wall at my back, I slid sideways and bolted out. Cold air slapped my face and the rain stung. It froze my brain. My heartbeat thundered through my head. Though impossible, I imagined I still heard the grandfather clock.

Tick. Tick. Tick.

Victor was shouting, and it took me a moment to tune in. He glared at me, his mouth moving, but I heard only that ticking sound. Behind me the shadows whipped and twisted into the wet afternoon. They thinned and shrank back, darted forward again and immediately retracted as though unsure to leave the house. Perhaps I heard them groan in frustration. I fancied I even saw a thin wisp of darkness curl like a finger, beckoning.

"Leo!" Victor screamed. "Press the button!"

Button? I blinked, no longer hearing the clock, no longer mesmerised by the shadows. I turned to him. Then I understood. I fumbled for the car key. My breath was sharp in my lungs, and my knee was killing me.

The house groaned—that's what I heard, not the shadows—and the sound of shattering glass made me take a final look. The darkness seethed at the threshold, unable to enter daylight. Through the windowpanes, glass spitting, the smoky phantoms tried to reach out.

With slick hands, I yanked the car door wide, threw myself in and started the engine. I even found it an effort to close the door, so I left it wide.

"Just lesser-shadows," Victor said as he pulled his seat belt. I dropped the handbrake and shot off after Lucas's 4x4. My door slammed shut as I tugged the steering wheel.

Mud and rain smeared the windscreen in twin arcs as I whacked the wipers on.

We made it away from the farmhouse. From the shadows. From the shrivelled corpses.

From the madness.

CHAPTER 21

The drive to Lucas's bookshop had been fast, too fast. I still felt as though the shadows, or the *lesser*-shadows as Victor had put it, were behind me, and I constantly checked the rear-view mirror for any pursuing darkness.

Once out of the car, things were no different. I didn't stop throwing glances over my shoulder until I'd followed Lucas into his flat above the shop. We spent time in the bathroom cleaning up as best we could. While Lucas threw some new clothes on, Victor took the bathroom first. When it was my turn, I made certain to put the light on, even though daylight blasted through the frosted glass. I wondered if Victor had done the same.

In the lounge, with Lucas and Victor in the middle of the room, I hovered by the window and watched the road below. I stared without seeing, stuck in a constant replay of the madness at the farmhouse. My temples pulsed.

On the gleaming surface of a glass coffee table, aligned parallel with the edges, sat a pile of movie magazines. Next to these was an empty fruit bowl and three remote controls—again perfectly aligned. All a contrast to the shop downstairs, with piles of books and split boxes strewn about the floor.

"You've done well, my friend," Victor said to Lucas. His face was cleaner, his gloves too, but there was still mud in his hair.

Lucas said nothing.

"Thank you so much," Victor added.

In his lap, the book remained covered. It sat in the folds of filthy cloth. The material fell over his knees, one edge draping the floor. Earth still caked his clothes.

"Don't think I've forgiven you," Lucas said, but his voice was softer. I thought of the way he'd looked at Victor when he pulled him from the shadows. Maybe they were closer—albeit slightly—than when we'd met at the farmhouse, before everything went crazy. That felt like such a long time ago.

Victor pulled the cloth away and it fell to the floor. Inside, tied with string, the book was wrapped in brown paper; torn in places, spotted with smudges of mud and age. Nothing on the outside of the package gave away its contents. He pinched the two ends of string. "I've spent years searching for this."

I had no doubt that inside the grubby wrapping was *The Book of Leaves*. It was something else to drag me into a world of witchcraft and corpses and magic knives. Plus, with recent revelations yet to be fathomed, doubt and deceit. And now, even ordinary shadows played the game.

"Now the search is over." His voice was small, his eyes unwavering.

"Don't you want to open it?" Lucas sat on the edge of his chair. His voice had definitely softened. I hoped they'd finally settled their differences. Again, I wondered what really happened to them in the jungle. And what jungle was it?

Victor didn't move his fingers. I wanted him to open the damn thing, the suspense crippled me. Especially after all we'd gone through to get it, all we'd witnessed, and the feeling of those shadows as they tore apart the family's home. Their bodies thrown around. Even though I'd not seen the shadows grab them, I imagined them hitting the walls in scattered bones and flapping clothes.

Lucas traced a finger down the length of his scar. "I'm too old for all that Indiana Jones shit."

Victor's eyes focused on somewhere else. A frown tugged at his forehead.

"The older I've gotten," Lucas continued, "the closer those calls. I don't know whether to cringe or smile at the memories of us two. Too many times we came close to death…."

"We did, my friend. Far too many."

"Still here, though," Lucas said, and then added, "Even after today, we're still here."

"We are."

"I have my contacts in the game now. Thomas was one of them."

"It's not a game any longer," Victor said, a slight edge to his voice. "It was never a game to start with."

Lucas scratched his chin. "No, you're right, it never was," he said. "Still isn't."

"You're still the same, Lucas. You proved that today." Victor's eyebrows raised. "I'll sort out a bank transfer for you. Give me a few days."

"No rush, it's Friday after all. I'm closing up shop tomorrow and heading to my sister's for the weekend. She's having a barbecue on Sunday." He motioned to the dining table: bread rolls, charcoal briquettes, lighter fluid. "At my age, it's about family."

Finally, these two were speaking normally. As normal as could be, given the recent events. Again, I thought of the shadows in the farmhouse, the way they'd slithered from the corners, coming alive and reaching for us; Lucas tripping and the clock exploding.

A sudden tug of Victor's gloved fingers and the string fell away, draping his knees. He hefted the book from one hand to the other, and the covering tore slightly.

I rubbed my forehead, a dull throb pulsed behind my eyes. Perhaps it was eyestrain, or even a dehydration headache. I wasn't sure.

Victor revealed the edge of the book, leather-bound, as he'd described it. Brown, stained, and aged.

A stab of agony shot across my forehead, blasting behind my eyes. I grunted, not loud enough to draw attention. All eyes were on the book as Victor slid away the final sheet of wrapping. I lost focus for a second. In front of me, the two men sharpened and then blurred under another bolt of pain.

The Book of Leaves sat in Victor's lap, cradled in folds of paper. He caressed its front cover. His fingers made a subtle rasp.

I blinked and frowned. A greyness clouded my vision and my head throbbed. A darkness swept over me and swallowed my periphery. It left a narrow tunnel of light where only the book remained. Even though it was a bulk of dark pages, the thing glowed.

The streaks of darkness pressed in with increasing force. Victor and Lucas were talking again. Their voices too far away, overcome by the wind rushing in my ears like a train thundering through that tunnel.

The light expanded slightly, with occasional glimpses of other things. Greyness at first, shimmering at the edges. Brief flashes of something...somewhere else; row upon row, on all sides, were books. Not books, *boxes*. Metal containers sporting an emblem which I failed to make out.

As suddenly as the image appeared, it quivered into a wave of shadow. Vanishing...

Again the wind roared, no longer resembling a train. It howled.

The tide of conflicting scenes crashed into me like being in two places. The main one—the real one—was a room where Victor and Lucas stared at me. The other was a transparency placed over my eyes, tricking me into seeing something else; a glowing bare bulb over many shelved boxes.

My mind buckled with that insistent bang and roar of the train, and those shadows pushing down. I wanted to escape. Bile crept up my throat; I wanted to run, vomit, collapse, to fly...and there I was, with Victor and Lucas now reaching for me. They came too slow. They couldn't help me. They wouldn't get there in time. Again, the image of those metal boxes smashed into my mind. The bulb was too bright.

What was this? A memory?

Rapid, alternate scenes flashed between my companions and the room of boxes. On and off, in and out. A strobe effect between reality and unreality. It was as if a determined tide dragged me under. I gasped, lungs tightening, and I clutched my throat with rubbery hands. The surge of images crashed down around me.

My mind reeled. This wasn't a memory. The room of boxes was *not* a distant place from my past.

It was something else entirely.

I squinted and tried to speak. Then I collapsed.

* * *

Victor's voice slid through the darkness and my eyelids cracked open enough to allow light to creep in. I felt fine—if strangely sleepy. No headache. No dizziness. And no odd visions. All was normal.

Victor's face hovered close to mine. His wrinkles were canyons.

"Leo," he said, "are you okay?"

I blinked a few times, my head swimming. I was slumped on the floor against an armchair, limbs awkward and with no idea how I'd got there. My breath came in short gasps.

Both men looked down at me.

"Victor?" My voice sounded weak. I felt small.

"You were lucky," he said. "Lucas managed to catch your fall."

"What happened?"

Victor shook his head. "I honestly don't know."

"You've been saying that a lot recently." Maybe everything had finally been too much to take in. After all, in only a few days my understanding of the world had been torn into strips.

"Yes."

As I shifted into a sitting position, Lucas went into the kitchen. He shortly returned with a glass of water. Inside, zigzags of reflected light shot around as though trying to escape.

"Here." He crouched beside me.

With a steady hand, I took it from him. The cold liquid sharpened my senses and I sat up straighter.

"I remember seeing boxes," I said. "Lots of boxes. Rows of them. Metal ones. A room full of them."

"What do you mean, boxes?" Victor took the glass of water from me.

Pressing my fists into the carpet, I got to my feet without a problem. I stood for a second, stretching, and lowered myself into the armchair.

Victor handed me the glass. Taking a large gulp, I waited for them to sit before continuing. *The Book of Leaves* was nowhere in sight. Between mouthfuls of water, I told them how I'd felt and what I'd seen. Neither of them interrupted.

"I was there, yet not there," I concluded. "Weird."

"As soon as you saw *The Book of Leaves*?"

"Yes!" I said, embarrassed that I'd shouted it. "Yeah."

"I've wrapped it up again," Lucas said. "It's in the kitchen."

"Good." Victor rubbed his forehead.

"This is your territory, Victor." Lucas took off his gloves. "Not mine. I just find these things for you."

"I know, my friend. You did well. Thank you."

"You're telling me you don't know either?" My elbows thumped my knees as I leaned forward, glaring at Lucas.

"Sorry, pal." He shook his head—a familiar gesture all round, and it was getting annoying. I gritted my teeth.

From the kitchen a combination of clatter-clang-smash made us all turn our heads. The three of us froze and strained our ears. I wanted to get out of my chair, but didn't want to make a noise in case something else happened.

Silence. Nothing more.

Lucas slowly stood up and headed for the kitchen.

Victor and I watched the big man leave the room. There was a short hallway leading to the kitchen, next to which the stairs vanished to the lower floors.

While a few seconds passed, I pictured Lucas crouching and picking up a pot or a pan, frowning at the mess of a piece of shattered crockery. Moments later, he returned, framed inside the doorway. From behind him, the lightshade gave him a crude halo.

"A pan fell off the rack." He shrugged. "Damn thing broke a plate."

Victor's shoulders slumped. I shook my head and took a sip of water.

"I'll clean it up later," Lucas said.

The hallway light went out.

Lucas frowned, turned, and looked up. A darkness had spread across the ceiling, swallowing the light. It resembled a puddle of dirty water, only it defied gravity. Its smooth edges shifted and seethed, moving towards Lucas.

Victor said something as Lucas's bellow ripped into the room. Several tentacles of darkness burst from his stomach in a red mist, yanking him upright.

I dropped the glass and water soaked my trousers. It hit the floor and cracked.

The ends of those black limbs twisted and squirmed. Blood gushed from jagged holes, soaking Lucas's clothes. Like a puppet, his arms and legs flailed and his face contorted.

This was nothing like the shadows at the farm. I'd seen and felt this presence before. At Stanley's house. It was the Shadow Fabric.

A black coil speared Lucas's neck. Another haze of red, splashing the walls. His head flopped sideways as the slithering darkness whipped the air. His legs buckled. The weight of his lifeless body supported only by tentacles of varying sizes. Their ends curled like beckoning fingers.

In a collective tug, they tore Lucas's body to pieces.

CHAPTER 22

"Lucas!" Victor roared, and the two of us leapt to our feet.

A lump clogged my throat and I forced it down. I'd never seen anything like it, certainly not beyond the TV or cinema screen, and I knew there was nothing remotely similar in my unremembered past.

Pieces of Lucas were everywhere. A few tendrils of shadow prodded and stroked the chunks of his flesh. Beneath their touch each piece shrivelled and crackled, losing its wetness. The redness darkened to grey. Those tentacles retracted and the bulk of the shadow pulsed. Clinging to the top of the doorframe, it shimmered like tar.

"Think we've found the Shadow Fabric," I said.

With the darkness in front of us and the evening sky pushing on the window behind, we were closed in. Trapped. The Fabric blocked our only exit. It didn't move. It packed out the hallway, and even as I watched, its size increased. Already its bulk had expanded since the last time I'd seen it—thinking of the redundant violin case back on Stanley's dining room table. It must be ten times larger now.

"Victor!" Sweat beaded my brow; bile rose to my throat. "What can we do?"

"We can't allow the Fabric to take the book." His gloved hand clamped my arm.

For a moment, I dragged my eyes away from the Shadow Fabric, and I saw Lucas's gloves beside the sofa. I grabbed them, my eyes returning to the Fabric as I pulled them on. Far from a snug fit, but they were all I had. Given that Victor always wore a pair, I guessed it was time for me to get into a similar habit.

The tentacles slithered back into the body of Fabric, and in one movement it shifted through the doorway. It still clung to the ceiling as it dragged itself half into the room. The light dimmed further. Its seething bulk throbbed once and settled. It dipped in the middle like a black canopy, the surface neither rippling nor shimmering.

"What's it waiting for?" Victor said, glancing at the window.

"What are *we* waiting for?"

He peered out into the street. "Our only exit."

"You're joking!" My eyes leapt to the table of barbecue supplies, and then to the Fabric. "We'll break our necks from this height."

Still the Fabric hadn't budged, and without taking my eyes off it, I sidestepped towards the table.

"We have another exit." I grabbed the bottle of lighter fluid. We had fire.

Victor saw my intention and pulled from his pocket a lighter. It was similar to the one I'd bought for Goodwin.

"This and a pair of gloves," he said, "is all we need."

"And maybe the Witchblade."

"Yes."

"If it wanted to kill us," I said as I unscrewed the lid, "it would've done so already."

Victor swiped Lucas's weekend supplies to the floor, kicked a chair away, and heaved the table from the wall. One of the chairs tipped and fell with a sickening thud onto a part of Lucas's remains. It was hard to tell, perhaps it was his trousers. My heart thumped with each passing second. We had to get out of there. Now.

Victor shoved the table into the doorway.

Waiting until he retreated, I squirted the lighter fluid at the table and the walls. "This could go horribly wrong."

The Fabric still didn't move.

"It's our only way out." He flicked the Zippo wheel a few times. The spark eventually created a flame, and in an underarm throw, he tossed the lighter at the table. The flame arced through the air and skidded across the surface, coming to rest halfway. Orange and yellow, plus traces of blue, surged as the fire fanned outwards. It coated the table and climbed the walls.

On the ceiling the Fabric shuddered, stretched itself out, and pulled its mass further into the room. I cringed, waiting for a tentacle to reach for us, to rip us in pieces as it had Lucas.

Nothing.

Victor darted underneath the burning table. I ducked and threw myself after him. Everything was bright. Knees banging the floor, I scrambled under the fire, dragging and pulling myself through the doorway.

I ignored the pain in my knee as I scrambled into the hall. The Fabric still hung from the ceiling, mostly in the room behind, held back by the flames. Smoke drifted out as the crackles intensified.

Victor ran from the kitchen holding *The Book of Leaves*. Remembering what happened earlier, I was relieved to see it wrapped. Loosely, but still out of sight.

I charged downstairs with Victor a short distance behind me.

On the first floor landing, I stepped aside as he caught up. I turned and pointed the bottle of lighter fluid up the stairs and squeezed. The jet of liquid caught the flames in the doorway, and immediately the fire spread along the carpet. I hoped none of the fire would run back into the bottle—this was one dangerous game.

As we were about to descend the final set of stairs, flames burst through the upstairs wall and part of the staircase. Carpet and plaster heaved as both fire and darkness fell on us. The black of the Fabric did little to dim the inferno now engulfing the top floor.

The heat stung my face. Smoke, heavy and bitter, filled my mouth. My lungs were tight. This was insane.

Victor made a noise and staggered away from me, clutching the package close to his chest. The floor tilted, lifting us upwards, and shifted sideways. A tentacle, thick as an arm, forced its way up from under us. It smashed part of the wall.

"Victor!"

He was gone.

On either side of me the walls were jagged sheets of plaster and skirting. Flames licked everything. The ceiling creaked, and with each passing second, the heat snatched more air away. Smoke stung my eyes and tears blinded me.

A bulk of shadow loomed on the edge of the flickering light as it tore through the upper floor.

"Victor!" I coughed and spat.

I tilted backwards, the floor heaving. Something cracked and splintered from behind and below. Both my feet slipped forward. With arms flailing, I peered over my shoulder—the snapped floorboards and split balusters peered up at me. Fire lashed between broken furniture.

The staircase was no longer there, replaced by vicious stakes and splinters. A mantrap like those I'd seen in Vietnam: lethal traps constructed from household objects such as tables and chairs, hidden beneath the forest floor by the Viet Cong. Desperate to remain upright, that was all I thought.

One hand still clutched the bottle, the other searched for a wall no longer there. I waited to fall, to be impaled by a mantrap of splintered balustrade and broken flooring.

A crash and a roar rushed over me as part of the ceiling collapsed. The world was blinding.

My feet shot out from under me and I fell.

I shouted something, my voice lost in a roar of fire and darkness, the heat unbearable.

Gravity tugged at me. It would be a short fall onto those deadly spikes, then a gloved hand yanked me to a stop. It jarred my neck. I grabbed Victor's forearm, my feet perched on the edge of wooden splinters. He held me with one arm, *The Book of Leaves* under the other.

He hauled me up and my feet found buckled floorboards. His eyebrows twitched, eyes determined. The flames licked the ceiling. There was a lot of darkness behind that—I couldn't tell if it was the ruined upper floor or the Shadow Fabric.

Shadows—normal ones, I hoped—flickered and danced around us.

Victor's foot slipped and I fell back. He dropped the book and it slid down broken boards, disappearing into the room below. With a *humph*, he clutched me and I swung to the side. I kicked my legs for purchase and my knees slammed into the remains of a wall. Finally, my feet found something solid.

Teeth clenched, heart in my throat, I nodded to Victor and he let go. Any doubts whether I could trust this man vanished the moment he dropped the book. With a few grunts, I levered my body onto stable ground and collapsed against the wall, my breath fierce, my throat ragged and burning like the building.

Coughing, Victor pulled me up. The bottle of lighter fluid rolled at my feet. With so much fire destroying the house I doubted I needed it, yet I grabbed it regardless.

Victor slithered into the bookshop below and I followed, managing to snag my trousers and bang my head. Clean air rushed into my lungs as I clambered over a busted bookcase. Flames raged overhead.

Then darkness blocked it out.

I gasped, coughed, and brought the bottle up. Squeezing the last of the fluid into the hole I prayed none would splash down on me. Flames leapt around jagged floorboards and ripped carpet, and in the Fabric's retreat, a roar shook the ceiling.

As I made it to ground level, a huge portion of a far wall gave way amidst a tangle of strip lights. They exploded.

A black mass leaked through the ceiling. Fire raged and fell through, covering the bookcases and broken shelves. Flames claimed them.

Darkness filled the room. With so much burning plaster and floorboards, and now books and shelving, the Fabric failed to come closer.

I ran to Victor who crouched over a mountain of books. His hands slapped at them.

"The book." He coughed. "Help me find it."

I didn't want to help, I wanted to run. My clothes stuck to me. Smoke clogged the air and crawled into my lungs. My eyes stung. Another part of the ceiling fell and fire spilled down, obscuring the Shadow Fabric. Both fire and shadow were close to killing us, and we had to find a single book amongst a pile of others. My eyes jumped back and forth, desperation must've been etched into my face as it was in Victor's. Every other breath had become a sharp cough, my vision blurred with tears. I had to fight the urge to leave him to his ridiculous search. He wanted to destroy *The Book of Leaves*, after all. I knew that. I also knew we couldn't leave it for the Shadow Fabric to claim.

There it was, among hundreds of scattered books. As if drawn to it, I pointed and darted for it, grabbing it without hesitation. Perhaps it was confidence in wearing Lucas's gloves, or having the Fabric above, which drove me to snatch it. I clutched it to my chest and lunged for the archway.

"Got it." My mouth tasted of smoke. A sharp cough leapt from my throat as I stumbled over books.

Victor close behind me, we sprinted through the bookshop. No more than fifteen seconds later, I had my foot jammed on the car's accelerator and with squealing tyres, we headed away from the inferno.

CHAPTER 23

"Headlights," Victor said, and coughed.

I'd been driving for a few minutes, oblivious to the oncoming cars as they flashed their lights, trying to tell me mine weren't on. My eyes were on the road, yet all I saw was Lucas torn apart, chunks of his flesh flying about the room, and the Shadow Fabric chasing us down through the floors. That, and my vision of the metal boxes. What the hell did it mean?

An orange glow spilled into an edge of the rear-view mirror and I spotted blue lights, flashing between distant trees.

Occasionally, I coughed. My heart thumped in rhythm with a roar in my head louder than the car's engine. I let the road take us wherever. The headlights cut into the night and forced back shadows which reminded me again of poor Lucas.

My voice shot from a raw throat. "The Fabric tore him to pieces, Victor."

"I know."

"Crazy." I eased my foot off the accelerator, dropping the car to the speed limit. I'd been doing fifty in a thirty zone. I didn't want the police to pull us over, especially as we were headed away, stinking of smoke, from a bookshop blaze.

"The Fabric came for the book," Victor said, "not us."

I glanced at the book in the rear, loose in its wrapping and seeming to take up half the back seat, then said, "You think Stanley is controlling the Fabric?"

"Quite possibly."

"It appeared when you got the book out." I shivered, thinking of Victor unwrapping it.

"It does seem to be linked. Nothing explains why you fainted, Leo. That's the troubling thing."

"Troubling? Fuck that!" I shouted. Softer, I said, "Lucas is dead."

"I know."

"Tore him to pieces."

We travelled in silence for a few miles.

"Where am I driving to?" I'd been following the road, keeping perfectly within the speed limits, which may have been suspicious in itself.

"We must destroy the book. Before that…"

"What?"

His face was in shadow.

"I have to show it to Goodwin," he said. "He believes *The Book of Leaves* to be a legend."

"We can't trust him." Saying that left a sour taste, a weird combination with smoke clinging to the back of my throat. I wanted nothing to do with Goodwin.

He added, "I know Goodwin is hiding something—"

I laughed without humour. "Hiding something? Victor, he's hiding a lot."

"I have to show him *The Book of Leaves*."

After all that had happened, I didn't want Goodwin to see the book. I didn't want him near it. And why did I see metal boxes when Victor had unwrapped the damn thing? I couldn't believe he wanted to show it to Goodwin. Victor annoyed me.

Finally, after a long drive with nothing else said, we reached Periwick House. The reception desk was empty and our first stop was the toilets. We had to clean ourselves up. I spent most of my time at the sink splashing water on my face and gulping some to soothe my ragged throat. It didn't eliminate the taste, or smell, of smoke.

I returned to the foyer, Victor behind me. I didn't want to speak to him—I was still pissed off. I didn't want to be here. Around the corner from the restaurant, raised voices reached us.

"I can't believe you've taken it!" It was Suzy's voice.

We entered the restaurant as she dropped a crate of sparkling glasses onto the bar top. It was a surprise they didn't break. With all this madness, people were still going about their business; everyone, not just here, but the whole of the human race was oblivious to the darkness beneath what they assumed was real.

Joe, the resident barman, stood with his hands on his hips, his jaw set.

"Suzy, I—" He knocked his head to the side to remove floppy hair from his face.

"I don't get it," she said. "You turn the lights off and things just disappear, is that what you're saying?"

"Suze, I wouldn't steal from you."

"Things don't just disappear."

The pair had a small audience, people I'd met earlier in the week. The father and daughter sat in a far corner. He cradled a pint of lager and peered across the room with the typical expression of an eavesdropper, while his daughter thumbed a magazine. The only other occupied table was taken by the couple whose argument had blocked my way into the foyer. The grimace on the woman's face suggested she crunched ice cubes. She rolled an empty tumbler between her palms, eyes burning through a menu. I recalled her name: Pam. Her husband, Mick, wore a blank expression, his eyes on the bar. He sipped a half-pint of Coke.

Goodwin sat on a bar stool with his back to us.

A twist in my gut reminded me this guy had been my best friend—my mentor—over the last two years. He'd paid for everything since my accident, and I thought I'd known him. All I could think of was his silhouette in the cave while he oversaw the herding of a dozen handcuffed men under gunpoint. I wanted to turn and walk away.

All eyes were on Suzy and Joe. Except for mine. They were riveted to the back of Goodwin's head. The sound of Suzy's voice had already fused into a chirping noise.

Victor grabbed my arm as we made our way towards the bar. Against his chest, he held *The Book of Leaves* wrapped tight in its packaging.

"Please leave the talking to me," he said in a low voice. "No matter what."

"That'll be difficult. Goodwin is up to something and I've just seen your friend get ripped apart."

"Please, Leo." He gripped my arm tighter. "I mean it."

"Okay, okay," I said.

He released me.

Goodwin followed Joe's gaze and nodded to us.

I pushed a smile onto my lips and hoped it was convincing.

Joe's stance hadn't changed in the few seconds it took us to join them. Suzy screamed into his face: "How can I trust you?"

"I promise you, Suze," he whined, "I didn't take your money. Why would I do that?"

"All day things have been going missing, and now this."

"I—"

"I told you to keep your voices down!" Goodwin shouted, cutting off Joe's mumble. "Now, hang on. What else has gone missing?"

"I don't care about anything else. I care about my purse. My money."

"I know you do, Suzy." Goodwin's voice did little to calm her. She rounded on him, fists thumping the counter. A splash of spilt drink flicked up her shirt.

"Joe was the last one with it."

"Yes, but please tell me what else has gone missing today."

"Loads of things." Her shoulders slumped and she leaned against the counter. Her hands unclenched and her gaze lowered. "You've said to me before about leaving stuff around the place. This is different."

"Go on."

"Silly things have gone missing, mostly little things." Her eyes were moist, chin trembling. "Like mops, buckets, cloths, not the stuff people normally nick."

Why did we listen to this pathetic argument? I'd just witnessed a man get ripped apart by the fucking Shadow Fabric.

Joe took a couple of tentative steps back and grabbed a can of furniture polish.

"And these things, too," he said. "I swear we had one under the counter, but I had to get another one this morning. I know it sounds stupid, but I know my bar."

"Not at all." Goodwin winked at Suzy. "Looks like you're not alone."

"It's as if we've got gremlins running around nicking stuff for the fun of it," Joe said, more to himself.

"Still doesn't explain my money, though, does it?" It was impossible to ignore the chemistry there, this pair were more than work colleagues.

"Suze…" The way he said her name was another indication of their relationship. "You know I wouldn't take your purse. That's stupid."

"Don't call me stupid."

"I didn't."

"You—"

"That's enough." Goodwin stood up. "Both of you."

They froze, faces slack like children rebuked by a father.

"Leave it with me and I shall look into it. Trust me, people."

Trust me…

* * *

"You have the book?" Goodwin said and sat behind his desk. At some point, he'd put on gloves.

Placing the package in front of him, Victor stood back while I sat in a chair on the far side of the office. I didn't look at it. I didn't want to have another episode and faint again. Not only that, I didn't want to look at Goodwin. I heard the wrapping fall away as Goodwin revealed *The Book of Leaves*.

Victor eyed me as he sat opposite Goodwin. His look said, *don't say anything about our mistrust*. Well, I trusted Victor—obeying him was another matter. I already found it difficult to remain quiet.

Perhaps Goodwin noticed the way I avoided shaking his hand when we came into his office. I hoped so. My stomach twisted into a tight, heavy lump.

"There it is," Victor said. "As described in all references to the Shadow Fabric. Bound in leather. Pages made of leather."

"I once believed the book was only legend." Goodwin slumped and exhaled. "And it contains the shadowleaf of witches caught in the 17th century. Do you think that's true?"

"That book contains a few thousand shadowleaves."

"There were that many witches?" Goodwin asked.

"Those discovered, yes."

I heard the slow rasp of turning pages. Somehow, I managed to resist looking.

"This is incredible," Goodwin said.

"It is."

"Almost four hundred years, and this book has stood the test of time. Look at it."

I gave in, and looked.

The Book of Leaves sat amongst a nest of dirty cloth. Opened wide, its brown pages appeared innocent enough, kind of like a carpet-sample book. The only difference being each swatch was black. To my relief, nothing happened, no dizziness or queasiness. No visions invaded my mind. I sat up and saw that the pages held a dozen shadowleaves. Each not much larger than a thumbnail.

Victor told Goodwin about the last couple of days, starting with the mystery girl ramming us off the road, and the discoveries at Stanley's house, the emails from Tulip Moon, and the dried-up corpse. Goodwin's reactions appeared genuine: shock and disbelief mostly. Occasionally, he'd glance at me and shake his head. Each time, I'd avert my eyes. Skipping the part about my 3 a.m. phone call from the middle of a field, Victor went on to explain his ransacked flat. Here, Goodwin sounded sympathetic, and when he heard about the discoveries at Polly's cottage, he became agitated, especially when learning our mystery girl was Tulip Moon, who turned out to be Annabel.

He reached for his phone, speed dialling. Eventually, he said, "Polly's not answering."

Victor nodded. "We couldn't find her either."

Telling Goodwin all that happened at the bookshop, including my faint, Victor struggled with his description. It was the part about when the Shadow Fabric tore Lucas to pieces.

"Victor," Goodwin said, "bloody hell, that's awful. He was a good man, and did a lot for us."

I avoided Victor's gaze and eyed the book. I didn't want to look at either of them. Hearing the story told like that was strange, and I wasn't certain if it made things clearer or more absurd. Either way, it was completely crazy.

"So," Victor said and sat up straighter, "here we are. There's *The Book of Leaves.*"

I was still waiting to faint.

"A book," Victor continued, "containing the shadowleaves of captured witches. Put on trial by the Witchfinder General himself. A marvellous piece of history."

Victor was leading up to something, I thought.

"And," he said, "one of few artefacts to survive those dark times of the witch trials...the other being the Hourglass."

I waited for Goodwin's reaction. His face revealed nothing. I looked at the pad on his desk and wondered what he'd done with his doodle. And what of the invoices?

"Over the last week," Victor added, "we've found the Witchblade and *The Book of Leaves*. Even the Shadow Fabric has turned up."

Again I thought of Lucas exploding into pieces.

Goodwin slowly ground out his cigar. The ash reminded me of Lucas's body parts.

"Yet the Hourglass remains elusive." Victor pointed at the book. "We have proof of its existence right there. Each one of those shadowleaves extracted by use of the Hourglass. There is no other way to remove a shadowleaf from a person. Witch or not."

"Possibly," Goodwin said softly, "that particular artefact has been lost through the ages."

Victor didn't say a word. I wanted to say a lot...too much. I clamped my jaw tight to stop myself screaming at Goodwin, telling him how I'd trusted him over these last couple of years. I wanted to admit that I saw him as a father. And I wanted to ask why he was out in the woods with handcuffed men—at gunpoint.

Eventually, Victor said, "You might be right, Goodwin. You might be right."

Victor was playing a game. It felt as though the two of us were against everyone else. He reached for *The Book of Leaves* and dragged it towards him.

"I'm going to burn the book." Victor slammed it shut. As the leather pages came together, the slap filled the room like a thunderclap.

"You've got to be kidding!" Goodwin shoved his chair back. "You can't do that."

"Why not?" Victor had the book in his lap, pulling the cloth over it.

"Because it's a remarkable artefact, a fantastic piece of history."

"It's dangerous. Imagine the potency of evil should these leaves be stitched."

"We must keep it." Goodwin's face reddened, his eyes bulging.

"We don't need it. It serves no purpose to our greater goal. It can't help us in destroying the Fabric. It's not a tool we can use against the darkness."

"No, but we can use it to learn more about the Witchfinder."

"We don't need to do that. You know we don't." Victor pulled string from his pocket and tucked it under the package.

"We can keep it, locked up tight."

"There's no point. No need." Between nimble fingers, Victor made a bow with one end of the string and looped the other around it.

"You can't destroy it, Victor." Goodwin came to his feet, fists knuckling the desk. "What the hell are you playing at?"

I stared at him. *What are you playing at, Goodwin?*

Victor said nothing.

"This is absurd." Goodwin towered over the desk.

"It's absurd to think you want to keep it. What can you—we—possibly do with it? Can we learn anything more about the Shadow Fabric?"

"That's beside the point, we can't just burn the thing." Goodwin's eyes were ready to pop from his face.

"I said this book is dangerous." Victor pulled both ends of the string tight. "Its concentrated evils could be the unmaking of everything. Its darkness could leak into the world. Stitch this lot, and there would be no stopping the Shadow Fabric."

"And like this to infinity," I said.

Goodwin glanced at me and his head tilted, then his attention dropped to the photo frame next to him.

Several seconds passed, and Victor stood up. I took that as my cue, got up myself, and walked to the door. I grasped the handle—Goodwin's presence burned behind me—and I pulled it open. Victor joined me.

"I don't believe you're telling me everything, Goodwin." He strolled out of the office. Over his shoulder, he said, "Leo, we have a fire to build."

I paused on the threshold. Goodwin on one side and Victor on the other. He was already halfway across the foyer. Goodwin's attention remained on the photograph of his father.

I followed Victor.

CHAPTER 24

Victor struck a match. His hand and face glowed, and he held the flame against a bundle of twigs at the base of the pyre. Near the top, wedged between branches and covered with dry bracken, sat *The Book of Leaves*. It was still wrapped in cloth.

A short distance away, a waterfall surged over rocks and into a stream that curled into the woods and the darkness beyond. Its rumble soothed my tumbling thoughts.

The drive hadn't been too far into the countryside when we found a secluded area, and once the headlights were off, the darkness hid us from the road. Besides, we doubted anyone would be travelling through the lanes so late at night.

With our fire only hip-high, when the flames flared, it soon became an impressive pyramid. The wrapping caught quickly, and the leather bubbled and shrivelled.

The stink was incredible, like overcooked and still-smoking meat. We stepped back.

"Polly should be with us," Victor said. "She deserves to be here."

"Where could she be?"

"Annabel must have her."

I chewed my lip. I still found all this difficult to believe.

Victor shook his head, the fire dancing in his eyes. "She obviously knows we're onto her. She doesn't want us to interfere with her plans."

"And what are they?" I wondered how many more people would die before this ended. If it ended.

"I can only assume she's in it with Stanley. Both of them want to stitch the Fabric."

"We've stopped them getting the book," I said. "Can they stitch another way?"

"The Fabric can continue to grow. But it would be slow. Not the same as stitching shadowleaves. Its evil wouldn't be as potent. However, it would intensify the more life force it absorbs."

"People can be absorbed."

"Once it's powerful enough, the intensity of evil within the Fabric would manifest to such a degree, there'd be no stopping it."

I thought about that for a moment, the darkness taking over everything. "Still think Goodwin has the Hourglass?"

"I certainly have no doubts now."

"I was close to confronting the guy."

"I know, Leo. Thanks for not saying anything. I didn't press him about his secrets. Long ago, I learned that answers eventually come."

"You think he's working with Tulip Moon or Stanley?" When I asked that, I knew my face screwed up.

"No."

I relaxed.

"If that was the case," he continued, "he wouldn't have let us out of his office."

The thought horrified me. I couldn't believe Goodwin would do anything to hurt us. Not after all he'd done for me. And given the history these two men shared, it was difficult to accept the possibility Goodwin could harm Victor. Yet, given recent revelations…

"Goodwin either knows where the Hourglass is," Victor said, "or he actually has it."

"And he hasn't told any of you guys."

"That's one question on the list, with why he was rounding people up at gunpoint."

"Yeah, back in his office that's all I could think about."

The Book of Leaves hissed and spat. It shifted to the centre of the fire and flared. I threw another bunch of twigs onto it. The leaves instantly crackled.

I said, "He didn't want you to burn the book."

"That, my friend, is what worries me."

Flames surged around the curling leather pages and a cloud of smoke belched outwards. The stink crawled into my nostrils. I coughed and stepped away.

"If anyone should want to keep the thing, it should be you, Victor."

Tiny fires reflected in his unblinking eyes.

"You're the book collector," I added.

"I am. But this isn't one I wish to keep." For the first time, he looked old. Someone had ransacked his flat, his books torn and heaped in a mess of broken shelves, he had finally come to a kind of reconciliation with his friend Lucas, who the Fabric then ripped apart.

Beyond the light of our fire, shadows flitted between the trees. Real, normal shadows. I hoped they *were* normal. There was a difference between ordinary shadows and the Shadow Fabric—the presence of the Fabric, it clogs the head. Heavy, like a lingering cold blocking the sinuses. The country air was crisp and fresh, a typical spring night, and not the heavy atmosphere I'd recently experienced.

Occasionally, Victor and I heaped more twigs onto the fire, burying *The Book of Leaves* deeper into its heart. When there is a campfire, there is always something to do to it. Even if it's a prod or two, something to move the burning branches and logs around, and in this case the book. It's never a proper fire unless it's being stoked. Fire connects with us all at a subconscious level. Somewhere, deep within us, is the prehistoric man, the caveman who first brought flame to life in order to banish the darkness.

The fire dwindled to charred branches and heaps of embers, *The Book of Leaves* little more than a clump of smoking goo. Tiny flames leapt in places.

The dark sky pressed on the trees, and an impenetrable black squeezed us in. It took a while for my eyes to adjust to the darkness, having been staring at those flames for a long time. Dark adaptation, a phrase I'd learnt from Goodwin when stargazing.

I stepped away, leaving Victor silent and unmoving.

From the road, a fair distance behind the car, a pair of headlights flashed through the woods. The beams snapped us alert. Given the tumbling of the nearby waterfall, we hadn't heard the vehicle approach. Blinded, we stumbled and shielded our eyes. The car skidded to a halt, kicking up a flurry of leaves and dirt.

I couldn't make out the car through the glare of its headlights. Was it the police? Had they found us after the bookshop burning? Was it Annabel?

"Victor!" I shouted. "Get into the car."

I squinted, my face still hot from the fire, and watched him dash for our vehicle. He held a gun.

CHAPTER 25

In the car, I forced it into reverse with a crunch. We faced the same direction as the stationary car. In my mirror its headlights were a pair of blinding orbs. At any moment, I expected a door to spring open, or the car itself to rush forward and smash into us. Perhaps even gunfire.

Surrounded by trees, it seemed impossible to manoeuvre, yet I tried. I shoved and yanked the gear stick from first to reverse, reverse to first. I palmed the steering wheel and stamped my right foot from the accelerator to the brake and back again. My breath hissed between my teeth.

Victor had wound down his window, his gun now held in both hands.

The other car still hadn't moved, nor was there any sign of the driver.

After many curses, I got the BMW to face the blocked exit. I now saw what car it was and recognised it immediately: a red convertible. Its soft-top was in place—unsurprising, given the chill of the night. It was our mystery girl again, no longer a mystery.

"Tulip Moon," I said. "Annabel."

The headlight glare switched to sidelights and dragged in the shadows from all sides. A moment later the driver's door popped open and a slight figure stepped out. She walked in front of the vehicle, becoming a silhouette. Hooded, her face was in shadow. With all my hectic manoeuvring, I hadn't even turned my lights on. I flicked the switch. A hand came up to shield her face, yet she still strode towards us. She wore the same outfit as she did when she stole the Witchblade from Victor at the beginning of the week: dressed in black, with a red scarf looped about her neck.

I sat there, keeping the revs up, ready to ram her if she pulled a firearm on us. My heart twisted with the thought. Could I really do that? Maybe she'd use the Witchblade against us…or the Shadow Fabric. I revved the engine more. Again, I wondered if I was truly capable of running someone over. I hoped I didn't have to find out.

Victor leaned sideways and pushed his gun out, still in both hands. I heard a metallic click as he pulled back the hammer. Annabel stumbled to a halt and shot both hands up. She reached high.

"Put the gun down, Victor," she called. There was a slight accent to how she said his name. She sounded strange.

"Annabel, how many more times are you going to try to kill us?" Victor shouted, levelling the weapon on her.

"It's…" I said, realising something. "It's not—"

"I'm not Annabel," she interrupted and pulled her hood down. "My name is Isidore, and I've come to you because I'm scared."

I switched the car's headlights to full beam and the girl averted her eyes in a tumble of blonde hair.

"I am not Tulip Moon either," she added.

Given a brief glimpse of her face before it hid behind those curls, a memory slapped me hard. A recent memory. I recognised her, my mind racing back in time. I'd seen this girl before at Lucas's bookshop. She was the one who caught me checking her out.

Victor threw me a glare, keeping the gun on the girl. "Leo, why are you laughing?"

I didn't realise I was. "She's been following us all week. In her little red convertible."

"Not the van, then?"

"No, we know that was Annabel. This is the girl who stole the Witchblade." If this wasn't Annabel, then meeting Isidore now kicked up a heap of new questions.

"Two different people." Victor frowned. He shoved open the door, the gun steady, and slowly got out.

Isidore remained where she was, her face still obscured by her mane of hair. I left the engine rumbling and joined Victor. Keeping her in sight, we stepped towards her.

"Isidore, is it?" Victor said, and we stopped in front of the car, blocking the headlights.

In response, she raised her head. It was her, pretty features and dark eyes. Attractiveness aside, she'd been following us, threatened us at gunpoint, and stole the Witchblade.

Victor kept his gun raised, now head-height. We wanted answers.

"Please," she said, "lower your weapon. I'm not here to do you any harm. I want your help, and I'm thinking you need mine."

"Really?" Victor said.

"I have your magic knife."

"Of course you do. You stole it."

"I did and I'm sorry." Her accent was hard to place.

"Why steal it?" Victor asked.

"I was under instruction."

"Go on."

"By a person called Tulip Moon."

Victor's eyebrows twitched.

"At first," she continued, "things were good. The money was good." Her eyes glistened and her voice trembled. "Then I was a witness to the devil's work."

I leaned against the bonnet. Here it comes again, all that witchcraft bullshit.

Victor lowered his gun, the barrel now aimed at her feet.

"Last night I saw Death," she said, "and it spoke to me. I heard its voice. I heard many voices. I tasted fire, could smell the fear and see the pain, and when I closed my eyes, I knew something wanted me—something large, powerful, and perhaps even greater than God. The opposite of God. It wanted to show me pleasure and desire and the answers to all questions. At the same time it wanted to be me. Eat me and kill me. Drown me and burn me. It wanted me to kill myself. It wanted me to starve, to jump from a roof. It wanted me to bang my head against the wall...and it wanted to love me. It told me it loved me, and inside those words, I saw my head bloody as I smashed it against the wall. I felt its own desire and pleasures. All it wanted was my death. It wanted to suck in my life and blow it out as darkness. And that darkness was all there was. And this frightened me more than anything. More than the other strange things I saw. It wanted me to exist as nothing. A darkness so much more than Death's offering."

Victor's arm dropped to his side, pointing the gun at the ground.

Isidore lowered her hands. Her shoulders sank into her already small frame, and she cried.

* * *

Isidore told us how she'd come to this country searching for release from a world of burglary and drugs. Leaving—or rather chased from—Greece, she'd hoped to start afresh in England. Wanting to begin a new life here in the Southeast, in Kent to be precise. After all, she'd heard so much about the Garden of England.

And she'd found more than a picturesque countryside.

She sat sideways in the passenger seat with the door open, and Victor and I listened to her story. Occasionally, she would wipe her cheeks with a sleeve. She told us how temptations were hard to resist when networking online. Things soon became serious when she met a user named tulipmoon73. This Moon paid big money for small jobs. The kind not to be found at the employment centre, or advertised in agencies. Those which yanked her back into her past—unfortunately, a past she wanted to leave behind.

The offer of such ridiculous money had been hard to refuse, and given her illegal entry into the UK, and difficulty at gaining a respectable new career, she soon said yes. Petty theft to begin with, and Isidore believed Moon was testing her loyalty. The jobs escalated to subtle threats, and then to violence. She admitted to having no idea how that came about. Plus, on occasion, there would be arson. Still having never met her employer in person, the money kept coming, and eventually Isidore lived a new life of greater crime than before. Not only was she back to being a thief, she'd also become a criminal in everything short of murder. Her bank balance outweighed morals, and it got easier to accept the jobs. She'd been manipulated by Tulip Moon, something she'd known all along.

"Things went bad." She wrapped my jacket tighter around herself—earlier, I'd been a gentleman.

Victor hadn't said much while she spoke, and neither had I. I hoped what she had to say would explain everything.

She shivered. "I wouldn't have pulled the trigger on you. I am not a killer, I'm a thief. Just a thief. That's all I am. I didn't want to do anything else."

I thought of how it was to stare into the barrel of her gun.

"Oh?" Victor's voice contained an edge I'd recently been hearing a lot.

"The threat was good enough," she told him. "I'm glad you didn't push it, because I don't know what I would have done."

"Why have that gun if you're just a thief?" I asked. With her puffy eyes and red cheeks, she was still attractive. Her blonde hair did little to disguise her Mediterranean origins, betrayed as they were by her olive complexion and intense brown eyes.

"Money." She scratched her cheek. "It always comes to money, yes? Stealing is one thing. Threats and violence? That is something else. Black magic of the devil is another thing entirely."

Victor's forehead furrowed. The glow from the interior light gave his face an almost plastic sheen.

"Last night," Isidore said, "I saw strange things going on, and that prompted me to seek you out."

"What happened?" I crouched beside her, shoulder against the car.

"I contacted a hacker friend. Old habits. Breaking my own rule of contacting anyone back home." Isidore offered a weak smile. "He managed to trace Moon for me. Yesterday, I decided to watch her, this Tulip Moon, to see what she was doing."

"What does she look like?" Victor asked.

"A tall woman. Very skinny. With dark hair and piercing eyes." Isidore's own eyes flashed wider. "And what I saw was evil. There is no other word for it."

I nodded as I recalled the time when I'd first met Polly's assistant. Tulip Moon was the same person, the person behind everything.

"She went out last night," Isidore continued. "Driving a van. The front was badly damaged."

Victor turned towards me. I didn't look at him—we thought the same thing.

"I followed her to a farm." Isidore's voice wavered. "Hiding, I saw four men get out of the van. They were tied up. Then they were taken into an old barn."

Victor and I exchanged glances. We knew which farm she spoke of. I thought of Thomas, Lucas's contact, with the shard of mirror rammed down his throat, his body pierced like a pin cushion. I thought of the family sitting at the table, hands together as if in prayer, with their bodies drained of life. I was conscious of my breathing and I tried to slow it down.

Isidore hung her head. "I recognised all the men. They were those I'd threatened last month. Four men that I'd been cruel to. More than cruel. I'm sorry for that. When I saw them yesterday, they looked like broken men. Beaten up. Sad. I never did see the fifth one."

"Who were they?" Victor stepped forward to the open door and leaned on it, folding his arms across his chest. He no longer held the gun. Clearly, he had the same idea as I did about Isidore. She'd been a proverbial pawn in this game of light against dark.

Isidore moved her head slightly. "Keepers of something or other."

Victor puffed out his cheeks and let out a long breath. "Something to do with the Fabric, by any chance?"

"Yes." Her voice was small as she looked up. "Moon tracked these men down herself, and offered me a big payment if I was successful. It could have been my last job, and of course, Moon offered me even more money to stay working for her."

"You got them to hand over pieces of the Fabric, didn't you?" Victor said. It wasn't a question.

"Yes. I didn't know what they were at the time. Four leather bags, each holding a piece of black cloth for all I could tell. When I opened one of the bags, I was sick, really sick, and I had strange thoughts." Her eyes flashed wide and wet. "I never did that again."

"By this point," Victor said, "you still hadn't met Tulip Moon?"

"No, it was all by email. I left the package at the usual drop-off. Inside were the leather bags."

"Back to last night." Victor knelt and held her hands. Gentle, undemanding. "What happened to these men?"

"I got closer to spy on them, finding a part of the barn wall which had broken away." She swallowed, blinking away tears. "Inside was lit by lanterns. Not a lot of light and it was difficult to see. Those men looked weak. Drugged perhaps. They had collapsed against stacks of hay."

Perhaps it was the same one I had peered into, the hay bales, the piled clothes in the centre. Maybe those clothes weren't empty.

"What else did you see?" Victor released her hands. "Was there a blind woman?"

She shook her head.

"No. No. I did see another person inside the farmhouse with Moon, but I couldn't tell if it was a woman or a man, and the way they walked around, they didn't look blind."

Victor dragged his hand from his forehead to his chin, then to his neck.

Isidore continued. "In front of the men was the package I'd left at the drop-off. Its side had split and all I saw was darkness. It oozed out like some kind of liquid."

A wind rustled the leaf-strewn ground and I shivered.

"Moon handed them something," she said. "Something small. And they moved their hands together as if they prayed. Like that, they...they..."

"Go on, Isidore," Victor said.

"Sitting straighter, they began to move. Slow rocking at first, like madmen. After a minute or two, their heads shook. Then their bodies as well. It was like they had a seizure."

I hunched and my hands became fists. Those clothes heaped in that barn weren't empty after all.

Isidore wiped her eyes. Her cheeks sparkled in the soft light.

"I don't know how long it lasted." She sniffed. "But I watched their heads become skulls. Their skin shrinking, eyes falling into their faces." She raked fingers through her hair. Her eyes bored into Victor's. "Death," she said. "That's when I saw Death."

Victor stood up.

"No," he said. "Stitching. That's what you saw."

CHAPTER 26

Saturday

I made a decision that it was time for me to approach Goodwin. About everything. Fuck Victor and his game. I wanted answers.

With the morning sun spotlighting her, Isidore strolled from the bathroom, towelling her hair. Like the first time I'd seen her, she caught my eye. This time, I didn't look away, and she gave me a different kind of look. I liked it. I couldn't deny it: I fancied her. Somehow, she managed to take the edge off my thoughts of Goodwin. She wore the same clothes from the previous day, as did Victor and I.

His gentle snore broke the moment and I grabbed my boots. My thoughts returned to Goodwin and his deceit. Who the hell was he to me? Was he a friend of the family? And what of my family? Were they who I thought they were? I only knew of them through Goodwin's stories. Stories? Were they just that?

After meeting Isidore in the woods and learning her story, we'd explained how Annabel and Tulip Moon were the same person. We also explained Stanley and Goodwin's involvement—or the little we knew of Goodwin's involvement, at least—and we shared our concern as to Polly's whereabouts. We didn't, however, reveal much about the Fabric or *The Book of Leaves*. I guessed things would be answered in time for all of us. Then we returned to her hotel, close to the motorway services. Luckily, she'd been able to get a family room, so it was comfortable for us all. Victor had the double bed in the main area while Isidore took the kid's room. I'd taken the sofa without bothering to remove my clothes. Isidore made a lot of noise, keeping me awake for a while. I suspected she blocked the door with furniture.

I tied my bootlaces as Isidore disappeared into her room. She returned moments later tugging her hair into a ponytail.

"Do we wake him?" She nodded at Victor.

I shook my head. "Not yet."

"I am awake, my friends," Victor said.

His eyes popped open and he sat upright. The sheets slipped off and collected on the floor as he slid a hand underneath the mattress. He pulled out a familiar box. Its surface, although coated in matt-black lacquer, reflected the room's lamps in a dead kind of way.

I laughed. "You slept on it?"

He scratched his silvery whiskers, eyeing the box.

"I wouldn't have done that," said Isidore. "There's something about that knife…"

"Isidore," Victor said, "you're not the one who ransacked my flat, that was Annabel searching for the Witchblade."

She nodded.

"Makes sense," I added.

"I'm sorry I took it," Isidore said.

"Not at all." The corners of Victor's eyes crinkled.

"I was supposed to leave it at the drop-off, but didn't. The day after I took it from you, I hid for a while. I needed time to think. I already knew things were getting bad."

"Oh?" Victor's thumb hovered over the box's clasp.

"Moon ordered me to follow you to your brother's house. I saw what happened. I saw the darkness come out of the violin case. I saw what it made you do to him."

Victor's eyebrows twitched and his jaw clenched.

"I saw him disappear," she added. For a moment, she'd lost her radiance, and she resembled the fearful girl from the previous night. "Things were getting even stranger, and all I could think about was money. I didn't want anything more to do with Moon, and so I hid for a couple of days. That's why I tracked her. Found out where she lives and ended up spying on her."

Victor sat on the edge of the bed and stared at his bare feet. He rubbed his gloves together as if washing his hands. He'd placed the Witchblade case beside him.

"I wish I hadn't spied on them," Isidore said, "I wish I'd said 'no' a long time ago. It's all about money. Always has been."

I knew how she felt and remembered how I'd squeezed the cash in my pocket when looking at Stanley's blood on the carpet.

Always, it was about money. Yet this wasn't how I expected my new life to evolve.

It didn't take us long to get ready, and skipping breakfast, we made it to Periwick House in excellent time. Isidore's convertible kept up with me all the way, although I suspected she jumped one or two red lights. It was an old Mazda, sun-bleached red with its soft-top torn.

She pulled into the parking space next to the BMW as I slammed the door shut. Victor hurried towards the House's main entrance, his jaw firm. He held the Witchblade case tight to his chest. On our drive over, he announced it was time to approach Goodwin. I didn't mention that I'd already made that decision.

The morning sunshine reflected from several cars already in the car park, and I watched as another vehicle crunched into reverse and slid into an empty bay. Then I remembered: it was Saturday, and tonight was the concert.

Victor had disappeared into the House and I shot my head over a shoulder at the sound of gravel underfoot. Isidore stood beside me, watching Victor.

I stifled a yawn.

"Fast for an old man," she said.

I nodded. "Yeah, he is. Doesn't wear any socks either."

She laughed. "I've noticed."

I said, "Come on."

Inside, Victor hammered on Goodwin's office door. By the time we'd joined him, ignoring Dean's bemused attention, Victor had already entered.

"Goodwin?" he shouted into the room. "Goodwin?"

I pushed my way past Victor. I had no idea what I intended to say to Goodwin. Too many questions stormed my brain.

Isidore followed us inside.

"Where is he?" I said, my pulse quickening. I needed answers. To everything. I left the office and headed for reception.

The manager's eyes widened as I approached.

"Dean." My voice filled the foyer. "Where's Goodwin?"

His frown leapt from me to the gaping office door, and back again. "What are you up to?"

"Where is he?" I leaned against the desk. Heat rushed to my face.

Dean's eyelids peeled back further and he scratched his chin. "He had a visitor earlier. Not long ago, half an hour, I think. It was that man, Stanley."

I thought of Polly's disappearance and of Stanley dying in front of me, yet not truly dead. What about Isidore's story of those men stitching? And where was Polly? And Goodwin? Even though my trust for him had crumbled, he remained a part of my new life. I still saw him as a son would a father, despite everything, I still cared. But what part did he play in all this?

"Where are they now?" I asked.

"They should still be in his office." Dean's cheeks reddened with each passing second. "He always buzzes to let me know he's going for a walk in the gardens, and they haven't come out."

From across the foyer, Natalie's voice bounced towards us. "What's going on?" Her curious eyes followed the movement in Goodwin's office. She wore a figure-hugging shirt and skirt— not her usual beauty therapist uniform.

Immediately, I thought of Isidore, of how uncomfortable she'd be in such an outfit. I looked back at her, standing close to Goodwin's desk. She stooped slightly, leaning to read something. She wore her own clothes well. Very well.

My gaze returned to Natalie, and I gave her a smile I didn't really have.

"Not sure," I mumbled. And it was the truth. I sprinted across the shiny floor and into the office, pulling the door behind me. It slammed shut.

Isidore spun, eyes wide. She almost dropped some papers.

"Look," she said and handed them to me.

I heard Victor rummaging in the other room.

"Your friend Goodwin has interesting contacts," Isidore mumbled.

Each sheet contained a list of names, none of which I recognised. There were three columns on each page: the first contained the name, mostly male, the second listed a County. It was the contents of the last column that concerned me the most. What did all this mean? My lips parted to say something as Victor charged into the room.

"Nothing." He clenched and unclenched his hands, the leather gloves creaking. "We have to find Goodwin... What's that?"

He pointed at several gouges in the parquet floor.

"Looks recent." I bent down.

Their depth suggested the desk had been shoved under a great weight, and next to them was a collection of red flecks. I gingerly prodded one.

Victor and Isidore loomed over me.

Suddenly, I felt small. "Blood."

Both of them remained silent.

"Dean told me that Stanley's with him," I said, and stood up.

Isidore's nose twitched. I knew the feeling. It wasn't safe in the room. Nothing was real anymore. She sidestepped towards me.

Victor motioned to the papers bunched in my fist; I'd forgotten all about them. I handed them over. After several seconds listening to my pounding heart and watching Victor's furrowed brow deepen, he threw the sheets on the desk.

"What has Goodwin been up to?" he said. "Tranquillisers. Handcuffed men. Now this."

I shrugged, somehow feeling responsible for Goodwin's deceit. It was as though I should've known what was going on, I should've been aware something was up. Emotions clashed in my head in time with my racing heart. I was worried about Goodwin and hated him for his deception. I dragged my feet towards the French doors and shook the handle.

"They couldn't have gone outside, it's locked."

"They must've gone back through the lobby." There was an edge to Victor's voice.

"Dean didn't think so." I pressed my forehead against the glass. It was cold and quite soothing. Across the terrace, in the gardens, was Neil. A row of recently planted silver birch swayed behind him.

"He must've blinked." Victor shoved a hand inside his jacket and pulled out the Witchblade case. He flicked it open and removed the athame. Throwing the box on a shelf behind him, he slid the blade behind his belt. It reflected the blue of the morning outside.

"I think you need to see this." Isidore's voice came from beneath the desk. She traced her fingers along a cable, revealed because of the shifted leg. It joined a tangle of wires from the computer.

"What's that?" I squatted next to her.

"It's the only one separate from the computer leads. The one which doesn't end at the wall sockets."

Victor and I tore out the plugs, tugging the extension leads away, while Isidore continued to follow the cable. I yanked too hard on one lead and the monitor slid towards me. I threw an arm up and grunted. The monitor stayed where it was and I relaxed.

Victor carried on untangling the wires.

"Found it," Isidore said. She had a hand hooked awkwardly under the desk, near the drawers.

"What?" My eyes watered and I rubbed my nose. I managed to contain the sneeze.

"A button," she said, and pressed it.

I winced, hoping it wasn't an alarm, or worse; some kind of lockdown. I imagined blast doors shooting from the doorframes, sealing us in the office. Nothing moved. However, from somewhere nearby, a hum of motors brought us to our feet. It must've been about ten seconds, when eventually a bookcase behind the desk rolled sideways. The Witchblade box flew to the floor and broke at the hinges. It clattered near Victor's feet.

Lights from the clean, steel confines of a lift poured into the office. Reflected in the polished interior like the amusing warped images in a Hall of Mirrors, the three of us stared back with mouths agape. I never knew this existed. Incredible.

At hip height on the wall, a panel revealed a red button—one destination.

Without a word we stepped into the lift, with me wedged between Isidore and Victor. Bathed in artificial light, the almost futuristic walls reminded me of something in a sci-fi movie.

Victor read my mind. "Kind of like Star Wars."

"I gather you two didn't know about this." Isidore stood so close, the smell of her shampoo filled me up. Apples? It made me hungry. Damn it, even in circumstances as crazy as this, I still found times to be a bloke—I annoyed myself sometimes.

"There's a lot about Goodwin we don't know," Victor said.

On countless occasions, I'd been in that room without knowing the lift was a few strides away.

Isidore moved slightly and with a rigid, pink-tipped finger, she prodded the button. The wooden panels of the bookcase slid back into place. A second later, the metal doors came together with a soft clunk. Victor's reflection was on my left, and Isidore's on the right, whilst mine had a vertical split from crotch to head, dividing me in two. Without a jerk, thump, or grind typical of any lift, a hum vibrated through the floor.

"Downwards," Isidore announced. "Exciting."

I couldn't make the girl out. She caught me looking at her, which she had a knack of doing, and those dark eyes held mine for a moment. Then she lowered them.

"I guess this is some kind of rescue mission," I said, and ran my hand down the cool panels of the lift.

Isidore held her gun to her chest.

"Goodwin's in trouble," Victor replied. "Assuming it's his blood we found. And Polly, assuming she's also with Stanley."

"You think she's here as well?"

"I can only assume she is."

"And Annabel?"

"Again, we can assume Annabel and Stanley are working together."

"You're assuming a lot…"

"I saw another person in the barn that night," Isidore said. "It might have been him, it was difficult to see."

I thought about what she'd told us when witnessing the men stitch.

"Quite possibly," Victor said.

The hum softened and the lift came to a stop as if resting on a cushion.

"Comfy ride." I'd said that to avoid saying anything else, like: *I don't want to do this. This is crazy.*

Victor slid the Witchblade from his belt.

"Magic knife." Isidore eyed the blade. The reflected light gave it a jagged appearance. Deadly.

"We'll put it to the test," Victor said.

My distorted image parted, and the doors gave way to a short corridor of yellow walls and glaring strip lights. The scuffed floor stretched ahead and ended at a door. It was ajar.

I emerged from the lift, with Victor and Isidore following. A tangy, damp smell overwhelmed the scent of her shampoo.

Having been a resident at the House for the past two years, I had no idea this area existed—Goodwin never once hinted. We moved along the corridor and I imagined Periwick House above, business as usual. Its daily routines, the normal lives of visitors and staff, of me calling it home, and the concert later that evening. A glance at my watch revealed it had just turned midday.

Our footfalls bounced around the corridor. As I reached the door, I held my hand flat against its surface—I still wore Lucas's gloves—and as I nudged it open, I expected it to creak.

Silence.

The frame was rotten in places, and there were scratches on the wall and on the door itself. Slowly, I craned my neck and peered in. Another corridor led off to the left and the right.

No one around.

When I walked through, Victor laughed through his nose.

"Anti-climax," Isidore said.

With no markers or signs to indicate what lay in either direction, we huddled together, undecided.

"Don't split up." Victor moved his head as though ready to cross a road.

"Which way?" I asked.

He headed left, his strides revealing bare ankles. I kept pace with him, Isidore close behind me. I suddenly wished I'd brought some kind of weapon. Victor had the Witchblade, which was okay for him, and he had a gun. There was no way I wanted to touch a firearm. Isidore still held her gun, the same one she'd waved in my face four days before. It's funny how we can forgive someone without thinking about it. Things had happened at such a pace, it was ridiculous I hadn't the foresight to protect myself. Knowing how fire had saved us from the Fabric back at Lucas's bookshop, I should've at least thought about making myself some kind of flamethrower. I hadn't even considered it, and there we were, the three of us beneath the House on a rescue mission, to face off someone controlling the Shadow Fabric.

Victor paused, his back to the wall, and looked round a corner. He made a small noise in the back of his throat as he moved out. We followed him into another corridor, only wider. It ended at a set of double doors. A series of single doors lined one wall—ten at a quick count—evenly spaced. All of them housed a vision panel, most just a dark hole in the wood, and the furthest two doors sent distorted patterns of light onto the opposite wall. Along the corridor's length were a number of trolleys, mostly empty. One of the strip lights was out.

A damp stink clawed up my nostrils. Here black marks criss-crossed the floor, the walls chipped in places. One other thing occupied the area, and Victor had already reached it: a gurney. Its frame was rusted, wheels clogged with sticky dust, and stained linen heaped the mattress.

My nose wrinkled. "Nasty."

"So is that." Victor pointed to a leather strap, its rusty buckle protruded from beneath a pile of bed covers.

"Hey," Isidore said. "You need to see this."

She stood before one of the doors, her head framed in the light of its vision panel. On tip-toes, hands on the wall, her nose pressed the glass. I moved up behind her—the smell of shampoo much nicer—and peered over her shoulder. When Victor joined us, she moved aside.

It was no surprise to see a man in a gown strapped to a gurney. He threw his shaved head around, lips quivering. The bare bulb above him gave his flesh a sickly glow and created the illusion of sunken eyes and hollow cheeks. He reminded me of the corpse at Stanley's house, only his eyes weren't dead. The pupils shot from left to right, up and down, searching for something. Maybe he wanted help. Whether he didn't see us, or he didn't have the lucidity to recognise we were there, we'd never know.

My hand reached out to the door knob. Why was this guy in there? Where was he from? Was he one of the handcuffed men from a couple of nights ago? I wanted to yank it open and release the poor guy from his restraints, but a metallic clatter echoed from another room. It came from our left, from beyond the double doors.

The three of us backed into the centre of the corridor. My ears were hot. We heard it again, and maybe a voice this time. Victor and Isidore darted towards the double doors, and as they got there, Isidore raised her gun. She mouthed something to Victor. Witchblade in hand, he went to the opposite side of the doors.

There I stood between the two of them, empty-handed. I straightened my back, mouth dry. I somehow managed a grin. More to reassure myself.

The pair of discoloured, rubber-edged doors were scuffed along the metal trims. Black paint, chipped and peeling, coated the vision panels. These doors were like the ones in a typical hospital. Yet this place was not a hospital, this was something else. The cold, bleak expanse of corridor was at least laid out like one, although it lacked the atmosphere of a hospital. From what I'd witnessed down here, the patients weren't the typical kind.

Standing with my companions, without a weapon, I held my ear up to one of the doors. Isidore's knuckles whitened around the grip of her gun, her jaw set and two vertical lines formed between her eyebrows. With Victor at my back, I knew I was in good hands.

On the other side of the door, I heard nothing. Two, three, four seconds passed and still nothing. I placed a hand flat against the door, and with the slightest of pressure, I pushed a fraction at a time.

When I looked into the room, my jaw dropped.

CHAPTER 27

On the furthest side of the room a nurse stretched over a gurney, unfastening straps. The buckle clanked and the leather slapped the floor. Although free from most restraints, the patient remained still.

Patient and nurse, nothing wrong with that. Wearing a hat and hair net, a mask hiding her face, she looked innocent enough. As did the patient, gowned and rigged to an intravenous drip. Yet something about this scene wasn't right.

"What's going on?" I said, and thought of the guy in the room behind us. And now this.

Isidore and Victor squeezed beside me. I didn't budge, not allowing them to see in. I sensed their impatience, but couldn't move. My frown deepened.

With most of the strip lights switched off or not working, the glare of a spotlight swamped everything.

"Leo?" Victor said.

I shook my head.

The patient wore a kind of swimmer's cap. A spaghetti-tangle of wires sprouted from it and coiled into a towering machine behind the nurse. A panel of instruments blinked rainbow reflections over her uniform. Other monitors sat on a desk with displays of patterns, charts, and text. Whatever I'd done for a living before I lost my memory, I certainly hadn't worked in this profession. Her shadow leapt across the floor as she cranked the mattress to a seating position. The man remained utterly submissive, his legs still strapped. A tribal tattoo snaked up his neck and around his ear.

"Leo." Victor bumped against me.

"Hang on."

There were other gurneys in the room. Most contained a patient. They were all men: shaved heads, blank expressions, intravenous drips stuck into a vein. Beyond them, an archway led to a corridor and a partitioned office. When the nurse turned her back, I nudged the door further open.

"Look." I leaned sideways.

My companions edged in.

"Oh, Goodwin." Victor's voice hissed. "You fool."

I peered over their heads.

From a machine that resembled a coffee percolator, the nurse removed an hourglass. Its glass bulbs, framed between wooden supports, reflected the blinking instruments. Sand had collected in the lower section. Not white as you'd expect from a standard hourglass. The sand was black.

The nurse tightened the handcuffs around her patient's wrists. The ratchets echoed. His eyelids flickered, his head lolled, and the coloured wires quivered. Saliva bubbled at his lips. With her back to him, the nurse detached connectors which ran from the Hourglass. Each coil sprang back inside the main machine. Along the top of the equipment, with its steel surface bathed in the spotlight's harsh glare, was a row of test tubes. Each contained a different level of bubbling liquid.

"It's like crazy Baron von Frankenstein," Isidore murmured.

The nurse placed the Hourglass back in its housing. She pulled on gloves and slid open a drawer at its base. With tweezers, she hooked out a small black square.

"What is that?" Isidore's breath touched my ear.

"A shadowleaf," Victor and I said simultaneously.

The edge of her mouth curled upwards.

After inspecting the leaf, the nurse placed it into a machine which reminded me of a miniature photocopier, though I doubted that's what it was. She clicked a glass lid in place. The tweezers clattered as she dropped them and pulled a keyboard closer. With rapid key strokes, she typed a series of commands and a beep crackled from the computer.

She walked over to the office. Her shoes slapped the tiles. Sitting in front of the window, she appeared to write something; keeping a record, I guessed. No doubt there were many records for the other men. Those poor bastards drugged, restrained on the gurneys. One of the closer ones had veins almost splitting the skin of his forearm, the leather straps cutting into his flesh.

Maybe from repeated muscle flexing, whether consciously or not.

None of this made sense. What was that woman doing to the guy? And what was Goodwin's role?

The nurse scratched her nose through the mask and stood up, tugging on a jacket and then slipping a handbag over a shoulder. The main room dropped further into darkness as she switched off the light. She returned to the patient and removed his cap, revealing a shaven dome like the others. The instrument panels blinked off. Bending, she prodded a switch and the spotlight went out. The room plunged into a murkiness lit only by several strip lights and the glow of monitors. Moving behind the patient, she pushed the gurney. Its wheels screeched. Pausing briefly, she tugged her mask. Its elastic snapped and she threw it on another patient's stomach. Shadow hid her face and she kept her hat on. Again, the gurney wheels turned in protest, the patient's stare unwavering, his mouth dribbling, and they vanished down the corridor.

Screech…screech…screech.

The three of us dared not move as we listened to the receding sound. We eventually entered the room. Victor headed straight for the Hourglass, while Isidore and I weaved between the gurneys, eyeing the patients. Each held a similar expression: vacant.

"All right," Isidore said. "Shadowleaf? What was that woman doing?"

Her question reminded me we'd only explained so much.

"A shadowleaf," I said, "is what's created by the Hourglass. It's a refined substance of someone's evil, extracted and made into something solid."

"Nicely put," Victor said. He examined the Hourglass, his elbows on the counter.

I zigzagged between the gurneys, not really wanting to see the patients. There was a lack of lucidity to their stares, no different than the patient who'd only moments before been wheeled away. I grabbed the nurse's discarded mask and threw it to the floor, crushing it underfoot. "Stitch them together—"

"And we have the return of the primordial darkness." Victor stood back from the Hourglass, hands on hips. "The black void.

The nothingness which existed before the words 'let there be light' were uttered."

"Serious?" Isidore's eyes reflected the red of the monitor. Its display blinked on and off. The coloured half-light did little to diminish her good looks. "Actually, I believe it."

"Goodwin had the Hourglass all along." Victor's eyebrows twitched to his grinding thoughts.

"At least we know where those men were being taken." I shrugged. Was I getting too dismissive towards the situation, to the weirdness going on? Maybe, maybe not. Perhaps being in the presence of Isidore somehow balanced me.

"And," Victor said, "to what purpose is he extracting their shadowleaves?"

"Where are these men from?" I said. "You don't just pick random people off the street."

"Those men," Isidore said, "aren't off the street."

"What?" I clawed my chin.

"Have you forgotten what we found?" She pointed to the ceiling. "In your friend's office."

"The list of names," Victor said. "Of course."

Alongside each name and County, the third column on the list we'd found contained words such as, fraud, assault, manslaughter, murder, rape, and worse. An icy draft tickled my neck. I doubted it had anything to do with the dampness in the room.

"That," I said, "explains the black shadowleaf."

"Evil." Victor ran a gloved hand over the Hourglass. "To the core."

"Are you saying the crime is in that little black square?" Isidore pointed at one of the hunks of technology.

The machine was the one I'd thought resembled a photocopier, only with innards visible through the glass casing. The extracted shadowleaf sat in a cradle of wires and circuitry.

"Not the actual crime," Victor said. "The shadowleaf is an imprint of the evil mind behind the crime."

"On a sliding scale from white to black, with white being the purest," he continued, "well, you can guess how evil that man was."

"Is," I said, thinking of the way the poor bastard dribbled at the ceiling as the nurse wheeled him away. "He's still alive."

"Barely."

"They're all still alive." I waved a hand towards the occupied gurneys. It was as if Goodwin collected these criminals to experiment on them. But to what end?

Victor scanned the monitors.

"I have no idea what any of this means." He crouched before the Hourglass, hands on thighs, and ankles on show. "Or what Goodwin is up to."

I hadn't taken much notice of the sand heaped in the lower bulb of the Hourglass. As the three of us stood there, the black sand greyed moment by moment. Within seconds, it became white again. Pure white, like any typical hourglass, or egg timer.

Bad eggs.

* * *

We left the Hourglass laboratory and followed the corridor the nurse had taken. Assuming she headed home, seeing she'd taken her handbag, we could remain exploring. All the while keeping as quiet as possible—she had, after all, taken the patient somewhere else and we were uncertain if the woman had left entirely. We still had to find Goodwin, and perhaps Polly, if she was down here. I wondered about Stanley and what would happen when we found him. Or he found us.

So far the route proved similar to the previous corridors, and just as creepy. As yet, nothing else seemed out of the ordinary, simply rooms containing linen and cleaning materials, medical supplies and the like. Many were empty, some with gurneys covered with leather straps. No more patients. And we hadn't yet come across the tattooed patient.

We continued along the passages, taking lefts and rights, and headed through a number of double doors. There weren't a great number of alternative routes beneath the House, and I guessed most linked back to the main area. I had no doubt we still followed the nurse, and every room we entered, I expected to find her either wheeling the gurney or operating on the patient, undertaking another weird experiment.

"Must be another lift somewhere," I said. "Wonder where it comes out."

"I doubt Goodwin would want people coming in and out of his office," Victor said.

"I doubt everything about Goodwin, full stop."

Isidore held her pistol again—I'd lost count how many times she'd pulled it from her waistband, popped the magazine to check it was loaded, and slipped it away again.

Before we came to another set of doors, a concreted area stretched out beside us and became an uneven expanse of bare rock. I ducked beneath a lintel and entered, stopping beside Isidore. Victor had ventured a little further inside. We remained in the glow of corridor light. The echo of dripping stalactites bounced around us. No lights here, and by the looks of it the area was unfinished. More like a construction site with its heaped rubble and masonry, and I assumed Goodwin was expanding further, creating another room for more bizarre experiments. No downed tools, though, only rock rising from the ground. It was a cave, and reminded me of Goodwin's silhouette at the entrance to the place in the woods. Was this where it led to? Perhaps this wasn't an expansion at all. The drips reverberated. Modest stalagmites dotted the immediate area, and further back a slanted rock face acted as a backdrop to our shadows. It was more than a cave…it was a cavern.

Isidore visibly shivered.

"Want my jacket again?" I said.

"You're not wearing one."

"I know."

A noise from deep within the cavern killed her amusement. Victor held up a hand, with the Witchblade in the other. Even in the semi-darkness it glinted.

I had an image of Lucas ripped apart by tentacles of shadow, and I stepped in front of Isidore. She grabbed my arm, trying to pull me back. Already, she had her finger curled around the trigger of her gun.

My heart hammered, and a warmth throbbed in my ears.

From somewhere beyond the reaching light, a chain rattled. *Chink, chink-chink*…followed by a rasp of metal over stone. Then a rapid pounding of feet and a splash, and the grunt of someone—something—fast approaching.

The shadows came alive. A solid hulk of darkness dislodged itself and came at us.

Victor said something.

I clenched my fists, unworried that I had no weapon, and I hunched. Fuelled by adrenaline, I stepped sideways, keeping low and shot my arm up. I blocked the charging shadow as it swung at me with a rock.

It was a man.

His forearm smacked into mine and he roared, teeth bared, spittle flying. Between us, the rock crashed to the ground. In the half-light, the man's eyes were burning orbs of hatred and fear. He was out for one thing: survival.

And we'd stepped into his domain. His territory.

The stink of shit and sweat fogged my senses and I took several paces backwards.

With one leg behind him, supported in the air by a taut chain, the veins in his neck bulged like threads of rope. His muscles flexed and he swung each massive arm. He hissed and grunted and whined as if unsure which reaction to display.

Filth dripped from his shaven head, rage contorting his features, while he clawed the air with nails chipped and raw.

I'd taken another step back, and flanked by Victor and Isidore, we gaped at this man. This madman. This beast...

"Victor," I said, my breath heavy. "Is this a necromeleon?"

"No, they're worse than this. This man is still human."

CHAPTER 28

Having left the cavern and followed more corridors, another pair of eyes locked with mine. This time the guy raged behind reinforced glass. His tongue wriggled in a toothless mouth, froth collecting around his gums. The tendons in his neck, taut and huge. He pummelled his fists against the glass one final time, broke eye contact, then stomped away, giving me an over-the-shoulder glare. His jeans, bloodied and soiled, flapped around bare feet. His back slammed into the far wall. High above his head a pattern of bloody smudges streaked the steel surface.

There wasn't even a bed for him. Nothing. Only an empty cell. Grabbing his knees to his chest, his toes curled upwards and he sank his head into his arms. His shoulders heaved.

"What's wrong with these men?" Victor walked towards Isidore, whose silence said everything.

"Guess we've found why Goodwin needed tranquillisers," I said.

The two of them continued to pace the corridor. On both sides, between two sets of familiar double doors, every cell offered a similar scene. Each contained madness, some more than others. The cells, with soundproofed glass, accessed by heavy-duty doors with a keypad entry, were numbered one through twelve. A couple of the occupants wore expressions of loss and loneliness. Others, simple confusion. Most, however, wore a bestial glare of little more than violence.

There was something about the silence of that place, the way the mute hammering and yelling of these prisoners closed in. With my periphery clogged with silent screams and rage, I had no idea where to turn.

We pushed on through the doors and into another area.

Darkness and silence greeted us, and the familiar stink of damp…and something else. Something heavy. The light behind us did little to penetrate the room, and in the dimness, I could just make out steel surfaces reflecting blinking lights. Victor found a wall switch and thumbed it. The sudden glare of overhead lights made me squint for a second.

"A morgue." Suddenly I felt cold.

"This place is wrong," Victor said.

Isidore shook her head repeatedly as she glared around the room.

A dozen gurneys littered the place. Each, unlike elsewhere, covered by a black plastic sheet and showing the unmistakable outline of a body. The smell, I assumed, must've been formaldehyde and it clogged my nose. There was a mixture of something else—I guessed it was the smell of the dead. A strange smell, and stranger still to be among them. Again. Unlike the other bodies I'd seen this week, these weren't drained of life force. Beneath the sheets, the outlines were too full. Too normal. But what is normal?

Steel panels and the sickly yellow walls seemed to be the general decor throughout this underground network of rooms and corridors. In this room, between huge panels of dull steel, many compartments covered one wall. I headed for it, gripped a handle and pulled it open. Inside, as expected, lay a dead body. Toe-tagged, like in the movies.

Isidore joined me. "Horrible."

"Yeah."

"Your friend Goodwin's behind this?"

"Yeah."

"What's he playing at?"

I slammed the door shut and mumbled, "I don't know." A part of me didn't want to know what game Goodwin played. All of this was way above me.

She circled a couple of the gurneys while I stood motionless. I didn't want to know anymore. I felt defeated and cheated.

I dragged my hand—always gloved now—from my forehead down to my chin. The leather rasped against stubble. I pinched my jaw and blew air between bulging cheeks. I was hungry, unclean, and I'd just seen a dead person's feet.

I stepped away.

A rumpling, stiff sound claimed my attention, and there was Isidore pulling back one of the black sheets. Underneath, dead eyes stared at her. Curled around the ear and running down his neck was a tattoo, a tribal design.

"Our friend here didn't make it." Her hand was steadier than mine would've been.

"She killed him?" I said through dry lips.

"Yes."

"How did he die?"

"He looked more drugged than dying."

Victor stood at a desk in front of a computer. With one hand on the back of a chair, he slid the Witchblade under his belt and prodded the keyboard. The computer hummed into life. As it booted up, he slid the chair back and slumped into it.

I walked over to him. Behind me, I heard the sheet rustle back into place.

No company logos or password requests flashed on the screen. I'd expected it, as I'm certain anybody would. It displayed the usual desktop screen: black background, a few icons, and a taskbar.

Near the desk, a door I'd failed to notice creaked open. Slowly at first, and then it swung inwards. It whipped wide and smacked the wall beside Victor. I jumped, my breath catching.

Victor leapt to his feet and reached for the Witchblade. He brandished it like a sword, legs wide, jaw firm. His eyebrows wriggled above unblinking eyes.

And there stood the nurse, hands on hips. Her red hair accentuated the outrage in her eyes. Her voice echoed. "What is this?"

"Katrina?" Victor said, and lowered the Witchblade.

CHAPTER 29

"Missed you last night, Victor." Katrina ignored Isidore's raised gun. "You said you'd be there."

I frowned so hard it hurt. This was Victor's yoga instructor.

Victor said, "What are you doing here?"

"More to the point, what are *you* doing here?" Her eyes retained their anger, and possibly fear. "You shouldn't be here."

Victor's eyebrows twitched.

Stepping fully into the room, Katrina dropped her handbag on the desk. Her eyes moved from Victor and rested on me for a moment, and then to Isidore and her gun. "Please, put that away."

Isidore hesitated, flicked her eyes to Victor, whose nod was enough, and she lowered the weapon.

"Thank you," Katrina said.

I had a bombardment of questions and didn't know where to begin, and I suspected Isidore had many herself. I'd let Victor handle it. After all, he had some kind of connection with this woman.

"Goodwin isn't going to be happy when he finds out about this," she said.

"What's he up to?" Victor collapsed in the chair, his leg hooked beneath him, the Witchblade now hidden.

"Where to start..." She touched her hair, her face softening.

"Whatever can help us understand. Not only this, but everything else that's happening."

"What do you mean?"

"We're all in danger. Goodwin's in danger, too."

"Why?"

"Just tell us what these experiments are about. From the beginning."

For a moment, she didn't blink. Then her lips parted, her tongue moved, but she said nothing.

"Katrina?"

Her shoulders rounded. "Goodwin has developed a means of combining ancient apparatus and modern technology to remove evil from the thoughts of man."

I scratched my chin. Goodwin the scientist? I didn't...couldn't understand.

"Years ago," she continued, "he discovered the potential to cure the darkness which consumes some people. His theories are intense."

Victor leaned back into the chair and it creaked. The sound reminded me of the dead bodies behind me.

"He has nothing but good intentions. He's desperate to rid the world of its evil."

I almost laughed.

"Okay," Victor said, "I won't ask how this is even possible. Clearly, you have the equipment here to play such a game. But those men you've been experimenting on are either mad or dead."

I said, "Even the guy you experimented on earlier is dead."

Katrina's lips whitened.

"Yes," she said eventually. "Over the years there have been many failures. Too many. And we've never given up. The potential is there."

"Are you saying you've never been successful?" Victor's mouth twisted.

"I'm not saying that." She averted her eyes, settling on her feet. "It's all for the good of mankind. That's what Goodwin always says."

It sounded like exactly the sort of thing he'd say.

Victor said, "These men are taken from a prison—"

"Willingly." Katrina dragged her eyes to meet Victor's. "They see it as a ticket to freedom."

"Even with the chance they'll die?"

"Not all of them die."

"This can't be legal," I said.

"Goodwin has contacts very, very high up in the ranks."

"Ranks?" I raised an eyebrow. "You mean the prison system? That's crazy."

"Goodwin has influence in certain circles. It's as legitimate as it needs to be."

"It's corrupt. That's what it is." My ears felt sunburnt.

"So," Victor said, and stood up, "these men willingly hand over their lives so you can possibly cure their evil ways by extracting their shadowleaves. Do you realise how dangerous this is? Playing with such dark power?"

"Victor," she said, "please. You don't understand—"

"Enough to see the madness in it."

"No, Victor—"

"Those poor men out there. Mad. All of them. Mad, if not dead. Your ideas and theories, just as mad!"

"Tell us about the mad ones." Isidore's voice sounded distant. "Can't you cure them?"

Katrina barely nodded. "Afterwards, everyone shows different symptoms, all have different results. The side effects are varied, always. One claimed she saw angels."

"She?" Isidore's voice was no longer soft. "You experiment on women as well?"

"Of course."

"Drain their minds," I said, "and leave them as vegetables. Unable to cure them. It's sick."

"No," Katrina said, "you don't understand. The science behind this is incredible. Goodwin's theories are sound. Solid. We're so close."

"I can't believe this." Victor shook his head.

"Our results are impressive," Katrina continued. "We've made such discoveries. Such progress."

"You're my yoga instructor, for God's sake."

She gestured at the computer. "This is what I do. Yoga is a front."

"You're not joking." Victor almost spat the words in her face.

She took a step back. "I'm a scientist."

And there we were, I thought, *thinking you were a nurse.*

"This is the wrong kind of science." Victor darted for the

nearest gurney, his shoes stamping on the tiles. He yanked back a sheet covering the head. "This is madness."

"Victor, you don't under—"

"Stop saying that." Victor pointed at the dead man's face. "This poor bastard, regardless of his crime, doesn't deserve to be your guinea pig."

Their crimes had been listed like a shopping receipt, and I wanted to speak out, to tell Victor I disagreed with him. Granted, it was utter madness, but each one of those prisoners had chosen this. Maybe these people deserved their fate. Each played a dangerous round of roulette, a chance for freedom, and so possibly free to commit their crimes again.

I settled on saying, "It's all messed up."

Katrina's eyes were small and wandering. Her lips quivered. "Victor…"

He tugged the sheet back over the head.

Isidore said, "Show me the CCTV monitors. I want to see what you are doing."

I gawped at her, and she pointed up into a far corner.

"Smile," she said.

A camera spied on us.

"Didn't notice them," I admitted.

Victor laughed. It sounded false.

Isidore nodded. "I looked out for them as soon as we got down here. There aren't any in the corridors."

"Oh," I said.

"I'm a thief, remember? I look for these things."

Katrina threw a thumb over her shoulder. "Down there, second door on the left. Help yourself."

"Too right I will," I heard Isidore say as she left the room, and I considered following her.

"Tell me," Victor said, "where's Goodwin now?"

I decided to stay.

Katrina tried to smile and failed. "He was here earlier."

"How long ago?"

"An hour or two."

"Was he alone?"

"Funny you should say that…"

Victor arched an eyebrow.

"He was with your brother." She raked fingers through her hair. "They were acting strange."

"How so?"

"Not sure. Recently, I've noticed Goodwin's been on edge. Paranoid, you could say."

"Where did they go?"

"They headed for the other side of the complex."

"Doing what?"

"It's where the main machines are. Over here is just routine stuff."

"Routine stuff?" Victor frowned, and grunted. He nodded at the computer. "Show us what's in there, Katrina."

The screen saver—random coloured patterns—spread across the screen. Katrina removed her jacket and draped it over the chair. She sat and opened a program. Minutes passed where no doubt Victor and I had similar thoughts.

"You said Goodwin has been paranoid recently," Victor said eventually. "Why?"

"He fears his collection has attracted some attention. Unwanted attention at that."

"Collection? What collection? Whose attention?"

Katrina started to reply, when Isidore's voice leapt along the corridor, reaching us in an echo.

"Hey, you need to see this."

I was getting used to her saying that.

* * *

A bank of monitors, stacked three-by-three, featured static images of rooms much the same as those we'd already seen. Isidore sat at the console, her face a white-blue sheen. One screen, *CAM 5*, showed activity: Polly in fast reverse, her face impassive as she traced rapid hands over a gurney's empty mattress. She was alone. No Georgie, nor Annabel. Various machines and apparatus loomed behind her, and a computer terminal sat in one corner. Its screen was blank.

"Wait." Isidore released the back-arrow key and leaned into the chair. "Watch this."

CAM 5 continued its forward motion.

"How long ago was this?" Victor said behind me.

"About half an hour." Isidore swivelled in the chair.

"Where is this?"

Katrina stayed in the corridor. "The Operating Room."

"Nice," I said.

"It's not what you think. We don't *operate* on our subjects."

"Just tell us how to get there." Victor's head rested against the doorframe. The screens bleached his face into a cold mask.

"Wait," Isidore said again. "There's more."

"How did she get there in the first place?" Victor asked.

"She walked through from the corridor."

"No Georgie? Her guide dog."

Isidore shook her head.

"There are only cameras in the main oper—the main rooms," Katrina said.

We watched for a few seconds longer, and the unmistakable frame of Goodwin entered the room. As always, an eddy of smoke surrounded his head.

In short, what followed was confusing. Their hug looked awkward, and Polly wasn't having any of it. As they parted, she stepped back and bumped into a gurney. Her lips were a rapid movement. Both gesticulated.

"Are they arguing?" I asked.

From the corner of my eye, Victor nodded. "So it seems."

After a last outburst from each of them, Goodwin walked away. Giving her a final verbal blast and a dismissive hand gesture, he stomped from the room into the corridor. He yanked the door behind him, but it bounced in its frame and remained ajar.

Alone again, Polly's lips moved, and then the lights blinked out. No one had touched a switch. The vertical strip of light from the doorway did little to illuminate the room. A white flash leaked across the screen as the transition from normal light to infrared flared and settled into a grey fuzziness. Polly's eyes pierced the gloom like LEDs. She couldn't know the lights were out.

Now in two types of darkness, she stayed where she was, leaning against the gurney.

And then it got weird.

At first it was as if water leaked into the room. A shimmering grey coated the floor near her feet, spreading like an overflowing bathtub. Only this had a kind of accuracy, a determination. Several more 'puddles' collected beneath the apparatus and the machines. They advanced. It reminded me of the shadows at the farmhouse.

Shadows, heading towards Polly. They flowed and thickened, and linked with one another, darkened. They no longer resembled water.

White light burst into the room, and as the glare shrank— cancelling the infrared—a distorted silhouette of a man entered through a swinging door. The outline sharpened as he walked over the writhing shadows.

Stanley.

With bulging forearms, showing little effort, he carried Georgie. The dog's tail wagged. By now the shadows had stopped approaching, having surrounded Polly. She remained against the gurney. Stanley spoke and he placed Georgie at her feet. She fussed over the dog and the room became a fraction lighter as the shadows retreated to a corner, beneath the machines. Some slithered higher and clung to the walls. Occasionally the mass would throb, its surface rippling.

The pair hugged and began speaking—civilised compared to the exchange with Goodwin only moments before.

"What's with these two?" I said.

"She doesn't realise the Shadow Fabric is there," Victor whispered.

"Surely she'd feel it." I remembered the sickness I felt in its presence.

"It's possible to shield it when required. Only when in the right hands."

"Or wrong hands."

"Quite."

Katrina started to say something and Victor shushed her. Onscreen, the pair's exchange continued for a few moments longer, and then Georgie led Polly to the door. She left Stanley behind. He sat on the gurney, and there he stayed, swinging his legs.

It wasn't long until the Fabric closed in again, blocking the corridor light.

Again, the infrared kicked in. Nothing glowed. No lights remained. Where Polly's eyes had contained a strange glow, Stanley's did not. No lights in Stanley's eyes. His were impenetrable holes in an expressionless face.

"Those eyes..." I said.

Victor inhaled sharply.

A spiral of shadow dragged a kicking Goodwin into the room. His body seemed to ooze from the dark mass of the Fabric. Words froze on my lips. What was this?

Behind Goodwin's struggling form, Stanley swung his legs. It appeared as though Goodwin had been gagged, yet I knew it wasn't by a typical piece of cloth or fabric. It was a piece of Shadow Fabric. It writhed over his lower face like a highwayman's mask in the wind. The terror in the man's eyes was enough to make my stomach lurch. The darkness fell from his mouth and he grimaced and spat.

The shadows erupted in a mass of tentacles. They lunged for him.

Before he managed to protect his head, an arm of shadow smashed into his face. His neck snapped back. Blood sprayed from his mouth and his face twisted in agony. He dropped, covering his head, and tucked his legs in. This did little for protection, and soon his arms slapped at the limbs of shadow. His feet kicked at them.

The Fabric ravaged and beat him, played with him like an unloved doll, all the while Stanley's legs thrust forward and back. His eyes revealed only darkness. When it was over, with Goodwin's chest heaving and his nostrils flaring, the Shadow Fabric released his body. He curled up, still alive. Barely.

Stanley slid from the mattress and walked to Goodwin. He kicked him. Once, twice. Behind them, the Shadow Fabric erupted. Tentacles thrashed. The gurney shot backward and crashed against a wall.

His face creasing into a smirk, Stanley stepped away from Goodwin.

I felt sick.

The Shadow Fabric billowed like a tsunami, enveloping Stanley. And he vanished—first he was there, then he wasn't. The darkness receded as the Fabric slipped into a far corner, retreating from Goodwin. It, too, disappeared.

I squinted at the screen. Goodwin looked dead, though I swore he still breathed. I hoped.

"Oh my God." Katrina's hand muffled her words.

"Unconscious," Victor said.

"Stanley is a necromeleon?" I glared at Victor.

His eyebrows came together. "If that is the case, then Stanley is dead."

I thought of the corpse back at the house.

"The body at his place isn't his," he said, as if reading my mind. "A necromeleon is the reanimated dead, possessed by the Fabric."

"A different type of necromeleon?"

"What in God's name are you talking about?" Katrina pushed herself into the room and faced Victor. She pointed at the screen. "And what was that?"

He ignored her.

Isidore reset the monitors and stood up. "Goodwin is still in there."

"Katrina," I said, "take us to your Operating Room."

She began to protest and Victor barged past her into the corridor. Isidore and I followed, leaving the woman stunned.

"I need to get my handbag." Katrina headed to the morgue.

Standing in the corridor, the three of us no doubt replayed it all in our heads. My jaw ached, and reluctantly, I relaxed. Then I saw the door. An ordinary door, just like the rest of them; scuffed wood and a tarnished brass handle. No panel to peer through, either. Just another closed door and it had got to the point where I did not want to discover any more secrets. Yet, there was something about this door. What lay beyond it? I had an overwhelming urge to open it.

So I did.

The light from the corridor flooded the room and I stumbled back. I stepped on Isidore's foot and she yelped. Victor said something, but I didn't hear him. Kind of like déjà vu slapping me about the head, my senses whirled and my jaw dropped. My throat dry, my hands curled into fists. Ears burning, my blood steaming through every vein.

Rows of metal boxes, floor to ceiling, packed the room—exactly like the ones I'd seen as Victor unwrapped *The Book of Leaves* at Lucas's shop. That was before the Fabric came and ripped the man apart. These boxes had been revealed to me back then.

And they were here. Here was the room.

Light reflected from the boxes and shelves, shining before me in a teasing glory. *Here I am*, each of those tiny reflections said.

I took another step back, Victor and Isidore grabbing me. My legs buckled, nausea swallowed me. Crumpled, on my knees, my hands flat in front of me, I wanted to spew.

"Leo?" Isidore's voice sounded so far away.

Tears blurred my vision. I strained my neck to watch Victor run into the morgue. Twisting slightly, I collapsed onto my side. From there, I had a view of half the room, which was enough. Did the gurneys move? *That can't be right*, I tried to say. It wasn't the gurneys moving, it was the black sheets that covered the corpses.

Something twitched beneath each of them.

One of the sheets slipped from a corpse, a grey hand flexed and clutched at the air.

Katrina's scream pierced my already jammed senses.

CHAPTER 30

Necromeleons. The reanimated dead.

Wisps of shadow coiled around the gurneys. At first, a faint slithering greyness—insubstantial almost. From my viewpoint, crouched on the ground, I saw more than Victor could as he charged into the room. He shouted at Katrina. She continued to scream even as he grabbed her. He seemed unaware of the shadows at his feet, glancing at the corpses as they stuttered awake.

Like my legs, my tongue refused commands as I tried to warn him of the shadows crawling across the tiles. Tried to warn them both, and couldn't. I wanted to get to my feet and run to him. Even my arms tingled with a peculiar numbness. With my head flushed with nausea and a weakness in my limbs, I grunted. My vision churned.

Isidore remained with me as Katrina and Victor gaped at the waking corpses. They took deliberate steps backwards, heading towards us. I don't think Isidore saw the shadows—I'm sure she would've warned Victor.

"That's impossible." Isidore's body tensed, her breath cold on my neck.

Katrina's hands turned into rigid claws. The first corpse to have awakened, sat upright. Victor curled a gloved hand around Katrina's arm. They were too close to that corpse, and I was unable to warn them. So far, it was the only one to have removed its cover. The only one to have sat up.

Isidore tugged at me, groaning as she struggled to get me on my feet. She said "Impossible" a few more times. My legs still didn't respond, neither my arms. I rocked back and forth, desperate to move, to get up, help Victor. My scream roared in my head, failing to reach my throat. Why couldn't I move? This was pathetic.

There must have been a dozen corpses there. Another couple had now risen. The sheets slid off, falling to a heap in a crinkled mess. Their blackness disguised the swelling shadows that converged like a lynch mob around the gurney wheels. The necromeleons' white flesh shone in contrast to the poor light. Darkness filled their eyes.

Frustration roared through my head again. Isidore managed to drag me sideways, while my brain's commands failed to reach my sleeping limbs. Even my arms didn't play the game.

Victor's voice bounced off the walls as he shouted, "Come on!" He yanked Katrina's arm and she staggered back.

The nearest corpse reached out and swiped at the air.

With the Witchblade raised, Victor continued to pull her.

Most of the corpses were on their feet now. A few pushed themselves up and tiptoed as if testing the solidity of the floor. Some were naked. Others wore gowns. One even wore jeans, and on the belt buckle it said *Proud to be your Bud*. I didn't think they served Budweiser in prison, and I knew they'd not allow belts for risk of suicide attempts. Regardless of my lightning thoughts as to where this guy came from, he was dead. A necromeleon. All of them.

They advanced on stiff legs.

"Get..." Isidore yelled in my ear, tugging beneath my armpits. "Up!"

The dead walked, and I couldn't. I was dead weight in her arms and I helplessly watched Victor and Katrina continue their retreat as the dead advanced like playground bullies. Mouths drooped, eyes full of death and darkness and determination. With arms ending in white claws, their pace quickened.

Like a sudden slam of thunder, a thump echoed through the room. It came from one of the compartments. Then another. And another. Bang, slam, thump, from the inside of those small chambers. The doors shook. The light reflecting off the steel warped beneath each impact. Slam. More and more beating, echoing, drumming as more corpses came alive.

Isidore proved her strength as she lifted me off my arse. Only for a second, as my legs folded. Their life remained far away. My jaw ached, my heart was ready to explode.

And still the advancing necromeleons gained distance. Although Victor and Katrina hurried, neither wanted to turn their back on them.

"Leo!" Isidore's scream pierced my skull. She yanked hard, growling, and managed to drag me further into the corridor. My arms still didn't work properly. I felt pathetic.

Some of the compartment doors buckled, shaking from the impacts. Each handle heaved beneath the rapid kicks from the corpse inside. Many feet stomped an irregular rhythm, now a frantic soundtrack to an unbelievable scene.

I winced at a *snap-crash* as a handle broke. It flew across the room and smashed into a monitor. Sparks and glass erupted. The steel door of the compartment bounced once and creaked to a stop, revealing the kicking feet of the occupant. Another door burst open…and another. More compartments gaped wide, pieces of metal flying and doors swinging. In seconds the tables shot out on steel runners, the corpses jerking upright. One table gave way and the corpse fell to its knees, while the others gained footing on unstable legs.

Dizziness stabbed my head from all corners. Isidore pulled at me.

"Leo, move!"

If I didn't already feel nausea drowning me, I'd have been sick anyway. I knew I was disabled without knowing why, and my fear boiled, but it was the sound of the advancing dead which got to me.

Now the drumming had stopped and the corpses were free. My ears roared as God knew what emotion steamed through my head—whether amazement at seeing the dead walk, anger at being unable to walk myself, or fear of what was happening. The necromeleons lumbered towards us, open mouths uttering not a word—not even a moan. I heard nothing apart from the shuffle of bare feet.

Isidore released me, finally giving up the effort to yank me to my feet. A gunshot shattered the silence. My right ear rang. Isidore's targeted corpse jerked, a bloodless hole in its chest oozing clear fluid and darkness. A tendril of shadow licked from the wound.

Still the thing advanced.

I couldn't decide what was worse, seeing death or watching it walk.

The gun cracked another couple of times, and still they came.

With a bell tolling in my head, my legs tingled. Regaining some kind of life, it was as if those gunshots had reminded them to get moving.

"Move, Leo," Isidore said. "Move. Now!"

With both palms flat to the floor, I shoved myself upright. The coldness of the tiles leaked through my gloves. My feet were still numb, if at least a little responsive.

Isidore stood aside.

A necromeleon—it was Bud—sprang forward, evidently one of the more energetic ones. He clutched at Katrina's scrambling limbs and clamped an ankle. She sprawled and slipped sideways. Her head smashed into a gurney's frame and sent it wheeling away. Her scream sounded far off, strangely muted by my temporary deafness.

Victor lost his grip of her and staggered into a crouch. As he reached for her with one hand, with the other, he swung the Witchblade.

That knife really was powerful.

An arc of flame cut the air diagonally, creating a barrier between them and the advancing necromeleons. As one, they halted, the darkness in their eyes bulging from hollow sockets. The streamers of fire held for a few seconds, then burnt out as Victor went to Katrina's aid.

Too late.

Bud had his mouth at her throat in a mess of red spurts and flapping flesh.

Everything was happening too fast, and I was too slow. Katrina stopped screaming.

"Shit!" Isidore's voice echoed.

Victor, his suit saturated with Katrina's blood, continued with backward strides as sparks flared around him. I caught the faint whiff of ozone—almost cleansing.

I punched my legs, desperate to encourage more life to return. My breathing burned as if I'd been running, and I should've been doing precisely that.

Isidore's gun roared several more times, and still the necromeleon ravaged the poor woman. With eyes wide and blank, Katrina's head wobbled from side to side; Bud's face buried into her. Back straight, hands flat on the floor with fingers splayed, the dead man looked to be doing press-ups.

"Bastard!" My voice had returned. My senses, too, were back as finally I regained control of those important limbs.

Isidore slammed another magazine into her gun and fired again.

"Victor!" I screamed, my throat dry. "Come on!"

He stood erect, pale faced and swiping the Witchblade left and right. More flames cut the air. His suit glistened with his yoga instructor's blood.

Katrina's body twitched, and it had nothing to do with the Budweiser-swigging necromeleon vampire at her throat—it had everything to do with the shadows looping into the ragged mess above her collarbone. Her arms straightened and her fingers hooked as the shadows claimed her. Both legs kicked and a knee jerked between Bud's legs. He didn't flinch. Bullets didn't deter his friends, so a knee to the nuts certainly wouldn't.

Victor gave the Witchblade another series of jabs and more fire burned around him. The smell of ozone drifted on the air. Flames sputtered and flared, giving clearance for his retreat.

Katrina rose to her feet. Her eyes reflected darkness.

As the fire dwindled, Victor again slashed back and forth, and again the flames created a temporary barrier. Burning slices of bright yellow seared my vision even from a distance. The man must've had his eyes squinted shut in the glare.

Isidore pulled off another couple of shots at two of the closer necromeleons. Both came to a brief standstill. One tripped, stumbled, and continued advancing. The other already regained its pace.

A necromeleon charged, barging the others and ran into the strips of flame. The collection of fire strands shredded the thing as if shoved through a meat slicer. A burst of flame enveloped the pieces of undead flesh and bone as they flew in all directions, trailing fire like meteors. The fiery chunks scattered and scorched the tiles. Each tiny fire sputtered out to leave shrinking pieces—nothing more than ashen lumps of bone. Several quivered as the shadows within burned away. The more intact limbs crackled as the flames devoured the remaining undead life. The stench of burnt flesh clogged the air. Black tentacles of shadow flicked to and fro, the fire eating into them. They shrivelled to nothing. A few pieces of flesh and bone crackled as they greyed to ash.

Now on my feet, I tested my weight. Uncertain, unsteady, I stood nonetheless. My ears screamed in a mute kind of way.

Isidore stood beside me, her gun gripped between steady hands.

"Victor," I shouted again. "Come on, man!"

He'd almost reached us, and wasn't any more than ten paces away from reaching the corridor. Once there, it would act as a bottleneck, and the approaching dead men would only be able to come through two abreast. Then, I guessed, we'd run our arses off. Providing I could manage it.

With more zigzags of flame burning before them, the necromeleons charged as one. Those in front, the first to break the barrier, succumbed to the fire. Pieces of meat exploded around Victor and covered him in sputtering flame—harmless to him, fatal to the necromeleons. Each chunk, trailing fire, scattered in a blackened heap.

Behind dwindling fire strands, dead Katrina and her dead friends leapt at Victor. Onto him. And he went down beneath their weight. First he was there, backing up and waving the Witchblade before him, and then he wasn't.

Not until after he said, "Run, Leo!" did he scream.

CHAPTER 31

Isidore yanked and urged me on, her face as pale as the corridor walls.

"No," I told her, knocking away her arm. "We can't leave him."

"We must," she yelled into my face, and jostled me towards the doors. "Go."

And so we ran. Fast. As fast as my legs would allow. Yet, who would be proud of running? Leaving a friend to die beneath the weight of a dozen reanimated corpses. It sickened me. With our footfalls slapping the tiles, echoing as we burst through door after door and room after room, Victor's screams dwindled. Even when it would have been impossible to physically hear him, I believed I still could.

Soon, it was clear the necromeleons didn't follow us. I guessed they were otherwise occupied.

"We've got to find Goodwin." I slowed my pace and stopped. My chest heaved and my knee ached like hell.

Isidore's eyes shone, sharpened with adrenaline, and her breath hissed. She still held her gun in white knuckles.

"How are you feeling?" She nodded at my legs.

I shrugged. "Victor…"

She dropped her gaze and slid her backpack to the ground, tugging at a zip. In a swift movement, she reloaded the gun and poked another magazine into her jeans' pocket.

Since leaving Victor, each turn had been another extension to the ridiculous labyrinth below Periwick House. Whether room or corridor, each was no different from the last, with weak strip lights casting a familiar gloom over empty gurneys, computer terminals, and other apparatus.

In the room we'd now entered, along one wall, a row of filing cabinets squatted. They reflected years of misuse.

Isidore's gaze shot past me and into a far corner. Beneath a counter supporting an array of peculiar machines and equipment, a collection of shadows gaped like a black hole. Normal shadows, I assumed. I hoped.

"What is it?" I asked.

"They're moving." She raised her gun.

Those shadows warped, albeit slightly, and they burst open. A smudge rushed towards us, its claws a series of rapid clicks against the tiles.

Isidore lowered her weapon.

"Georgie," I said, and exhaled.

Stopping between us, Polly's guide dog mewled. I crouched, removed a glove, and offered a reassuring stroke. Perhaps for the pair of us. I pushed my fingers into the dense hair, the warmth beneath reminded me of life. Time disappeared for a while. Only vaguely was I aware of Isidore at the cabinets, nosing through manila envelopes. Victor's scream echoed in my head, and the image of him disappearing under the bodies of necromeleons replayed in my mind's eye. No way could he have survived. By now, he would be another member of the walking dead. And he'd had the Witchblade, the only tool which worked against the Fabric. That and fire. If only I had the foresight to make myself some kind of flamethrower. I had to find a means of protection. Isidore had a gun, even if it did little to stop the dead.

Slowly, I straightened and pulled my glove on. A familiar pain flared across my knee. I grunted.

Isidore zipped her rucksack and slung it over a shoulder. "We've got to get out of here."

"Not without Goodwin," I said, not knowing what I'd say when we found him. Did I want to save him or strangle him? Georgie stood attentive at my side, and I added, "And Polly."

"Fair enough."

"The Operating Room, according to Katrina."

"All of these rooms could qualify."

"Yeah."

We bustled out of there with Georgie in tow, and into another room like any other. I had little faith in finding anyone alive. Dead, yes. Not alive. And as we reached another set of doors, I expected to be faced with more necromeleons. More corpses with shadow-filled eyes, walking, jerking, reaching out with dead hands. Both Goodwin and Polly were most likely dead. I only hoped they weren't walking.

It wasn't long before we found Annabel, strung up. She writhed in the shadows like a spindly insect caught in a web.

"That's our Tulip Moon, right there," I said to Isidore as she pointed her gun at the woman.

Pinned to the wall by clumps of shadow, Annabel squirmed. A smirk distorted her face. Was there contentment there? This bitch was where she wanted to be. Tangled with the shadows, her dress bunched in places, torn and blood-stained, and revealed a lot of leg and one skinny breast. Her hair hung in clumps and she dribbled saliva. Her eyes reflected the flickering strip lights.

"Good God," Isidore murmured.

Annabel's eyes rolled and her back arched as much as the shadows allowed. "Ah, you've caught me. Caught me in the act."

When she spoke it was as though ice slid down my spine. Isidore visibly shivered. At my feet, Georgie growled.

Fingers of darkness flexed around Annabel's shins, caressing her. She wore only one shoe. Her body moved in slow motion as tiny feelers of shadow walked across her skin.

"You're here, but too late," she continued, speech as slurred as her movements. "Too late. It's already starting."

"What?" I shouted at her. "What do you mean? Where's Goodwin?"

She chuckled. Deep, low.

Georgie made a fearful sound which became a series of vicious barks. The poor dog was as uncertain about all this as I was.

I yelled into Annabel's face: "What have you been playing at?"

Isidore had now grabbed me and gently pulled me away. I wasn't aware I'd stepped so close to the shadows. Too close. The dark, curling limbs seemed to concentrate on restraining the woman. They kept her clamped to the wall, keeping her entertained.

Her eyes sharpened as they fell upon Isidore. A smirk cracked her face. "Little slut!"

Isidore didn't flinch.

"Stupid slut. Gullible, greedy little bitch." Spittle flew from her mouth. "Playing a game you thought you could win. Spying on me. On us. Like a little bitch-slut!" She laughed. "My game! I won. I'm here. We're all here. The Shadows are here. And so will he be."

"Who?" I said. Did she mean Stanley? She couldn't be talking about Goodwin.

"He. Him. Don't know his name. Hasn't got a name."

"What are you talking about? Who? Goodwin?"

"Don't be stupid, little man. Goodwin is as good as dead." More laughter. "Dead. Like your Victor."

I wanted to punch her. I wanted to kill her. I wanted to grab her head and smash it against the wall. I wanted to…touch her.

"Yes!" she yelled. "The shadows talk, don't they?"

I stared at her breast. Repulsed and aroused at the same time. Her nipple stood erect. I shouted, "Stop it!"

Her eyes settled on me, her mouth suggesting too much.

"Stop it," I said again, shaking my head.

With tight lips, Isidore stepped forward, her gun raised higher.

"Where is Goodwin?" I said between clenched teeth. Blood surged through my head. Rushing to where I didn't want it to go. The more I thought about it, the harder—and the more difficult—it got. "Where is he?"

"Not telling."

"Who's coming?" My fists burned. "Who will be—"

"Nope. Not telling." And like a child, she closed her mouth, her lips tightening into a thin line, and she moved her head to the side to avert her gaze.

"People have died because of you." I stepped back. Strangely, I heard my watch, its tick loud, reverberating, as though I held it to my ear.

"More will die." Again, she laughed, shrill and piercing. It echoed around us in a hollow kind of way as though the shadows in the room absorbed the sound—and the darkness closed in. "So many more will die."

"Just shoot her!" I snarled, amazing myself. *Tick, tick, tick.*

Before Isidore could pull the trigger, an arm of shadow shot from the body of darkness and forced its way into Annabel's mouth. *Tick.* She gagged, eyes bulging. *Tick.* Her laugh became a gurgle. *Tick.* Snot bubbled from her nose. Mucus and blood dribbled down her chin. *Tick.* Her whole body convulsed as the shadow forced itself deeper. *Tick.*

Whatever the hell that thing did to her insides, it killed her in seconds.

I no longer heard my watch.

"That saved a bullet," Isidore said.

I frowned. I had no words for that.

Georgie barked once as though speaking for me.

And again we ran—at least I jog-limped the best I could.

* * *

When we found Polly, things were a lot different. Dressed in a red t-shirt and blue jeans, she sat at a table with her hands placed before her as if waiting for lunch. She did not resemble the woman I'd first met. She was in a staff room of sorts. A place with a little more décor than elsewhere in that labyrinth of corridors and rooms beneath the House. Pictures of the ocean and sunsets lined one wall. Above a sink, pasted to a cupboard door, was an upside-down no smoking sign. On the counter, sat a microwave, a toaster, and a cordless kettle, its lid gaping like a mouth. A fridge crouched beneath the counter, alongside more cupboards. Everything needed a scrub. Cleanliness, it seemed, proved to be in short supply down here. Nonetheless, the place was more inviting than elsewhere. I guessed the faint smell of food had something to do with it.

She said nothing as we charged through the doors. Nor did she flinch. Georgie barked and bounded over to her. And still no reaction. Her blank eyes, along with her blank expression, fixed upon nothing.

"Polly?" I reached the table and rested both fists on the stained surface. I leaned forward a little. "Polly, are you okay?"

Again, no response.

"Victor's gone. Annabel's dead, too. Did you know who she was? Did you know she tried to kill us?"

Isidore opened the fridge.

"And where's Goodwin?" I asked. "Polly, what's going on?"

Nothing.

Next to a set of condiments was Goodwin's lighter. *Godwin. A Good Friend*—the man I'd known had been leading another life beneath Periwick House. I'd bought him the lighter as a small thank you for his generosity towards me. All the while, those poor men and women were being experimented on, driven mad, or dying. For the good of mankind, apparently.

"Polly," I said into her unseeing eyes, "tell me where we can find Goodwin."

Polly's expression remained as it had been the moment we entered the room. My lungs deflated, my head hammering, and after a few more seconds, I grabbed the lighter and Polly's arm.

"We have to go," I told her.

Pulling her up, her chair screeched, caught a chipped tile, and clattered to the floor. I winced and hoped it wouldn't bring any unwanted attention. Particularly from the shadows.

Georgie moved with us, keeping at Polly's side. Still she said nothing. It was strange to watch her walk as if in a trance. How did this happen? I guided her to an archway leading off along another corridor.

With Isidore close behind, eating a sausage roll, we rounded the corner. We had no idea where we headed. I had to find Goodwin, that's all I knew. Each new corridor was the same as the last, leading into new rooms and further walkways, some up or down steps. The further we walked, the more my head burned. Hair clung to my forehead and my lungs were tight. With a palm held out as if to stop traffic, I slammed into yet another door. It swung inward. Another room beyond. Everywhere, the same. I held the door for the two ladies and allowed it to swing closed.

By this time, Isidore held Polly's hand, helping her towards the other end.

"This," I shouted, "is useless!"

Isidore stopped and glared at me. Polly immediately came to a standstill, and Georgie, too.

"Leo…" Isidore said.

"Seriously, we're wasting time wandering around."

"I know, but—"

"From every corner, every corridor," I said, "I'm expecting the shadows to come alive."

"Leo, I—"

I stepped forward and leaned close to Polly's face. My ears rang and my face burned. My hands clenched and unclenched, as though belonging to someone else.

Georgie barked.

My hand shot out and gripped Polly's shoulder. Knuckles white, fingers arched like claws, the thing didn't belong to me.

"Where is Goodwin?" I shook her.

"Leo!" Isidore shoved me away.

I stumbled, but still had the woman's t-shirt bunched in a white fist. Ignoring Isidore, I pushed my face closer into Polly's blind stare.

"Tell me!"

Isidore screamed my name again. The blood rushing through my head drowned her voice. She tugged me aside, away from Polly. I clung onto the woman's clothing.

I heard myself yelling, "Where is Goodwin?"

Isidore grabbed my hand and yanked it free from Polly. "Leave her alone!"

I spun and glared at her. My teeth tight, baring them.

"What's wrong with you?" She demanded, her face turning ugly.

A growl came from somewhere—my first thought was Georgie, and then I realised it came from my throat. My hand twitched and flew upwards, arcing towards Isidore's furious face. It smacked into the side of her head.

Her eyes blazed. Stunned into reflex, she levelled her gun on me. "Get away from us."

I wanted to hit her again. And I wanted to hit the stupid blind bitch. Kick the dog too, to shut it up. The damned thing was barking again, but not at us. He faced back where we'd come from.

Three dark shapes rounded the corner, approaching from the semi-darkness. Men. Each dressed in suit and tie, official-looking—like security—coming at us with square shoulders and firm expressions. One thing though: their faces. They weren't quite right.

Their eyes contained a blackness. Death.

Necromeleons. All three. Not the shuffling dead as before, the ones which had taken Victor down, these guys were sharp, neat, and determined. Intelligent, perhaps.

The roar in my head had subsided. My jaw relaxed and I stopped growling. I wanted to be sick, to purge my system of whatever flushed my brain. Then I remembered. I'd hit Isidore. Before I could give her a pathetic—and most likely useless—apology, the three Fabric-infested men charged and wrestled us to the floor. So quick, Isidore didn't have time to shoot anybody.

Pain erupted from every nerve in my body as the world rushed into darkness.

CHAPTER 32

From far away, a jingling sound beat a wave of consciousness into the dark. Footsteps, too. It sounded like I'd been wedged at the bottom of a well, and it was the bucket I heard, its chain rattling at the top of the shaft. I pictured exactly that: me, trapped in a dried-up well, the light at the top broken by the rising bucket, swaying and shrinking to a black dot.

As my eyelids cracked open, brightness flooded my vision. I tried to move. My wrists and ankles wouldn't budge, and my head swayed on a neck of rubber. Squinting, I saw someone's hairy, callused hands strap my right wrist into a leather harness, awkwardly twisting it. The cold buckles pinched my skin. I was seated in a chair, with my other arm bound to the armrest, restrained not by rope but coils of shadow. As were my legs. There was a dampness to their touch. They caressed my watch, licking the glass and playing with the strap. It felt like spiders crawled over my arm. I shivered.

I arched my back to allow some leverage, to ease my cramped arm. Whoever stood behind me pressed down on my shoulders. I puzzled at having one arm strapped in a leather harness, held still by clamped fingers. Pale, dead fingers.

And that's what I could smell, a necromeleon. The stink of unwashed clothes and dead—albeit reanimated—flesh. Sweet, sickly. My nostrils flared and my lips moved, my tongue refusing to work. As my senses sharpened, I realised I'd been gagged as well as strapped to the chair. I guessed my mouth had been stuffed with shadow too—such a bitter taste.

I recognised my surroundings: the gym studio, with sunshine pressing on the windows along the upper part of a wall. Exercise mats and dumbbells sat in one corner. At the other end of the room a *Staff Only* door stood ajar, with darkness beyond. Along the opposite wall a row of mirrors reflected the room: me and my necromeleon friends. One stood behind my chair, his eyes black, face expressionless.

Feathery shadows rolled across the wooden floor between the legs of Stanley's dead henchmen. Polly was strapped and gagged too, her face as emotionless as it had been before.

No sign of Isidore.

Then I remembered how I'd gotten there. It hadn't all been darkness since the time those three smart necromeleons captured us. Where was Georgie? And, oh God, I'd hit Isidore!

At some point we'd been taken into a lift. We headed upwards, away from the maze of corridors and rooms. All I had was a vague recollection of Polly's silence and Isidore's yells. At some point on our way to the studio, one of the suited necromeleons knocked out Isidore and carried her over his shoulder. I'd followed, doing little else. I also remembered their eyes: darkness, like a pair of bored holes. And also Stanley. He'd been there to greet us when we arrived.

Dizzy, I strained against my ties.

"Excellent, you're back in the land of the living," Stanley said, his voice drifting from the *Staff Only* room. As his laughter thundered into the studio, he entered and approached me. His eyes, bright and blue, showed no trace of darkness. He didn't look dead. This was the man I witnessed die by the involuntary hands of his own brother. He stood with a bunched fist, suited like his necromeleon henchmen, except his tie was loose and his top button undone.

The way he held his fist suggested he hid something. Or perhaps he intended to hit me. I relaxed as he poked it into his pocket. When it slipped out, the fingers wriggled—evidently he had held something.

I grunted into the shadows stuffed in my mouth. Why wasn't I dead?

"All impressive stuff, back at the bookshop." Stanley laughed again. "Don't look so confused, I saw it all once *The Book of Leaves* came into the light."

I flexed against the shadows. Attached to my awkwardly angled right hand was the Hourglass. I hadn't noticed it before due to my slow focusing, I guessed. The last time I'd seen it, it had been in a mess of wires and tubes, linked to Goodwin's machines. This time, it was the device on its own, the glass a web of scratches, and its wooden supports equally scarred with age. White sand heaped in the lower bulb. A short distance away, my gloves clutched the ground like severed hands. I thrashed against my restraints. Useless. I thought of Victor, dead beneath the weight of necromeleons.

"What a waste," Stanley continued, "burning *The Book of Leaves*. Impressive your Victor did it so quickly, without even hesitating. Such a waste of evil. Could have been useful, but it doesn't matter. There's plenty more to play with, plenty more to stitch."

Why did Stanley say 'your Victor'? What did he mean by that? I strained against my bonds. The shadows tightened and the leather straps dug into my flesh.

"Time to play with this marvellous tool." Stanley grabbed hold of my arm, and even though it was bound to the armrest, he forced it over, and inverted the Hourglass. "It will take a while."

I groaned into the mouthful of shadow as a collection of darkness slithered towards the Hourglass and fastened on my arm. The pain of pinched skin subsided, the awkwardness relieved. The sand fell from the top bulb in a silent whisper and the grains tumbled over one another.

My muscles ached as I heaved, but my arm didn't move even a fraction. A numbness spread up my arm and into my shoulder—cold, like putting a hand in the freezer. I expected it to continue to my chest, around my body, and eventually to my head. It didn't.

Images of the madness we'd witnessed in the rooms below the House raged through me. The poor bastards who'd been driven mad or had died when attached to this device from the dark ages. Watching the sand run down—run out—was like seeing my life coming to an end. If so many emotions hadn't been driving through me then, I'd have rationalised that those men and women had died due to Goodwin's experiments, his weird alchemy of high tech and ancient magic.

Stanley's mouth curled into a smile I wanted to punch. His back straight, and with hands clasped behind him, he stood between the towering hulks of two necromeleons. Their eyes were as black as Stanley's suit and shadows boiled at their feet. I tried to scream, and only succeeded in making a pathetic muffled groan. I rocked my upper body, and immediately, the necromeleon behind me smashed the side of my head and leaned on my shoulders, clamping me to the chair.

"Sit still," Stanley said, "and let it do its work."

My face heated like a furnace and I slumped.

Polly hadn't moved—the poor woman still had no idea what was happening. What precisely had made her mind tune out of this madness? Sadly, perhaps that was it: she'd been driven insane.

And where the hell was Isidore? And what about Georgie?

A sudden movement from behind and to my left made Stanley and his dead henchmen snap their heads sideways. One necromeleon charged into action and I saw Isidore, scrambling to her feet. Evidently, she'd been unconscious until then.

I struggled beneath my binding, my right arm still numb. Helpless. In my mouth, the stuffed shadows were a bitter reminder of my inability to scream. I wanted to tell Isidore how sorry I was for striking her, yet couldn't. I silently pleaded for her forgiveness, hoping she'd read it in my face. Hoping she understood, hoping she would know I hadn't been myself. It was as if someone had controlled me. Like I'd been a puppet. I never meant—never wanted—to hit her.

One of the necromeleons gripped her midriff. She heaved and grunted, and shouted something, and in an instant a block of shadow shot into her mouth. Her eyes flared in panic.

She saw me, and the panic switched to anger.

I bucked and shook my head, she had to know I was sorry. I never meant to harm her.

Twisting her shoulders, she squatted and tore herself from the dead man's grasp, sprinting towards me. Her jaw set, her eyes feral, and as she reached me, her leg swung upwards. An explosion of pain shot through my face as her boot connected with flesh.

Then the necromeleons brought her down. She let them. And through a tangle of limbs, her eyes burned into mine.

* * *

Stanley lifted a metal box above his head, the studio lights glinting from it, and he slammed it to the floor. An eruption of black squares burst like gothic confetti. The clatter died and the shadowleaves fluttered about his feet. He stepped back and glanced at a necromeleon. With the smallest of acknowledgements, the dead man left the studio. The main doors swung shut.

Stanley laughed. "Doesn't matter about *The Book of Leaves*. Your society has some fantastic evils."

I couldn't speak, shout, or scream because of the mouthful of shadow, and my face still roared as if someone had smashed a rock into it. There was a stickiness on my brow. Isidore had every right to kick me—I thought nothing less of her. Even though I'd been powerless, I deserved it.

The shadowleaves were silky in appearance, no larger than a postage stamp, and they attracted my gaze like something taboo. And there were dozens of them.

Beside the pile, the metal box—about the size of a shoebox—gaped open. I'd seen the likes of it before; many of them stacked in the room beneath the retreat. I managed to make out the Ministry of Justice emblem where a leaf slightly hid it.

The white sand cascaded into the lower bulb of the Hourglass, piling on top of one another. White over white. An hour was proving a long time. I looked at my watch; its second hand moved around the dial. Slowly.

Isidore was curled on her side. Her wrists and ankles bound by the shadows, as was the lower part of her face. She stared at me through small eyes, her hair a mess of blonde tangles. I hoped she knew how sorry I was. My face still throbbed and my head and neck felt disconnected. She had one hell of a kick.

Sunlight poured into the room as the main doors swung inwards. The sentient wisps of shadow had pulled the door open to allow a staggering Natalie to enter. She was dressed in her therapist's uniform, her wrists and mouth restrained like the rest of us. A necromeleon followed her, his face as impassive as only a dead man's would be. The girl's eyes glistened, her nostrils flaring and her chest heaved. She saw me and her eyes widened.

Stanley smirked.

Natalie bustled further into the room. He pulled her against him, seemingly to sniff her hair. She struggled, and her muffled desperation flooded the studio.

I screamed into my gag. Not Natalie, the poor girl. I had to do something. I bucked in the chair and the necromeleon behind me grabbed my head. His fingers dug into my skin. I winced, certain those dead digits would invade my brain and kill me outright. I glared at Stanley. From the corner of my eye those white grains of sand continued to pile up.

From a caress of Natalie's lower back, Stanley's fingers walked up her spine like a bloated pink spider and clamped her neck. Her moans became a higher pitch and he shoved her to the floor. Both knees banged in a double thud, and he continued to force her closer to the pile of shadowleaves.

Her struggles ceased and a wave of silence spilled into the room. No longer did she resist, no longer were her eyes so fearful. No more muffled protests. As she relaxed, the coiled shadows fell from her face to reveal smudged lipstick and an emotionless mouth. Her face went slack and her wrists were freed. Like water along a gutter, the shadows disappeared past Stanley into the darkness now leaking from the *Staff Only* door.

The Shadow Fabric. It trembled in the corner, absorbing both sunlight and spotlights.

Laying there, her face pushed against the collection of black squares, Natalie's breath settled and her eyes shone. No evidence of fear remained, nor pain or panic, only a longing. A want. A desire. I knew where this was going.

With deliberation, almost in slow motion, she shuffled into a sitting position. She even took time to toe off her shoes before she came to sit like a child in playschool, legs crossed and back slightly hunched. She reached out and touched a shadowleaf with a probing finger. As her flesh came into contact with it, the pinkness paled to grey, yet this didn't bother her. I doubted she even noticed, such was her eagerness to 'play'. That was what it was like, watching a child discover a new toy. Just like opening a birthday present, unfolding the wrapping paper and giving the toy undivided attention. Nothing else mattered.

Natalie, expressionless, now held the shadowleaf in her palm. She picked up another leaf. Holding one in each hand, her skin tone changed. Subtle at first, as though the lighting dimmed, her flesh paled, turning grey to match her finger.

And there she sat, as if in some meditative state holding a shadowleaf in each palm, like an image of Buddha leaking black stigmata in blasphemous contradiction.

Long seconds passed—more of the white sands tumbled down into the lower bulb of the Hourglass—and Natalie brought her hands towards her face. Before eyes which focussed not on the task before her, but into distance, she pressed her hands together. Like in prayer, as Isidore had said, and that it was like seeing the very nature of Death.

And that is precisely what I witnessed.

Natalie's shoulders moved slowly forward and back. Her eyelids drooped as though tired, widened again, and then closed fully. With her eyes closed and her shoulders rocking, it appeared as if she tuned into music only she could hear.

The greyness in her flesh darkened. It spread along her wrists and up her arms, disappearing under her uniform. Wrinkles appeared along her fingers and her nails cracked. They yellowed and appeared to be extending, due only to the shrivelling skin.

With the necromeleon holding me in the chair, I could do nothing. Anger surged with a muffled outlet, screaming into the shadows. My cheeks bulged and succeeded only at creating a rawness in my throat.

Natalie's movements sped up, her rocking now charged by a faster rhythm. Occasionally, her face would twitch, her lip curling with a sideways flash of teeth and an eye squinting like she'd bitten into something sharp. Her face would relax, her skin continuing to grey. The darkness spread into her cheeks, across her nose, around her eyes. All the while, her movements became less rhythmic and more rapid. Irregular shudders wracked her body, and she still held her palms together.

Her flesh wrinkled as the life force ebbed.

By this point, I stopped screaming—it was useless. I wanted to look away, yet couldn't.

Natalie's elbows lurched outwards without breaking the obscene prayer, and on a scrawny neck, her head moved forward and back. Her dark hair had now lightened and her scalp was showing. The sudden jarring of her head dislodged wispy strands. Cheekbones and chin prominent, her body shook as if in a seizure.

Stitch-stitch-stitch as the drained life force flowed into the shadowleaves still hidden between her emaciated hands. Her legs had already become like the rest of her: thin, shrivelled, and grey.

On a final backward snap of the head, wisps of hair detached from her scalp and silently floated. Her eyes shot open, a pair of black orbs rimmed by grey flesh at the back of sunken sockets—sockets in a skull's mask with a wig of trailing white hair. The darkness in those eyes where once a brilliant green had shone, lightened. Wrinkles shifted to cracks and her face paled in death. The black of her eyes, only lasting a moment, lightened to brown, and to yellow…and her eyeballs shrank.

Something crackled as the dried husk of her body settled. And it collapsed.

Gnarly hands, still clutching the shadowleaves, sat atop shards of bone and a dusty uniform. Natalie's skull rolled away and knocked into Stanley's boot. It rocked once and cracked open in a plume of dust.

CHAPTER 33

Of everything I'd so far witnessed, this was the worst.

I thrashed against my restraints. Will this never end? Now the necromeleons shoved two more people into the studio. I recognised the pair as the arguing visitors from a few days before: Mick and Pam. Mick held a paperback in his shadow-bound hands. Most of his head was wrapped in shadow, too. Pam, however, wore a dressing gown which sported the familiar embroidered script: *Periwick House.* I guessed she'd been in a treatment with Natalie while her husband patiently waited for her. The shadows coiling around her were a lot larger and suggested she'd put up more of a fight than her husband. I had no idea how much more I could take.

In the Hourglass, sand tumbled into the lower glass bulb. The white sands had almost run out and I estimated there remained another ten minutes or so. I had no idea what Stanley intended to do to me, or to Isidore. I guessed that after me, it'd be her turn with the Hourglass. What did he intend to do with us afterwards? Indeed, what was he going to do with my shadowleaf when the hour was up? And what would happen to me?

Stanley's eyes weren't dead like his henchmen. Clearly human, he still walked amongst the dead as if he was one of them, flanked by the Shadow Fabric. There was some crazy objective to this. The bastard wanted to bring the primordial darkness back into the world. Just as Victor had said.

Victor dead. Natalie, too. Isidore, alive and shrouded in so much shadow. And there I was, also restrained. The frustration in my chest was as tight as the shadows binding me.

Stanley regarded Natalie's gnarled fingers laying across the folds of her uniform, and a smirk tugged at his mouth.

The dead girl's spindly digits twitched and parted slightly. A darkness oozed and slipped from the twisted confines of those skeletal hands and ballooned. Its surface shimmered like a diesel spill. Pulsing, it rose up and shot sideways into the mass of Shadow Fabric.

My eyes watered as bile burned my throat without escape.

As the bulbous portion of shadow joined the main bulk of the Fabric, Stanley nodded to the necromeleons and they thrust Mick and Pam onto Natalie's dusty remains. A plume of decay puffed into the air, and undiluted horror flashed across the pair's faces.

The Hourglass sand had almost run out, now piled in the lower bulb in a brilliant white mound. Remembering what Victor had said about the use of the Hourglass, I was relieved there were no black grains. There had to be a few black ones in there, surely. No one was perfect, but what of my mysterious past? God only knew what I'd got up to before this life. Before this madness. If this thing could be trusted, then my past was free of any crime. Good to know.

Stanley stood overseeing the beginnings of Mick and Pam's stitching. The shadows binding them had now left their faces and hands, sliding from the pair as they had when Natalie became a stitcher.

Natalie: I recalled her questions about the classical concert and whether I needed a date. This had been the morning after I witnessed Victor stab his brother, when I first laid eyes on the Shadow Fabric. No surprise I hadn't acted on Natalie's not-too-subtle flirt.

My eyes wandered to Isidore. The shadows had almost entirely cocooned her like a sleeping bag. I guessed she'd put up a massive struggle. Quite an impressive kick she'd given me. But how was I to get out of this? I could only watch as the sand tumbled into the lower bulb. There were only a few minutes remaining, and I closed my eyes. In my head, I heard an angry rush of blood.

Stanley loomed over the stitchers.

"In your own time," he said to them. Both now held their hands together and sat crossed-legged, rocking their heads back and forth.

Isidore looked at me, and perhaps she nodded. Did she know I hadn't been myself, that somehow I'd acted like a puppet?

Stanley then bounded across the studio, his eyes focussed on me. The top bulb of the Hourglass was now empty. With delicacy, he detached it from my unresponsive hand.

"Time to play," he said. When the small compartment at the base of the Hourglass slid open, he froze. His eyes widened.

The deadness in my arm was absolute. I tried to move my hand. Nothing. I glared at the bastard who stood before me. He clutched the Hourglass in one hand and my shadowleaf in the other.

"This," he said, "is useless to stitch."

The leaf was white.

He wiggled it between his finger and thumb, close to my face. I wrestled beneath the heavy hands of the necromeleon behind me and grunted into my mouthful of shadow.

"I thought as much." Stanley threw the leaf onto the floor.

My dead friend gripped my shoulders and yanked me to my feet. Having been separated from the Hourglass, the leather strap swung from my wrist. It slapped my leg. I flexed my fingers as sensation returned. I wanted to hurl myself at Stanley even though my legs were untrustworthy. Dizziness burrowed into my brain, only the necromeleon's hold kept me steady.

"No matter," Stanley said. "I still have this one." From his jacket, he pulled out a dark grey shadowleaf.

The way he held it suggested an importance, yet I puzzled how he—clearly not in any way dead—was able to hold it without becoming a stitcher. Stanley was ahead of us in this dangerous game. This guy had control. And I was certain he intended to make me stitch.

Natalie had stitched. Her remains not far from me. The poor girl had crumbled into dust and bone shards. So too had Mick and Pam.

Stanley strolled past Polly, ignoring her—I'd forgotten she was there. She appeared unconscious, bound by shadows in a similar way to how I had been. Stanley then came to Isidore, still encased in folds of shadow. Her nostrils flared with each breath.

I attempted a step forward, but the necromeleon's strength was incredible.

Stanley crouched and grinned into Isidore's face, showing her the shadowleaf. "Why else do you think he's being an arsehole?"

She threw me a desperate glance and my heart tumbled into my stomach. I had to get us out of this. I could, surely? After all, I was no longer bound and strapped to the chair. I licked my lips. I didn't have any shadows stuffed in my mouth. How had I not noticed being released? My throat was dry and words failed me. I'm not sure what I tried to say, no doubt a stream of obscenities were well overdue.

Stanley still held the dark shadowleaf between thumb and forefinger, and he appeared to rub it. He wore a smirk I needed to smash in. My fingers curled into fists and heat charged through me. I had to do something.

During the time I'd been standing there, one of the other necromeleons had detached the leather strap from my arm. Again, how could I possibly not have felt it? Perhaps it was due to the numbness.

Isidore's blonde curls obscured most of her face. Stanley hunched over her. He resembled a hungry predator preparing to bite its victim. He still held the Hourglass.

I stepped towards them, the necromeleon behind me having released me. Stanley stood up. I attempted another step and failed, my legs felt glued to the floor. My dry lips parted and still nothing came from them.

Then my legs moved. Only I wasn't the one commanding them. I took two steps forward and stopped. I glared at Stanley's amusement as he thumbed the shadowleaf.

"Confused?" He approached me, continuing to run his fingertips over the shadowleaf. "I knew I had the right Leonard Howard."

I puzzled over the way he said the surname, Howard. Who was he? It wasn't me, was it? My surname was Fox. What was Stanley talking about?

"You can only have one shadowleaf." He waved the grey one in my face. "And the white one proved that."

I frowned.

Stanley's face changed. His jaw set firmer and his eyes flashed at me, still a brilliant blue. Something shifted behind them. "What a waste of time that was."

Leo Fox, Leo Howard? Leonard Howard. What was this? Although Amy couldn't move—

Amy? What? I meant Isidore. That was her name. Not Amy. *Isidore*. Although she couldn't move because of the shadows wrapped around her, I was unable to move due to something else entirely. Some other power outside my control.

Who was Amy?

My hands remained fists and my feet again took me forward. I headed towards Isidore, and Stanley stepped aside. Frustration screamed in my head and I urged myself to stop walking. I didn't want to do this. I didn't know what I was going to do, although I knew one thing. That bastard Stanley had control over me. How was this possible?

I could feel my limbs, yet they weren't my own. I felt my bruised face, strangely disconnected. Stanley was the puppeteer. The key to which he held in his hand, the dark grey—nearly black—shadowleaf. I guessed it was mine. If my shadowleaf was that colour, then it opened up even more questions. And what about my white one? Suddenly, I had no desire to learn of my past. Was my past as dark as that leaf? Who had I been? My stomach somersaulted and my mind twisted with it. Was I a criminal like those under the House? Should I now be bashing my fists against a cell wall? Perhaps I should be in the morgue.

And then I realised I'd been one of Goodwin's experiments. That's what I was to him. No longer Leo Howard, criminal, I was Leo Fox. This was my new life. And here I was, wrapped in this madness without any control over my actions. I pushed aside thoughts of what my crime might have been.

Inside, I raged. Outside, I obeyed.

Fully under Stanley's control, I yanked Isidore to her feet. Her head snapped backwards—I hated myself for that. I vowed then to save her. To save us all, and further still, to save the world. In any other situation, I would've laughed, yet right there, under the twisted guidance of a man cloaked in humankind's evil, this was my word. And even if I didn't know much of my past, I knew I was good to my word. Never had I gone against a promise, and as I dragged Isidore's shadow-shrouded body to the chair, I desired nothing more than to fulfil that promise. Somehow, I would fix this. I would save this girl I now thrust into the seat.

Although she kicked out at me from beneath her shadows, Isidore's eyes reflected a resigned understanding. She knew I wasn't behind my actions, and for that, I was thankful. There was desperation there also. And a pleading. If telepathy was at all possible—and who's to say it wasn't in light of recent occurrences—I wanted her to hear my promise. I gave her my word.

Most of the shadows slipped from her body, leaving only her arms, ankles, and mouth covered. I knew what came next, and as a necromeleon attached the leather strap to her wrist, I took the Hourglass from Stanley's outstretched hand.

He nodded.

I forced Isidore's fingers into the Hourglass straps and pulled tight the buckles. With a flick of my wrist, I upended it and the white sands flowed.

I doubted even my eyes held any of the apologetic fear I hoped Isidore could read as I stepped away, leaving the necromeleon with her. His calloused hands clamped her shoulders and she slumped into herself.

"Now get me more stitchers," Stanley said into my ear.

* * *

Being commanded remotely was one hell of an experience, not unlike hypnosis. To my knowledge, I had never been hypnotised. The difference here was that I remained lucid throughout. I felt everything and helplessly obeyed Stanley's instruction to find more stitchers. Every minute under that bastard's control, I gazed out of my own head, entirely at his command. I guessed it would last throughout the hour while Isidore's sand counted out the time.

Flanked by two necromeleon henchmen, their impressive bulks hung in my peripheral, all dark suits and death. Those guys were no doubt menacing when alive, let alone now that they were dead—God only knew where Stanley found them.

My feet took me from the studio and into the walkway.

How long would I last? How long before Stanley got bored playing with me? I wanted to hit something, someone. To hit out at the pair of dead men walking beside me. And my rage seethed, unable to do a thing.

The emptiness added to our shuffled echoes as the three of us headed alongside the gym, past the beauty rooms, and across the thankfully empty foyer. Dean was nowhere in sight, and I guessed he was at the marquee, given the classical concert would begin in a couple of hours. Sounds from the restaurant and bar echoed towards us. Clearly, that was where most of the life was right now. Life…death. Such a thin line between them.

We stomped up the staircase and headed for the suites. Stitchers. Stanley had ordered us to collect more stitchers. I guessed we'd collect a few individuals, not yet grabbing a crowd. How many were in the bar? What about the restaurant? And how many seats were in the marquee? The potential there was too much to grasp.

My legs took me upwards onto the first floor landing. I didn't want to find anyone. I hoped each resident was out for the evening. I wanted everyone to have left the House and driven into the neighbouring village in search of a restaurant, or for a different form of entertainment. I knew otherwise. Rooms two through twelve were no doubt occupied. It was a busy time of year, regardless of the House hosting a concert. As the softness of the carpet silenced my feet, I prayed there wasn't anyone getting themselves ready for the evening.

The Bach Suite was first, and as we came to stand before it, one of the necromeleons pulled out an all-access keycard. I recognised it by the luminous green sticker and the smiling face drawn on it: Suzy's. Where was she now? I hoped she had the early shift and was home. Safe. Away from this madness.

After the lock mechanism clicked open, without pause the dead men bundled in. I waited at the threshold, standing guard. My head moved to the left, taking in the short landing and four steps downwards, then it moved to the right. Another hallway, containing six more rooms, and beyond these, another staircase curled upward.

My ears strained as did my eyes; no one around. It pained me to think what I'd be made to do should anyone come. Indeed, if—when—we found someone in one of the suites. All I heard was the necromeleons searching Bach.

Moments later they filed out, to my relief, empty-handed. My hand reached for the door handle, grasped it, and pulled the door closed. Seeing my hand obey a command I had not given was like watching myself in a vivid dream.

A few paces down the hall, we came to the next room: the Handel Suite. The necromeleons reached it before me, and when the door opened on silent hinges, they stepped aside, allowing me passage. I walked into the small entrance hall. The room beyond was fairly large. Sunlight burst across the modest lounge and fell into the inviting cushions of a sofa.

Soft noises came to me from behind the bedroom door slightly ajar.

I strolled forward, leaving the dead men at the threshold. The closer I got, the more certain of those noises I became: a gentle rhythmic movement with the undertones of heavy breathing.

CHAPTER 34

Suzy's head snapped up, her eyes wide. Her breasts bounced between the folds of her uniform. Beneath her in a mess of pillows, Joe's eyes flared and his mouth gaped. In any other circumstance, I would have politely closed the door and left them. It must've been an act of snatched passion, given neither had fully removed their clothes.

The girl leapt from the bed, sending the covers to the floor, and pulled down her skirt. The barman yanked up his trousers and coughed, unsure where to look.

"Leo—" Suzy buttoned her top. She frowned at me. Besides getting caught in such an act, she recognised something wasn't right. I guessed it was how I stood unmoving, the way I must have come across as a sleepwalker.

Joe remained silent as he buckled himself. His face red, his movements frantic. His scowl said it all.

I said nothing. I wanted to apologise for walking in on them. I wanted to tell them what was happening downstairs. Emotions clawed behind my face, unable to break through. My feet moved towards them. I didn't want to do this. Another footstep followed, then I stopped. My necromeleon companions came to flank me like bodyguards.

Joe stuffed his shirt into his trousers and his expression switched to dismay. "What's going on?"

By this time, Suzy had composed herself, but her cheeks still glowed. She squinted when she took in the two dead men. A single crease broke across her forehead and her jaw dropped.

In a displacement of light, the necromeleon's faces shifted into a knot of shadows, wreathed in grey phantoms as traces of the Fabric oozed from their eyes and mouths. Two streams of liquid darkness shot into the awestruck faces of Joe and Suzy. They had no time to react as the black lumps wrapped around their heads, leaving only their noses free. Joe staggered and smacked his shin into the bed, while Suzy dropped to her knees and fell against the dressing table.

Their screams were muffled behind masks of shadow.

I yanked Suzy upright. Her legs were unresponsive as though she had lost consciousness. No, it wasn't that. She immediately kicked out, arms flailing. Her hands bunched into fists and pummelled my chest. It was short-lived as the shadows around her head leaked downwards. A few tendrils wriggled over her shoulders towards her legs. Each shadow now bound her firmly.

I wanted to scream, to apologise as I dragged her thrashing body out of the bedroom, leaving her bra behind us—it was frilly, flowery. Somewhere in the corner of my eye, I saw one of my dead companions do the same with Joe.

We threw them onto the sofa where more shadows collected, enveloping them. I assumed we'd keep the pair there for later. The Handel Suite would become our storeroom.

With my dead friends, I went from room to room, from the Tchaikovsky Suite to the Rachmaninov Suite, to Strauss, Beethoven and Haydn, then up to Mozart and Grieg, Boccherini and finally Wagner. We didn't go into Goodwin's room, the Holst Suite, because it would've been empty. The man was still somewhere beneath the House—dead or alive, I simply didn't know.

The horror of what I was doing twisted in my core, tangled with frustration. I hated myself for my actions, and I hated Stanley for his control over me. Whoever I had been before this, whatever was in my previous life, I didn't want it in my new life. Maybe I'd been bad once—perhaps I still was—and now I had a role to play in Stanley's game.

We collected more potential stitchers, yanking them from their business, wrapping the darkness around their startled expressions. Some of those faces I recognised, others I didn't. Some put up a fight, others didn't get the chance. The three of us would steal into each room like kidnappers and capture the occupants. Two rooms were empty, and in total, we collected seventeen stitchers for Stanley's screwed-up game. Seventeen people who would soon stitch, to become nothing more than empty husks. Drained of life.

As I dragged another person along the hallway and threw them into the Handel Suite with the other moaning bodies, the voice in my head screamed denial. I knew it was another potential death on my hands.

I was with Death, and I could do nothing about it.

* * *

I had always pictured memories as compartments in my head, little cabinets and drawers accessible by the grasp of a mental hand, opening on silent runners to reveal files and folders of varying widths, colours, and condition—much like filing cabinet divisions. Not like an office, no. Nothing so impersonal nor cold. Nothing so uninviting.

My bank of cabinets were locked up. And somewhere some bastard had the keys. I could see the blank-faced compartments, all of them, yet was unable to access the damn things. Perhaps one contained a list of my crimes. Was I a bank robber, a murderer, a rapist? Was I imprisoned for grievous bodily harm? Who was Amy? Had it been domestic abuse against her?

This was worse than not knowing anything about my past. A sickness churned in my stomach.

Under Stanley's control, as my feet took me through the House herding potential stitchers, it was as if the occasional sheet of memory would poke out of a drawer. The shadows leaking into an odd compartment, pulling out a random memory.

It happened first when I dealt with the father and daughter. When I'd first seen them a few days before, back when I met yoga instructor, come nurse, come scientist Katrina for the first time, the teenager came across as a spoiled and bored young girl. And the father, he simply looked troubled.

As we let ourselves into the Grieg Suite, the girl wasn't around. The father sat beside the window reading a newspaper. He gave us a slow, quizzical look.

I ran at him.

The man opened his mouth to speak and I punched him. With a sound like a heavy book dropped on a leather sofa, the contact between fist and face surprised me, let alone him. Blood dribbled from his split lip and he dropped the newspaper. He groaned and cupped his hands to the gushing wound, his eyes tiny.

I dragged him towards me—the man was heavy. His bloody hands slapped uselessly at my arms.

In a wet voice, he said, "What the hell is this?" A redness coated his teeth as though he'd scoffed strawberries.

I wondered how many times in my unremembered past had I inflicted such pain on others.

As I held him, an image of someone else scratched across my eyes like a phantom, shimmering behind reality. For a moment, I saw the thuggish looks of a much younger man with a burning aggression, not like this father whose face oozed blood and terror. The ghost—was that it?—was like a glimpse beneath the mask of Man. Yet it wasn't that simple, this was something else.

There I stood, my hands acting not of my own command, holding a terrified man, while another was there in the same place. Two images overlapped one another. One existing, the other not at all. The face—an incorporeal flutter—was from a memory. One of my memories long before my accident. The crash…the red car…was it real? Never before had I reason to doubt. And if it never happened, then someone please explain my knee injury?

This was the first glimpse I had of those leaking cabinets in my bank of memories, and as quickly as the image came it vanished, leaving me to question if I'd seen it in the first instance.

My thoughts tumbled as my limbs obeyed Stanley's commands.

The father was shouting something and I forced myself to tune in. "Emily! Emily, get out of here!" Blood leapt from between puffed lips. "Emily!"

One of the necromeleons darted into the bedroom, while the other remained beside me. I heard a gurgle from his direction like a rumble low in the belly—it wasn't hunger the necromeleon experienced. He stepped forward, a streamer of shadow burst from between his dead lips and fired into the father's face.

I held the poor man. The blackness clamped around his head like a wet towel, leaving only his nose visible. Suffocating moans escaped him, and his nostrils flared as panic escalated.

Behind me, I heard his daughter being dragged into the room. I pulled the man sideways and on stumbling legs, he came with me. There was Emily. She wore a gag of shadow, her eyes a petrified daze. I heard the beat of music from her earphones. The late afternoon sunshine filled her glistening eyes, which created another phantom for me, another blast of a ghostly image. Snatched from a forgotten past was Amy, with eyes brimmed with fear and tears. Amy. Her brown hair clumped to the wound on her head, her lips swollen and saying my name, over and over.

Amy. Who was Amy?

And again, as swiftly as it came, the image—that memory—vanished. I saw a scared teenager, wires coiling from her ears, shoved along the hall by a dead man.

I followed, hauling the father with me. His hands were now restrained by more shadows. My head thumped almost in time with the music. The other necromeleon closed the door behind us and we headed to the Handel Suite.

These two were the last to join the nest we'd created there.

Soon, I bundled Dean, my final captive, into the studio. On entering, he tripped and staggered, and I kicked the back of his legs. He dropped to his knees.

The studio had darkened, having little to do with the late afternoon. In the centre of the gloom, like the hub he indeed was, Stanley stood with his chin firm. He still held my shadowleaf between thumb and forefinger. I wanted to knock the thing from his hand, but of course, I was incapable.

Isidore was still attached to the Hourglass. The sand had nearly run out, and a heap of dark grey had collected in the lower bulb. If Annabel had her way, eventually it would have been black. As Isidore had admitted, she'd started with small crimes and it escalated into everything short of murder.

Not long after I entered the studio, the two necromeleons came in with more captives: Joe and Suzy. They passed me, and reaching Stanley, a loop of shadow tripped the pair and they fell.

Stanley's lips curled into a smirk and I wanted to leap at him. To punch the bastard for being my puppeteer. Evil, evil bastard. The box of spilled shadowleaves was at his feet, the black squares waiting to be stitched, waiting to become part of the Shadow Fabric. Behind him, it quivered as if a breeze stirred its surface.

"Make yourself useful." Stanley threw a shadowleaf into Dean's lap. It was my original, dark grey one.

My legs buckled, both knees smacking the floor. An agonising flare lanced up my thighs, more so in my already damaged knee, and I cried out. I had bumped into Dean who had been attempting to sit up. His eyes, questioning, fixed on mine.

I focused on my surroundings, my head no longer clogged, and I vomited. Its bitter taste was welcoming, like a purge of the system dispelling all traces of Stanley's control. Its stink burning my nostrils, it was a surprise no shadows had come up.

Dean's shadowy restraints slipped away as curiosity overwhelmed him, inspecting the shadowleaf he held. His eyes flicked in my direction.

My head swam, and although I once again had control over myself, I couldn't move. The leaf in Dean's hand was mine, I knew this. How else was Stanley able to control me? Earlier, he held not the white shadowleaf which came from the Hourglass, but a dark grey one. Victor had said we all are sinners regardless of our good intent. Was Dean's cursory glance as he held my leaf an acknowledgment of my sins? Was it even possible? That in itself led to further questions…and where *did* Stanley get this leaf from?

Huddled and shivering, not far from the arrogant stance of my puppeteer, I glared at the man. He was the evil one here. Not me. It hadn't been long ago my shadowleaf came out white. That had to mean something. The extraction was from my new life, not a reflection of my past. This was my new life.

The three dead henchmen walked past me and out of the studio, to collect more stitchers I guessed. I sat up ready to stop Dean from stitching.

Stanley laughed.

"You—" I began to say, when a portion of Fabric detached itself from the roiling mass and clamped shut my mouth.

Stanley ignored me and crouched before the pile of leaves. Straightening up, he tossed another leaf at Dean. Now having two, one of which was mine, the manager's confusion vanished. His face relaxed. From my collection of captured people, visitors, and employees alike, Dean was the first to stitch.

With wide eyes, Joe and Suzy froze, watching Dean begin. His face serene, so peaceful as the first signs of his life force ebbed. At some point, while I stared helplessly, Stanley threw a couple of leaves to the other employees. Their faces slackened as the stitching took hold.

Regaining my strength, I pushed myself up. No longer was I wrapped in nausea, no longer was I to sit and let this happen. I had to stop this.

And more shadows came. They whipped around my wrists, fastened my ankles, and once again fully restrained me. Gagged and bound, I uselessly struggled. The hate, the terror, the frustration raged.

Isidore had an expression which I suspected mirrored my own, and I was aware of my constant grunts. Her sand had run out.

"Ah." Stanley turned towards her. He wasted no time undoing the Hourglass straps and removing her shadowleaf.

Isidore's eyes were fierce and glistened.

"This is more like it," he said. Her dark leaf flapped between his thumb and forefinger. "Leo, your white one was useless."

Dean had now shrivelled into his suit. His grey skull still had wisps of hair attached to it, and it lolled. Joe and Suzy were rapidly losing colour. They rocked, hands held as if in prayer. Their black eyes charged in sunken sockets.

Steadily, they stitch-stitch-stitched. I watched, helpless as ever.

Stanley cupped Isidore's leaf in his palm. "Leo, this is lighter than your original one." He dropped it onto the pile in the middle of the room. He headed for Polly. I'd forgotten about her, sitting motionless. When he reached her, he strapped her to the Hourglass. Already the sand had lightened from black to white. Purer. Free of sin.

Behind and above me, something creaked. I strained against the shadows. My neck clicked as the door opened a fraction. There stood Victor. He was ravaged, beaten. Blood caked his hair. Clothes torn.

I moaned, slumping into myself.

Both his eyes were sunken and dark. Black...filled with shadow.

CHAPTER 35

And like this to infinity

Seeing the Shadow Fabric and experiencing its overwhelming presence, there was no doubt its evil suggested more than any childhood fear. Not like the time as a kid when we're afraid of a coat hanging on the wardrobe door appearing as a monster's silhouette. Not like the harmless, silent spectre in the shadows of a corner, familiar to us during the day, and come night, it morphs into a chasm of unknown depths. It's the very substance which belongs at the core of every evil since the beginning of time.

There can be no doubt the Fabric was fuelled by an evil born from the primordial darkness long before light came into being.

And when the man I'd come to know, no matter how short a time it'd been, looked back at me with eyes of an impenetrable darkness, I physically felt the light dimming. Victor had brought me there, not for his ills or selfish desires, for I had willingly joined his quest against the darkness. No, I had accepted my hand in this, and for all my courage and determination, I could only accept my fate. Our fate.

We were fucked.

The Shadow Fabric swelled, pulsed, and expanded against the far wall of the studio, growing as more stitchers stitched. By now, I guessed the Handel Suite must've been empty. I hadn't been counting.

The twitches of father and daughter—Emily, her name was Emily—flickered in the corner of my eye. Around them were too many shrivelled bodies to count. People I'd known, people I'd spoken to, all now little more than heaped bones and dusty clothes.

With resignation, I shrank into myself, not even wanting to look at Isidore to whom I'd vowed to save. Save the world, no less. All the while the Fabric did precisely the opposite.

I glimpsed the Witchblade. It glinted where Victor stood in the doorway holding it. The blade shone around him, even in the failing light, the athame reflected a reminder that there *was* light. There will always be light…and it also reflected hope.

There will always be hope.

He clutched the Witchblade to his chest. The last time I saw Victor, pressed to the floor by the bulk of necromeleons, I thought he was a dead man. Indeed, moments ago, I suspected he was a necromeleon. His eyes were buried not in shadow, but blood. Mostly his own, I guessed, and perhaps Katrina's, and that of the dead men who'd brought him down.

He acknowledged me only briefly as he lifted the blade. One of his eyes was bad, nearly swollen shut, while the other was bloodshot. No shadows.

He lived. He was of the living, and not of the living dead.

With bitter shadows clogging my mouth, I breathed heavily through my nose. God knew how Isidore felt—she'd been gagged the whole time.

Polly sat motionless, with her hand attached to the Hourglass. I had no idea how much sand had run into the lower bulb—it hadn't been long since Stanley inverted it. As I tried to peek, the shadows surrounding Polly's legs bubbled around her. They clawed up the chair and encased the Hourglass.

Stanley stood over the shells of Emily and her father, their remains a stark contrast between greyed limbs and coloured clothes. The newly stitched pieces of Fabric slithered from the bodies, snaking and lifting. Each throbbed and headed for the darkness which encompassed almost half the studio.

Although hope had returned at seeing Victor alive, the presence of the Shadow Fabric overwhelmed me. Nausea came in waves and I wanted to vomit. My head pounded. The evil spoke to me, its raw power rushing through every fibre of my being. It charged through the shadows in my mouth, almost like an electric current. I tasted copper. Blood perhaps.

I guessed it was only me who saw Victor. Any moment now, Stanley would feel the light from the Witchblade, if not see it.

With the Fabric's presence draining the light from the room, the majority of its bulk obscured the light from the windows. It blocked out some of the ceiling lights.

In contrast, the Witchblade spread liquid gold across the wooden floor. It had to be a distraction to someone. Why hadn't Stanley already seen it? Or the necromeleons? As the glow oozed into the room, one of them surely must see it. Victor now shone like a beacon amongst the darkness. Why couldn't anyone else see this? And what about the mirrors and the gleaming reflection?

Isidore's eyes had widened above the binding shadow. Had she seen Victor? There was hope in her expression and she glanced at me. The light shone from her skin. Her hair appeared on fire. She was closer than anyone else. Still, why hadn't anyone else seen it? Surely they felt it, too? It looked like it should be hot, generating warmth like a campfire.

Victor came fully into the room. Each furtive step he took forced light into the darkness. The shadows on the opposite side of the room remained where they were, while the three necromeleons and Stanley stood vigil over another stitcher, an older woman I'd snatched from the Grieg Suite. I guess she must've been in her early 50s. She'd been on the telephone at the time, with her back to me, and she'd turned at the sound of my footsteps. I yanked the phone from her and slammed it in its cradle. It was strange to think I'd been under Stanley's control earlier, and I hated myself for it.

As this woman stitched, she had greyed more than her actual years.

Victor made it further into the room, his pace deliberate as the golden hue spread around him. Angelic, that's what it was. He appeared like an angel—albeit one in a bloodied suit, and not wearing socks—striding into the path of evil with the confidence of a man blessed with light. The Witchblade drenched his entire body in a golden fog, pressing back the darkness.

Stanley still hadn't noticed his approach, and Victor stood behind him. The light bleached everything. Bathed in a solar glare, the gently rocking woman continued to stitch.

One of the necromeleons moved and scanned the room. His black orbs lingered on me for a moment, then on Isidore. Then on Polly. And finally back to the stitcher. He hadn't seen Victor. The dead man's gaze had gone straight through him. The man was right there. Any moment, I expected someone to see him in a mirror from one angle or another.

The golden glow now lit the entire studio. It swallowed the darkness and left only the Fabric to shimmer and bulge as it always had done—still growing with every newly stitched piece—yet not recoiling, or even hinting at retreating from the light.

Stanley shifted and the golden glare passed across his face. The light reflected in his eyes, yet he still didn't react. He was oblivious to it. I didn't know how it was possible for Victor's presence in the room to be shielded by the Witchblade. It shrouded him in a safe light, a light which itself was equally invisible.

Victor, remaining invisible, walked around Stanley, who still observed the twitching woman. No doubt his actions were just, but I couldn't work out his intentions. Standing before his brother, emotion hard to read in a face obscured by swollen eyes and so much blood, Victor raised the Witchblade. There was no way a necromeleon could brandish that blade like he did. I doubted the dead would even touch it. The living dead, and Stanley, couldn't see it, nor were they aware of the man standing directly in front of them.

The light blasted from the blade as Victor brought it to arm's length.

Already that light saturated the room. It pushed back the darkness and gave the impression Victor was made of gold. Like a statue gripping a dagger, shining on a pedestal for all to see. Only it was Isidore and I who saw him, no one else.

As the athame arced up, fire crackled around the blade, spitting orange and yellow streamers. Delicate at first, then thickened and spread outwards. Victor's jaw squared and his teeth clenched. The pool of light shifted from yellow to white, brightening with each passing moment. The way he held the blade high, with one downward swipe, it would spear Stanley's head.

Sniffing the air, taking reassurance from the hint of ozone charging the atmosphere, I waited for him to kill the bastard.

Victor's lips moved. At first, I assumed he recited some type of ritualistic text, some passage with which to stop this madness. I was wrong. His lips formed the words *God help me*, over and over.

Tiny flames showered both of them like a sparkler on Guy Fawkes Night, tumbling over their shoulders. Still oblivious to it, Stanley watched the stitcher at his feet, as were the three necromeleons beside him. They didn't move, obediently standing beside their master.

The Shadow Fabric moved. It shifted sideways, enough to make it obvious. I wanted to warn Victor, yet couldn't, gagged as I was. I had no idea of Victor's intentions, the way he held the Witchblade above his head. Would he slam it down into his brother's head? Would he really stab him again? Last time had been a cruel moment where the Fabric itself had pulled Victor's hand forward into a fatal strike. This was different.

In a sudden jerk, Stanley snapped his head back and roared. It drove into my brain, made my teeth ache, and froze my spine.

The necromeleons still hadn't moved.

Victor remained where he was. His lips now still, jaw set. The Witchblade unmoving in the air with the flames showering him and his brother.

Stanley screeched like I'd imagine a pterodactyl would when swooping through a prehistoric sky. The pitch rose. I shook my head, bucked, and squirmed beneath the restraining shadows. From the corner of my eye—unable to take my eyes off the spectacle across the studio—Isidore did the same.

Victor held his ground as Stanley's mouth issued that inhuman scream. The man's jaws opened wide, spreading his lips further apart. His tongue squirmed, its colour shifting from fleshy pink to a grey pallor, then blackening, even under the glow of the Witchblade. Stanley's skin darkened as traceries of veins surged beneath. His hair became blacker. And his eyes…their whites shifted to black as though a switch had been flicked. Darkness oozed from them. It dripped over his long cheekbones and curled down the elongated face.

And still the scream rattled my brain. It was thankfully losing its pitch, lessening enough to take the edge off.

Stanley's dark flesh altered: from where the tongue protruded, the lips peeled back. Like some obscene blossom, the skin curled and split without any spray of blood. The black tongue flicked sideways and melded into the grey skin as his face continued to stretch. His head warped, defying human anatomy. No longer did his hair resemble hair, nor did his face resemble a face.

The light of the Witchblade poured over the two men, and a flurry of sparks tumbled about them.

The scream dwindled.

Stanley's clothes had lost their colour, their sharpness. They *blurred*. The fabric of his clothes shifted out of focus, diluting as though sidestepping reality. His dark skin melted to become less than human, nothing more than a lumpy, man-sized blob. No longer a man. Once, yes, Stanley had been Stanley, back at his house when I'd first met him. That had been the last time anyone had seen him alive. Victor had, after all, killed his brother—albeit under the guidance of the Shadow Fabric.

I guessed we knew whose corpse it was back at Stanley's house. So, this wasn't Stanley after all. But what was happening to him? An entity existed within the Shadow Fabric as Victor had suggested. He'd said that once the Fabric became strong enough, an entity would begin its haunt.

Sweat spotted my forehead.

The Fabric remained where it was, bulging and heaving. It hung as a backdrop to the spectacle like black curtains, a transient shroud of evil. It shivered in a coruscation of black folds and impenetrable darkness.

The entity, haunting via the Shadow Fabric, had taken on human form to walk on our plane of existence, the world in which we live oblivious—up until now—to the terror behind the light. Like an actor taking on a role, indeed on a stage upon which stood humankind, the entity had walked among us. In doing so, it had put into motion its plan for our undoing. It wanted, as Victor once explained, to return the universe to the primordial darkness that once was, to pull the curtain closed one final time.

The Fabric quivered, charged by newly stitched evils, and pulsed behind the ghostly form of the entity.

Flames spat from the Witchblade and bounced off Victor's shoulders as he glared at the entity. The thing had neither shape nor form, only a greyness, spreading up and outwards—a gurgling mass of nothing. Like an old photograph of a ghost where a grey spectral image floats through the air, insubstantial, yet holding an eerie presence, smothering the image. Hanging in front of Victor, trailing wisps of dark energies, it stole my focus. I had no choice, I had to see it. I tried to look away, and immediately my attention snapped back as though on a rubber band. Grotesque and incredible, it was mesmerising.

The three necromeleons remained motionless while the last stitcher's body fell. A chalky plume puffed outwards as though its final breath escaped. The shell collapsed under folds of clothes.

My eyes returned to the entity. Its presence seethed against the bubbling darkness at Victor's feet. He yelled and swiped the Witchblade downwards, fire tracing the air. Flames erupted as the blade tore into the entity's dark body. Its scream filled the room, and I would have sworn my ears bled. Flames licked Victor's gloves. Apparently not burning him, the damage was only to the entity.

I thrashed against the restraining shadows, my frustration groaning into the gag…and the entity's shrill cry tore through my brain.

The quivering mass pulled away from Victor. The Witchblade dislodged and created more flames. The pair separated and circled one another like boxers in a ring. On one side, Victor thrust the glowing blade, fire crackling; while on the other, the entity shimmered beneath crawling flames.

Victor's chest heaved. His jaw set as he waved the Witchblade. Fire splashed the entity. With each move of his hand, Victor stepped forward. The bulk of greyness shifted backwards. It squirmed, heading towards the Shadow Fabric, perhaps attempting escape. Would the Fabric then vanish? I could only hope.

With a series of sudden flicks and jabs, Victor created a pattern of fire. It clung to the air. A collection of symbols with intricate curves and lines. It seemed to be enough to hold the entity there. Its spectral shivering framed against a backdrop of absolute darkness, it froze, briefly shrinking, hunching almost—only to remain still, caged by the fiery script. The symbols swirled and sent traceries of spitting flame in all directions. They flared into white arcs to dissolve like shooting stars.

No longer did the entity scream. I heard only the sound of crackling flames.

The necromeleons still hadn't moved, as though the three were tailor mannequins, just for show. Anytime now, I expected them to jerk into life.

The Shadow Fabric hadn't moved since Victor had cornered the entity against it. Its sharp edges no longer a roiling mass of blackness, it now hung motionless. Watching Victor stand behind those flaming symbols was like nothing I'd ever seen...at least from what I could remember.

With another combination of intricate hand gestures, Victor scribbled more symbols around the entity. The thing jerked backwards, and its incorporeal being clung to the Fabric. Like mixing paint, the contact between black and grey churned, bubbled, and blended. The grey diluted instantly.

The transition as the entity shifted into the Shadow Fabric left no visible trace. Relief flushed through me.

Victor almost danced as he scrawled another set of symbols around the clinging mass of shadow. The Fabric's presence was still incredible, yet strangely subdued. I strained against the shadows which held me, hoping that securing the Fabric as he had, the rest of the shadows in the room would release us.

No chance, they still held me firm. Isidore's eyes fixed on mine.

Victor lowered the Witchblade.

"Get me out of here!" I screamed into my gag.

CHAPTER 36

The flaming symbols still spat delicate streamers in the air. Victor stepped away from the Shadow Fabric and walked across the studio towards me. His wrinkled forehead relaxed. One eye half-closed, glistening red, the rest of his face was blood and bruises. Finally, I was going to be released.

The three necromeleons rushed him.

He leapt sideways, brought up the Witchblade in an arc of fire, and severed the dead as they ran into it. All three henchman came to a sudden stop and their bodies tore into fiery chunks. Each piece hit the floor with a sickening slap. A few smouldering ribbons of suit and shirt fluttered in the air. An arm twitched, the fire already dying as it burned away the last traces of shadow. With flames trickling over its surface, a dark tentacle flicked outwards to escape its crackling confines. Victor kicked it towards a flaming torso and it was consumed.

Silence.

He wasn't idle. He released us with the Witchblade. Isidore was first, careful as he pried out the packed shadows in her mouth. She grimaced, spat, and rubbed her tongue over her teeth. Then he cut me free. The shadows fell away and dissolved, not even attempting to return to the Fabric. I assumed that due to its confinement, the Fabric's hold over such lesser shadows had weakened. Victor stabbed at several lingering patches and they burned quickly.

As I straightened—my knee killing me—Isidore came to stand at my side. Her eyes roamed my face, and with the back of a hand, she stroked my cheek. It was where she'd kicked me. There was an angry bruise on the side of her face. It's a curious thing, hating yourself for a physical act you had no control over. She offered me a smile and I took it. And her, mine. I understood, so did she.

Victor crouched beside Polly, a pained expression on his face.

"Polly." He grabbed her hand, the one which wasn't attached to the Hourglass. She didn't respond. The blind woman's eyes were closed and her chest gently rose and fell. It was as if she'd passed out. Only the top of the Hourglass was visible and revealed plenty of white sand remaining. The lower half was sheathed in shadow.

"I don't know what would happen if I released her in that state." Victor let go of her hand. It flopped to the side, palm up as though she begged. I wondered why she had passed out rather than remaining awake like when I was attached to the Hourglass.

"You can't just leave her," Isidore said.

The remains of the many stitchers lay at our feet, mounds of dust heaped about the floor. In places, bone shards protruded from chalky clothes. I felt dirty just looking at them.

"Victor." I walked towards him. "Surely—"

"No, Leo, we can't risk it." He stood and met me in the middle of the studio.

"What do we do now?" I asked, wanting to walk away. Wanting to ignore the revelations of my past. I'd been a criminal and had no idea what crimes I committed.

Victor took his time to answer, and when he spoke, his voice was soft.

"This is all a mess," he said. "Stanley. Katrina. Those people, the stitchers."

Isidore joined us. Her knuckles glowed against the black metal of her gun.

The Shadow Fabric remained behind the wall of fire, its edges sharp and unmoving. The black surface gleamed and reflected the occasional flame. Chunks of dead flesh littered the ground, resembling little more than volcanic rock or bits of coal. Several cauterised limbs lay around; my gaze didn't linger on those. And there were the remains of the stitchers... Natalie, not my fault. Dean, the Periwick manager, entirely my fault. As were all the others. My old life had leaked into my new life. I was no better than before.

"This is madness," I said.

My thoughts strayed towards my white shadowleaf. It proved I was pure again. Right?

Victor spoke, "The Fabric is held at bay. We're safe."

The Fabric, like a magnet, kept pulling my attention. Its thrall had lessened, yet it raged behind those intricate patterns. It was as if I could sense its frustration.

"Safe for now," Victor added, and groaned as he rubbed his neck. "The entity is back inside the Fabric. Locked within the darkness again. I don't know how long we can prevent its haunt. It will still fight, and seeing how the Fabric is so large, I have doubts the fire will contain it for much longer."

"We need to stop this thing." I glared at him. He gripped the Witchblade in bloody gloves.

"If it fights," Isidore said, "we fight."

I gritted my teeth. Looking at her gun, I wondered if I'd ever used one, whether I'd ever shot anyone. Maybe that was my crime.

She waved her gun towards the mass of Fabric. She had a weapon, not that bullets proved effective against the dead. Nor the shadows, for that matter. Victor had a better weapon— powerful and one with serious results—and there was me without any protection. Lame, standing between blade and bullets, empty handed. I straightened my back and puffed out my chest, and felt pathetic.

"That's all we can do," Victor said, eyeing the Fabric.

I grabbed my gloves from the floor, thinking of Lucas exploding into pieces. It was reassuring to pull the leather over my hands.

"Stanley and Polly once had a thing together," Victor said.

I frowned and flexed my fingers. "Really?"

"He was different. Kind of, but Polly loved him. Then, as always, Stanley would muck it up." He swallowed hard. "And then he really mucked it up."

"What happened? What did he do?" Whatever I'd been in my previous life, I hoped I wasn't on Stanley's level.

"What did he do to Polly? What did he do to make us all hate the vile, evil bastard?" His lips parted to say something. He dropped his gaze to Polly and he snapped his jaw shut as though whatever he'd been about to say would finally break him. In silence, he took steady steps towards the remains of the stitchers, and stopped at a metal box. There were several shadowleaves scattered about the floor. He dropped to a crouch. "Where did these come from?"

"Under the House," I said. "There's a lot more down there."

Victor's bloodshot eyes widened.

"A lot more," I added.

Isidore nodded.

Victor looked up at us and waved the Witchblade in front of him. Flames spread across the shadowleaves and they flared. As the rush of fire shrank, smoke curled from the shrivelled clumps that remained. The smell was like burning rubber. Putrid and lingering.

He coughed and said, "If each box contains shadowleaves, we've got to burn them. All of them."

"That thing," Isidore said, pointing at the Fabric, "was here before humans, right?"

Victor snapped his head in her direction. "Most entities were here before life, yes."

"Before there was light," I added.

"Before there was fire," Victor mumbled. "Come on."

"Where to?" I asked, hoping he'd say away from there, away from the House. But I knew the answer, I knew we couldn't leave. Not yet.

"I need a closer look at those boxes," he said, clutching the Witchblade to his chest.

"Don't you want to get cleaned up first?" I asked him. He looked awful.

"This is more important," he said as he walked away.

CHAPTER 37

"The concert, Victor," I said, checking my watch. Its second hand stuttered around the dial: *tick, tick, tick...* "It starts in about an hour. We need to get those people out."

We entered the foyer where a few guests were heading into the restaurant and bar area. A busy hum floated out to us, reinforcing my concern. All those people ready for an evening's entertainment, not to mention those in the marquee or walking the gardens.

"We can't just tell everyone to leave. It would create hysteria." Victor ran ahead into Goodwin's office. Being covered with blood and sporting a bruised, puffy face wouldn't look good if anyone saw him.

"We can pull the fire alarm," Isidore said.

"That would alert the services." Victor slammed the door behind us. "We can't have them seeing this."

"Good point."

"What about all those people?" I said.

"The marquee must seat a few hundred." Isidore grabbed my arm.

"Maybe a thousand." I winced. "Not to mention however many are in the orchestra."

"We can't do anything about that right now," Victor told us. "Leo, our mystery corpse was actually Stanley after all."

It took me a moment to realise what Victor meant. "And we thought he was a necromeleon."

"It couldn't have been the case. I should have realised even when we'd suspected it."

"Why?" I had Goodwin's lighter gripped tight like a lifeline. I was glad I found it back where we'd found Polly. That seemed a long time ago, and it had only been a few hours.

"Necromeleons can't speak. Tongues. That's what I'd been struggling to translate. Tongues. The dead can walk but not talk."

"This is crazy," Isidore said. "Absolute madness."

I agreed with her, but said nothing. My head pounded and I doubted I could handle much more. As always, my knee was screaming. Victor favoured one leg himself; with every step, he'd been grimacing. Standing before Goodwin's bookshelves waiting for the lift, he spoke of the entity. Mostly for Isidore's sake.

Victor explained how he believed the entity to be *The* Entity, and it needed an earthly being—in this instance, it was Stanley—to begin the unrolling of its plans. The Entity's aim was to stitch all humankind's evils into one all-enveloping Fabric, and return the universe back to the original primordial darkness. In creating a new Shadow Fabric, its expanse would be powerful enough to absorb the life force of all living beings, no longer needing actual stitchers. Eventually, each pocket of natural shadow around the world would become a separate piece of Fabric as every being on the planet was absorbed. No longer stitching the Fabric, but fuelling it.

"Since time immemorial," Victor concluded as we made it into the corridors beneath the House, "the Entity—the very presence of darkness itself—has hidden behind a veil of precisely that: darkness. Since its near success back in the 17th century, humankind's evil has reached such a potency that the Fabric is able to be stitched. Once it's large enough for a complete haunt, the Entity will break through onto our plane and mutate the Fabric into darkness. Returning the universe to how it was at the beginning of time. Before there was light, life, you, me…everything…"

The way he said it chilled me to the core. I gritted my teeth.

"Haunt," he added and stopped walking. His eyes bulged. "The entity, Haunt. How could I have been so stupid?"

Isidore and I gaped at him. What the hell was he talking about?

His lips tightened and he shook his head. "There are many levels, or ranks, if you prefer. The darkness is home to infinite abominations. In all the text I've read, there have been many references to a haunt and how it's achieved. Something I overlooked…"

"What?" Isidore's eyes leapt to mine, then back to Victor. "What are you saying?"

He stared at his bloodied shoes. "According to sources, the entity born of the shadow from Man's first sin dubbed itself *Haunt*. Referring to the way in which it came into being. They are all arrogant bastards."

"Reflections of Haunt?" I asked, remembering the shattered mirrors at the farmhouse.

"Precisely!" Victor shouted, then lowered his voice. "Haunt has been referred to as a demon. Mistaken for a fallen angel. He is also known as Turlamov, one of the first entities. Born, as I said, of Man's first sin. Think about it."

"I am thinking about it," I said. "It's crazy."

"You've seen enough to recognise that I'm not making this up." Victor pulled at his gloves. "But understand that I've read extensively about the shadows, about haunting. About everything which exists between the folds of darkness around us. Yet there is only so much I know. Turmalov, the entity known as Haunt, has been rumoured to be part of the big picture. I always assumed the texts referred to haunt as the gateway and not Haunt, the entity. I didn't understand."

"I guess you can't know everything," I said, not knowing what else to say.

"I'm too old for this." He raised one leg and shook it. The bloodied trousers hardly moved.

Isidore shrugged, almost saying something. Her lips whitened and she averted her gaze. I, too, felt for Victor. He was a mess, and defeat tugged at his face.

"Haunt," he said, "the entity, is said to answer only to the Being of darkness. The main Entity. Absolute evil, it has no label. Turlamov bows only to this Being."

"From the beginning," I said, "I thought the Shadow Fabric was the bad guy."

Isidore looked at her gun and her mouth turned down slightly. She knew it was a useless weapon. "Which entity are we dealing with?"

Victor glanced at me. "Evidence could suggest either one. However, I doubt it's Haunt."

"Why?" I asked.

"From what I understand, only the Entity itself can possess someone. The lesser entities could never be powerful enough."

"Haunt sounds powerful." I thought about Lucas's contact, Thomas. The shrivelled body pierced by countless slivers of mirror. *Reflections of Haunt.* And I remembered the massive shard rammed down his throat.

"Reflections," Victor said. "Yes. He can only exist in reflections."

"Plenty of mirrors in the studio." I rubbed my face, thinking how much damage could be caused by all that glass. "Haunt could've used those like it did with poor Thomas. We'd be dead by now."

"We're dealing with the main Entity. The Being of absolute darkness." Victor headed for the next set of double doors. "And it's playing a game."

Isidore and I shared a quizzical look, and followed Victor's hammering footfalls into the corridor beyond. We made our way in silence to the room where we first encountered the necromeleons. It was where Victor had been overwhelmed by the dead. Where I thought he'd died.

"How did you escape?" I asked him. Then I heard the noises, a kind of frantic shuffle, and as we rounded the bend, there was my answer.

Strip lights flickered. Some dangled from the ceiling in broken casings and coils of wire, some lifeless. Below the stuttering lights, the familiar traceries of Witchblade fire encircled a crush of undead bodies. In the centre of the ambient oranges and yellows, necromeleons knocked into one another. Their black eyes darted about, their skin a mix of dead pallor and fiery reflections. Around the ring, strewn over the charred floor, were several blackened limbs. The stench crawled up my nostrils and filled my head.

"The longer I hold the Witchblade, the more I understand it." Victor smiled—evidently a painful effort behind those bruises.

Isidore raised her gun, taking furtive steps into the room. Dead eyes stared at her through the flames.

"I don't suspect it can hold them forever," Victor said. "Not with the Shadow Fabric being as powerful as it is."

"The Fabric is contained," I said.

"For now."

A few paces further and we came to the CCTV room. The screens were as lifeless as the necromeleons. Even the console was dead. Everything was dead. Except us.

"Where is Goodwin?" I asked.

Victor had paused in the doorway. He ran the Witchblade down the wall, its blade scoring the paintwork. "I have no idea."

"We can't just burn the House." Suddenly, almost stupidly, I understood our intentions.

Victor's eyebrows wriggled across his bloodied forehead.

"This is crazy, Victor."

"Too much is at stake," he said.

"We have to find him."

"For the greater good, sacrifices must be made."

My jaw dropped. My mouth was dry. "What—"

"Leo, for the light of humankind, we have to fight against the darkness."

"What you're saying—"

"What I'm saying is, Goodwin would do the same. We're on the same side."

"Are we, though?" I took a step towards him.

"He—"

"Is Goodwin on the same side? How do we know?" My face burned as I shouted and waved my hand. "Look at all this shit, Victor. Look at it. You had no idea he was doing this?"

"Leo—"

"Did you?"

"Leo—"

"Please, you two," Isidore said. "This isn't getting us anywhere."

I ignored her. "Victor, did you know?"

He shook his head. "No."

"We can't burn this place to the ground with Goodwin still here. Somewhere, he's down here."

"He could be anywhere."

"Yes. We've got to find him."

"We don't have time, Leo."

"And what about Polly? We can't leave her here."

"We know where she is, and we can grab her. Even though she's attached to the Hourglass." He paused, clenched his teeth, and added, "And we'll run while this place burns."

"Victor." I wanted to grab him. "Goodwin's down here somewhere."

"We don't know where he is."

"We have to try." I needed to find Goodwin, to confront him.

"He…" Victor wiped a gloved hand across his forehead, smearing blood and sweat. "He could be dead."

"We've got to look for him at least."

"We haven't got time, Leo. For any of this."

"We have to make time. We have to try, Victor. We can't abandon him."

Pushing himself away from the wall, with nothing else to say, he headed off to the room we came down for. Isidore's face was unreadable, and without a word, she followed him.

"Victor!" I shouted. "Don't walk off."

We reached the room. And in the dim light, the boxes seemed to taunt me—each one I knew contained many shadowleaves. I stood back, staying out in the corridor as Victor and Isidore entered. I glared at the back of Victor's head. My tongue refused to move. My breath was sharp, my head hammered…but not from nausea. Not like last time. This time it was the exertion of getting down here so quickly. I waited for the sickness to hit. I leaned against the door frame and gripped it tight. My eyes glued to the room and what it held, what it represented: humankind's evil. Every vile thought turned into action. How many were similar to my crime?

Victor flicked a switch and a bulb lit up the collection of metal boxes neatly aligned along chrome shelves that extended from floor to ceiling, wall to wall. In contrast to the shiny racks, the boxes were dull, stamped with the Ministry of Justice emblem. There must've been a few hundred of them, equating to thousands of shadowleaves.

Isidore noted my hesitation to follow them fully into the room. She nodded. The way she looked at me made me believe there was hope. For all of us. For me.

I stepped into the room. Surprisingly, my feet obeyed and no nausea wrapped its cloying hands around me. Coming to stand beside her, I already had Goodwin's lighter flipped open. My thumb rested on the wheel—this was my weapon. Victor had the Witchblade, Isidore her gun. And there was me, with a lighter. Only a tiny flame, yet I knew what fire could do against darkness, and I had no intention of losing my weapon. As before, it would've been better had I made some kind of flamethrower. Too late now.

Standing in the centre of the room, it was easy to feel closed in. Such oppression, knowing each box held the heinous crimes of convicted men and women from across the country. Goodwin had collected those shadowleaves over the years, and stored them beneath Periwick House. Incredible, yet somehow, Goodwin had the resources to do it. I didn't know Victor at all, having known him for a lot less time than Goodwin. They were friends. And what was Goodwin to me? Who was this man who'd paid my way in a new life after my accident? All while he carried on with his weird experiments, right under my nose. He claimed to be a family friend…was this true?

Victor reached out and ran his gloved hand along a row of boxes. He curled a finger around an emblem. "This high concentration of shadowleaves is perfect fuel for the Entity."

I stared at him.

"I've no doubt," he added, "it's the Entity that's here."

"So, where's Haunt?"

"I don't know," Victor said, slowly. "That entity may never have been here in the first place. The broken mirrors at the farmhouse may have nothing to do with Haunt. Rather, it's the Entity—the Being of darkness—and its haunt into this plane of existence."

I frowned and clenched my jaw. This was getting confusing. My ears rang.

A familiar voice echoed from the corridor: "I thought I heard voices."

Isidore swung her gun round and aimed it at the doorway.

Goodwin stood there, framed in the white glare of the strip light, bloodied as Victor. He squinted through one swollen eye, the other gummed shut. "And you have found my collection…"

CHAPTER 38

"Don't you realise you've built a store of ammunition here?" Victor shouted as Goodwin stumbled into the room. "Should the Entity stitch this lot, we've lost."

Goodwin brought an arm up and rubbed the back of his head. He winced. Filth caked his clothes and he was missing a shirt sleeve and both shoes. When Victor appeared earlier, I'd mistaken him for a necromeleon, but there was life in Goodwin's eyes. He was real. Even through all the bruises, I could see that. He was the Goodwin I knew...or thought I knew.

"I'm..." Goodwin dropped his gaze, "I'm sorry."

My anger rose again. A rush of noise flooded my head. I wanted to yell at this man who'd lied to me. Lied to all of us. Sorry just wasn't good enough. Who the hell was this guy? Who was he to me? I actually had a lump in my throat.

Isidore had lowered her gun, now angled towards Goodwin's feet. I guess her trust had been damaged, and she didn't even know him. I sighed and perhaps she heard me, because she took a few steps in my direction. Her finger slid away from the trigger.

"Goodwin." Victor walked towards him. "Tell us what's been going on here. Where have you been?"

As Goodwin talked, I couldn't look at him. After all this time hating him, wanting to confront the deceitful bastard, I couldn't face him. After doubting him, I had a thousand more doubts about myself. I wanted to know, yet couldn't ask. If I knew the true Goodwin, then I'd finally learn my past. I knew I'd been a criminal in my old life. Now, faced with the chance to know more, I didn't want to take it.

"I've only just come to," he said. His teeth were bloody. "All I remember is Stanley becoming darkness. I remember the shadows bursting from the walls and how they dragged me through the corridors. I must've been beaten unconscious. What time is it? How long have I been out?"

It was quarter past six. I said so, trying not to say anything else.

"Stanley came to visit late morning…" Grimacing, he ran a hand down his ribs, reminding me of the CCTV footage.

"Goodwin," I said, giving in to myself. It was surprising how soft my voice was. "Tell me what you've been doing."

His shoulders slumped. "Perhaps it is time to tell you."

"Everything." Victor locked eyes with his old friend.

"Yes." Goodwin coughed. "Let me put it this way, Vic, all that I didn't believe is now right before my eyes."

"You're not wrong there," I said.

"Leo, please," Victor whispered.

Goodwin ignored me and continued. "In truth, I've always turned to science and never once believed in the supernatural. I always rationalised things scientifically. Coincidentally, if necessary, never supernatural. Yet here it all is."

"Forever the sceptic," Victor said. "I never knew you were a scientist, Goodwin."

"I am." He nodded gently. "And have been since before any of us met, Vic."

"Katrina…" Victor pulled at his gloves. "Katrina is dead."

Goodwin shook his head. His lips moved, yet no sound came out.

Victor continued, "She said you found a means of combining ancient apparatus and modern technology. To remove the evil from a man."

"I have."

"In doing so, you have the potential to cure the darkness that turns a man into a criminal. Whatever the crime, you found a way to suppress it?"

"Yes. All for the good of mankind."

I wanted to punch him for that comment; it was lame. What of those who turned mad? What of the dying man on the gurney before he became a necromeleon? For the good of mankind, they had all reanimated and become the walking dead. I could've been one of them.

"It's madness, Goodwin." Victor paced the room. "You created mad men and mad women. You even killed people."

"Indirectly, you could say that."

"Good God, listen to yourself."

"I knew the Hourglass had a power. I knew it could extract evil."

"Even though you didn't believe in the supernatural yourself?"

"I saw it as a piece of scientific equipment. Primitive, yet its potential was incredible. I could not ignore it."

"So you found it. You kept it from me. From all of us."

"I wanted to make a difference in the world."

"You've extracted more than enough evils," Victor whirled his hands about him. "This crazy collection is more than enough for your experiments. Why so many, Goodwin? Why didn't you stop at a few?"

"Every man and woman is different. Every prisoner has their own agenda, their own reasons, their own ideals."

"Your ideals are mental." I spat the words at him. "What am I in all this?"

"Please understand..." Goodwin's eyebrows pinched together as he raised a hand. "You've no idea how far I've come."

"Not interested," I said. "You've betrayed our trust. Old friends and new."

Victor tugged at his gloves. "What amazes me is the sheer scale of the operation here. I mean, you collected thousands of shadowleaves. Are they all from prisoners?"

"The majority, yes."

My heart had replaced my tongue. I could not speak.

Victor said, "How on earth did you manage such a thing?"

For a moment Goodwin remained silent, and finally said, "Money."

Isidore nodded, biting her lip.

"You bought them?" Victor's eyes widened. "You bought the prisoners?"

"I have a great many contacts in the justice system."

"Did you believe anything at all of the supernatural? Did you just go along with everything for your own means?"

Goodwin shook his head. "Forever the sceptic."

"Goodwin," Victor shouted at him, "you obviously realise the danger we're in."

"I… Yes, I do. I know now."

"Precisely when did you come by the Hourglass?"

Goodwin took a moment to answer. "1975," he said, and coughed. Red spittle flecked his lower lip.

"You had it from the beginning?" Victor's voice lowered. "Where did you find it?"

"Lucas, rest his soul. He acquired it. Somewhere in Eastern Europe."

"Lucas?"

"He was loyal, we cannot deny that. Loyal to each of us."

Victor slowly shook his head. "I never knew he found it."

"Why would you? You guys were never really on speaking terms."

"That was between me and him." Victor stopped pacing. "You could've told me."

"Money," Goodwin said again as though to justify it.

Beside me, Isidore said, "It's always about money."

Victor glared at Goodwin.

"So," he said, "let me get this straight. You had the Hourglass all along and built the House with these rooms beneath it. As a cover, obviously. All the time believing you could cure humankind's evils. You paid for the release of prisoners and collected their shadowleaves. You also experimented on them. Some dying, some going mad…"

"And," I said, "you did it because someone murdered your father?"

He stepped back. "Something like that, yes."

"Did you even know my father?" My throat burned as I shouted. "Did you know any of my family?"

Goodwin's swollen eyelid fluttered as he tried to hold my gaze. He didn't reply.

"Goodwin, seriously. Was everything a lie?"

Still nothing.

If he hadn't already been beaten and bloodied by the Fabric I would've done it myself. The deceiving, lying bastard.

"Did I mean anything to you?" I lunged forward and Victor caught my arm, his grip tightened on my bicep.

"Leo," he said. "Come on, my friend. This will get us nowhere."

"Vic—" My heart wanted to leap from my throat. I stood there with my head hammering, fists clenched. Then a ridiculous calmness washed over me, which annoyed me further. I was angry at myself for being angry in the first place. Stars spotted my vision for a moment and I swayed. Victor tightened his grip. My breath softened and I stared at the ground.

"The prisoners, Goodwin," he eventually said, and released me. "Did you cure any?"

Goodwin's chin dipped to his chest, but his eyes stayed on Victor. They drifted to Isidore, and then to me. He didn't say a word.

"Well?" Victor spat. Perhaps even he found it difficult to contain his anger.

"Yes," Goodwin replied. "There were several cases where the patient became normal."

"Define normal, Goodwin."

"Like me," I said, "I was a patient. A criminal. Have I become normal?"

A long silence followed, and I believed everyone could hear my heart pounding against my ribs. Goodwin didn't know where to look, and when he spoke, his words came slowly.

"Normal is no longer wanting to wrong another man. No longer having the urge to break the law, or to push aside morals or ethics." Almost in a whisper, he added, "There were side effects, however."

My ears burned. "How did you know our minds were free of evil?" And I wondered if my mind was exactly that: free of evil thought. What was I capable of? Moments ago, I wanted to beat the shit out of him, so perhaps I wasn't entirely cured. Or maybe, when it truly came to it, a mental block would crash into place and freeze my fist in mid-swing.

"With such advances in technology over the last thirty years, I had everything in hand, and I developed a process to enable us to see into a man's mind. I call it my dream camera." Pride glimmered somewhere amidst the bruises. "Put to the layman, it categorises thought processes. In remarkable detail, in actual fact. We can see beyond the grey matter, we can see the black and the white. The good thoughts and the bad."

Victor rubbed his forehead. "We're wasting time."

"What can we do?" Goodwin coughed, covering his mouth. His fingers came away spotted with blood. "Stanley is—"

"Stanley is truly dead," Victor interrupted. "The Entity possessed him. It tricked you. Tricked us all."

"I know that now," Goodwin said, and coughed again. "I knew from the moment I closed my office door. He changed from the bastard he always was into something even worse. The shadows came out of him and he made me take him down here. Under the House, to reveal my theories. But he knew. He knew about everything."

"He knew…" Victor said. "No, the Entity knew you held the key to its success."

"The shadowleaves."

"Yes. We're dealing with the most evil Entity known to humankind. The darkest power there is."

Goodwin, Victor, Isidore, I didn't know any of them. I caught my reflection in one of the chrome shelves—I didn't even know who I was.

"You're such an idiot, Goodwin." I barged past him into the corridor with Isidore close behind.

"We managed to contain the Fabric," I heard Victor say. "For now."

"Let's get out of here," I mumbled to Isidore, who simply nodded, eyes closed and massaging her temples with both hands. My head was fuzzy, not unlike my nausea before. I needed fresh air.

Victor and Goodwin joined us in the corridor, and with Victor rubbing the back of his neck and Goodwin looking like shit, I reckoned we all needed some air.

And so the four of us left the oppressive room behind, with our mission to destroy those boxes entirely forgotten.

* * *

Returning to the studio, it was a relief to see everything as we left it. The Shadow Fabric remained immobile, walled in by the fortress of Witchblade fire. The dusty smell of the stitchers clung to the air and I tasted the familiar hint of ozone.

"Victor?" Polly said. "Cubs? Is that you?"

Victor ran to her. "Yes, it's me."

The shadows had left her. She strained against the leather restraints, veins bulging as they dug into her forearm. Her blind eyes were wide—searching without seeing.

"Good to have you back." Victor unfastened the straps of the Hourglass. I wasn't sure how long it had been since the sand ran out. It was white. No hint of black there at all.

"Dear God," Goodwin said. He came to stand beside me and Isidore. His attention was on the Shadow Fabric and the screen of crackling flame around it. He leaned against the wall, his chest heaving. Our ascent back to the studio had clearly been an effort for the man, and on the way we'd stopped several times for him to recover from a coughing fit.

"Why was she in a trance, Leo?" Isidore asked. "We weren't like that."

"I've no idea."

"Maybe it was all too much for her."

"Yeah, maybe."

Goodwin groaned and his legs buckled. He slid to the floor, limbs sprawling. I reached for him and he knocked my arm away.

"Leave me." He managed a smile which must've hurt. "Leave me be."

With reluctance, I straightened. Isidore hadn't moved, hadn't made any effort to help him. I couldn't blame her for not wanting to. This madness stemmed from his experiments. His playing with the Hourglass and using dream cameras to see into people's heads. I, on the other hand, had been quick by his side. Had I forgiven him? Perhaps. With his crumpled body at my feet, there was also pity there.

Something else took our attention.

Polly and Victor.

She was on her feet now, and Victor slowly backed away from her. She held the Hourglass in one hand and its compartment in the other.

"Polly, I—" He raised the Witchblade.

"What colour is my shadowleaf, Cubs?"

Cradled in the rectangle of wood, there was no mistaking its colour. Her leaf was black.

CHAPTER 39

Polly placed the Hourglass onto the chair, taking a moment to make certain it sat centrally. She set the compartment beside it and squinted as she removed the shadowleaf. Her eyes were no longer a blind stare. They were black as the leaf she held. The way she composed herself and looked directly at Victor suggested she could see. The darkness in her eyes had somehow given her sight.

She wiggled the shadowleaf at Victor. "Cubs, what colour is it?"

Victor came to a stop, as did Polly. "Your eyes," he said. "Polly, your eyes."

Her mouth twisted into a smirk. "What about them?"

"You can't be a necromeleon. The darkness…"

She laughed at him.

"Where is Polly?" he demanded.

"I am Polly. I am flesh and blood. Don't think I'm anything else."

"Then what—"

"Oh, Victor, you're more intelligent than that." Her dark eyes wandered about the room and settled on the Fabric.

"Tulip Moon?" Victor asked, and I knew he was right. Polly was behind everything.

She nodded without looking at him. "Well done."

"But—"

"Annabel?" Her once-blind eyes roamed across the gleaming surface of the Fabric. "We both played the role of Tulip. I needed someone who could see. In case you haven't noticed, I'm blind, or was."

I tasted the evil in the air and the pungent scent of decay, something dead. The remains of bodies—the stitchers, shrivelled to dry skeletons—heaped the floor in places, yet this was different. I heard something too, a hum as though an engine approached. No, more a rumble. Like an earthquake. Or a bestial growl rising from the depths of some creature's gut.

Isidore experienced it too. She had a hand to her throat, rubbing it. Her eyes darted about the room as if in search of something, and they settled on the Fabric. It pulsed. Still encased in the flaming wall of intricate script, it now pushed at the confines, teasing its way side to side, up and down, testing its limits. It wouldn't be long until it escaped.

Already the surrounding shadows—the lesser shadows—slid across the floor. They circled Isidore and me, forcing us closer to Goodwin and away from the door.

"Some people are known to have stared into the sun and gone blind." Polly laughed. Her black eyes were deeper, more piercing, than a necromeleon's. "Whereas, I simply stared into the darkness."

Victor's mouth hung wide, his eyebrows twitching as he dragged his gaze from Polly to the Fabric.

"Did you people forget something?" she asked.

"What?" His forehead creased.

"You went beneath the House to burn the shadowleaves," she said. "And forgot all about it when you got there. Clever, yes?"

My head ached.

"How—" Victor began.

"Don't be dim witted, Cubs. You of all people shouldn't be surprised."

"The Fabric," he said. "It channelled through you."

My mind raced. Forgotten what? What were they talking about?

"It did, Cubs, it did." A smirk cracked her wrinkly face in two like an egg.

"What have you done?" Victor asked.

"I command the darkness, I have been the gateway, and now it's here."

"Why, Polly?"

"Simple answer…" Her eyes widened, the darkness in them impenetrable. "Why should I be blind when others can see?"

"Polly—"

"Shut up, Victor. Just shut up. Think about it, you know why I went blind."

His mouth opened a fraction.

"You know."

He hung his head. "Yes."

"I tasted evil." Her mouth twisted. "I tasted evil the moment your brother forced himself on me...in me."

"Polly, please—"

"I said shut up!" She snapped her head forward. "The sun went down on my life then. You know how young I was. You know I was impressionable, innocent."

Victor's shoulders slumped and the Witchblade hung from his hand ready to drop.

Isidore and I huddled against the wall, unable to move with the shadows shifting about our feet—showing no evident signs of danger. Isidore pointed her gun at Polly and all I had was fury. Speechless, I watched as Victor stood before Polly. Looking at the small woman, I couldn't believe she'd been behind it all.

"Cubs, when you showed me no interest, when you told me you didn't feel the same about me, of course I ran into the arms of your brother. I was a heartbroken little girl. Weak. Pathetic." She spat these last words. Her back straightened and she continued. "How was I supposed to know he'd take me, and in any way he chose? Locking me in that room for days on end. Only wanting one thing from me."

"I am so sorry, Polly. I am. You know I am."

"No!" She took a few steps back. "No, you're not. No one is truly sorry. No one knows the hell I went through. My eyes simply switched off like a light. You and Goodwin may have disowned Stanley, the two of you may have taken me under your wing like the good guys you try to be, but look at you now."

Goodwin mumbled something. His eyes had closed and his chest rose and fell rapidly. A tight ring of shadows now surrounded the three of us. We had nowhere to run. Not that I wanted to; I wasn't leaving Victor again, I would be with him to the end.

"Both of you," Polly was saying, "are as pathetic as each other. Beaten down and worn. The light isn't going to shine through. The darkness is already here."

Victor shook his head.

"It's going to be dark for a very, very long time."

"Infinity," Victor said.

And like this to infinity was something I recalled from one of his books. I still had a cloud of confusion in my head, blocking something more. What else had I recently forgotten? Something to do with boxes? Earlier, Victor mentioned something about channelling?

"And as for you and that foolish brother of yours," Polly said. "You two were perfect to play against one another. It simply wouldn't have worked with anyone else. It had to be the feuding brothers. Time to get you at each other's throats by giving one the Fabric and the other the Witchblade."

"But the man in the antique shop…" Victor said.

One side of Polly's mouth curled. "I knew you'd offer to help, so I sent you there. By channelling, the Shadman with the Witchblade was already waiting for you."

Victor grunted. "He was an original Shadman?"

Polly sniggered. "And easily influenced, having witnessed the death of his companions and gone quite insane."

"What about the shop owner?"

"He was just stupid."

Victor looked down at the Witchblade in his hand.

Polly pointed at him. "Your hatred was fuelled by that knife, and when you killed Stanley, it gave the Entity a being to take. Stanley was evil anyway, no denying it. Could there have been anyone else so perfect for the Entity to possess?"

"You played us," he said. "You knew what would happen."

I gaped at Polly; the clever, manipulative bitch.

"That is how the Entity managed to regain so much power," Victor added. "To manifest enough and to absorb Stanley's dying life force."

"Of course," Polly said. With a flick of her wrist, she threw her shadowleaf towards the Fabric. It glided through the air and the fire parted. The surface of the Fabric bulged and split, opening like a toothless mouth to swallow the leaf. Its mass bulked up as though it flexed its muscles, and the fire surrounding it warped and cracked in places. Hissing as parts of the barrier broke, the flames dwindled. The Fabric heaved against its confinement.

I kicked away a shadow which had crept over my boot, and Isidore did the same. The coiling tentacles evidently saw no threat in Goodwin, and it was only us they concentrated on. They snatched our ankles, wrapped around our legs, and then yanked us upside down. My shoulder crashed into the floor as Isidore's gun bounced near my head. The shadows dragged our thrashing bodies up the wall, and forced us against the ceiling high above Goodwin.

The side of Isidore's head gushed red.

The final spirals of fire sputtered out, no longer able to confine the Fabric—inside which, the Entity forced itself to the surface in scintillating waves.

My shoulder screamed at me and my whole arm was numb. I flexed my fingers, urging life back into them. I'd landed on that shoulder. As the shadows pressed me to the ceiling, the pain gradually subsided.

Victor faced Polly without showing any signs of fight. It was almost as though he had given in.

Hemmed in by squirming shadows, Goodwin lay motionless. One eye peered through his swollen face. I still didn't know how to feel about him.

My arms had a little movement, and more importantly, my head remained unrestricted—unlike before when bound up and gagged. Such a relief not to have a mouthful of shadow. I caught Isidore's eye. Shadows covered her torso as they did mine. Blood trickled along her cheek.

"Not again," she said.

"You're telling me," I muttered. "This has been happening to me all afternoon."

Polly was staring Victor down and he appeared to shrink beneath her gaze. He hung his head. She grinned.

Surging to life, the Shadow Fabric bulked and shifted from the corner. So much darkness in the room, with the lesser shadows snaking over the floor. They licked the remains of the stitchers.

There I was, helpless again, pushed against the ceiling. Strung up, useless, and the shadows tugged off my gloves. They fell in a double slap. Why didn't the shadows simply kill us?

Their floating darkness had now swallowed the dumbbells and mats, and most of the floor. And the Hourglass was still on the chair. Further away was the upturned box of shadowleaves, with its contents spilled like a discarded jigsaw puzzle, the pieces all black. With piles of dusty clothes and skeletal limbs heaped in places, I couldn't decide where to look.

Something else was there, too. Something which glowed bright like a beacon in the darkness. It was my shadowleaf. My white one. The one which had been extracted from the Hourglass after Stanley—the Entity in human form—had forced me into the straps. Even though Stanley had managed to find my grey shadowleaf and had somehow controlled me with it, there was my white shadowleaf.

Two lives, two leaves. What did that mean? Not only that—if Stanley could control me, how many others had he controlled, or did he intend to control? And what else had he done with other shadowleaves? At least Isidore's leaf had been lost amongst the rest of the discarded pile. Stanley hadn't been at all concerned with hers.

More questions. And it wasn't the time to ask. I had to do something. I thrashed against the shadows, trying to force my arms out. Like before, I failed.

Beneath us, roiling shadows circled that white leaf as if repelled.

Isidore saw it too.

"Leo," she said. "Look."

"I know."

Victor cried out as an arm of shadow knocked the Witchblade from his hand. The athame spun across the floor. The shadows parted, each wispy tendril careful not to touch the blade. Another tentacle clamped around Victor's head and looped around his neck. He choked and clawed at it with both hands. Polly laughed.

The Shadow Fabric rippled as if energised. It puffed out as though inhaling, as if it held its breath, ready for something. The air, heavy, clawed down my throat. I felt dirty, as foul as the Fabric. It shuddered, once, twice, and blasted through the wall in an eruption of brick and glass.

I shouted something as the destruction rang through my head.

A part of the ceiling groaned as gravity snatched it in crumbled masonry and twists of timber frame. Dust drifted into the room over scattered glass.

Then silence.

I didn't realise I held my breath. With the Fabric no longer in the room, the mind-fog cleared, replaced by an image of the box room. We hadn't burned the boxes—this was what Polly referred to. We forgot to burn them. No matter our intentions, we simply didn't do it. After all our deliberation, standing in the room with me persuading Victor to hold tight, not to burn the boxes. At the time we'd not known where Goodwin was, and that had been my case. When Goodwin joined us, bruised and broken, we left the room without further thought, without further discussion. Victor and I had voiced our mistrust and disappointment, and we left. Isidore followed us without a word regarding our initial intentions. That would explain our fuzzy heads. All of us had symptoms of an outside influence, a channelling, as Victor had said.

All of us had forgotten.

And so we retreated, by no conscious thought of our own. Not having burned the potential ammunition, we returned to the studio in time to witness the extraction of Polly's shadowleaf.

The Entity can influence others by channelling its powers via a perceptive mind. In this case, it was Polly. Her lack of sight gave way to the heightening of other senses, essentially creating a sixth sense. With the capabilities of mind control—despite the Fabric restrained by Witchblade fire—the powers writhing behind the veil of darkness were strong enough to bounce from Polly's mind and into ours. Channelling.

So we'd left the box room without following through with our plan. We'd gone to use fire, yet didn't get around to it. Distracted, as simple as that…clever.

And now the Fabric raged into the evening.

CHAPTER 40

The Shadow Fabric filled the view beyond the studio's crumbled wall, blocking what little light remained of the day. It was impressive, there could be no denying it.

I struggled behind the restraining shadows. Isidore too, desperate for release.

"Leo!" she screamed. Her hair stuck to her blood-streaked face in clumps. "We've got to get away."

My teeth clenched. There was nothing I could do.

The Fabric throbbed, hovering above the gardens. I saw Neil—working late, as always—manoeuvring a wheelbarrow. He stopped and looked up, his mouth and eyes wide. The darkness lunged downwards. One moment, Neil stood there, hands clamped around the handles, and the next, he wasn't.

He and the wheelbarrow had vanished.

A second later the barrow burst from the pulsing Fabric, followed by bone shards falling to the ground. Torn clothes fluttered and his skull smashed onto the pathway.

I bucked against the shadows—too many good people were dying. I'd known them for the last couple of years and all of them were like family. I slumped into the shadowy embrace and shook my head. A wind pushed into the room and its chill dried my unblinking eyes. In the distance, rain clouds formed.

With shattered glass glinting at her feet, Polly nodded at her achievement. Framed by splintered timber, she placed her hands on her hips, and as a chunk of masonry fell from the ceiling, she stepped casually aside.

Seeing her like this, I knew she deserved to stand proud. She had, as she'd admitted, been the gateway to allow the Entity into this world. And she had succeeded. There it was—The Entity—riding the Fabric with nothing to stop it. She had accomplished it and I admired her. I wanted to be down there with her. I wanted to stand by her side and laugh at the world…I wanted…

"No!" I threw my head back. It smacked the ceiling and the shock cleared the mind-fuzz. I strained at the shadows, breathing in short bursts.

Polly laughed.

"I can hear it talking to you, Leo," she said.

"No," I said again.

With shadows snaking each footfall, Polly moved from the ruined wall and came to stand beside Victor. A collection of shadows formed around his legs.

"You can't blame me for everything, Cubs." Without taking her eyes from him, she pointed at Isidore. "She helped me."

"Montelius…" Victor whispered, shaking his head.

"I had no idea." Isidore squirmed beneath the shadows. "I didn't—"

"Yes you did." Polly's dark eyes shot up. "She did, Cubs. She found the whereabouts of the four keepers of the Fabric. Those remaining folds left over from a burning London. And in doing so, she even found the Shadman who simply handed the Witchblade over to you."

As though accepting his fate, Victor allowed the shadows to embrace him. Perhaps, if he still had the Witchblade, he would've lashed out at them. With his eyes downcast and the way he shook his head, I doubted even that.

"Victor!" I shouted. "Don't give up, man."

Polly walked around him and headed for the Witchblade where the shadows kept away. She picked it up by the sharp end.

"Over the past three hundred and fifty years, the four pieces of lifeless Fabric were handed down from generation to generation. The protectors were sworn to keep each piece far from the others." She smacked the Witchblade's hilt against Victor's chest. "Bet you didn't know that."

The shadows now squeezed him, and for the first time, he reacted. It was a lame attempt. "You don't have to do this, Polly."

"With Isidore's excellent skills, she found the four men, and when I got them in the same room…" She slapped the Witchblade in her palm. "I simply allowed the pieces to stitch themselves together again. The life force of those men was enough to set it all into motion."

Victor's eyebrows pinched together, and he shifted against his restraints. Isidore and I continued to heave against our shadows.

"I want the darkness back." Polly dragged her little finger along the blade. Blood hit the floor and a passing shadow balled into a frenzy and licked it up. "I want the Entity to regain control."

"Polly," Victor said, "if the darkness returns, even you won't be here. There will be nothing."

"I've been in the dark long enough, Cubs. Now it's time for me to embrace it."

"You're mad," I shouted at her.

"Perhaps I went mad the moment I went blind."

Since devouring Neil, the Shadow Fabric hadn't moved. It clogged the view through the ruined wall. Maybe it waited for something.

Polly strolled towards Goodwin, again slapping the hilt of the Witchblade in her palm. She leered as he made to move, but the combination of his weakened condition and the binding shadows allowed little manoeuvrability. Several limbs of darkness coiled around his arms and legs.

"Stay there," Polly said. Sparks crackled around the Witchblade's hilt as it smacked her hand. Being so close to them, the shadows recoiled from the knife's presence.

The Fabric hovered closer to the studio, bubbling against the wreckage of joists and brick. Definitely waiting.

Goodwin looked at me, and then at Victor, and through bloody lips said, "I am so sorry."

With one final smack of the hilt, Polly gripped the Witchblade and brandished it high. Tiny fires sparked from the blade, tumbling over her head and shoulders.

In one motion, she rushed forward and slammed the blade into Goodwin's chest.

CHAPTER 41

I shouted Goodwin's name. I couldn't stand this. Everyone was dying around me. Now Goodwin, for all the hate I had for him, he didn't deserve this.

The Shadow Fabric gushed back into the studio. Masonry crashed behind it. In a whirlwind filling half the room, it hovered above Goodwin's body. And swallowed it.

Polly stepped back. Her arm hung by her side, the Witchblade dripping blood. Victor screamed something as he struggled against the sleeve of shadows. He remained upright as darkness spiralled around him. Finally, he was fighting. My frustrations again threw me into a frenzy and I thrashed against the shadows. Useless. As always.

Inside the Fabric, as its glimmering surface flattened, the bulge of Goodwin's body started to shrink. It seemed to collapse in on itself as the Fabric consumed him. Then Goodwin's withered remains oozed out and I wanted to spew. Partially clothed, the husk crumpled. Goodwin's body was a shrunken heap of wrinkled skin, a fraction of the man's actual size.

Isidore and I raged against the shadows still pinning us to the ceiling. My eyes wanted to pop from my face, Goodwin's name on my lips. For all the man's faults and deceit, he'd been no less to me than a father to a son. To watch him die this way…so swift, so final…

I had so many questions for him.

Polly stood a respectful distance from the Fabric, her face now relaxed. Her black eyes sparkled.

The Fabric slid away from the hollow shell of Goodwin's body. Now drained of life force, there was little holding it together, and the skull—with its curls of sparse hair—rolled away. The jaw dislodged and several teeth broke loose.

The flat area of Fabric bulged, its surface gleaming. No longer an impenetrable darkness, it glimmered like a pool of diesel, rainbow colours swirling.

Polly smirked, her chin jutting forward.

The rising bulb of Shadow Fabric lightened, becoming grey. Tiny lumps appeared down its flank, one either side of the rising column of…flesh. It looked like flesh. Grey, and lightening still. It softened to white, and then it showed soft hues of pink. Human skin.

Two nubs protruded and stretched downwards to become spindly arms. The trunk thickened and became a torso, upon which the lump of a head grew. The form expanded, rising as if from the murky depths of a swamp.

The rest of the Shadow Fabric pooled around its legs.

It had taken the form of a fully clothed man. And as I recognised the short, round frame, a set of human features wrapped around the face of the thing, a fresh-faced and smiling Goodwin.

He blinked and scanned the studio. It was the most incredible—if horrific—thing I'd ever witnessed. The Entity had become Goodwin, as it had with Stanley.

"Now," Isidore said through tight lips, "you're telling me your mate Goodwin there is the Entity?"

I nodded, my mouth dry. The shadows pulled tighter across my chest as if daring me to struggle.

Victor's eyes were bursting from his face. The shadows rushed tighter over his body. They held him, allowing his head only the smallest of movements.

"Yes," he said, "the Fabric still isn't large enough. The Entity still needs a life force to ride. Its haunt is not quite complete."

Finally my tongue came away from the roof of my mouth, yet I couldn't dislodge my tumbling thoughts.

Goodwin grinned at Polly.

Out in the grounds of Periwick House, music started to play.

CHAPTER 42

The event organiser, Jocelyn, had done a fantastic job. She had proven she could indeed pull it off. *Even if there was a hurricane*, she had said. With music floating on the evening air, a vortex of shadow heaved behind the new Goodwin. The way the darkness swirled as a backdrop to the Entity's present form, Jocelyn hadn't been far wrong, even in a hurricane of shadows.

Victor looked as helpless as I felt, and Isidore's frustrations were equally as evident; all of us wrapped in shadows.

"Polly," Goodwin said. The man was immaculate. He walked across the layer of Fabric. It bowed under his weight, and he came to stand beside a pair of shrivelled corpses. "You have served your purpose. I release you now."

"What?" Polly had been swinging the Witchblade like an absentminded child. Now she stopped.

Between them, the overturned box sat atop a pile of shadowleaves. Some of the ordinary shadows toyed with its edges. Shadowplay. From outside in the marquee, wind instruments and violins rose up in beautiful oblivion.

"Drop the knife," Goodwin said.

Polly did as she was told, her black eyes questioning. The blade thumped in a spray of blood. Fleeing shadows disappeared under the dumbbell rack.

Goodwin crouched and grabbed a handful of shadowleaves. Bunched in his fist, the black squares poked through his fingers. He straightened up and stepped towards Polly.

The shadows weaved around his legs and the husks of stitchers, and more curled around Victor.

Goodwin and Polly faced one another. He smiled while her frown deepened. Her black eyes greyed and lightened further, becoming white. She blinked, shoulders rounded and her blind gaze darted about the room. Her hands shot up and slapped at her face. She clawed at her eyes.

"Why?" she demanded, her chin quivering. "Why have you done this?"

The shadows at her feet made way as she stomped on uncertain legs. Goodwin had his arm out towards her, with shadowleaves clutched tightly. As Polly reached him, he pressed them into her hands. She stopped short of bumping into him and immediately clamped her fingers around the leaves. A few fluttered to the floor.

She dropped to her knees and the stitching took her.

As if composed for that moment, the orchestra played a magnificent crescendo. The music filled the room as much as the evening air, and the Fabric ruffled behind Goodwin. It embraced him. Its edges caressed his shoulders, his arms, his legs.

"Plenty more potential stitchers out there," he said as darkness folded around him.

He and the Shadow Fabric vanished.

* * *

My muscles ached. I couldn't have been pinned to the studio ceiling for long. Five, maybe ten minutes. I wasn't certain. I had to get out. And why had we been spared? Why hadn't we been made to stitch? Or, even simpler, why hadn't we been killed? I didn't understand, and Isidore's face suggested her confusion mirrored my own.

Goodwin's potential stitchers numbered around a thousand, and would no doubt provide enough life force to energise the Fabric, allowing the Entity passage into our world. No longer would there be a need for it to ride the energies of a human, its haunt would be complete. I had to do something.

Trapped as the three of us were, we shared the knowledge that Goodwin, as the Entity, had plans for the occupants of the marquee. I forced away thoughts that led to Goodwin's death. More pressing matters at hand: the shadows. I had to get free.

The music fell into a gentle rhythm of woodwinds, and now that the Fabric had left us, the studio was much lighter. And my head was clearer. But the lesser shadows still held me.

Below me, almost directly, Polly sat crossed-legged. A pool of shadows churned around her as her body swayed. She had already crumpled, her flesh greying beyond her years.

Another heave against the constricting shadows and I grunted through clamped teeth. I knew it was useless.

Isidore was equally desperate. Hair hung over her face, jaw clenched, and she wriggled under her restraints. Victor lay on the floor, his face obscured by the teasing shadows. It was difficult even to recognise a man crouched inside the trunk of darkness.

Several lesser shadows were playing. Each one snaked around the dumbbell rack and toyed with the wilted remains of stitchers. In places, bodies huddled in twos and threes—wherever they'd stitched, they had fallen. The box of scattered shadowleaves seemed to be the main area of attention for shadowplay, where occasionally a leaf caught in a whirlwind of shadowy wisps, only to flutter to rest once more.

A fair distance away was the weapon which could save us, the Witchblade. Absurdly, I willed it to leap into the air, to cut away the shadows around me. To help us with its magic, but its powers weren't linked through telekinesis. The shadows continued avoiding any contact with the athame. They had, however, licked up the flecks of blood which spotted the floor; life force, no matter how small, wasn't to be wasted.

As the Witchblade was a source to avoid, so was my white shadowleaf. Each slithering phantom was clearly repelled by its presence. What significance did its purity suggest? All too much, that's what it amounted to. I couldn't grasp everything.

The music still played, and I guessed Goodwin—the Entity—hadn't gotten to the marquee yet. If he intended to get the entire audience stitching, then he would need to collect plenty of shadowleaves first. And there was only one place he could get them from: the box room beneath the House. We failed to burn the boxes, and now the Entity had a battery of ammunition and potential stitchers numbering a thousand or so. All enjoying the chamber music, oblivious to what was coming.

At any moment, I expected the music to stop as the stitching took hold.

Surely there was still time to use fire, and if so, how? There was the athame, too far away. Goodwin's lighter? Where had I put it? I rewound to the last time I had it: helping Goodwin as the poor guy stumbled from under the House to here, I'd put the lighter away. It was in my pocket—one of many pockets in my combats. If only I could move against the pressure of shadows. No longer struggling against them, they had slackened slightly, allowing me marginal arm movement. Combats, always handy. The pockets were large and baggy, easily accessible. I hoped.

Victor nodded, perhaps knowing my intentions.

I twisted awkwardly, pain lancing my shoulder as my joints strained. Using both hands, my fingers prodded and probed—I couldn't remember where I'd put the damn thing. The downside of combats is that any pocket could contain what we're searching for, and so accelerates frustration in an already panicked situation. And if someone—some*thing*—had pulled thoughts from my mind, then of course, I was less likely to know which pocket the thing was in.

On top of that, with the distant music and knowing that at any moment the mass-stitching would begin, I heard time race by with the sound of stringed instruments.

Coins…keys…a packet of mints…wallet…more coins…

I found the lighter. My hand closed around it.

Isidore frowned. She knew I was up to something.

Pulling my arm back, I held that magnificent Zippo lighter—the one I bought in Hong Kong for Goodwin as a small thank you gift. The thought of dropping it terrified me, watching it clatter to the floor, hope lost as the shadows looked up and laughed at my despair. I held my arm away, flicking the Zippo open and straightening my elbow. I didn't want to set fire to my clothes.

I thumbed the wheel.

Fire shot up my fingers, across my knuckles, and over the back of my hand. I screamed, and at the same moment the shadows relaxed—perhaps I even heard them scream as they scurried off. The pain was intense, but I now had full movement. Shadows clung to the rest of my body, but they squirmed, still pinning me to the ceiling. I pushed the flame towards them. My hand wasn't on fire, although it felt like it was. I swore I heard their screams, like they projected their agony directly at me.

The shadows released me and gravity grabbed me. I slammed to the floor. My bad knee struck first, taking my body weight. Pain, a brief moment of disorientation, and I was on my feet, favouring one leg. I picked up the Witchblade.

I sensed rather than heard the athame speaking to me.

Holding it felt wrong. I knew it wasn't my time. Maybe it was the voices probing my mind. *Not yet*, they said. It was as if the blade granted me use for no longer than a minute. It allowed me to brandish it—*just for now*—to cut away the shadows which held Victor. Each wispy phantom shied away from the glowing edge as it sliced them, freeing him. Every lesser shadow darted into the corners of the studio.

Victor emerged out of the darkness and I handed him the athame.

"Nicely done," he said, and peered up at Isidore.

"Come on!" she yelled. "Get me down."

I rubbed my hand, desperately wanting to run the damn thing under cold water. My flesh was red. My knee screamed at me to sit and do nothing. Regardless, I was thankful I no longer held the Witchblade. I shivered.

At arm's length, Victor held the blade towards Isidore and a trail of flame shot up and tore away the shadows. She dropped into my arms. In another place, at another time, I would have enjoyed the moment, but my aching limbs protested and I steadied her to her feet. I tried not to grimace and didn't mean to ignore her as she began to say something. I saw my white shadowleaf and bent to pick it up. The thing intrigued me.

"You may want to keep hold of that," Victor said.

Isidore eyed the white leaf.

I ignored the lingering pain of my burnt hand and cupped the shadowleaf in my palm. I stuffed it into a pocket. I kept hold of Goodwin's Zippo, the engraving reminded me of its brief owner. *Godwin. A Good Friend.* I chewed my lip as Victor handed me my gloves. I poked the lighter into the pocket and pulled them on. I felt safer, marginally.

Around us the lesser shadows retreated into corners. Some vanished entirely as the tracers of Witchblade fire chased after them. We stood together, composing ourselves, while the streamers fizzled out.

On a chill breeze the chamber orchestra's music floated through the shattered wall.

I faced Victor. "We must stop Goodwin."

"It's not Goodwin." Dried blood coated his forehead and caked his eyebrows.

"It's a monster," Isidore said and she tightened her rucksack straps. Her gun waved around and I squirmed when the barrel pointed at me for a second.

"The Entity," Victor corrected. "It has to be stopped."

My head throbbed and my shoulder screamed when I moved my arm. "Why have we been spared?"

He shrugged, which annoyed me. "I have no idea."

I hated that phrase, yet I was equally as guilty using it. Tugging my sleeve up, I checked the time—old habits—and noticed the second hand had frozen. There was a crack in the glass and the face had darkened as if burnt. Perhaps the Zippo flames had scorched it.

The ruined wall presented us with no easy exit, and with a row of hedges separating us from the gardens, we chose to head back to the foyer. As the three of us hurtled past the pool area and treatment rooms, our feet pounding the floor, I spotted something. Someone had left a chambermaid's trolley against the wall, and on top of it, beside some towels, sat a cardboard box.

"What are you doing?" Victor asked. He ran past with his trousers flapping around bare ankles. Isidore was close behind him.

"Protection," I called after them. I grabbed the box and hefted it under my arm. It wasn't heavy, only awkward to carry. When I picked up my pace again, it was all I could do not to drop it. Every other step was like broken glass grinding into powder, using my knee socket as a pestle and mortar.

Even though I had paused to take the box from the cart, I caught up with the others as they crossed the foyer. Outside, gravel crunched as we sprinted towards the music and reached the side of the House. Finally, there was the marquee, still a distance away. Beneath the evening sky its white canvas glowed in contrast to the Shadow Fabric overhead where it thrust back and forth like an excited dog waiting to be fed.

Isidore now sprinted in front, followed by Victor. I was losing speed, the glass inside my knee a constant smash and grind.

Occasionally, the Fabric would rush down and sweep over the rippling canvas of the marquee roof. A line of silver birch bowed as if in awe. Collecting overhead, dark clouds threatened rain.

We ran. Fast. The marquee seemed miles away. Nasty splinters fired up into my knee...I gritted my teeth, and limp-sprinted.

As I rounded the hedges, hugging my cardboard box, the white walls of the marquee exploded into view. There was Goodwin, heading through the main entrance between a pair of spotlights. He held to his stomach two metal boxes, the top one without its lid. Behind him maybe twenty necromeleons—some male, some female—all carried at least one box. Most wore patient gowns, some were naked. All of them held the same stare: dead and determined.

Between me and the marquee, Victor and Isidore flicked up dirt as they ran. All I wanted was to stop running and hold my bastard knee. Hot needles boiled inside it. Tears streaked my face.

By now, Goodwin's dead followers had disappeared inside the marquee.

The music cut off and the screams began.

CHAPTER 43

I bounded into the dimly lit marquee. The audience was on its feet, screaming as people collided. The seats had been closely arranged, and everyone tripped over upended chairs and each other.

Victor had taken out two necromeleons, the rancid stench of scorched flesh sharp on the air. Chunks of burning limbs lay scattered at his feet, while Isidore's gunshots tore into the evening. The Witchblade's flames still flickered around them.

Onstage, the orchestra were in as much of a mess as their audience. Abandoned instruments and scattered chairs lay about the raised platform as the entire ensemble scrabbled to get away, shoving one another. Some still clutched their instruments. One bow-tied man dragged his cello and it bounced off a music stand, smacking into the shin of a woman who ran with a violin above her head. She crashed to the stage and her violin disappeared under the stampede.

The conductor crouched with hands to his ears, while beside him the event's organiser, Jocelyn, still stood. Her arms were folded. They wore similar expressions of confusion and terror.

Goodwin ran towards them, holding in each hand a metal box. The lids were off. His fingers seemed abnormally long and he raised his arms. And they lengthened. None of the musicians managed to flee as he launched the boxes at the stage, his throw perhaps charged by the shadows, and propelled in equal measure by his stretched limbs. The contents of the boxes spilled over everyone's heads like a swarm of insects, and as one, the musicians came to a halt. They reached out and grasped the fluttering shadowleaves. The conductor and Jocelyn held a handful of leaves, and together, they sat like obedient children.

The musicians also began stitching.

Between the stage and us, the necromeleons ran down the aisles among the uprising crowd. They all held metal boxes, more shadowleaves.

Men, women, and children scrambled to flee. They slapped aside chairs, bashed into people, and clawed through the bedlam. A man knocked down a woman and stepped over her. People, old and young, were frantic for their lives while the dead rushed in.

As Isidore reloaded her gun, I pulled open my cardboard box. Furniture polish cans rolled inside. God bless Suzy and her forgetfulness. I grabbed one and knocked off the lid. With a moment's fumble, I flicked open Goodwin's lighter—awkward because of the gloves—and thumbed the wheel. Holding it at arm's reach, I aimed the can's nozzle at the flame.

My eyes searched for a target.

Isidore fired a couple of rounds at the nearest dead men. They each held a metal box, the lids chattering as they ran. The bullets didn't slow them.

Victor cut down several more necromeleons. Still they came through the side entrances, carrying more boxes. Occasionally a container would drop, the shadowleaves flying—it didn't help the dead were running, their legs unable to keep their bodies upright.

Unlike the necromeleons we'd seen so far, these were quick. Energised, I guessed, by the stronger Shadow Fabric.

I squeezed the nozzle and fire roared at an approaching dead man. He screamed as flames licked his head and he threw the metal box into the crowd, as had the other necromeleons.

The stench of burnt hair and flesh wafted over me. I coughed and spat. Isidore did the same, her face contorted. Victor leapt towards us. With quick wrist flicks, he created a shield of flame above our heads. Tracers of orange crackled. It made me squint, while the comforting smell of ozone fell around us.

Arcing overhead, dozens of boxes spewed shadowleaves over the fleeing crowd. They exploded like devil's confetti.

People jerked to a halt as the leaves touched them. Some frantically reached out and grabbed them unknowingly. Others faltered, and several stopped when seeing the majority of their neighbours stop. Confusion etched into every face as all around them people sat down, some on seats while others dropped amidst upturned chairs.

With their way blocked by blank-faced stitchers, those still lucid exchanged glances. From an audience of around a thousand, there must've been fifty or so left standing. This number swiftly decreased as several necromeleons rushed them. The dead men, their gowns flapping, smashed their legs into the sitting stitchers. Chairs tumbled as the necromeleons hurled a handful of shadowleaves into the remaining stunned faces.

A final scream echoed.

The frantic sounds of escape no longer filled the marquee and the following silence was incredible. I heard an occasional shuffle as the stitching got underway. We had failed. With all these stitchers stitching, this would energise the Fabric and the Entity would soon complete its haunt. Isidore, Victor, and I stood side by side, helpless. Isidore's weapon shook as she pointed it at each necromeleon, though she wasted no more shots. Victor would occasionally wave the Witchblade to reinforce our canopy of flame. The shadowleaves flew over us and flared on impact with it. As they burned away, the protective fire dimmed.

The necromeleons who'd entered the crowd now stood still, while most of the others flanked the perimeter of the stitching audience like sentinels. Several were onstage with Goodwin, who towered over the conductor. The man sat cross-legged. He held a shadowleaf in both hands and pressed them together. Next to him, Jocelyn already stitched.

To the back of the stage, a cellist—the guy who'd been dragging his instrument—dropped his cello as he concentrated on the shadowleaf in his other hand, and he fell to his knees. The cello boomed the last note of the evening.

Goodwin wore a smirk that did not belong on his face. I had to remind myself it wasn't Goodwin, it was the Entity.

The diminishing wisps of flame fell around us without harm, and Victor stepped away. His chest heaved and dismay brought his eyebrows together. Another flurry of Witchblade swipes and another ring of fire protected us. Isidore remained close by my side as she lowered her gun. I lowered my can of polish. I was ready to use a second can if necessary. My head hammered, my lungs burned, my knee throbbed, and my eyes ached. Between the stage and the three of us, an uneven blanket of upright bodies twitched as one like a sea of rippling waves. Beneath dim lighting, the main focus was the stage where the musicians now played very different instruments.

And there was Goodwin, standing centre-stage, palms open and slowly raising his arms. His voice came like a bark. "Let's begin."

It was as though the crowd were in prayer, worshipping him. Stitch-stitch-stitch.

A darkness crept into the marquee. The light dimmed, albeit slightly, as the lesser shadows entered. Grey ones, elongating and flitting, and then the Shadow Fabric oozed through the side entrances. Its black mass bulged through the doorways, every exit now blocked. As it pushed inwards, the canvas tore. The poles bent and popped from their housing. The rigging collapsed in a tangle of supports and cables. In sections, the lights sparked out. More canvas shredded, leaving only skeletal supports as the Fabric rushed in like a black river.

"Victor!" I shouted.

"Stay there, Leo. Wait."

"Wait for what?" Isidore glared at him. "Let's get out of here."

"We'll be dead the moment we try!" he shouted over the tearing canvas and clanking metal. He swung the Witchblade, encircling us with flame. "Stay where you are."

Great strips of the canvas flapped as the Fabric whipped into a frenzy. The main body of Fabric surged over the stitching crowd, pulling away the final portion of sheeting, then hurled it into the fields.

"Victor!" I screamed at him. "We've got to do something."

While there were only a few disconnected supports, most of the marquee rigging remained in place. The two spotlights now poured their brilliance over the stitching crowd. Its glare highlighted the nightmare before us.

The stitchers continued to stitch as we stood shoulder to shoulder. I glared at Victor. *Stay there*, he'd said. I clutched Goodwin's lighter and a can of furniture polish, watching as the Shadow Fabric hurled itself upwards. It spiralled above the tree line and abruptly altered course, accelerating in an arc, and slammed into the gardens. Spitting chunks of hedges and dirt, the earth erupted as the Fabric burrowed beneath us like some gigantic worm. The ground rumbled and I staggered, clutching tight my pathetic can. My leg gave way. I fell onto my hands and knees, and Isidore tried to pull me up. Her wide eyes searched my face. They reflected my own fear.

The shattering of windows tore into the evening, and from the south wing of the House, glinting shards poured into the gardens. Chunks of masonry fell away in dusty resignation.

With the ground heaving and a thousand or more stitchers twitching, Goodwin stood before it all with hands on his hips. Parts of Periwick House crumbled as the earth shook its foundations.

"What can we do?" Isidore crouched beside me, holding me. The Witchblade fire sparked overhead. "This is madness."

"I have no idea." I grimaced, not wanting to move. My bad knee throbbed and sent hot spikes into my thigh.

"You okay?" she asked.

A weak smile was my only reply as I managed to stand. Beyond her, out in the car park, I saw something...

The gravel bulged and the vehicles rippled as the Fabric surged underground. Several headlights flashed as alarms squawked. The rumble subsided for a moment, and in an upheaval of cars, the Fabric blasted out from its burrow. More alarms wailed in cacophonic protest as the vehicles catapulted into the air. A motorcycle spun and smacked into the House's roof in a scattering of tiles. Its front wheel hooked onto the edge and hung there. Cars flipped and crashed, windscreens shattered, and metal and plastic rained down. Hunks of tarmac shot into the earth. Cars crashed atop cars. There were no Hollywood explosions, only an inky darkness rushing through the bedlam.

Isidore's hair was a flurry as the Fabric corkscrewed, whipping up dirt and debris. The air rushed into my ears and added to the roaring blood coursing through my head.

I saw Victor running from us.

"Victor!" I screamed. What was he doing? With flashes of bare ankles, he hurdled the stitchers. He stumbled occasionally, zigzagging towards the stage. Sparking fire trailed behind the Witchblade as he raised it. The closer he got to the stage, the brighter the strip of flame. It seared the retina, yet I couldn't help staring. Like a burning rope, it flared and lashed the air behind him.

All this time, Goodwin watched him approach, amusement smeared across his face.

With his arm raised, Victor moved the Witchblade in circles, and a charge of fiery energies coiled into a lasso. With a flick of the wrist, he sent the streamer at the man standing on the stage. The blazing rope looped around Goodwin's neck and jerked his body rigid. His arms dropped and his face shifted from amusement to something else. The features melted like wax. His head swelled and warped as the Entity seethed beneath the mask of Goodwin's face. Its powers were escalating, yet still restricted by its human form.

An almost welcome relief of darkness passed before us as another crash shook the earth. Shrouded by the Fabric, another portion of the House crumbled and flattened a row of bushes. Mud and debris flew.

Under the continued protection of fire, Isidore and I stood aghast, inhaling the smoky destruction. Both of us coughed. Small fires were everywhere. I didn't know where to look, the Shadow Fabric, the stage, or the House.

I felt helpless. *Stay there…*

The Entity reached outwards and dimmed the light. No sooner had the darkness drenched the flame, another fiery blanket burst from the Witchblade and wrapped around Goodwin's false body.

I yelled at Victor—I had to *do* something. I wanted to help.

"Isidore, I—" My jaw ached.

She gripped her gun in both hands, eyeing the devastation.

Now completely immobilised, the Entity struggled as Victor, dragged by the Witchblade, flew up towards the stage. Both his feet left the ground as the fiery streamers pulled him up.

Isidore's hair rested on her shoulders as the Fabric calmed itself. It now hovered above the ruined car park. Why the sudden cease in its destructive rampage, and what was the thing waiting for? The answer came immediately. Its surface rippled and hundreds of tentacles shot out. Probing, wriggling, and whipping. Searching...

And the whispers began. Indistinct at first, revealing their presence. They came from the Fabric. They suggested I should run. To escape from the canopy of protective flames. The voices writhed through my brain. I wanted to run as fast as I could. I wanted to fight. To cry. Hide. Kill myself.

Isidore held her arms over her head. "Tell it to stop!"

The fire around us blazed brighter still and erupted in a sputtering wall. The voices—those teasing murmurs—faded into darkness. My shoulders slumped and my head emptied. Isidore dropped her arms. Her cheeks were moist and her eyes glistened.

"This is too much," she told me.

The stitchers were collapsing into dusty heaps, their shadowleaves now stitched, and floated away in dark clouds. Those transient shadows merged with the lesser shadows, hooking into new pieces of the Fabric. Given the spotlights, the various fires, and the spreading darkness, it was difficult to see detail. The necromeleons remained inactive, with new strands of Fabric snaking up their legs. Tentacles from the main body of the Fabric snatched at them and pulled them down. As the stitchers fell, so did the necromeleons. Each collapsed body and dead henchman slipped into the Shadow Fabric.

Victor and Goodwin wrestled onstage in a match of Light versus Dark. Sputtering streamers whipped the air.

The Fabric's intruding whispers echoed, though their suggestions meant nothing. The only thought remaining was to fight, yet I dared not emerge from the Witchblade's shield. I could only peer between the tracers of fire Victor had created for us. I wanted—no, I *needed*—to help.

Isidore screamed in my ear, "Leo!"

Reluctantly, I let my gaze snap off and I gritted my teeth.

She grabbed me and shook me, glaring past my head. "Leo!"

An arm of Fabric had crept behind us and flattened into a scoop of darkness. It blocked out the sky. I flicked the lighter and brought up a can of polish. A roar of fire pushed through the fiery canopy into the Fabric. The black folds pressed down onto the skittering traceries of our shield.

Isidore shouted something, her body against mine.

The scorching flame crackled and flared intermittently, and my fumbling fingers dropped the lighter. Idiot. I bent and groped for it.

The light dimmed.

We were going to die.

Victor and Goodwin grappled. With the Fabric obscuring my view of the stage—so much darkness—I saw Goodwin snatch the flaming lasso from his throat and shove Victor to the floor.

I gripped the lighter.

Victor crumpled, pain twisting his face, and the Witchblade flew from his hand. It landed amongst the remaining stitchers in the audience.

The darkness lowered. Onto us. In one hand, I held Isidore close, and in the other I clutched the Zippo—my fingers too weak to use it.

The fire shield sputtered out and the light faded to black.

Voices invaded my brain and I cried out. Isidore said something I failed to hear through the cacophony. The filthy, mind-intruding darkness clogged my ears, my brain, my every fibre. Isidore pressed herself against me, still screaming into my ear. Our collective fear roared, twinned with millions of shrieking voices. All I tasted was death.

I could smell a mustiness, the heavy presence of the Fabric. Darkness squeezed, tighter.

That's all there was. Darkness.

CHAPTER 44

The Shadow Fabric arched over us, and in a vortex of black waves, it shot away and slammed into the House. Brick and glass exploded. In an instant, the voices snapped off.

I gasped and Isidore relaxed in my arms.

The Fabric tore through the wrecked masonry.

Inside the roiling mass of shadow, half submerged as if trapped in tar, were the bodies of necromeleons and stitchers. The rush of darkness was like a tsunami, tearing down all it struck, dragging more bodies en route. Drowning its victims— although these were already dead. Unlike the natural course of such a destructive wave, governed by momentum and gravity, this torrent of charged evil had a life of its own. Even slices of turf and trees were pulled into the Fabric.

The majority of people had ceased stitching, now drained of their energies, and clouds of newly stitched shadows floated to join the darkness which continued to creep in on them. More stitchers collapsed. Few remained alive. All were shrouded in shadow, yet only Isidore and I were left alone as though the Fabric, and the recently stitched patches, had spared us.

"What…" Isidore's eyes were wide. We still clung to one another.

I shook my head. I knew what she was asking. "No idea."

"Why aren't we dead?" She gently moved away from me.

"No idea." It weakened me each time that pathetic answer rolled from my tongue. Still, it was the truth.

No longer were there any traces of Witchblade fire around us, the Fabric having extinguished every last protective streamer.

The Fabric's slithering tail vanished beneath the foundations. Crumbled masonry and wooden splinters buckled in a tangle of cables and plumbing, followed by a belch of dust.

I pressed the lighter and the can of polish into Isidore's hands. Without a word, I left her and ran towards the Witchblade.

Victor was now on his back. Goodwin leaned over him and pointed a finger. Behind them the last of the musician stitchers fell, a dark wisp of newly stitched Fabric floated away. It seeped into Goodwin's shoulders. His image rippled as darkness squirmed beneath his false flesh.

I ran, and it was difficult to ignore the crack of bones beneath my boots as I sprinted as best I could over the bodies. At first, I tried to leap over them, but it was impossible. Dust puffed around me, and on several occasions my feet tangled with clothes and almost pulled me down. With this and my screaming knee, I waited for the moment I would drop amongst the dead and be consumed by shadows.

I reached the spot where I believed the athame to be. My head moved from side to side. Somewhere here, somewhere...*somewhere*.

The ground still rumbled as the Shadow Fabric displaced the earth. On the perimeter of the gardens, great oaks and silver birches groaned and crashed in bursts of leaves, branches, and splintered trunks. Dirt and paving slabs spat out as if the ground coughed.

As I rummaged between the bodies my stomach churned; my gloves had whitened, covered in the dust of the dead.

Somewhere... somewhere here...

On my hands and knees, a glance at the stage showed me that Goodwin no longer resembled the man I'd known; even though I knew it to be the Entity, I couldn't help seeing it as him. Dark patches covered his face, bubbling beneath the flesh. The Entity was contained, still restricted to the form of man, yet its power was swiftly escalating. Victor sat up. The mass of deformed flesh towered over him.

Slapping aside fragile bones, my hands fumbled watches, wallets and rings, bracelets, earrings and necklaces. I gritted my teeth as my stomach somersaulted. *Somewhere here...*

Again, I glanced up, this time to Isidore. Short bursts of flame from the can she held forced back the darkness. Her mouth was small, eyes in a squint, a stance to be reckoned with.

Then to Victor, and I saw the Entity pressing him to the stage. Shadows flitted around them.

Somewhere…

And then I found it. The Witchblade was warm to the touch and perfectly snug in my grip. I sprung to my feet as a crowd of voices filled my head. Each one an echo of affirmation, confirmation—the blade was mine, all mine. Holding the Witchblade was like brandishing a sword. Undeniably powerful. Such was the power in my hand, I was energised. No longer did I hurt anywhere. I felt taller, incredibly giant-like. No, not a giant. I was like a god.

Inhaling the ozone, I ran to the stage with my arm outstretched, led by the sparking Witchblade. No longer was the agony tearing at my knee—it was as though the Witchblade acted as a kind of anaesthesia, its voices soothing me all the while.

The Entity—now looking less like Goodwin—leaned over Victor. Tentacles emerged from Goodwin's stomach and wrapped around Victor's exposed ankle.

"Victor!" My voice wasn't as loud as his agony.

Cool fire circled the Witchblade. There wasn't any warmth, yet at the same time there was a tingle. And those voices, reassuring me. I reached the stage and the flames whipped around my arm. Near my feet, the clothes of fallen stitchers caught fire.

From inside the bulbous body of what was once Goodwin, the Entity pushed outwards. It was like seeing two images, overlapping one another; reality being challenged as an echo of absolute malediction thrashed against the shell of that cruel impersonation.

I was witnessing the completion of its haunt.

With renewed energy, I bounded onto the wooden platform and rushed to Victor's side. Where the shadows looped around his exposed ankles, his flesh blistered. It smouldered. His sweaty face told me the rest.

The stink of burnt skin made me gag.

I lunged and rammed the Witchblade into the tentacles that held him. Fire exploded along the lengths of darkness, and they drew back into Goodwin's stomach. The jacket neatly linked together as though nothing had protruded from it. The image of Goodwin, however, greyed swiftly. Failing perhaps. It darkened in places and became less vivid. No longer was it glaringly false, yet the Entity's true form was still evident. Haunting.

Darkness rippled behind Goodwin's face, and the impassive expression shifted as the Entity altered that mask to an arrogant smirk. All I wanted was to be rid of it, to smash my fist—my *blade*—into the face which didn't belong there.

From Goodwin's eye sockets, streams of darkness shot towards me. The two jets became one. I braced myself and held the athame high as fire rushed outwards, then I twisted sideways.

The shadows smashed against my fiery shield.

Victor's legs were a bloody mess of torn trousers and flesh. His lips moved.

Under the strain of holding back the shadows, my back and shoulders ached. They burned. My legs buckled. Sweat prickled my forehead and my arms screamed.

My leg slipped.

I dropped onto my side. With my knee exploding in agony, I cried out. The flaming shield thinned, sputtered, and crackled. It was losing intensity. I still gripped the Witchblade in both hands, but the moment of disorientation had broken my mental link with it. Just the tiniest of moments was all it took, and the flames failed to protect me. Failed me and Victor…

As fleeting as the moment was, that was all the Entity needed.

A relentless energy surged behind Goodwin's form. It fuelled the pummelling shadows and they broke through. They rushed past me and speared Victor's body. His stomach burst open, the shadows thrusting into him. Blood sprayed and offal erupted.

"Victor!" I ignored my protesting knee and spun the Witchblade around. It sliced into the serpentine shadow that coiled into his body. Too late. His body jerked as the Entity roared and retracted the shadows. They whipped away, avoiding the protective fire now spreading around Victor's body.

So much blood. So much mess.

Victor's dead eyes stared at nothing.

CHAPTER 45

With Victor's name on my lips, I sprang to my feet. The Witchblade's cool fire encircled me. Looking nothing like Goodwin, the Entity's burning eyes pulsed.

And it knew it couldn't touch me.

Although it still held the shape and size of Goodwin, there was no mistaking its mask. There was a subtle displacement as the Entity raged beneath the image of the man I once knew, the man I once trusted. The flesh bubbled and spat. No longer was it even bipedal, just a shifting mass of shadow. Not of this world. Its haunt so close to completion.

I glanced at Victor's lifeless body and my grip tightened on the Witchblade. I tore my eyes from the mess of my friend's torso and advanced on the Entity. My jaw ached from my clenched teeth.

In a deluge of stygian black, the Fabric absorbed most of the stage, the musical instruments, and the husks of stitchers. It spread and took out the remains of the marquee and part of the garden. It rushed down the gaping crevices of what was once the car park, and raged outwards into the woodlands. Roaring, circling us, the Fabric closed in on the Entity, and it puffed up like a cobra ready to strike.

And it did.

With a snap, it devoured the grey lump of the Entity. Together, the Entity and the Fabric churned in black folds. Shadows coiled and streamed, knotting in a frenzy.

"Shit," I said. My heartbeat crowded my head. I raised the Witchblade and sparks flew, tumbling over my gloved hand. The smell of ozone was rich in my nostrils. Straight-backed, legs wide, I glared at the Fabric as the Entity's carmine eyes throbbed within.

So, the Entity was out. Released. Its haunt complete, and existed in this world through the medium of the Shadow Fabric. Strong enough to be without the life force of the dead, able to move freely within the Fabric itself, free to exist within our universe.

And like this to infinity...

Staring out of the Fabric, the burning eyes intensified and expanded. They separated and became another pair, equally brilliant. The four eyes flared and grew and became eight eyes, and more popped open. Many, many eyes. From where they were, a stem of shadow protruded from the Fabric like a grotesque neck. It saw me through dozens of eyes that reached into my core. Each was an accusation, mocking me. It was like gazing into the night's sky where the stars weren't blue ice chips against a black backdrop, but burning yellows and oranges, like too many Jupiters. Or maybe Mars by the power of a thousand... Mars, God of War.

Only this wasn't war. This was pure evil. There I was, in a face-off with undiluted Evil. The bastard burrowed into my soul, tearing my thought processes down, stripping them into baser instincts where Man's own darkness dwells. As the Entity connected with that primal nature which exists deep within us, I roared, spit flying. I stepped forward, without any idea what made me do it. Perhaps it was Modern Man conflicting against the Cave Man. And for all my arrogant stupidity to face down such an enemy as the Entity, the lumpy head with those burning eyes flinched, albeit slightly.

The heat of the Witchblade—*my* Witchblade—intensified and fire erupted like a geyser. Above the House, above the trees.

Tracers of flame curved outwards in every direction. Some crackled, some roared. Thousands of fireballs scattered across the Shadow Fabric, and beneath each impact, its surface bubbled, blistered, and hissed.

Witchblade sparks showered my face, ozone pouring into my lungs. The power pumped my muscles with adrenaline. It was as though a god-like energy charged the fibres of my tiny mortal body.

I slammed the blade into the Fabric, between its many eyes. Again and again. I hooked it around and pinned the cursed thing to the edge of the stage. The boards were blackened by small fires, and more leapt across the grass where the floor had come apart, scorching a wider expanse.

The dark head writhed under my power. Its banshee wail stormed into my mind. Where the athame sunk into the Fabric, flames sputtered and the eyes blinked out, leaving only one pair in the dark void of its bulbous head.

They were Goodwin's.

No, I told myself, *they only* look *like Goodwin's. They're not actually his.* A sickness washed over me as those eyes drew me in—focusing on an essence of life. And it spoke to me. Just me. No one else. It held promises. It told me I'd have her back, I could have Amy back.

"Amy?" I whispered.

Amy, it said, *she can be yours again.*

I moaned, my lips numbing.

Everything can be the same again, it told me. *You must release the Witchblade. Discard the athame. Lose it. Bury it.*

Bury it? Amy was—is—buried! My head, my shoulders, my whole body constricted as though hundreds of kilos of earth pushed down on me. I choked on it, feeling it scatter down my throat. It stuffed my windpipe. Smothering me...

Amy. I saw her. Could smell her. There she was, the image of the girl I once loved—still love! Her hair, her smile, and the way her cheeks bunched up when she laughed. *Laughs...* When she laughs...she can laugh again.

And the Entity promised to bring her back.

It wasn't earth that clogged my throat, it was tears. The dampness cooled my cheeks. Soothing, like the Witchblade fire rushing along my arm as it held the Entity.

Promises...

Goodwin's eyes held me. *Trust me*, they said. *She can be in your arms again.* Trust. Goodwin? I wanted to laugh, yet couldn't.

Yes.

And the eyes became Amy's. Sharp, piercing, a shade of green. There was love there. There always had been. Still was...

Can be again.

Amy's face shimmered in the darkness.

"Amy?" I said. "Amy!"

Agony fired up my leg—from my knee—and I wrenched my gaze away. Not Amy's eyes at all. Nor were they Goodwin's.

They belonged to the Entity.

Filling my mind as the trance broke, the Entity's shriek clawed through me. I shook my head as a wave of nausea threatened to drag me into my own darkness.

The searing pain kept me lucid.

A streamer of fire had hooked itself around my knee, one end still attached to the Witchblade. The stink of burning material and singed flesh crawled up my nostrils.

"Bastard!" I twisted the Witchblade even further into the thrashing lump of the Fabric.

Isidore was now closer to the stage. She shook a can of furniture polish and waved the Zippo before her. Her hair obscured her face and I could just make out her wide eyes.

The shadows were closing in on her. Fast.

And an explosion tore the sky.

It was from the House, the restaurant now a rush of fire and masonry and shards of so much glass.

CHAPTER 46

The erupting walls of Periwick House lit up the evening as if the sun had returned. I staggered and my grip of the Witchblade slipped. The blade was still buried in the Entity's head, and I fell back, landing on my arse. With rapid breaths, tears streaming down my face, I somehow kept hold.

Rubble and patches of fire settled throughout the scorched gardens. Amidst the collapsed part of the building, the fireball had retreated and now remained a flicker of tree-high tongues. Fires had broken out everywhere, smoke adding to the hazy darkness. Amazingly, the spotlights still glowed like a pair of lighthouses in fog.

With the Entity pinned by the blade, I tightened my grip with renewed resolve. My teeth ached and I grunted, pushing down against the thing. Still dizzy from the explosion, I searched for Isidore. There she was on the ground. For a moment my stomach lurched as I thought she'd been brought down by the shadows, but no, she was on her knees. She tore the cardboard box open and shouted obscenities. I guessed there were no more cans of polish left.

The Shadow Fabric spread to such an expanse it was difficult to tell where it ended and the natural evening shadows began. The edge closest to Isidore was a rippling mass of tentacles, like some mythological leviathan of the deep, breaking the surface of a midnight ocean and flailing its limbs to bring down its quarry in a fatal embrace.

Isidore's eyes reflected fear and fire.

The crash of trees in the distance snatched away the sound of roaring flames. Along the perimeter of the grounds, the Fabric wrenched them from the earth and sucked them into its darkness. The sharp crack of breaking trunks echoed around us.

I straightened. My head reeled and my ears rang. With the Witchblade deep in the lump of darkness, I yanked. In a crackle of orange sparks the blade split the head in two and the Entity's scream tore through my mind.

The head, now eyeless, slithered into the mass of Fabric as the flames broke away. Fire crawled along the edge and across its surface. A wall of flame shot into the sky and swept outwards over the Fabric. Blinding.

I grinned and yelled, "Yes!" as the lake of darkness succumbed to the Witchblade's fire. In seconds a dome of comforting flame encased the mass of the Fabric. Yet several patches still managed to defy the fire.

The Entity's shriek rattled in my head.

The seething Fabric outside the flames stretched and clumped into tentacles. They thrashed as small fires ate into them. One lashed at Isidore.

She stumbled.

I shouted at her and squinted into the flames like I stared at the sun. Sweat and tears drenched my face. She fell into a crouch and brought up her can. The snake of darkness went to strike her and a roar of fire whipped it away. It exploded. Small chunks of darkness smouldered and the sparks dwindled.

I bounded over the stitchers' bodies. This time not even attempting to avoid stomping on any. Witchblade fire sputtered around me. Several fireballs shot at the remaining limbs of shadow.

Reaching Isidore as she straightened, I eyed the remnants of shadows. The fire consumed them. My head hammered and I heard the Entity raging from inside the Fabric, imprisoned within that fiery dome.

"What else can we do?" Isidore's eyes were wide.

"Don't know." The Witchblade crackled in my hand. "Victor's gone. Goodwin's gone. This is so messed up."

She shook her head and screwed her eyes tight. "It's horrible."

"You can hear it, too?"

She nodded and opened her eyes.

Inside our heads the Entity continued to scream.

More flames ate into the House and parts of the roof collapsed in great plumes of dust and smoke. Another rush of fire. So bright, we held our arms up, squinting, looking away.

Something was happening to the perimeter of the fiery dome. It swelled—breathed almost—and then it shrank. In thickening clouds of darkness, the dome closed in on the bulk of Fabric leaving a ring of singed grass. Fractionally, second by second, it continued to shrink.

I blinked at the smoke scratching my eyes and coughed as it stuffed itself down my throat.

Isidore clutched the Zippo and brought it up to her face. "Like this back?"

"Keep hold of it." I coughed again.

Before she replied, a dog barked from inside the ruined House.

"Georgie!" Isidore grabbed my arm. "We have to get him."

I had no say in the matter, because she sprinted across the burning gardens. She dodged smouldering masonry and headed towards the entrance to the House.

With a glance at the shrinking dome, I felt a strange sense of calm. I had defeated the Entity. Hadn't I?

Isidore had already covered a considerable distance and with the Entity's voice still echoing in my head, I ran after her. The back end of the House was mostly in flaming ruins, while the majority of its frontage remained intact. As I rounded the corner, I almost slammed into Isidore. She stood looking across the immense burrows where the Fabric had churned up the ground. Her eyes darted around, searching every dark corner. We leapt over the heaps of earth and cracked paving, and jogged towards the entrance. My knee throbbed.

The Entity's voice had lessened, yet I sensed it reaching out, influencing something else: the shadows. Such was the Entity's power, although the flaming dome continued to force the Fabric into a tighter bundle of darkness, it was still capable of manipulating the shadows around us. They merged into one—shadowplay in the making. It wouldn't be the Shadow Fabric as such, but close enough to be lethal. I'd witnessed too many times the capability of ordinary shadows. Even as we approached the entrance, those shadows rippled with sentient menace directed en masse by the Entity.

Georgie's sharp barks suggested he saw us. We couldn't see him.

I followed Isidore over the threshold and into the foyer. My heart lurched. Beyond chasms of rubble and earth and flitting shadows, the crumbled staircase curled behind the remains of the reception area. Somewhere overhead and past the splintered balustrades was my room. This place, the only home I remembered, had been my sanctuary. Goodwin, for all his deceit, had welcomed me and given me somewhere I could call home. Had he really cured me?

My home was now destroyed.

From beneath the foyer, lumps of concrete had cleaved the marble floor and burst through at jagged angles. Given the Fabric's burrowing, the devastation wasn't a surprise.

Through the smoke, I saw something: several buckled rods of metal pinching a mattress. Dark stains covered the material and a wheel pressed into its soft edge. The twisted bulk was a gurney from under the House where Goodwin's experiments had taken place. Where he experimented on me. Even cured me? I could've died like most, or perhaps gone mad. Or worse, I could've been one of the reanimated dead.

I remembered all the necromeleons down there and knew why the Shadow Fabric had burrowed into the ground, tearing up the foundations.

It wanted to get to something—many things...

As I followed Georgie's barks and manoeuvred around gaping holes, the first of many dead hands clutched at the jagged edges. They clawed and reached out into the smoking air.

CHAPTER 47

Isidore screamed and leapt away as a metal box bounced between us in a flutter of shadowleaves. It skittered across the lobby floor and shot down a fissure. The Shadow Fabric's earlier burrowing had a purpose when it heaved up the House foundations—to release the reanimated dead from their cells.

It succeeded.

Remaining where she crouched, Isidore slipped a full magazine into her gun. A moment later, her hand recoiled as the sharp crack of her weapon shocked my ringing ears. Her target's head snapped back and darkness dribbled from the hole in its forehead. The necromeleon still clambered out of the ruined floor. Isidore targeted others and pulled off another three or four rounds. Still they came.

It was time to see what else the Witchblade was capable of.

Careful to step around the shadowleaves, I held up the Witchblade. It streamed fire in short bursts to protect us. Cool flames spread around my arm, my muscles tingling. The comforting smell of ozone teased my senses and displaced the thickening smoke.

From all sides, as half a dozen necromeleons clambered into view, the shadows closed in. The condensed darkness further dimmed the light of the foyer. From a crevice near my feet, dead eyes stared at me, the face framed in unmistakeable red hair. With an outstretched arm, Katrina's reanimated corpse grabbed my hand. I yanked myself away and left her with my glove. I swung the Witchblade around and down to drive it between her eyes. Fire blistered behind her face, and the black orbs of her eyes burst in a spray of pus and shadow. She fell back into the gloom, taking my glove with her.

With only one glove, I didn't have time to be concerned—I would have to be careful not to touch any shadowleaves should any come my way.

Most of the other necromeleons held one or two metal boxes. Their vacant eyes contained the evil that charged them.

My stomach wrenched when I glanced at Isidore. She had stopped moving. In her palm she held a shadowleaf. I assumed it had floated into her hand. Curiosity wriggled across her face, mesmerised by the dark energies within the leaf.

Her fingers curled inwards. Slowly.

"No!" I shouted, and with my gloved hand, I slapped the thing from her. It shot into the air and spun like any normal leaf would. It disappeared into the buckled floor.

For a moment, Isidore looked ready to hit me, her eyes narrowing beneath a bloody brow. Confusion wiped away her fury, and with a shake of her head, she mumbled an apology.

I didn't reply, but swept the Witchblade overhead. Its flames snatched more of the fluttering shadowleaves from the air, each one flaring and sizzling. As the tiny fires died, a necromeleon stepped through the smoke, lit up by the raging flames. Absurdly, I recognised the walking dead man when I saw his belt buckle: Bud. His mouth dripped red, messy, still caked with Katrina's blood. Behind him, more dead men and women emerged from the smoke and darkness. Their pale flesh reflected the sprouting fires. Bud didn't move towards us. Indeed, they all allowed the shadows to play around their ankles, each of them settling dead eyes on us.

It was as though the shadows had stopped their advancement.

I didn't waste time. I mimicked Victor's moves from earlier and twirled the Witchblade above my head. With every revolution, the flames thickened to light the area. Sparks bounced harmlessly from me as I quickened that circular movement. The familiar, fresh smell of ozone displaced the smoking air, doing little to calm my racing heart. Round and round and round, brighter and brighter, and with a sudden jerk of my arm, I let fly the fire.

It shot out and spread towards the necromeleons.

The closer the sheet of flame got to the waiting dead, the wider it fanned out, and just before it enveloped the crowd, it separated into dozens of fireballs. Each one aimed at the chest of a chosen victim, engulfing it individually.

All of them exploded in a brilliant flash.

I turned my head and screwed my eyes tight as the brightness overwhelmed everything. Pieces of burning flesh flew around us. Something hot and wet hit my cheek.

The Entity raged from within the Fabric. I sensed it smashing against the flames of the shrinking dome. Its scream pierced my brain and I yelled in triumph. I hoped it felt its minions burn. Seconds passed and the fire dwindled. At some point, I'd grabbed Isidore and held her head to my chest. We were safe—at least for the moment—from the Entity, yet the shadowplay appeared to be intensifying. The rippling phantoms meshed together. What was happening now?

The shadows darkened…solidified, to become a newer, fresher, stronger, Fabric.

A new Shadow Fabric? "Shit!" I shouted, and more Witchblade fire flared around us.

A snap and crack echoed from above, and the balcony crashed into the reception area. Part of the roof slid downwards and belched a cloud of dust.

"Georgie?" Isidore said.

There he was, backing into the darkness under the buckled staircase, away from the settling heap of debris.

Isidore ducked beneath the safety of the mounting Witchblade flames and ran towards the dog. Her hunched shoulders broke our protective barrier. In a swirl of criss-crossing sparks, the cool flames fell away.

I screamed her name and ran after her. As my leg came down on the uneven floor, my knee gave out and I shot sideways. I fell onto my arm, luckily not stabbing myself with the Witchblade. Pain fired up into my thigh as I pushed myself into a crouch, testing my weight on the damaged knee.

The new Shadow Fabric whipped an arm of darkness at Isidore. It smacked her to the ground and she tumbled close to a gaping hole. Fire licked along the marble chunks. As her head came up, the new Fabric closed in. A wall of eager shadows encircled her. They grew and allowed her one exit, a jagged burrow into darkness.

The new Fabric flexed behind her.

Isidore clutched the gun to her chest and a finger slid behind the trigger guard. She looked at me as I limped towards her. Damn my knee.

She shook her head, lowering her eyes.

"No!" I hurried. Each step sent lightning agony into my leg. This couldn't happen, I wasn't going to let it.

This new Fabric wasn't any larger than the original when Stanley pulled it from the violin case. Yet it seemed more lucid, more alive. I felt its evil invade my mind, seep into my thoughts. Snaking limbs of darkness reached for the scattered shadowleaves and snatched them up. They sparked on contact as strange energies criss-crossed the new Fabric's surface...and into it. Shadows within shadows, charging the black mass. Each leaf sparked as the Fabric absorbed it.

I yelled at Isidore as I staggered towards her and the new Fabric. Towards the fresh, brand new Fabric as it began to stitch itself. I saw those knitting threads of darkness interlinking and binding tight...

And it was stitching around Isidore.

"No!" I screamed. The essence of the new Fabric leaked into my senses. I tasted its influence, and God knew how Isidore felt.

Defeat spread across her face.

Eyes closed, she pushed the gun muzzle beneath her chin.

CHAPTER 48

I hurdled the yawning darkness and crashed beside Isidore on an explosion of pain. The new Shadow Fabric now surrounded us both. Although tiny in comparison to the one contained in the fiery dome, there could be no denying its power. On the edge of its folds the shadowleaves stitched, weaving threads of darkness.

Isidore's finger tightened on the trigger and the barrel sank into her flesh.

Throbbing like a heartbeat, the Entity's agony still raged in my brain. I clenched the Witchblade between my teeth and tore at the arms of shadow, wrenching them from the Fabric. They were slippery as my bare hand yanked on them. Clammy, sticky, slimy. It felt wrong and my stomach churned.

Eyes wide, Isidore lowered her gun. In the gloom, surrounded by darkness, it would've been hard to miss her red face and tears. She slumped into herself as I worked around her. I slapped away a few black feelers while grabbing others. Regardless that I wore only one glove, my hands attacked the tentacles in a frenzy. I heard a growl from somewhere close and realised it was me.

"Run!" I told her as I cleared an opening. I still had the knife in my mouth and was uncertain she heard.

Seeing the small arch of freedom through the stitching mass of new Fabric, she flashed apologetic eyes at me and darted out.

Having snakes of Fabric wrapped around my bare hand made me want to spew: I gagged, coughed, and again bit hard on the Witchblade. Cool fire sputtered down my chin. A trio of conflict raged through my head: the Entity's pain, the new Fabric's increasing power, and the Witchblade's voices.

The orange light flickered inside the envelope of darkness. The tentacles prodded and poked me in return, some still held shadowleaves and continued to stitch. I saw the tiny black fibres thread and loop, silvery sparks of energy knitting the leaves.

I grabbed the closest shadowleaf and yanked it from its incomplete stitching, tearing the fibres apart. Discharged energy dripped away and hair-thin threads of Shadow Fabric curled and extended, reaching out for the half-stitched leaf. It was as if it pleaded for its return, like a dumped boyfriend on a park bench. It was the beggar for a coin. It was the newly born baby and the severed umbilical.

In my palm, I held the shadowleaf, and silence fell on me. No longer could I hear the voices in my head, nor the roaring flames, or even the collapsing parts of the House. No more did I hear, or *feel*, the pounding of my heart, or the agony that was my knee. No more was the taste of bile in my throat threatening to reach up. Neither could I feel the blade between my teeth, nor the cool fire trickling down my neck as the Witchblade offered its help.

All I felt was the clamminess of the leaf. It was as though I looked at a black and white photograph of a stigmata; a white palm surrounded by slightly curled fingers, with an irregular dark blob of suggested sanctuary. Or misery, inviting revelations, promises, and a chance to go to Heaven.

No chance.

There I stood, holding such a promise, surrounded by crevices that had given birth to creatures which belonged in Hell.

But the stitching. That's what was important…

Stitch.

I must stitch.

And so I did.

Stitching, the edges of the Fabric clammy to my touch, I accepted the invitation from a wisp of Fabric. The shadowleaves whipped around me and licked with the smothering darkness. Slivers of Fabric grasped my own fingers to join the stitching.

I fell to my knees, feeling no pain from where I knew there should be. Nothing, only the energies pulsing within, rushing from me and into the tiny patch of darkness—of someone's personal evil—in my hand. The Fabric, in a burst of renewed energy, took fuel from my life force and gave birth to more tentacles. Firstly in twos, then tens, then hundreds. Each of those tiny feelers slapped at the remaining shadowleaves, and they fluttered like the devil's blossom.

As I succumbed to the stitching, so did the Fabric resume stitching itself.

From my peripheral, my gloved hand arced into view holding a white square. Neat, perfectly formed, and promising. Did this one hold a promise of sanctuary, unlike the irregular blob of corruption in my other palm?

Heaven and Hell. White and black. Good and evil. This was a face-off between light and dark, as stark and true as any war since time immemorial.

The white leaf in my hand—my shadowleaf, my impossibly white shadowleaf—burned fierce. My fingers were straight and proud. And in the other, my flesh greying, sat the black leaf. I raised my hands before my eyes. Both black and white leaves knitted with a loop of Fabric. Tiny threads linked and locked rigid with the darkness as if that segment of Fabric accepted an invitation to stitch.

My hands came together.

White and black, folding and pressing, they writhed as one. Stitch-stitch-stitch. Panicked. Hurried. Nothing else mattered. All there was, all there could be, was to stitch.

Stitch-stitch.

Darkness tangled my thoughts, plus what little memories I had. With my life force draining and fuelling the Fabric, blackness poured into my vision. It pushed aside the light…and the dark overtook it.

For a moment my sense of feeling returned and my jaw slackened, and the Witchblade slipped out. A coldness seeped into my veins. I wasn't sure if my eyes were closed, or if I was blind like Polly, or if my entire being had absorbed the darkness.

Betrayed by my own senses, I succumbed to the stitching. My shoulders rounded and my body sank. All I wanted to do was stitch.

Recognising the approach of death was incredible.

CHAPTER 49

And like this to infinity.

The cross-stitch of black and white leaf fibres stretched in all directions as the Shadow Fabric embraced me, like I was a traveller through a world of darkness stitched with darkness. The occasional thread zigzagged across my path, yet failed to restrict my speeding mind. Absent of feeling, I rushed through that black void, the curls of white twine now diluted by blackness.

Eventually it was impossible to see even the black threads. The darkness, absolute. And in this stygian expanse, there would be no mistaking my death. My life ending. Had it ended already? Was it over? Was there nothing else other than my soul racing into the great oblivion, greeted with outstretched arms into a void where there is an all-consuming darkness? An infinity. *The* infinity.

Where the stitching had taken over my will, it had transported my awareness into the very stuff which sapped my life force. As I travelled through that nothingness, I felt the essence of *me* shrink, my entire being diminishing into insignificance. This was an out of body experience to the extreme.

Outside my mind, my body would be only dusty remains in a heap of clothes. But my thoughts should be nothing like that, it was all about the stitching. As I raced through darkness without end, I was a proud contributor to this amazing piece of work, to assist with the stitching of such beauty, and to be part of the construction of this incredible piece of fabric. *The* Fabric. The Shadow Fabric.

Pure darkness, and there I was, travelling faster than light.

The exquisite surroundings pressed in and I heard laughing—my own laughter. I was excitable, ecstatic. I was there, riding the Fabric. The darkness. The black.

Without light…

Yet the threads could be seen again. There was an occasional ridge in the expanse of darkness, tiny tracers of colour—white—within the darkness…just ahead.

Why was this? How was there any colour in this great void? How could there be such a thing as light inside this infinite nothingness? Yet there was. There shouldn't be, but there was. I saw folds of light overlapping in the distance. They shined brighter the closer I got.

This isn't infinity, I heard myself scream into the void. *This is chaos.*

No one answered. Of course not, I was the only one there; the only stitcher. The last to complete the Fabric. This new Fabric, this *stronger* Fabric.

Ahead, I saw white stitches. Many stitches of light broke the nothingness. Glimmering imperfections in the dark turning the black to grey. Rushing like shooting stars, they streamed past me. My mind collided with the whiteness—the brightness—and my voice bounced back at me.

Isn't infinity…Infinity. Infinity.

Light streamed in. It shifted the grey whorl of darkness ever lighter. Strengthening it, surely? My velocity dropped. Not stars, these were not stars shooting past, nor were they streaking fireflies. These were white stitches meshing with blackness. Forcing back the darkness.

Infinity.

My echoing voice twisted with the whiteness now clouding the dark. It churned like sour milk in the pit of my stomach; like poison tearing down my immune system, shutting my organs down one by one. Only the whiteness couldn't, shouldn't, wouldn't be a poison to me or my mind. It would poison the darkness, and I didn't want that. The expanse of darkness, beyond this intruding brightness, must remain. Into infinity.

This isn't infinity.

In a flood of white, I sensed, more so than felt, my mind slam to a stop. I would be panting, gasping for air if my lungs had been with me, but they weren't. They were somewhere outside myself. Somewhere beyond.

No more was the darkness all-devouring, no longer was there only a black void. Now there was light. It merged with the shrinking—retreating—shadows. It was the light of so many zigzagging white stitches. They enfolded me.

From outside this beautiful and inviting cocoon of pure light, the darkness of the Shadow Fabric continued to press in. The stitched whiteness restricted the onslaught of darkness. No matter how it tried to seep through the white threads, it failed.

Perhaps I heard its frustrations.

And that soothing brightness bathed my mind and cleansed my soul. It forgave my sins, whatever they had been. It freed me. Was this freedom? Heaven, maybe? Was this the entrance to the pearly gates everyone talks about?

Shadows approached from all directions. Familiar shadows, whispers. Voices. I couldn't make anything out, yet they held promise. Hope. It all gave me hope. These weren't shadows in the evil sense I'd come to know over the past few days.

These were memories.

My memories.

CHAPTER 50

Black and white, cross-stitching fibres unlocked…

And there I stand beside the white panels of my car as it reflected a fiery sunset. My fingers are curled under the door handle. Noises from behind, a scuffle of feet. And the stink of body odour washes over me as the blur of a crowbar swings downwards.

A detonation of agony bursts in my knee and I collapse.

The black and white rush of zigzagging stitches clouded the memory.

I lie on the ground, my head soars in a dizzy kaleidoscope, hearing Amy screaming. All I see of her is the rush of an image, and the man—green coat, blue jeans, white trainers—has her by both arms, shaking her. Her fingernails claw his face. She is strong. Fit. But the man—the carjacker—is stronger, and he shoves her. She flies backwards, stumbles over the kerb into shrubbery.

Her brown curls bounce as she scrambles to her feet. She again grabs for the carjacker.

Frustration roars in my head as I struggle to get up, my knee—my leg—a useless appendage. Pathetic…

White and black scratches of shadows envelope the image, overlapping to become infinity once again, and Amy's scream fills my head.

My vision sharpens, and with me, sprawled across the tarmac, is Amy—her green eyes brimming tears, her hair clumped over bloody cheeks. Her puffy lips whisper my name over and over. Each time her voice floats towards me, it softens to become little more than quivering lip movements.

Black, white, grey shades interlink, rushing over the red and pink oval of Amy's dead stare.

I am up with a cry of agony from inside and out, my leg useless, yet I have the man in my arms. Kicking, punching, I slam the bastard against my car: blood sprays across the dented bodywork of my VW.

I roar. I am an animal.

The familiar shift of darkness mingling with creases of white, wrapping arms around my mind and pulling me into another scene.

The carjacker's face is a mess of split flesh, the jagged kerb beside his head, glistening, sticky, red. Another vacant, dead stare.

My trembling hands release the man's coat, my fingers streak blood over the green fabric.

Black. White. Threads of fibres break away and a glinting light explodes before me.

I hold Amy's limp hand in mine. The streetlight above me blinks on as if to spotlight my grief, and the ring—her engagement ring—reflects not only the roadside lamp, but a future denied.

White. Black. Flashes of shadow…

The brightness flares into shards of too many images, thoughts, and feelings. Grief, despair, fear. Self-defence. Suspended sentence. Prison.

Black and white, fleeting shadows. Mingling images and…

A white ambulance looms over me. Flashing lights. A car crashed…not the accident itself…just the wreck of a red car…not my car, though. My car was white. I was never in an accident. The accident was the carjacker's death. He killed Amy. I killed him. It was an accident, not a *car* accident.

Brightness gathers around me.

A white room next, it's my hospital room and the nurse has red hair. Red hair…Katrina? Victor's yoga instructor. My nurse is Katrina.

There's Goodwin and Katrina talking. She holds a hypodermic needle in one hand. In the other, she holds a leather strap.

White and black, rushing colours…red. Katrina's hair.

An hourglass. Katrina straps *the* Hourglass to my hand, and her smile fails to reassure me. Machines and technology stretch behind her, and I know the other guys have died. Some went mad. Sometimes I hear them in the other cells. And I recognise the possibility of this being the end. I don't care...I have no future. My future has been taken from me. This present can be my end. As the Hourglass links with the machines and connects with my sins—my past—I slip into a welcome oblivion.

My memories are taken, yet my life remains.

Darkness. Phantoms overlap one another, clouding my vision...

My grey shadowleaf clutched in a man's hand. It's Stanley. Victor's brother, using me like a puppet. And there he is again, this time throwing my white shadowleaf down after the second time I was strapped to the Hourglass. This time without any machine or technology dreamt up by Goodwin's crazy ideals.

A black and white flash, and there is Isidore. She cowers between the collected folds of stitching shadow. The *new* Shadow Fabric.

Darkness...entwining...stitching...

I am stitching.

Stitch-stitch-stitch.

I hurtle through the whiteness, my mind churning with the red of Witchblade flames...the crackle of so much fire...there are interruptions of blackness leaking orange...fire. Whiteness overcomes the searing orange, extinguishing the Witchblade's cool flames in an ever-shrinking dome.

The orange, yellow, and red tongues lick and smother the black. The whiteness overcoming the blackness. The light flowing through my gloved fingers, pushing the darkness back into a tangle of chaotic shadows. The nothingness shrinks.

No longer like this into infinity.

NEW LIFE

The sound of approaching sirens crashed into my other senses as I sniffed, coughed, and choked on the foul air. My eyelids flickered open and there was the tear-streaked face of Isidore. Her smile was reassuring, unlike Katrina's when she strapped me to the Hourglass, back in my other life. Before all this.

Georgie lay by her side and one of her hands absently scratched behind his ear. Her other hand clutched mine. She crouched, framed by massive trees.

"Leo?" she said. It reminded me of Amy, and my heart lurched as if my stomach had punched it.

My legs were stretched, my back against a red car. A familiar red car, though it didn't belong to me. It wasn't mine. Through the haze of a natural darkness, I spotted the ambulance, its bodywork a pale glow. Between unruly tufts of grass was a deflated tyre, squashed against a kerbstone.

Am I back in the car wreck? Dizziness drowned me in waves.

"What—" I coughed, my head thumping. It was as if I'd downed a pint of sand with a fire chaser. "How did I get here?"

And I remembered. I remembered all I'd seen while inside the Shadow Fabric, riding the nightmare within the stitched darkness. The car wreck had been staged to give me a new start. Goodwin had given me a new beginning. A new life.

Isidore ran a hand along Georgie's back. "I pulled you out of the House. From the fire. You kind of stumbled with us, but you made it."

"Yeah?" It hurt to move.

"I took you somewhere safe, away from the smoke."

I glanced at the wheels of the ambulance, at the length of winding kerb and the stretch of roadway with its four white lines. The secluded area was hemmed in by conifer hedges, and in a corner, obscured by overgrown foliage, once stood two stone columns. Only one remained upright, threatening to collapse. Between them an impressive sheet of iron lay crushed beneath masonry which must have flown from the House when the Fabric tore apart the building.

On a neck made of rubber, I turned my thundering head towards Isidore.

"Leo." She squeezed my hand. "It's over."

"New life," I told her.

She nodded.

Speechless moments rolled by as I listened to my heartbeat and thought of everything that had gone before. Of all that happened to me. And the things which *hadn't* happened.

Eventually, Isidore helped me up and, after a rush threatened to pull me back into darkness, I staggered towards the gate.

"Look," Isidore said, holding me. My knee protested even the slightest of movements. She brought me into view of the pyre which was once Periwick House.

Flames. Lots of flames. I sensed the dwindling cries of the Entity. It had failed. The dome of its final prison now merged with the burning timbers of the House. The sound of approaching fire services grew closer, and we watched the darkness retreat and coil into the hungry flames. Tentacles of Shadow Fabric whipped the air, no longer growing. No longer self-stitching. Faint murmurs, an intrusion on the roar of blood in my head, echoed one last time and I felt the Entity's anger vanish…into its own infinity.

I dragged a hand down my face. There I was with Isidore and Georgie in a separate area in the gardens of Periwick House, and behind me stood a crossover from my old life into my new. Here was a fragment of an unremembered past which leaked into my new life, a place once locked behind a massive gate, shielded from view. Shielding my memories. Here, a place where a car wreck and an ambulance had been hidden, both vehicles sitting on a false stretch of road. Goodwin had created that secluded area to build a fake memory, for any of us who survived his absurd experiments. It had existed as a memory for me, no matter how false. Now I knew the truth. Riding the

Fabric had shown me my past, my life. Amy's death. The carjacker and his accidental death.

I looked at Isidore: this was my new life.

Goodwin had staged it all while chasing his desires to cure humankind of its ills, the catalyst being the death of his father so long ago. There was me...and I knew what I had been to Goodwin, what I *truly* had been to him.

Isidore released me and I rested against the brick column, not thinking of its imminent collapse. She shrugged off her rucksack, sat down cross-legged, and wedged it in her lap. Opening it, she pulled out the Hourglass. Its leather straps flopped out and the buckles clanked.

"When did you get that?" I asked her.

She shrugged. "I have the magic knife in here as well."

My whole body ached and my knee throbbed. I sat— actually, I fell—in front of her. I grunted.

She placed the Hourglass beside her, and from inside the rucksack, she removed something else.

"I thought you might want this." She handed me a manila envelope.

Behind me, the flickering flames of the House illuminated it. In the top right corner, in Goodwin's impeccable handwriting, was the name: *Leonard Howard*. Not *Fox*, but *Howard*. I never realised Isidore had it, never realised she had found it. My fingers wanted to move, the rest of me didn't. All of me wanted to read its contents.

I wiped a hand across my mouth, eyeing her sideways. "I remember."

"Everything?"

"Not quite." I scratched my forehead. My hand came away black with sweat and soot, tinged with blood. I didn't know if it was mine—I hurt everywhere. "I still don't know what I'd been before I worked for Vic—"

Georgie interrupted me as he began to growl. He leapt away from Isidore and bounded across the grounds. He vanished into the darkness.

"Georgie!" she called. She leaned sideways and squinted at the Hourglass. "There's something—"

The glass cracked. The sound echoed around the enclosure. My heart flew into my throat.

The Hourglass exploded.

In a miniature sandstorm, pieces of glass flew into her face. None came my way, although I shielded myself. Isidore's screams filled my head. On her back, she clawed her face. She kicked her legs and rolled onto her side. Blood poured from the wounds. So many glass fragments stuck from her flesh, each sliver glinting. The one in her neck—the largest—gushed the most. And something else, something dark. Unlike the Fabric, unlike any sentient shadow.

This was different.

A scarlet puddle, shimmering with the reflected inferno of Periwick House, spread from Isidore's body and crept through the grass. It reminded me of how the Shadow Fabric moved.

Her last breath floated into the night.

My vision shifted in waves of dizziness…and a bright flash momentarily blinded me. A searing agony shot up my arm. I yelled, and the smell of burnt hair and flesh drifted upwards. Hot, burning pain tore through me…

My hand. No, my arm. On the inside of my wrist, still smoking, I had been marked. Branded.

I stared at the curls of twisted flesh, the pain raging through me. A pattern. A familiar symbol: two triangles, apexes facing and separated by a curved X. The triangles, one solid, the other hollow.

My future, my demons. The symbol, the darkness.